What People Are Saying About
The Dragon Forest

"Like all good fiction writers, she is able to draw the reader into the story, allowing you to "see" her world and making you want to know what happens next. About a third of the way in, Douthitt hit her stride, and I found myself running beside her, eager for more… *The Dragon Forest* is also a "coming of age" novel. Peter and his young friends have some growing up to do in a hurry as the great battle, fueled by the evil magic of Lord Bedlam, begins. They must make decisions which the adults in their world may not understand at first, much like the decisions Harry Potter and his friends had to make. There is a tension between obeying authority and doing what you know is right—something with which every young person must struggle." - **Mark Sommer, Fantasy and Book Review Editor for HollywoodJesus.com**

"*The Dragon Forest* is one of the most exciting stories I have read in some time. Douthitt really knows how to blend action with narrative. Her universe has a Lord of the Rings kind of feeling, but stands on its own. I would definitely recommend this tale to all fantasy readers and those who enjoy an exciting tale with loads of inspiration and hints at what is to come. I can't wait for Book 2!" –Scotty (Amazon review)

The Dragon Forest Series

R. A. Douthitt

The Dragon Forest

Book One

The Dragon Forest II: Son of the Oath

Book Two

The Dragon Forest III: The King of Illiath

Book Three

The Dragon Forest II
Son of the Oath

R. A. Douthitt

The Dragon Forest II: Son of the Oath is a work of fiction. References to real people, events, establishments, organizations, or locales are intended only to provide a sense of authenticity and are used fictitiously. All other characters, incidents, and dialogue are drawn from the author's imagination. The perspective, opinions, and worldview represented by this book are those of the author and are not intended to be a reflection or endorsement of the publisher's views.

Printed in the U.S.A.

THE DRAGON FOREST II

DEDICATION

To my editors Chris and Wayne:
Your extremely high standards have made me
a better writer. Thank you.

To Scott and Nathan,
Thank you for all your support and love.

To my students,
thank you for inspiring me to keep writing.

CROW VALLEY

THE DRAGON FOREST

THE BLACK HILLS

CARDION VALLEY

THE CORNSHIRE

THEADRON DESERT

Blue River

TO THE
EAST SHORE

Map
of
Théadril

ILLIATH

OGRE COUNTRY

ILLIATH

THE RANVIEG
MOUNTAINS

THEADRON DESERT

RÜNBRIOR
PRISON

THE WHITE FOREST

THE
JOURNEY
TO
VULGAARD

VULGAARD

"You must take this sword," the stranger said, his hands trembling. "Tell no one."

The Elf, an elder from the palace, hesitated for a moment, staring at the glistening steel before him. He recognized the filigree on the blade. He looked up at the stranger and studied his eyes.

"Take it, you fool!" the stranger shouted. Grabbing the Elf's wrist, he placed the hilt of the sword in his hand.

"Guard it with your life," the stranger said, gazing deep into the Elf's eyes. Then he wrapped his fur cape around his neck. "They will be coming for it soon."

He turned and left the Elf standing where he had found him, in the doorway of the darkened cave

PROLOGUE

In the early years of what is considered The Time of Man, the chroniclers of the history of Théadril put down in many letters their version of the quest for the missing swords and the trials of Prince Peter in the western lands. These writings were then placed into many books bound in leather and catalogued into the palace library of Illiath for safekeeping and future consideration.

During this time in the history of Théadril, the lands knew plenty and the people were contented and at peace. King Alexander continued to organize a party charged with the task of retrieving the lost swords in order for all the swords to be reunited and subsequently destroyed. It was understood by all ten rulers of the regions that when the swords created by Bedlam were destroyed, then the powers of Bedlam would cease, leaving all the lands free from the darkness once and for all. The King's conscription was met with great enthusiasm as many soldiers and knights throughout the kingdom were eager to participate in the search for the swords.

Since the Era of the Dragon had come to an end, the Time of Man had begun to greatly affect the surrounding kingdoms. More trade resulted in more commerce. Smaller villages and towns in outer regions started to flourish and these regions came with their own forms of local "government" under the rule of the King of each region. This was no cause for alarm since the people remained peaceful and respectful.

But it was the towns in the far western regions behind the vast Black Hills that caused concern for King Alexander. These towns were not adhering to the regulations set forth by the rulers and were enforcing their own laws without regard to the kingdom. Still, the people lived in peace with other regions and respected the boundaries set so long ago. None dared to enter into the Dragon Forest and, as long as it remained undisturbed, all was well with Théadril.

The King placed more importance on the quest for the swords than any other issue brought before him because he knew time was of the essence. Lord Bedlam remained quiet, but Alexander feared that at any moment Bedlam could try to start war with the ten regions yet again.

As Prince Peter completed his education in order to set off for his turn at Knight Training in the Crow Valley, the palace prepared for a grand celebration for the prince's graduation and departure. The Time of Man had come as the Dragon said it would. Peter knew his calling was to protect The Dragon Forest at all costs as his father had. He never realized what those costs would be or how painful a sacrifice his fidelity to the throne and the Oath of the Dragon would be. Nor could he have known. No one could have known.

But if the Dragon suffered, then all those sworn to protect the Oath must suffer as well…if the forest is to remain.

1 THE MEETING OF THE KINGS

"This quest has failed," said King Eulrik of Glaussier. His shouts could be heard from the hallway as King Alexander of Illiath entered. "It has been over three years since the knights departed for the swords and not one has been returned to us. I believe it is time to end this illusive endeavor and bring the knights home to their families and to their lands."

The men surrounded the large table in the dining hall of the palace at Illiath where so many meetings had occurred before. Historical meetings that settled disputes and created accords were held in the very same room for decades by King Alexander's father and now by him. But it was different this time. With the palace busily preparing for his son's graduation, Alexander was distracted. He entered the meeting late and sat down. He sighed heavily while the others spoke. He seemed withdrawn, too melancholic to argue. So, he patiently listened to the others while they discussed the terms of the quest. He wore his graying hair longer and had a thick beard along his chin.

"This quest has only begun," rebutted King Mildrir of Thorgest. "It is too soon to assess whether or not it has failed. Reports coming in have been negative, but the knights have reported that many of the outer lying towns and villages are assisting in the search. That brings great hope."

"Yes, it does, considering many were not involved in the Oath or Lord Bedlam's curse," said Iseif. "I find it comforting to know that others are concerned and want Bedlam destroyed."

Alexander rubbed his forehead with his hand.

"But finding all the swords…," argued Eulrik. "It is impossible! My son, Sir Leonius, a very brave knight, was last seen two years ago on the islands in the East Ocean. He was seen by pirates. Pirates! How can I trust the words of pirates? They said he had been captured and was being held on one of the islands, yet they had his belt and buckler with them. I suspect he is dead. I suspect they are all dead!"

This angered Alexander out of his trance. "They are not all dead. I refused to believe they are." He stood and produced the letter he received from Sir Roen. "The son of my good friend, General Aluein, has written me this letter telling me of the progress of the search. This letter arrived by carrier from south of Vulgaard."

"South of Vulgaard?" asked Eulrik. "That is farther off than we thought. That is dangerously close to Bedlam's realm of Ranvieg."

"Too close," said King Isleif. "What else did the letter say?"

Alexander hesitated to mention the death of Sir Lucas because of the mood of the meeting, but he did not want to withhold any information from the leaders. "Sir Lucas has been found dead," he revealed.

With that announcement, the others began arguing and yelling in the large room. Their voices echoed throughout the palace. Many servants stopped in the hallway wondering what was happening behind the closed doors. The words grew harsher with each passing moment, and Alexander rubbed his head as though it ached from the noise. Nothing would be decided with all the emotions and anger present in the room. He rose to leave without saying a word since hours had passed. He had to be up soon to prepare for the ceremonies. As he walked away from the table, King Eulrik's eye caught him.

"What say you, King Alexander?" he said as he walked across the room. "You cannot possibly leave now since this whole quest was your idea. This whole mess is yours to bear and yours alone!"

"Not so, Eulrik," shouted King Mildrir. "We all were present at the beginning. We all had a part in this decision to send out the knights. We all are responsible." He pointed his finger accusingly at Eulrik, who slowly walked back to his chair. He stood behind it and violently pushed it back into its place, making a loud clamor.

No one spoke. Eulrik made his way toward King Alexander, who stood in the entrance way of the room.

"We may have all discussed this, but it was his idea from the beginning. He gave up his sword in battle and now it is lost. He has nothing to lose. And why not? No one he loves is out on the quest," declared Eulrik.

Alexander faced the doorway. Slowly, he turned to face his accuser.

"I hear it is your son, Peter, who is leaving for Knight Training tomorrow," Eulrik whispered as he approached Alexander.

"Do not speak further, Eulrik," Alexander warned.

"And perhaps one day it is he who will be part of this quest," Eulrik continued.

Alexander watched him weigh his words carefully.

"And perhaps one day we will be speaking of his death at this table," he said, glaring into King Alexander's eyes. "Then what will you do, Alexander? Then what will you say? Will you still refuse to call this quest a failure?"

"That sort of talk is not warranted here, Elurik!" Mildrir shouted.

Alexander's eyes narrowed. He stared into Eulrik. Most in the room knew he had never liked King Eulrik, nor did he trust him. The words appeared to have struck deeply at Alexander's heart. All in the room were quiet as Mildrir walked over to the two men.

"Stop this now, Eulrik," Mildrir warned. "Leave if you must."

"No," Alexander said. "He has chosen to speak." Eulrik waited for a response to the question he put before Alexander.

"Yes, my son leaves tomorrow for training," Alexander said. "Perhaps this quest will continue when he returns. I know he will join in the quest. He has already said he will. I will not try to stop him. I will encourage him.

"But even if he does die in this quest, it will continue, Eulrik. It must continue, because it is bigger than any one of us. All of Théadril depends on the knights finding the swords and destroying them. I am weary from all this waiting just as you are. It has aged me. I grow weary of writing letters to mothers and fathers regarding their sons' deaths. It pains me more than you know as I know it pains all of you. But I know this quest will prove to be successful. I feel it. The swords will be found and returned to us so that we can destroy them and Bedlam once and for all. If I didn't know this, I never would have sent out the knights on this quest. You have to believe me. We all have to be patient."

Unsatisfied, Eulrik rudely pushed past Alexander and stormed out of the room without a word. One by one, the others followed.

Mildrir stood by Alexander for a moment, then placed his hand on the weary King's shoulder. "Get some rest, my friend." He sighed. "There will be more meetings in the future. But now you must concentrate on your son and the needs of your people."

"Thank you, my friend," Alexander said as he walked with Mildrir to the front entrance of the palace.

The meeting ended, leaving Alexander alone at the table where he sat thinking about what transpired in those early morning hours. He rubbed his eyes. The thought of Peter dying was even heavier on his mind. His son, his only son, was about to embark on a life-changing journey that could lead to his death in a horrific war against an equally horrific enemy. Yet, as with all the kings in the kingdom, Alexander knew this day would come when they placed Peter in his arms on the day he was born.

2 ENCOUNTERS

Stopping time was a dream to young Prince Peter, yet he clung to this dream as all youth do when the summer winds change, bringing with them the onset of autumn and the end of summer adventures. Peter longed to begin this new stage in his life as a knight in training heading off to the Crow Valley camps for young men, but summer had been so enjoyable. Three years had passed since the death of the great Dragon of the Forest, and since that time, Peter had undergone much training of his own, not of sword and muscle, but of his mind.

"Hurry now," Annika shouted. "We don't have much time left."

Peter winced at the words of his friend and classmate of three years as she made her way through the thick forest trees that lined the pathway leading to the palace at Illiath. She hiked up her long linen skirt with her hands while clumsily holding her fishing pole. The two quickly gathered their belongings to leave after fishing for hours in a small pond near the Dragon Forest.

"We're going to be late!" Annika shouted again. "And you know how Theo hates it when we come in after he starts his lecture."

Peter sighed and stood to leave. He gazed up at the sun. He had a feeling they were already late for their afternoon lesson with Theo, their tutor and mentor of the last three years. Simon and Crispin, Peter's other classmates, had already made their way back to the classroom after catching what would soon be considered a record number of fish for that small pond. A few inches taller than the previous year, Peter wore his brown hair a little longer with bangs that hid his large brown eyes. Peter brushed the hair from his eyes and looked at the leather pouch he used for carrying his fish.

It lay flat on the ground as when he placed it there. Peter and Annika had no such luck that day, so they stubbornly stayed behind to try and match the record, only to fail miserably in their attempt.

Huffing his way through the thick branches, Peter finally made it to the clearing in time to see Annika running down the path with her pole in one hand, her sack strapped to her back, and her long blonde hair flowing behind her. As she ran, Peter noticed she had passed an old wooden sign marker left by the side of the dirt path. Peter walked over to the old marker and stopped to read it. He traced the faded letters with his fingers recognizing it from years before.

"Beware the Dragon Forest," he mumbled as he read the sign post marking the famous turn off toward the mysterious woods.

He picked up the dusty, faded old sign attached to the post and studied it. "There's no need for a warning sign any longer," he said to no one in particular. He decided to leave the post where he found it.

Peter chuckled to himself as he remembered the first time he had entered the forest. Not knowing what to expect at the age of ten, he had entered cautiously with his horse, Titan. Smiling at the memory, he picked up his pole and sack of fish, turned to catch up with Annika.

Then he heard a noise.

Pausing at the entrance of the forest, he turned his head at an angle. He heard it again. He put down his pole and sack, took his sword from its sheath, and approached the entrance. "Hello?"

A few sparrows swooshed out of the bushes. He jumped and raised his arm to shoo them away. Peter stared into the darkened path leading into the forest. He gripped his sword tightly.

A cool breeze caught him from behind. The air felt good on his skin and the fresh smell of the pine trees calmed his senses. Peter, for the first time in three years, took a few steps into the entrance of the Dragon Forest.

As he entered, the branches of the trees entwined to make a canopy of sorts above him instantly blocking out the sun but allowing its rays to filter in between the branches for a most spectacular sight. Peter continued walking. This time, he walked with confidence, knowing he had nothing to fear from this forest any longer. It was as much his home as the palace. He touched the branches of the trees as though they were old friends.

"Hello?" he said again to no one in particular. I know I heard something.

He walked on until he finally saw the lake in the center of the forest. He could feel on his skin the cooler air with moisture as he approached the water. Peter wanted to jump in on that hot day.

He smiled. His mind flooded with memories that overcame him as he gazed across the water into the trees on the far side where once a pair of yellow eyes glowed between the tree trunks.

"It seems forever ago," he said wistfully, placing his sword back in its sheath. He looked up into the clear skies above and saw a few white doves flutter away. "And yet it seems like only yesterday."

Peter walked over to the spot where he had first met the Dragon. He turned and saw the spot where Peregrine was torched. Then he walked a few more steps to the place where he had mounted the Dragon's neck and rose higher and higher above the trees.

He sighed. "I miss you, my old friend," he whispered.

Peter hated the feeling of loneliness. It was as familiar to him as his own reflection in the lake. Like when one walks away from the mirror, Peter thought he had left loneliness behind, yet it had returned.

He picked up a stone and tossed it into the lake. The ripples disturbed the glassy smooth surface. Peter took one last glance around his sanctuary before turning to leave.

Suddenly, a large bird rudely flew past him, interrupting his thoughts. Peter jumped. It landed on a branch nearby. When he realized it was a white owl, he gasped. "What? Where—" he looked around.

The bird turned its head to the right. Peter took a few steps toward it. The bird turned its head back again and stared at Peter. In that moment, he recognized the bright yellow eyes.

"You!" He nearly fell backwards. Then he crept toward the bird. "But…how can it be?"

He tried to remember the last time he saw the bird but couldn't. He rubbed his eyes to see if it was a vision, a dream, anything but real.

But the bird remained perched on the branch. *It's just another white owl. It cannot possibly be anything else.*

He stared long at the bird whose feathers rustled. The eyes that glowed in the shadows of the trees were anything but normal. As Peter moved to touch the feathers, the bird flew off and circled above Peter's head. Instantly, it transformed into a dragon.

Peter fell to the ground in shock as the wind from the enormous wings flapped, sending leaves and twigs into the air. He crawled away and covered his face from the debris until the wind stopped, unsure if the dragon was friendly or not. It landed with an enormous thud a few feet away.

Peeking from between his fingers that covered his face, Prince Peter slowly moved his hands away and stared at the beast. It was not an ordinary dragon that stood panting before him.

No, indeed it was the Great Dragon of the Forest

§

The glistening scales were back in place. The wound in the chest was only a scar. The snout was no longer covered with deep gashes and the eyes shone brightly with a sparkle Peter only remembered in his dreams the last three years.

Peter laughed out loud. "I must be dreaming!"

The Dragon snorted air out its nostrils. Peter's hair swooshed back. He could smell the familiar odor of the Dragon's fire.

"Is this real?" Peter ran up to the Dragon's snout and stopped right before he reached it. The last time he stood so close to the beast, it was dying. Yet now its scales gleamed with a brilliance Peter had never seen before. Raising his hand, he gently rubbed the snout, feeling a warmth he hadn't experienced in many years.

He gazed into the large eyes. "But how? You died. I watched you die there in the desert plains."

The Dragon slowly nodded.

"I know I'm not mad. We all saw you die," Peter said. "How can you be here now?"

"Peter, I had to die," the Dragon said. "It was the Time of

Man."

Peter remembered the voice. He remembered the words.

"I had to give my life so that you and your father might live," it said.

"But why did you remain hidden all these years?" Peter's eyes stung with tears. "How could you remain hidden from me? Didn't you see me? Didn't you hear me cry out? I cried out for you so many times."

The corners of the Dragon's large mouth rose into what some would call a grin. "Of course I did. Leaving you was not an easy thing to do. To watch you from afar was most painful."

Peter began to walk away. "And yet you stayed away," he whispered in disappointment.

The Dragon lifted its giant head and exhaled. Peter sensed its frustration. He turned to see the beast standing on all four of its massive legs with its wings tucked along its sides. The tail swished along the damp ground.

The Dragon took a few steps and the ground shook.

"I'm glad you are here now!" Peter came back to it.

"The time has come, Peter," it said with seriousness. "I have watched man these three years from my home here within the trees. I have observed the comings and goings." It peered over the treetops with a pensive gaze. "And what I have seen brought me back." It turned its head toward Peter. "You have brought me back."

Peter saw a fierce light in its eyes he hadn't seen since the time Sir Peregrine was reduced to ashes.

"Me?" Peter asked.

"Your love, Peter. Your love for me, your love for your father. Your love for Illiath brought me back." The Dragon turned toward the lake and the shadow covered trees. "I know this is your time. I must be here for your time. As I was there for your father and his father before him, I will be here for you."

Its massive body moved along with its tail swishing behind. Peter couldn't help but touch the scales, if only to make sure he wasn't dreaming. He could see his reflection in them.

Peter stopped at the water's edge. The Dragon leaned over and motioned with its head for Peter to look into the water.

When Peter did so, he saw images within the ripples. His

mouth fell open with fright because he saw himself. "What is this?" He took a step back.

"Do not be afraid," the Dragon said.

The images moved by in the water, one after the other. Peter saw himself in chains, bound with others in some dark cave. "Where is this?"

He saw torches, rows and rows of people from other lands shouting and cheering. He saw black mountains illuminated by the moon.

"Peter, this is your future," the Dragon said. "It is time for your trials."

There was no response.

"This is the beginning for you," it said.

More images of battle and dragons spewing fire appeared in the ripples. Then, just like that, the images were gone.

"Am I to go to war?" Peter swallowed back the fear. "How can this be?"

The Dragon turned toward him. "Remove your sword from its sheath," it ordered.

Peter obeyed.

"Hold it up."

He did so.

"When you were but a boy you held a sword made of wood," it said. "Now you hold a sword made of steel."

Peter inspected his sword.

"A sword is more than a weapon. A knight, a soldier, a warrior is only as good as his weapon, Peter. You will learn this lesson soon. You will learn that to fight is more than defeating an opponent. You will learn the ways of the 10 dragon. And you will learn that you are prepared for more than you think."

"In Knight Training?" Peter smiled widely.

The Dragon swiveled its head toward him. "In the trials."

Peter took a step back. "I'm afraid I don't understand. Knight Training comes before the trials."

"Do not fear," the Dragon said. "You have nothing to fear. I will always be there with you no matter what happens."

"But I don't understand." Peter looked into the water. The surface was smooth again.

"You are bound for great things, Peter. And greatness takes

time."

Peter looked at his sword and carefully slid his hand along the blade. "This is the sword you made for me. All those years ago."

The Dragon nodded.

"I wanted to use it in Knight Training. But now I must go and face my trials first? But why now? Why like this? Do I not have a say in this?"

The Dragon grinned.

"I want to be a knight," Peter said. "I've been preparing for the last three years to leave for training. I'm not ready for the trials."

Regret shadowed the Dragon's face. It raised its head high to look over the trees again.

"I mean, it isn't fair." Peter threw the sword down, and it pierced the ground. "I deserve my chance, don't I?"

The Dragon listened patiently.

"Will had his turn." Peter crossed his arms. "Will is a knight now. He'll head out for his trials. Why am I not to do the same? Why must I face the trials first?"

The Dragon continued to stare off without a word.

Peter looked down.

"Over the horizon comes a darkness, Peter," it said.

"What? A darkness? Here in Illiath?"

The Dragon gazed down at the young man standing where a small boy once stood.

"How can this be? The land is so prosperous. The people are happy. There is peace," Peter argued.

"Lord Bedlam is almost ready," the Dragon said.

"Ready? Ready for what?"

But there was no answer. The two stood in silence as if the Dragon wanted Peter to think about the situation.

Finally, it spoke again. "His power grows because man's complacency has allowed it. And now Lord Bedlam's time has come."

The Dragon bent low to face Peter. He could feel its warm breath. "You must save Illiath, Peter."

Peter raised his eyebrows. "Save Illiath? Me?" he exclaimed, pointing to his chest. "Surely you must mean my father."

The Dragon shook its head. "Your father has fought his

battles. He faced his trials on the battlefield and fought valiantly. He was rewarded with a son."

Peter's face grew warm.

"Now it is your turn." It nudged Peter's side with its snout. "You are the Son of the Oath. You are the one to save Illiath."

With those words, Peter's mind raced and he closed his eyes. His body became numb. "I must be dreaming." He took a few steps as though in a trance. "I feel dizzy."

The Dragon inhaled and breathed out its cold blue fire onto Peter's face to wake him from the trance. "Listen to me. Now, you must return to the palace. Enjoy the celebration with your friends and with your father. Then, when all is said and done, you will depart for your trials, face them, and endure."

"But—what about Knight Training? I have no say in this?"

The Dragon sighed.

Peter took a few steps away from the Dragon. He rested his hand on a low tree branch and waited for the answer.

How can this be happening? I must be dreaming. This is madness. I'm leaving for Knight Training soon. I can't face my trials now without any training. I'm not ready. I'll face them after the training like Will and all the others did. Yes! That's right. After training I'll do what the Dragon says.

"Are you saying that this is a…choice…I must make?" Peter asked without turning around.

Instantly he heard the hissing he hadn't heard for many years. He knew what that meant. The Dragon of the Forest spewed out red hot flames that engulfed a pile of dead wood near Peter's feet, and Peter winced from the extreme heat. He leapt back as the flames just missed him. Panting with fright, he pivoted toward the Dragon as it raised its head high.

Instantly reminded of its great power and strength, Peter cautiously moved toward it. "I don't mean to sound…indifferent about all this," he said with hands raised. "Really, I don't."

The Dragon listened.

"It's just that I wasn't prepared for all this. A few minutes ago, you were gone forever, and I was a prince heading to Knight Training." Peter looked up.

"Now you are here again, speaking to me about a future I know nothing about."

"You do have a choice to make, Peter," the Dragon said as it stretched out its mammoth wings. "You can choose to be the king you were meant to be."

Peter nodded as though he finally understood what was being asked of him. "Will I—" He swallowed. "Will I die?"

"There is always that possibility," the Dragon answered.

Peter hunched over as though defeated. "Will I be alone?"

"Know that I am with you, always." The Dragon's tail swung around and the end of it gently picked up Peter's chin. "Always." The Dragon's eyes twinkled. "Now go back to the palace and tell no one what you saw here. The time will come when everyone will know."

As it spoke, its wings flapped, lifting its body off the ground. Peter covered his face with his hands as the twigs and leaves fluttered around him.

The Dragon transformed back into a white owl.

Peter reached out his arm and allowed it to perch. He stroked the soft feathers before it flew away into the trees. When it was gone, Peter stood alone in the sudden calmness of the forest with the sound of only a few sparrows nearby. The weight of the Dragon's words lay heavy on his shoulders.

Picking up his sword, he placed it back into its sheath. Then he ran out of the Dragon Forest toward home. Passing the old warning sign marker lying on the ground, he picked it up, stabbed the pointed edge of the post deep into the damp ground, and made certain the arrow once again pointed toward the Dragon Forest.

3 PREPARATIONS

Constable Darion, the King's most loyal assistant, finalized the arrangements for the night's graduation ceremonies at the palace. Suddenly, a loud crash came from the kitchen. Walking to the room, he noticed servants quickly cleaning up the spilt food from the floor.

"This is what happens when we rush," Darion acknowledged, remaining patient with the palace staff.

Everyone was working frantically to complete all the final preparations. Darion was used to the swift pace. With no family of his own, and still plagued with a limp from injuries suffered during the war with Lord Caragon, he lived within the palace walls. He loved King Alexander as a brother and enjoyed serving him with his skills as an inventor.

Entering the kitchen, he saw the scullery maids scrubbing the dishes in the giant sink as butlers and pantlers replaced the damaged food with freshly prepared food on the clean trays. Everyone did slow down a bit, not wanting to spoil the event. Many of the servants had been in the castle since long before Peter's birth, and this night they would be seeing him off to Knight Training in the Crow Valley. Perhaps many thought they would never see him again.

"He'll certainly not be the same Peter," the head cook said while she basted the roasting ducks over the fire pit.

"Well, that could be a good thing," said the butler. He tied on his apron. "No more practical jokes like snakes in pockets or spiders in bed sheets."

"That's true!" the head cook said. "It will do him good to be on his own."

"Yes, and the King will be pleased."

"I only wish his mother could be here for this, poor woman."

"Well, at least the King is here and all will be well."

"Yes, I suppose you're right," said the cook. She wiped her tears with her apron that still had flour on it from the early morning baking.

Constable Darion smiled warmly; everyone in the palace loved the Prince. "Let us all slow down and remember how special this night is, shall we?"

He exited the kitchen and entered the large dining hall, which had been cleared of the giant mahogany table and lined with chairs for the many guests. The food would be arranged as a buffet in the next room so the guests could mingle and talk with Peter as they ate. Darion stopped to inspect the work of all the servants and, as usual, was most pleased. "Well done," he murmured.

When he finished his inspection, he headed down the long paneled hallway to the King's study, and knocked gently.

§

"Yes, enter." The King glanced up from the book he was reading.

"Your Majesty." Darion bowed his head.

"How are the preparations coming along, Darion?"

"Almost complete, sire."

"I can smell the food from here, and it's making me mad with hunger." The King chuckled, placing his book on the desk and walking over to the fire. "Where are Peter and his guests?"

"Peter is upstairs, and the others have returned to their rooms in the palace. All will begin at sunset, sire."

"Well done. I shall go and see Peter before the night's festivities begin."

"Sire," Darion interrupted. "May I have a word with you?"

"Of course." Alexander motioned for Darion to continue. "By all means, speak."

"My Lord, about the quest."

"Yes?"

"More news has come in from Sir Roen."

"And?"

"Not good, I'm afraid."

The King slumped into the wooden chair by the fireplace. "What has happened?"

"In the report, Sir Roen has stated that another knight, Sir Lucas, has been found dead in the dales south of Vulgaard."

"That far west?"

"Yes, my Lord."

"I will pen a letter to his wife." The King rubbed his eyes. "He was a young man...not much older than young Will."

"Yes, my Lord." Darion bowed his head.

Alexander placed his face in his hands. The bones protruded under the loosened skin, as he had lost weight these last few months. The apothecary suspected an unknown malady, but everyone knew the weight loss was from worry. The lines on his forehead felt deep as he followed across them. More white hairs were visible in his beard and along his brow, he knew. The quest continued to rob him of the youthful vigor he had felt in the presence of the Dragon.

"This quest has gone on now for over three years and still no sight of the swords," he whispered through his fingers.

"We must be patient, my Lord," Darion said.

"I just hope it is over before my son returns from training. Otherwise, he will want to join the quest. Then who knows how long it will be until I see him again."

"It is a difficult time to be King, yes?"

"More than you know, my friend." The King stood and strode to his desk, where several maps of nearby regions lay across the desk top. "Some cities and townships are assisting us while others are refusing to assist the knights in their search. They claim they are not under Théadril jurisdiction and therefore have no reason to participate in the quest for the swords."

"No reason?" asked Darion. "Do they not understand what is at stake?"

The King leaned over the maps and in his mind marked out the areas that had been covered in the search so far. The areas were vast and boundless with many mountain ranges. It was hard for anyone to fathom the idea of men trekking along such land searching for something so small.

"So much land has been covered and yet no sign at all." He exhaled. "My worst fears are being realized before my own eyes."

"Sire?"

He straightened and swiveled to peer out the large window behind his desk. "Oh, Darion . . . I am afraid that Bedlam has fooled us all. I am afraid he has obtained all the missing swords somehow and is keeping them hidden. He knows that if they are together again in our possession, his plan will fail."

Darion stood quietly nodding in agreement. "Do you think the lands are safe? What about the Dragon Forest? Is it safe?"

The King gazed once again at the maps, spotting the Dragon Forest on the map of Théadril, and then staring intently into Darion's eyes.

"The land and I are bound," he said sternly, hands clasped together. "As I thrive, the land thrives. As the covenant states: 'As long as my heir lives, the Dragon Forest remains.'"

4 CELEBRATIONS

As Peter sat on his bed, he gazed through his window at the tips of the trees of the Dragon Forest. He did not smile. Instead, a certain heaviness descended. He realized he would soon be leaving this land for a long time, perhaps never to return. His boyhood days were over, and the forest took on a whole new meaning after speaking with the Dragon.

At that moment, his father knocked and entered.

"Oh good, you are here," Alexander said as he entered.

"Father!" Peter said with excitement, valuing any time he could spend with his father now more than ever.

"I see you have a new tunic for tonight." Alexander walked over to the feather bed, where a tan linen tunic embroidered with gold threads lay. The embroidering lined the collar and the ends of the garment gave it a regal appearance fit for a Prince. "It is fine indeed."

"Yes, Lady Godden sent it over as a gift for my graduation tonight."

"It is perfect," the King said. "How do you feel?"

"A little nervous, but excited." Peter stared at the bookshelves filled with his favorite books from his three years of study with Theo.

"I see the forest in the distance." The King stepped to the window. "So peaceful looking at sunset."

"Yes, it's strange, but I see it differently now," Peter murmured.

"Not so much as an anxious boy, but as a young man?"

Peter so wanted to tell his father about the Dragon and all that he had heard the day before, but he knew he couldn't. "Yes. I see it as a place that I must protect even if it means with my life." He joined his father at the window.

Alexander must have noticed his son's distressed expression. "That is something that won't happen for many moons, Peter. And you will not be alone in defending the forest or Théadril. When you are King, your knights will protect Illiath and Théadril with you."

Peter looked down.

"No need to put more burden on your shoulders than is necessary."

"Father…," Peter asked with a far-off gaze.

"Yes, Son?"

"Tell me about the trials again?"

Alexander chuckled. "Come now, Peter, we have talked about the trials so many times before."

"Is it true that each knight must experience his own trial?" Peter asked with a more serious tone.

Alexander cocked his head toward Peter. "Yes. This is true. But come now, there is no need to be concerned about any of that. You have training to endure first. Then you will face the trial set before you when it comes." He patted Peter's back with his large hand. "You have more exciting things to think about tonight. You're graduating! Then you head off to Knight Training and more adventures. Then the trials and all that." The King walked toward the door and opened it.

"You're right, Father. I had almost forgotten all that is to come." Peter smiled.

"So go ahead and get ready. Go downstairs to the entrance hall and greet your guests," the King said in a joyous manner, then exited the room.

Peter stared at the tunic on the bed. It was beautiful, and he felt special. After putting it on along with his brown trousers, he headed downstairs.

The frantic servants were carrying out the final preparations for the graduation ceremonies. The food had been sorted out on wooden platters inlaid with silver and gold. They prepared roasted turkeys and pheasants decorated with their long feathered tails, as well as fruits of all kinds sitting out for all the guests to see. Gold pitchers filled with fruit wines were placed next to the goblets for each of the guests to enjoy. Flowers from the gardens were arranged in vases made from hammered gold. They lined the tables and entranceway and added to the most pleasant aromas. Finally, the cook's finest pastries were displayed with care at the end of the long banquet table. Cakes and puddings as well as Peter's favorite cookies were set out in a tempting manner. It was a glorious sight.

Peter found his way to the entrance hall where his father stood alongside the Constable ready to greet arriving guests. But the smells from the dining room were too great to be resisted. Peter snuck off when no one was looking and inspected the treasures of the banquet table. Slowly he took in all the fine smells of the meats and breads until he spotted the plate filled with his most favorite cookies: honey snaps. Made with whole grains mixed with butter and flavored with rose petals and honey, these morsels would melt in one's mouth. He bent over to inhale the sweet aroma of the sugary delights. Then, looking around to make sure no one could see, he picked up one cookie and placed it in his mouth in its entirety. As he tried to chew, he couldn't help but close his eyes and let out a revealing moan of pleasure while the buttery treat melted in his mouth.

"Excuse me," someone said.

Startled, Peter coughed up a few crumbs and continued to chew quickly. Then he swallowed. "Yes?" he answered and coughed again.

"What are you doing?"

He turned to see it was a very surprised Annika speaking to him.

"Oh, it's just you," he said with relief. A few crumbs flew from his mouth. "I thought it was the butler." He dusted leftover crumbs off his new tunic and continued to inspect the food.

"You cannot eat now. Especially dessert!" Annika said with authority and her hands on her hips.

"Why not? Who made the eating rules that everyone abides by anyways? If I want dessert first, then why shouldn't I get it?" Then he bent over to smell the aroma of the cakes and puddings.

"Because your guests have not even arrived yet. Do you think they want to eat food that has already been pawed over by you and your unwashed hands?" She frowned. "Ick."

Upon smelling the pudding, Peter straightened quickly. "That one has raisins in it. I hate raisins." He frowned back.

He had moved on to the next pudding when suddenly a loud trumpet blast signaled that guests were making their way toward the entrance hall.

"Come now, we've got to take our places!" Annika ordered.

She and Peter ran out of the dining room and found their places near the entrance. Peter spotted Simon and Crispin walking in with Theo and positioned himself next to his father, King Alexander. Annika stood with her grandfather, King Baldrieg of Glenthryst, and assisted him. One of the eldest rulers in Théadril, Baldrieg was once a fierce warrior, but now he appeared feeble and weak with age. He was also the uncle of Alexander's late wife. Annika wore a long blue dress made from silk and embroidered with silver threads. Some gemstones lined the hem of the garment: amethysts, rubies, and other crystals. They sparkled in the light of the torches aligning the hall. Her usual tattered yellow hair was combed straight and pulled back tight. A thin golden crown with one purple amethyst centered over her forehead sat gently upon her head, revealing her royal blood.

§

When King Mildrir arrived to find his favorite grandson, Simon, waiting for him, he hugged the boy enthusiastically. The two laughed and walked into the hallway together. Simon had proved to be a superior student. He excelled in almost every subject except history. He often told the others that he did not like studying all the battles and wars of the past. But he finished all subjects with high marks and was ready to move on to an apprenticeship with a court astronomer in Thorgest. The city's position high on a cliff by the sea made stargazing most beneficial. Simon possessed a most enviable collection of telescopes, and he couldn't wait to return home to begin his research. He would miss his new friends, though. He had enjoyed their company immensely these last three years and hoped to see them again soon. In a way, he did envy Peter's journey to the Crow Valley to begin training.

Upon spotting Alexander, Mildrir eagerly approached him. "Any news of the quest?"

"Yes, and not good, I'm afraid. We will discuss this more after the ceremonies."

Mildrir nodded and then took his place in the entranceway.

§

Crispin scanned the gathering crowd for his uncle, Isleif, ruler of Gundrehd. Not sure if Isleif would make it to the ceremony, since he hadn't heard from his uncle in several days, he remained hopeful. But then, to his relief, he saw his uncle approaching. On Isleif's arm was Crispin's mother, Princess Leona. He ran over to the pair and embraced them both at once.

"I'd almost forgotten how much I missed you all," he said to them.

His uncle Isleif was more than generous to allow his entire family to live at the palace in Gundrehd, and he was a kind man with no family of his own.

"How are all my brothers and sisters?" Crispin asked his mother.

"All are well, my son. They wished they could be here," his mother said. "They cannot wait to see you again."

Together, they walked up the palace steps.

"Will he be joining the quest for the swords?" Crispin asked.

"I suppose." She sighed.

§

As the crowds entered into the grand reception hall of the palace at Illiath, the four graduating youths grew nervous and apprehensive standing in the hall waiting for their cue to enter. Near them stood Sir Theodore Sirus III, their tutor and mentor of the last three years, looking regal, dressed in a long black velvet robe with silk stripes on the baggy sleeves. Along the front of the robe was gold ribbing that stretched all the way to the bottom hem from the collar of the garment. He wore a blue velvet cap with a golden tassel that fell across the right side of his head. The Master's cap indicated his rank as Royal Tutor to the Prince of Illiath. Whenever he moved his head, it dangled like a charm banging against his cheek and caused his students to giggle. He gave them a stern look that quieted them down. In his arm he held a leather-bound folder with mysterious contents.

"Whatever can it be?" Annika whispered to Peter.

"Don't know," he replied.

"Shush!" admonished Theo. Then he beckoned the four students over to his side, lined them up behind him, and escorted them into the ceremonies.

The crowd's murmuring stopped. All eyes fixed on the procession. A trumpet sounded the commencement and the King stood from his throne to welcome his son and the others into the grand hall.

As the trumpet music continued, Peter and the others looked all around the room at all the faces staring at them. He could not recognize most of them, but they seemed to know who he was. Finally, they reached the throne when the music stopped and Theo spoke.

"My Lord, I am honored to present to you my graduating students. His Royal Highness, Peter, Prince of Illiath, Lord Simon of Thorgest, Lady Annika of Glenthryst, and Lord Crispin of Gundrehd," Theo said.

The guests applauded enthusiastically.

"These four students have successfully completed all assignments put before them with honors. All have shown great maturity and character. Ahem!" Theo cleared his throat as he looked up from his wire-rimmed spectacles to eye the four youths standing before him in order to signify his reluctance to continue reading. The students chuckled as they knew Theo was remembering all the pranks they had pulled on him and all the tardiness that tainted their lessons over the last three years.

"These students manifested a strong work ethic and loyalty to the regions in which they serve. All present should be proud of their accomplishments."

More applause came thundering from the crowd of people. Peter smiled at his father, who grinned proudly while he clapped.

"Without further ado, I humbly ask this court and all royalty present for permission to graduate these fine students. I ask that they be accorded all rights and privileges appertaining this day in the kingdom of Théadril." Opening the leather-bound case to reveal four lambskin diplomas with each student's name written in ink, he handed each student a diploma. They eagerly took them and read their names. When he reached the last student, Peter, he smiled and stood next to him.

The audience erupted in one last round of applause.

King Alexander stood and promptly asked for quiet. "Now, it is time for us to bestow our gifts on these graduates." He motioned for the Constable to approach with a large object covered with a red velvet cloth. "My gift to my son."

The cloth was removed, revealing a beautiful crossbow. Peter gasped at the sight.

"Every knight in training has one," his father said.

Peter took the weapon from Darion and inspected it. It felt heavy in his young arms, but he knew he would be able to use it once he entered training. He noticed the intricate hand-carved details in the wood that set it apart from all other crossbows. He smiled at his father, who seemed very pleased.

King Mildrir beckoned to his servant, who came carrying a large object also concealed with a red velvet cloth. Together the two stood in front of Simon. When the cloth was removed, he saw a beautiful, custom-made telescope, made of brass and polished to a glistening shine. Simon stared at the instrument with great satisfaction, pointing out his name etched in the brass.

"Incredible!" he shouted as he glided his fingers along the long brass tube. "It's perfect, Grandfather." The two embraced.

Next, Isleif motioned for his sister and their servant to approach Crispin. Neither carried anything, which at first seemed curious, but Isleif motioned for his servant to hand Crispin his gift—a small envelope sealed with red wax and a king's signet. When Crispin pried open the envelope and read its contents, a large grin appeared. He, his uncle, and his mother embraced. Then Isleif announced to the crowd that the gift was a notice of apprenticeship with Lord Asgeir, the great court philosopher of Gundrehd. All applauded the news. There was nothing greater to Crispin than the chance to sit at the feet of such a great teacher of debate and reasoning.

Finally, Baldrieg made his way over to his young granddaughter and led her over to the large picture window that overlooked the green gardens of the palace lined with lit torches.

As Annika stood gazing out the window, a sound came from the garden. At that instant Peter knew it was the most familiar and precious sound in the world to her young heart—a horse whinnying. Then, suddenly, a black stallion not more than two years old stood in the garden. Head held high, he looked defiant and proud with his black mane flowing in the night breeze.

"Oh, Grandfather!" She gasped at the sight of the magnificent beast, clasping her hands over her mouth. "How wonderful..."

"His name is Taj, and he is the colt of Aedán, the most excellent stallion of all Glenthryst," Baldrieg said. "And he is all yours, my dear."

Annika appeared frozen for a moment, then threw her arms around her grandfather.

The assembly erupted in loud applause as all the students beheld their gifts. Then off they went to gather in the dining hall for the grand banquet, where everyone laughed and seemed to be having a wonderful time. The students talked with relatives and friends about their studies and adventures as well as their gifts. Peter proudly showed his guests the diploma he had earned. Then he talked of the Dragon and his adventures in the Battle of Caragon. The ceremonies lasted until the late hours of the night.

When Peter noticed Annika talking with her relatives as well as Simon and Crispin, he wondered if they would ever see each other again. Suddenly, he felt sad as he remembered he would be leaving the next day for Knight Training. Glancing around the large hall at all the people laughing and eating, he spotted the large painting of the Dragon Forest behind them. As he slowly walked across the floor toward the painting and stopped to stare at it, Peter hoped no one noticed him. Many memories flashed, almost making him dizzy. He turned to see the painting of his mother looking so regal as the Queen Laurien of Illiath. As he approached, he was almost hypnotized by her eyes. He stopped in front of the painting, turned to see if anyone had noticed him, and when he felt sure no one was watching, took the compass from the pocket of his trousers and opened it. Sure enough, the painting opened like a door, revealing the hidden passageway behind it as it had done so many times before. Placing the compass back into his pocket, he slipped into the passageway, making sure no one spotted him. Then he closed the painting behind him.

Grabbing a torch from the wall, he led himself down the familiar passageway toward the classroom and library of Theo. To his surprise, it was lit with many candles. He walked into the room, sat on his assigned chair, and read all the titles of all the books in Theo's classroom. He sighed at the finality of the evening.

"Peter," someone whispered behind him.

Startled, he turned to see a familiar face. "Annika…what are you doing here?"

"I saw you come in through the painting. What are you doing down here?"

"I'm not sure."

"Remembering?"

"I suppose. Annika?"

"Yes, Peter." She sat in her assigned seat.

"Do you remember your mother?"

"No," she said wistfully. "She died when I was very young. My grandfather raised me. I do not remember my mother or my father."

"I see."

"Why?"

"I am having trouble remembering my mother. And it bothers me."

Annika nodded.

"Now that I am leaving, I wish I could remember her voice or her face when she spoke. But her memory is fading. It saddens me. What if, when I'm gone, I forget about this place?"

"Peter, you are off tomorrow to begin a wonderful adventure!" she took his hand in hers. "You mustn't be sad. This is such an incredible time for you. You've dreamed about this moment for so many years, and now you will be a knight, a royal knight!"

Peter managed a weak smile.

"How fantastic it will be for you to joust and sword fight with others. Then you will go to the trials and maybe even return to be part of the quest for the swords."

"Yes, I know." He was tempted to tell her about his encounter with the Dragon. But he held back.

"I envy you. I wish I could go along with you. I know I could be a great knight." She smiled at Peter. "Try to remember your mother as she was. I am sure she is proud of you."

Just then, more voices came out of the darkness.

"What are you two doing down here?" asked Crispin as he entered the room.

"The same thing you are doing down here," Annika said.

"I came down to see if I left my favorite book here by mistake," said Simon, following behind.

"And I came along with him," Crispin said. "There are too many adults talking out there. It's boring."

"What about you, Peter? Why are you here?" asked Simon as he searched through the books.

"I came to get away, too," he answered.

"Isn't it odd that we won't be here any longer, you know, to study together?" Annika asked as she thumbed through a book on the table. "It seems strange that we will all go our separate ways tomorrow."

"Yes," Peter agreed. "It will seem strange."

The other boys sat at the table.

"Three years is a long time," said Crispin. "But I must admit that I cannot wait."

"Me neither!" said Simon. "I want to go home and use my telescope. Weren't our gifts magnificent?"

"Yes, splendid," Crispin said. "We deserved them after all our hard work."

"Yes, I can hardly wait to ride my new horse!" Annika beamed. "And Peter, what about you? You'll be leaving for training in the morning. How exciting for you!"

Peter forced a smile. "Yes, exciting. But one thing…"

"What is it?" Annika asked.

"I find it interesting that all of us here in this room will be leaders of our own lands one day."

They all sat quietly in the room.

"All of Théadril will be depending on us to be good and honorable leaders," Peter continued. "What do you think about that?"

"I must admit, I haven't thought about it in a while," said Annika.

"I haven't thought about it either," Simon replied.

"Isn't it interesting that you are thinking about it, Peter?" Crispin added. "Future king and all."

"Well, I suppose since I am heading off to train, it has been on my mind," Peter said. "I often wonder what sort of leaders we will be. I know we are all intelligent, but will we be loyal?"

"Loyal to what? Our people?" asked Crispin.

"Well, loyal to the Oath…to the covenant," answered Peter.

"What do you mean?" asked Annika.

"I mean the Oath of our fathers and grandfathers…the one they made with the Dragon."

"You mean the dead Dragon? Come now, Peter," Simon scoffed. "You of all people know that that Oath no longer matters. The Dragon is dead. Théadril is fine now. We are prospering now more than ever before!"

"The Dragon gave its life for us," said Crispin. "There is no need for any Oath or covenant."

Peter sat and listened to the boys. It frustrated him that they no longer believed in the Oath. He felt himself becoming angry in his frustration. He wanted to tell them that the Dragon lived and that he had a choice to make, but he obeyed the Dragon's wishes.

"The Oath continues to matter," he said firmly. "Just because the Dragon is gone doesn't mean the Oath is erased. The leaders of each region swore to uphold the Oath. My grandfather swore. My father swore. And so will I."

Annika stared at Peter as though she suddenly noticed how he had grown these last few months. His facial features were more chiseled now. His eyes were deeper set. He no longer had a boy's face. He was beginning to look like the man he would soon become.

"I understand." She grasped his hand. "I know what you're saying."

"Come now, Pete," Simon said. "Look around! Théadril is growing by leaps and bounds. There are more townships and cities emerging than ever before. The people are prosperous. There are more places to discover. I, for one, can hardly wait to travel with my grandfather and visit the many islands in the East Ocean this coming summer. He says there are so many people settling on the islands, and they are wonderful places to visit. Théadril isn't the only land that matters any longer. You need to get your head out of here and see the world!"

All this sounded dreamlike to Peter. What the Dragon had told him was reality. What did these three know of reality?

"I have a kingdom to run when I return from Knight Training. My home is here in Illiath, in Théadril. I cannot afford to dream what other lands are like. I have people counting on me to uphold the Oath. I am sworn to protect the Dragon Forest from attack at all costs." He stood. "I made a promise. I, for one, expect people to keep their promises. I will keep mine."

Peter started to walk out of the room when Crispin hurried to meet him at the door.

"Look, Peter, let's not say good-bye this way. We all are friends. We all admire each other greatly. I admire you. You will be a king one day! That's fantastic. I know you will rule with honor and humility as your father has. I know you will be a great king one day." He placed his hand on Peter's shoulder. "It's just that not all of us are in the same position. If I become ruler, I will rule with honor and integrity even though I do not understand the Oath of my grandfathers. But the chances of me becoming king of Gundrehd are rather slim. My brother will probably rule long before I do and if he has a son, then he will become king."

"But if your brother goes off to the trials," Peter hesitated, "then you would be next in line after your mother."

Crispin briefly looked away.

"I'm sorry," Peter said. "I didn't mean to make you think about it. But I have been thinking about it. While we studied the history of this land, all I read over and over again in those books there on the shelf was that the Oath is what binds all the regions and the leaders together. Theo warned us not to forget the Dragon or the covenant. He told us to make sure we remember and teach it to our children lest they forget. Remember?"

"History is my least favorite subject, I'm afraid." Simon slumped.

Crispin headed back to the table.

"But if, by chance, I am ruler of Thorgest one day, I promise you I will uphold the Oath. I will come alongside you and the others to protect Théadril," Simon said.

All was quiet and calm in the chamber, though tension still radiated.

"I suppose we may never see each other again after tonight," Annika said. "Isn't that sad?"

"I guess you're right. After three years, it will seem odd. We will each head our separate ways and return to our lives," replied Simon. "Yet, that is a good thing."

"I know what we could do!" shouted Annika with great joy. "When Peter returns from the trials, I am sure we will all be invited to Illiath to welcome him home."

Crispin nodded. "That's true. When you complete your trials, Peter, you will return and, knowing Constable Darion, there will be a grand celebration arranged and we will all be expected to attend. Then we will all be reunited once again."

Peter smiled, but he knew in his heart this was not true. After what the Dragon told him, he knew he would probably never see any of them again. Even if they did reunite, they would never be the same. But he went along with the notion just to make Annika happy.

"Yes, I will make sure you all are invited to attend," he said.

"There, that's a much better ending," said Simon as he headed for the doorway. "We should all return to the banquet before they come looking for us."

Somberly, they all walked up the dark stairway together, Annika in front of Peter.

Deep in thought, Peter climbed the steps slowly. "It's as if I have a choice to make, Annika," he murmured to her.

"What do you mean?"

"I mean, on one hand, I could go to Knight Training as I've always wanted." Peter looked down at his hands, which were cupped as though holding his choices. "And on the other hand, I have this duty…this task I was given before I was even born. Something I cannot walk away from. Yet I do not feel prepared to handle it."

Annika crinkled her brow, as though trying to understand what Peter was saying.

"I want to go to Knight Training. But this task is expected of me. It's a choice I have to make, I suppose." He laughed a little.

"It will be all right, Peter." She took his hand into hers to assure him. "Everything will be all right."

5 THE DECISION

Way past midnight, after the guests left and the servants began to clean up the dining hall, Peter and his father climbed the long staircase toward Peter's bedchamber. Alexander held a torch in his hand to light the way. They halted at his door.

"Peter, I know you are exhausted, but…there is one more gift I want to present to you tomorrow, but I thought I would ask you about it first."

"What is it?"

"Well, Darion has informed me that you plan on taking Titan with you to training. Is this true?"

"Yes, he is my horse."

"Yes, but he is very old, Peter. He is almost fourteen years old now. That is very old for a horse."

"But he is my horse."

"I just wanted you to know that I have another horse for you to take with you, as a gift. You can see him in the morning if you'd like," Alexander suggested.

"No, I have my horse," Peter said while entering his bedchamber. "I have no need for another." He was loyal to the horse of his childhood, and Titan was special to him since the horse was a gift from his mother.

"I understand. Well, good night. Get some good rest. You have a very busy day tomorrow."

Peter walked into his bedchamber. His father followed, using his torch to light the candles in sconces on the wall. Peter collapsed onto the soft feather bed and moaned.

"Tired?" the King asked.

"Very," Peter answered.

"Good night, son," Alexander said as he stood in the doorway.

"I am proud of you." He closed the door.

Peter lay on the bed, resting his hands behind his head, and stared at the wooden beams on the ceiling. He would miss his room. He always felt safe here. Eyeing his bookcase with all his favorite books lining the shelves, he knew they would have to stay behind and wait for him to return. Then he spotted his sword. It was small, too small for him now. He would need a new sword to take to training. Next to the sword was the shield that saved him from the Black Dragon's fiery breath. The scale of the Dragon beamed in the light of the candles in his room. It had been years since he held it.

He got up and walked over to the shield. Peter took it and held it for a few moments. Turning it over, he slipped his forearm into the grip that was once the tendon that held it in place among the many scales on the Dragon's body. The scale was light yet sturdy as he remembered. Not one part of it had been damaged by the Black Dragon's fire.

Amazing. He ran his fingers along the smooth surface. It seemed so sacred to him now. He decided he would not take it with him to training. He didn't want to risk losing it or having it stolen.

"No, it'll remain here." Peter set the shield down. "I'll call for it later before I head to the trials. I've decided," he said to no one there. But he felt as though someone was listening. "I will go to Knight Training first and then face this task the Dragon spoke of."

At that instant Peter realized how much he would miss home, but he didn't want to think about it. It hurt too much thinking about being away from his father and how much he missed his mother. He lay back down on his bed. The last three years had been wonderful for him and his father. Their relationship grew stronger, and they were closer than ever, but he felt guilty not telling his father about the Dragon. He rolled over.

Would he even believe me? He would probably storm the forest and seek the Dragon's help with the quest.

His father had the quest for the swords on his mind. Hardly a word had come from any of the knights, and not one sword had been found in the three years since they left the palace. Peter was grateful for all the time his father had spent with him. Yet he knew it would have to come to an end this year, his thirteenth.

Peter's eyes drooped with exhaustion. "I'm not ready for such a task as saving the kingdom," he said out loud. "After training, then I will be prepared." He smiled. "Yes, that's it. After Knight Training…"

He tried to keep his eyes open, but it was of no use. As he thought about the Dragon, his friends, and the past three summers with his father, he slowly fell asleep.

§

King Alexander solemnly headed downstairs after saying good night to his son. It would probably be the last time he would say good night to Peter as a youth. He finally understood the torment his own father experienced when he left for Knight Training at such a young age. Alexander remembered the faraway look in his father's eyes when he rode out of the castle courtyard so many years ago.

Now it was his turn to say good-bye to his only son, the only family he had left. He sighed heavily. When he reached the bottom of the stairs, Darion stood waiting to lead the king to the grand hall for yet another late-night meeting with his knights regarding the quest for the swords.

Alexander stood in the now quiet palace, hating the silence. Then, ignoring Darion, he began the slow, solitary walk down the long hall toward his bedchamber.

6 DEPARTURES

Early the next morning, the palace prepared for Peter's departure. The castle staff swiftly served breakfast, and as the King, Peter, and Darion enjoyed the food, King Mildrir and Lord Byrén approached the main entrance hall.

"My Lord." Alexander stood to greet King Mildrir. "I had no idea you would be here this morning. I thought you and Simon had already left for Thorgest last night."

"The situation with the quest left me with a restless sleep," King Mildrir stated. "I stayed in the Solar near the chapel with Simon. I sent him off with my servants this morning. I will catch up later today. I feel we need to talk more about the quest for the swords."

Alexander's countenance fell.

"Do not worry, my friend," said King Mildrir. "I am on your side."

Lord Byrén served himself breakfast and sat at the grand dining table. He situated himself next to the Prince. "Excited this morning your Highness?"

"Very," answered Peter.

§

Later that morning, King Alexander led his son down the entrance steps and into the courtyard. The birds were singing. All the guests entered into the courtyard where Peter's horse, Titan, stood waiting for his master. Older and grayer, the horse was outfitted with a new set of armor and a new saddle sitting on a new scarlet horse blanket with the golden crest of Illiath stitched on both sides. Peter had never seen his horse with an armor shield on its nose before and the sight made him chuckle. Titan looked like a regal horse fit for a royal knight. Peter spotted his new crossbow, and other equipment required for the long journey to the Crow Valley was attached to the saddle.

Titan whinnied and stomped the dirt with his front hoof as he waited for Peter.

King Alexander continued to explain the day's itinerary to his son. "Lord Byrén will escort you to the Crow Valley for security reasons."

"Yes, Father."

"It will take you many days, so you will have to sleep in the desert hills."

"Yes, Father," Peter said. "We've gone over this many times."

"You're right. I had forgotten you already know all you'll need to know." He put his hand upon Peter's shoulder, as if amazed at how tall he was at age thirteen. "But I do have something for you," he said as he motioned for a servant to bring forth an object covered in a blue velvet cloth. When he arrived at the King's side, he dutifully unveiled the marvelous gift for Peter.

"A new sword!" Peter reached for the silver and gold hilt. "It is brilliant!" He inspected the detail in the hilt and blade, recognizing the filigree of his forefathers.

"You'll need it for training," Alexander said. "I had it designed especially for you. No other knight has one like it in all of Illiath."

"Fantastic!" Peter whispered as he held the blade in his hand. The double-sided blade was nearly three inches wide and settled to a sharply defined point. The steel glistened in the morning sunshine. The blue sky was reflected in the mirror-like finish and the gold carvings in the hilt sparkled. It was a sword fit for a future king of Illiath. He took it as a sign that he'd made the right decision.

"I shall never forget this, Father. "It is truly a magnificent gift. Thank you."

The two embraced in the courtyard as Titan nickered loudly.

"I suppose we had better leave now so we can get a good start," Peter said as he pulled away from his father.

Alexander reluctantly let go of his only son.

As Peter and his father walked out to the busy courtyard grounds, Peter caught a glimpse of Theo standing amongst the crowds of townspeople. He excused himself and greeted Theo, who looked very pleased with his former student. Theo was dressed in his black academic robe, buttoned up to his collar. Peter wondered if the man ever wore anything else.

"I am proud of you," Theo said, reaching out his hand. Peter shook it enthusiastically. "I know you will do well. How do you feel?"

"A little apprehensive," Peter confessed. "But very excited, sir."

"I have no doubt about that. Do you have all that you need?"

"Yes, sir. My father has made sure of it."

"What about the compass?" Theo asked.

"Yes, sir. I wouldn't leave without it. I have it right here in my pocket." Peter patted the side pocket, secured with a button. He could feel the compass. It made him feel safe.

"Good." Theo placed his arm around Peter's shoulders. Together they strode toward the entrance where the King and his guests were waiting. "Always keep it near your heart. Do not lose it. You will need it. Make sure you remember that much. You will be far from home now for many years. Returning to the palace may be a difficult venture in the future, and your mother knew this. That compass was made so you could find your way. It is important that you know this."

"I understand," Peter said, but his mind was on other things.

"Come back no matter what happens," Theo said sagely. "No matter what you may hear. Make your way back."

"Come now, son, it is time," the King interrupted.

Theo turned Peter toward his father and patted him on the back. He stood by and watched his young charge walk away with his father.

"Lord Byrén," the King said, "I hand over my son to your charge."

Lord Byrén motioned for his horse to be walked over to him. When the horse arrived, he quickly mounted and bowed his head to his sovereign. "I will watch over him, my Lord. We will send word as soon as we make it to the Crow Valley."

"Excellent," answered Alexander.

Finally, when all the servants and Peter were mounted onto their horses, they began to trot out of the courtyard and near the large wooden gates leading out to the castle ground. As the gate rose and the drawbridge was lowered to the ground, Peter's heart raced. He remembered watching Will ride through the gates and over the bridge to the hills when he left for training. Now it was his turn. He was almost too excited to contain himself, but he didn't want to hurt his father's feelings. So he pretended to be as saddened about leaving as his father was.

"Be careful!" King Alexander shouted.

"Yes, Father, I will!" Peter shouted, revealing his true feelings about leaving.

§

With those final words, Peter smiled a smile that would forever be imprinted in Alexander's memory. His son sat high on Titan's back with the golden handle of the new sword protruding from its sheath and the bright new sky behind him.

Peter dug his heels into Titan's side, and the two galloped over the drawbridge with the servants and Lord Byrén behind. King Alexander swiftly climbed a ladder leading up the castle wall so he could watch his son ride off. When he reached the top of the wall, Peter was already across the Blue River and heading into the desert hills north of Théadron Desert.

Standing silently on the wall watching his son ride off into the distance, Alexander remained deep in thought as he leaned against the limestone. None of the soldiers on guard along the wall said a word to disturb the king.

§

Darion and King Mildrir stood in the courtyard waiting for Alexander.

"Let me know when he comes down from there," Mildrir said to Darion. "Then we'll have our meeting."

"Yes, sire." Darion looked up at the curtain wall and waited for his king. Circling high above the courtyard, he spotted a white owl. "A bit odd for a nocturnal bird to be out hunting during the day," he murmured to himself. "You there!" he shouted to a guard.

"Bring me word when the king comes down from there," he ordered.

The guard nodded.

Then Darion headed into the castle and back to work.

7 THE DESERT PLAINS

Peter gripped Titan's reins as the two galloped onto the desert plains together. He could feel Titan's sinewy muscles beneath him. The ride felt good. The wind blew through his hair and he grinned at the feeling of freedom.

Remembering his escort, he pulled on the reins to hold Titan back. The horse let up and turned left into a slower gallop as the two headed back to regroup with the party. As he approached the others, he noticed how slowly the horse drawn carts trotted along with their loads of hay and water barrels. Peter knew this journey would take a while.

"What a beautiful morning!" he said as he approached the others.

"Yes, yes it is," Lord Byrén said. "But we must pace ourselves, sire. These horses have to pull our equipment through the gorge and out the other side."

Peter slowed Titan to a trot. After a while, the late summer sun rose high over the party as it came to the first gorge. Peter hopped off Titan to help lead the horse-drawn carts down a steep slope. After successfully maneuvering the slope, all the men helped the horses climb out of the gorge to the top of the cliff where the rest of the land was less hilly and rocky.

Peter mounted Titan again and rode ahead to find a good resting place for the evening. The land surrounding them was more beautiful than Peter ever imagined. The flat plains looked so peaceful and serene. He could just barely see the green trees of the Dragon Forest off in the distance, but this didn't bother him. He felt at ease in the land of his fathers. Soon all this land would be his to govern. He was glad he could finally survey it on his own.

The plains consisted of red dirt against dark rock with small patches of green trees and grasses occupied by goats and sheep.

Peter and Titan walked on the plains with the wide open skies all around them. He spotted a red-tail hawk circling above them probably searching for its next meal. It hovered gently in the air reminding Peter of his flight with the Dragon of the Forest so many years before. He gladly remembered the feeling of flying through the air and envied the hawk's freedom. The warmth of the sun on his face and the sound of Titan's hooves on the dirt made for a perfect day.

As the sun began to sink behind the looming mountains, the men decided to camp for the night. Peter dismounted, unpacked his saddlebag, and laid his crossbow and sword on the ground. Then he unbuckled his saddle and laid it on the ground. He watched as the other men rolled out their belongings and began to gather wood for the fire.

A loud thunderclap rattled the horses.

"We'd better get to work on the fire before it rains." Lord Byrén ordered his men to speed up the search for wood.

The clouds over the mountains were trying to block out the setting sun, but it continued to shine brightly through them sending colors of red and purple shooting through the sky toward the east. The sight was incredible to Peter as he helped pile up the wood in the center of the camp. His stomach growled from hunger, but he decided to feed Titan some hay first. Walking over to the servant's horses, Peter grabbed some hay from one of the carts. He dropped the hay in front of a grateful Titan who then began to munch quietly on his feast. A servant walked a water bucket over to the horses. Each horse trotted over to the water bucket and drank. Peter began to help the servants gather wood.

"Your Highness," Lord Byrén interrupted. "Please, allow my men to do their work."

Peter didn't realize that he, being a sovereign, wasn't supposed to assist the men in their task. Embarrassed, he sat down near his belongings and took out an apple to eat. Suddenly, the camp grew quiet. Only faint sounds of distant thunder could be heard. A slight breeze whisked through the horses' manes. Each standing side by side, the horses quieted themselves down for the evening. The air began to cool as day turned to evening. The stillness felt nice to Peter who had been rushed the last few months back home as he prepared for graduation and Knight Training.

Now he had time to reflect and rest before the real work began. All the men sat near the carts and horses as their horses ate oats and drank water. Lord Byrén watched one of his servants start a fire with two twigs. The constant rubbing of the two pieces of wood together caused some smoke and then, finally, a spark was seen. After a few moments, the Prince and the others spotted a small fire burning the grasses while the servant stoked the fire with twigs. Soon the woodpile caught fire and all the men cheered.

Peter smiled. Being an only child, he never really experienced camping out under the stars with anyone other than his father. Oh, there were the usual bodyguards several feet away at all times, but they never participated in the fun.

The fire grew larger and sent more sparks into the night air. The sun dropped farther behind the mountains. More thunder was heard, but it sounded farther and farther away. This made Peter feel better as he hoped it wouldn't rain that night. He didn't want to sleep on the wet ground.

"Peter," Lord Byrén asked. "How do you feel?"

"Excited," he smiled.

"Good!" Lord Byrén answered. "Hopefully it will not rain tonight. The mud will make it hard to ride out of the hills in the morning. But the cooler air is pleasant."

The men searched the skies for rain clouds, but only the higher thinner clouds covered the sky.

Peter decided to start a conversation.

"Did Peregrine have something to do with my mother's death?" he asked.

"Come now, Peter, let's eat some meat," Lord Byrén said.

His servant handed him some roasted pork wrapped on a stick.

"No, I want to know the answer to my question."

"Peter, you are too young for such knowledge."

Peter frowned in frustration. "If I am old enough to be sent off to training, then I am now old enough to handle such information about my own family."

Lord Byrén sat chewing his dinner.

"Now, tell me kind sir, did Peregrine have anything to do with my mother's death?

8 JOUSTING

Will sat high on his horse with the lance in his right hand resting on the earth below him. He stiffened his shoulders. The armor on his back and shoulders was heavier this day than any other. His squire stood nearby with an assortment of other weapons ready for the joust. Will's horse, a chestnut charger with long lean legs and a muscular body, stood ready for the order to charge ahead for its master.

Not adorned in full barding for the joust, the horse wore only a steel chanfron shield on its crown to protect it from the other knight and his lance. As dangerous as it was not to have the horse fully protected, Will found the heavy armor too distracting and inhibiting to his horse. He preferred his horse to have mobility in the joust. The red caparison with the heraldic emblem of Illiath embroidered on each side rested on the back of the able steed. Together, Will and his horse had won every joust that year in the list field of the Knight Training camp set deep in the woods of the Crow Valley. With the visor of his jousting helmet up, Will quietly and carefully studied his final opponent in the field as the crowds gathered that day into the arena stands.

He glanced up and noticed the sun sitting high in the sky signaling the beginning of the joust. A hush fell over the crowd as they noticed the knights lowering their visors and steadying their mounts. Will could spy his opponent through his metal visor, but the heat caused beads of sweat to fall into his eyes. He blinked steadily as the salty sweat stung his eyes. He gripped the lance tighter and shifted it in his hand. Then he lifted it into place under his right arm while he gripped the reins of his horse tightly in his left hand. With his loyal squire a mere few feet away armed with sword and ax, Will gently nudged his horse forward and together the two walked into the tiltyard. His opponent faced him at the other end of the yard where he stood on his mount, waiting for the white flag to be dropped.

Will's opponent wore more elaborate armor. The helmet of carved steel over his head gave the impression that he was a more experienced knight. Will had to conserve his strength to get through this last joust and prepare for when the battle took to the ground in hand-to-hand combat. He could hardly restrain the excitement building up inside him. He had recently divulged to his instructor how he loved to joust. He had wanted this all his life. Now he was experiencing it.

The white flag, held by a squire atop a platform several feet high, dangled in the breeze. The crowd grew silent with bated breath, waiting for the action to commence. Will's chestnut horse nodded its head up and down nervously. Will tugged on the reins and gripped the lance even tighter. So many unpredictable things could happen, and Will had to be ready for any one of them this day.

Will inhaled deeply and waited.

The white flag dropped and a raucous cheer arose from the crowd. The two opponents began the joust. With lances drawn and horses galloping toward each other, no one took a breath as the moment came. With fantastic speed and power, the two men met on the tilting field with full force as their lances clashed together sending both to the ground. The horses continued to run. Will quickly leapt to his feet first and motioned for his squire to bring him his sword while his opponent scrambled to his feet still dazed from the clash.

Will grabbed the sword and the crowd cheered again. He lunged forward toward his opponent who had his sword in his hands. As he raised the sword high above his head, Will swiped it down where it met the other sword with a clamorous sound sending both men twisting around. Will lunged forward again, pushing his opponent back and slashing him with the sword, but the metal met the armor of the knight. Sparks flew into the air.

The crowd whooped with joy at the sight of the two men fighting. In the Crow Valley, jousting was a popular sport. The people loved the tournaments and traveled from afar to attend them.

The clashing of metal clashing with metal echoed through the forest competing only with the cheers of the exuberant crowd. The two knights lunged toward each other with swords and bucklers in constant movement. Will's opponent held nothing back. With each blow to his body, he could feel all the man's power. Will was able to maneuver well and avoid several blows that would have ended the joust and sent him to the infirmary.

Will's youth and celerity were his most valuable weapons in the joust. He had learned much from his instructors and employed great skill with the sword. The two men continued to swing their swords forward and backward with grace and ease. Suddenly, Will's opponent yelled from deep within, catching Will briefly off guard. He lunged toward the youth with a shove to the chest that sent Will backwards onto the dry ground and his sword flying from his hands. As Will met the ground, his armor pinched his back causing great pain. Will yelled out, but then he rolled over two times, recovered his sword, and leapt to his feet, causing the crowd to whoop loudly for their favorite. He gained his balance, only to meet his opponent's sword clamoring down at him, and raised his sword in time to meet the steel blade. Then, turning around, he swiped at his opponent, striking his sword with such force as to propel it into the air, then hitting him in the face and also sending the helmet flying off.

It was only then that Will saw the identity of his opponent: Sir Reginald of Thorgest, a fine knight experienced in battle. Sir Reginald lost his bearings for a second or two, and then swiftly regained his balance as he stood up ready to fight. But his sword was nowhere to be found, so he motioned for his ax.

The crowd grew quiet.

They could see the anger and humiliation in Sir Reginald's face as he circled around the tilting field. He did not enjoy being bested by the young knight in training. Will quickly removed his helmet and threw it to the ground. Inhaling the air, he grinned, enjoying the coolness on his face, wet with perspiration. Then he held his sword with both hands as he studied his opponent. Round and round the two slowly circled, waiting for the opportune time to strike.

With great strength, Reginald raised his ax high above his head and lunged toward Will, who thrust his sword into the exposed flesh of his opponent's thigh. This caused him to awkwardly lower the ax to the ground, missing Will by several inches. But Will spotted the blood of his opponent, circled around, and sliced at the upper arm of Reginald finding more exposed flesh. His blood stained the silver armor as the crowd drew gasps. They knew the end of the battle was near.

Reginald stumbled and fell to one knee a few times as Will, sword held high, waited for another chance to strike. The pain caused his eyes to blur as the sweat poured down his face. He winced with each step he took, not knowing if Will would have mercy or not.

Finally, the pain was too much to take, and he knelt down on both knees. The crowd went silent in their shock.

"I yield to your mercy, Sir William," Reginald gasped.

Will lowered his sword and stood before his foe. Then, in the deepening silence, he gazed up at the crowd. He saw men, women, and children wondering what was going to happen. He smiled widely, knowing it would be his last joust, his last victory at training. Then, slowly turning toward Sir Reginald who was kneeling and bleeding from his wounds, Will stood for a moment before the knight and then reached out his hand to help him up.

The crowd roared its approval. Will helped his friend rise to his feet and limp off the tilting field. At long last, Knight Training had come to its glorious end on the jousting field where Will felt most at home.

As the crowd chanted his name, Will handed the wounded knight over to his squire and then bowed to the crowd one last time.

§

The final joust of the summer months had left Will battered and bruised, but he was ready for the trials. He had successfully navigated his way through several months of wrestling and fighting in hand-to-hand combat against older and more experienced men than himself. He proved himself over the short period of time without vaunting or conceit. He was the youngest knight ever to leave for the trials so soon after training. He had entered Knight Training at age sixteen and now only three years later he had mastered all of the skills with such ease, that General Aluein felt he had to let young Will go. He hoped Will would excel and return to be a fine member of King Alexander's Royal Knights.

Dressed in his finest royal armor with helmet, Will sat regally on his grey horse who was also outfitted in proper barding and royal caparison on its back. The two made an awesome sight to the new recruits. Will lifted the visor of his helmet up to reveal his intense blue eyes glaring at the new recruits situated only a few feet from him. They sat nervously on their horses awaiting orders to enter the fields to begin their training. As he inspected each one, Will noticed Peter was not yet among them. He motioned for his squire to approach.

"Has Prince Peter not yet arrived?" he whispered.

"No sir, he is set to arrive this evening or early tomorrow," the squire answered. Will could not hide his disappointment. He knew he would not be in the fields to welcome his friend because he was to depart in the afternoon for the Black Hills.

"Very well," he said, dismissing his squire.

Will trotted over to the young men staring intently at him. He rode up and down the ranks counting each man. He turned his horse around and continued his inspection.

At that exact moment, General Aluein arrived on horseback watching the scene. He trotted over to Will.

"What's this?" he asked Will's squire. "Inspection of the recruits?"

"Yes, General," the squire answered, bowing his head.

Aluein smiled as he watched young Will intimidate the youngsters.

What mostly caught the eyes of the young men that morning was the shield Will had dangling from his saddle. It was no ordinary shield, but a Dragon's scale glistening in the sunlight. As Will galloped on his horse on the green grass and into the sunlight, the young men noticed how beautifully the scale-shield reflected the light. The men no doubt also knew the legend of the Dragon. Only the best knights received the scales from the Dragon of the Forest on the last day of the battle of Caragon. Will, a veteran of that war, proudly displayed his shield.

Finished with his inspection, Will trotted his horse over to General Aluein. "Not much there." He sighed. "I am afraid you all are in for many years of hard work in order to make these young boys into royal knights." He purposely said the statement loudly so the new recruits would hear.

"Aye," said General Aluein. He dismounted his horse and walked a few paces back to the jousting field several yards away from the new recruits. "Have you decided what you will do when you return from the trials?"

"I think I will live here," he said as he gazed all around the field.

Surrounded with tall thin pine trees, the jousting field resembled an arena of sorts. Several royal banners made with brightly colored silks and satins with the Crow Valley crest and the Illiath crest stitched on them snapped in the wind across the wide open blue sky. All was quiet and serene in the jousting arena since training had ended.

"This place feels like home to me. My desire is to look after my ailing father by bringing him here and purchasing a parcel of land where we can breed horses," Will said.

"Sounds like a good plan, Sir William," General Aluein said as he walked his horse into the shade. "What about the quest for the swords?"

"I will gladly join in the quest if the King so desires. I have already written to my father. Any word on how the quest is progressing?"

"Not much news coming in as of yet, but it is still early. Do you know yet where you will be going for the trials?"

"Southwest of the Black Hills." Will gestered his head westerly toward the ominous mountains.

"You must be careful. Several fire-breathing dragons have been spotted. Also, many Baroks have been seen past Vulgaard and near Bedlam's realm of Ranvieg. The elves continue to flee from Vulgaard. The dark presence remains lo these many years," Aluein warned. "Be watchful."

"I will, my General," Will said. "I wish I could stay longer to welcome Peter. Please give him my best when he comes."

"I will, he will be sad he missed you."

"Tell him some tall tales about me! Make me look good!" Will laughed as he pivoted his horse. "I will see you soon, my friend." And with that, Will galloped off through the trees.

Aluein watched Will ride off, and remembered the time when a young inexperienced yet boastful Will entered into the camp as a recruit. Aluein smiled at the memory. Although Lord Caragon was dead, Bedlam remained as elusive as ever. The fight was far from over.

9 MEETING OF THE RULERS

Green and beautifully kept with rows of red roses and jasmine vines planted for the Queen many years before, the grounds adorned the palace like fine jewels. Tall trees lined the grass yard where King Mildrir and King Alexander walked as they discussed the ongoing quest for the swords. The two kings walked with hunched shoulders as though the quest weighed on both their minds, especially since young Peter wanted to join in after his testing in the trials. Both Kings understood that this could be a possibility since no knight had spotted the swords yet. At times, King Alexander felt his friend, Mildrir, was the only ruler who understood the importance of the quest and the collecting of the swords.

"The sight of the sword of my father being carried away by the black crow has never left my mind even after these many years," Alexander said.

"You must ease your mind, Alexander," Mildir said as the two walked the grounds. "You did what needed to be done to stop Caragon. We must keep our thoughts in the present and not in the past. What's done is done."

"But perhaps Eulrik is right. Perhaps the quest is over," Alexander said.

"Nonsense! Eulrik spoke out of emotion and not logic. With time to think, I am sure he will attend the next meeting with a clearer head."

"Perhaps. But I can't help but think that we sent those men out to die for a lost cause."

"Never. Our knights volunteered to do a noble thing. For their lands and people they search for those swords. It has only been three years. You and I know of quests that have lasted decades."

"This is true, but do we have time? What can we do to assist their search?"

King Mildir thought for a moment. Older than Alexander, his dark hair and beard showed some signs of graying, but his eyes remained clear. His strongly defined face looked serious, but hid a sometimes childlike personality that reminded Alexander of his father.

"I was thinking that perhaps they are looking in the wrong place. My scouts have been asking to venture in a different direction, but I wouldn't allow it. Now I am thinking perhaps they are correct in their assumption," he said.

"To where are they asking to go?" asked Alexander.

"Near the realm of Ranvieg."

"That's suicide," said Alexander. "Even the elves are fleeing from the region. I hear the darkness lingers near Vulgaard. We cannot allow it."

"Yes, that is true. It will be dangerous. But what if they are right? What if Bedlam has obtained, somehow, all the missing swords and is hording them in his realm because he thinks no man or Elf or Dwarf would dare enter to retrieve them?"

"It is too risky," Alexander insisted. "We would be sending them to their deaths. What would Eulrik say to that?"

They stopped near the pond to rest on a small bench made from twigs intertwined.

"I, for one, do not care what Eulrik would say or what accusations he would make, and I suspect you do not care either. We have to do what needs to be done to assist the knights on this quest. If we were able to get word to them of the precise location of one or all the swords, then we would be giving them the best assistance there is: reliable information…which is more than they have now," Mildrir explained.

Alexander walked over to the pond's edge. "I have thought about the knights out in the wilderness now riding from town to town not knowing if they would meet friend or foe, searching and asking about the swords. And I have thought about their families and their estates after all these years. Helping them is more important now than ever," he said.

"You are correct," Mildrir said.

"Although it is dangerous, we must try. Sending our scouts that far is a risk, but if they are willing to take it, so be it. I have often felt Bedlam had many of the swords. It is time to find out. I will send word to the knights that we are sending more scouts out as far west of Vulgaard as we can. This should give them hope," Alexander said.

Mildrir stood and stretched. Then he walked over to the King and patted his shoulder. "Alexander, don't you think it's about time to move forward?"

But Alexander continued to stare into the calm water.

"You know, now that Peter is gone to Knight Training..."

Finally, Alexander looked at him. "What do you mean?"

"Marriage, Alexander. Family," Mildrir chuckled. "Don't you think it is time to find another wife, have more children, and begin again?"

Alexander turned and walked away. "I was married already."

Mildrir followed him. "Yes, but there are so many young maidens at other kingdoms who could provide you with many children and years of—"

"I was married. My wife died. End of story," Alexander said curtly.

Mildrir smiled as a father would smile at his son.

"Understood," Mildrir said. "Come. Let's return to the palace."

The two walked to the palace gate in the eastern wall of the castle where Alexander ordered the scouts to gather in his chambers in the Solar.

§

In the castle of Alexander in the kingdom of Illiath, the regional rulers sat around the large table in the grand hall of the palace. All ten representatives sat waiting to discuss the quest for the swords. Sons and daughters now represented those leaders who had fallen or died years before. Each region had a say in the desperate search for the missing swords.

"As we gather here together once more, I am reminded of those who are no longer with us due to death in battle or by age.

Let us pause for a moment to remember our fallen leaders," Mildrir said. He lowered his head in respect. One by one, all of the rulers lowered their heads as they remembered past kings.

"All right, let us get on with this meeting," said Ronahn, heir to Hildron's throne. Carved out of a colossal mountain west of the Black Hills, Hildron stood ominously as a silent reminder of the high cost of betrayal. Ronahn resided south of Illiath because the castle at Hildron was no longer his. Ronahn's anger and bitterness toward his father for allowing the region to fall into Lord Caragon's hands continued to burn deep within his heart. He was a king without a land.

Lord Caragon, perhaps the worst of Bedlam's stooges, betrayed Alexander's father, King Aleon. The weak-minded fall easily into the hands of Bedlam, and Caragon was weakest of all. Bedlam used him to starve the people of the Crow Valley, forge weaponry, and experiment with the creation of foul monsters called Baroks to use in war. These half man and half creature soldiers were birthed at Hildron along with mysterious black metal used in the war. He took over Hildron castle until his death against the Dragon of the Forest. The castle had remained eerily silent, but Sir Ronahn cannot return and claim it for his own. Not until Lord Bedlam is dealt with.

"There is much to discuss," Sir Ronahn said.

"If we stop this quest now, all is lost. All of our regions will fall," said Eganir, heir to the late Niahm's throne. "My father will have died in vain. I cannot allow that to happen."

Princess Aemelia, there to represent her father Naál's region, smiled reassuringly at Alexander, who appeared exhausted and saddened by his son's departure. He rubbed his forehead as though worried.

"This blind quest has gone on long enough. There hasn't been good word from the knights in many moons. As I said before at our last meeting, my son remains missing and I want this quest to end," Eulrik insisted.

"As much as it pains you to look past your own concerns, Eulrik, we must realize that this quest greatly affects all the kingdoms. If we do not destroy all the swords…if even one remains….then Bedlam's powers remain. We cannot allow that to happen. Too much is at stake. My scouts tell me that the darkness is moving yet again. Many elves are fleeing into the higher country risking freezing temperatures to escape Bedlam's realm of darkness. Reports are coming about how men from smaller villages are mysteriously missing. Something sinister is coming," King Mildrir said.

"I agree," Isleif, heir of Gundrehd, answered. "It is far too soon to call this quest a failure."

"I decree, that we should hold on a bit longer," said Thorgaerd of Théadron. "Our knights are doing their best. We cannot let them down by calling off the quest after all they have given these last three years. All of them deserve our patience and loyalty."

Strangely, Eulrik sat quietly. Alexander studied him closely.

The decree was seconded and all the others raised their hands in agreement.

"This is a sad time indeed," said Mildrir. "Our lands are experiencing prosperity and peace unlike anytime in Théadril's history, and yet we cannot enjoy it, knowing that the swords are missing."

"Let us not wallow in what we cannot control. We must bring good spirits back to our people. Let us show them that this time of prosperity is not transitory, but long lasting. Let us set the example for our people," said King Beátann the Wise. "All is not lost. The swords will be found.

When the sun cast long shadows throughout the room, the meeting finally ended. Many of the rulers decided to stay at Illiath palace for the night. As the servants showed them to the rooms on the upper floors, Mildrir walked with Alexander.

"I noticed you were very quiet during the meeting," Mildrir said.

"Yes, Peter remains heavy on my mind."

"Everything will turn out alright," Mildrir said. "I remember when my son left for training. It was a hard time for me. Of course, having many children still in the palace helped ease the sadness, so I know this must be hard on you here alone in this large castle. But we've already discussed that. So…good night." Mildrir followed the servant to down the hallway.

Alexander lay in his bed, but couldn't rest. His mind raced with thoughts of Peter. He felt uneasy, the old pain in his side returned. Instead of trying to sleep, he got up from his bed and sat in the large chair watching the fire dance in the fireplace. He gazed up at the portrait of Queen Laurien hanging above the fireplace. The Queen wore a red gown and her dark hair was braided, framing her face . On her head rested a delicate crown of gold. Her lovely green eyes stared back at him. She had given him the portrait as a wedding gift. How could he remarry and replace the only love he had ever known?

Alexander returned his gaze to the fire as he wondered what the next few months would bring for the kingdom.

§

Peter sat near the fire, waiting for Lord Byrén to answer his question about his mother and Sir Peregrine.

"She died from illness. She was so young. Everyone mourned her death," Byrén said. "I do not think Peregrine had anything to do with your mother's death. She grew ill and that is the fault of no one."

"Yes, but, I saw something in a book and—"

"Really, Peter," Byrén sighed. "You cannot always believe what you read in those books written so long ago."

Peter remained unsatisfied. One day he would ask his father about it, but for now he would have to accept it.

"Well, looks like the men have already placed their bedrolls around the fire. We should join them." Lord Byrén stood and made his way over to the fire where his bedding had already been set out by his servants. Peter followed suit. It was the first time he had ever slept out in the valley without his father. It felt strange. He frowned as though saddened by something. He realized the memory of his mother was heavy on his mind. He gazed at the stars above.

Peter shivered and rubbed his arms. The air had turned colder, and as Peter climbed into his bedding, the fire's warmth soothed his uncertainty. As he laid his head on a folded blanket, he decided to try and count the stars above him to help ease his mind. Soon enough he would be entering into the Knight Training camp and into a hectic life for the next three years. He wondered what his father was doing at that precise moment. Then he thought of Will and his successful training. He knew that Will would probably head out west to begin the trials. He envied him.

Prince Peter fell asleep to the gentle bleating of the sheep in the distance.

10 RAVENSTAIL

The sky darkened quickly with the clouds blotting out the setting sun. Will looked at ease in his surroundings. He and his horse had made their way deep into the valley as they neared the foot of the Black Hills. The land was beautiful indeed. He had never been this far away from Illiath in all his life, but he felt more confident than ever before. He had passed through many quaint towns and villages with names such as Barrow Hallow, Wolfshire, and Riverdale. The townspeople seemed pleasant and welcomed the royal knight as he rode through and ate with them. He told them stories of training at Crow Valley, and they told him folklore about Lord Bedlam and of nearby dragons searching for prey. Will listened intently to the stories of the dragons knowing that he would face one sooner or later. The townspeople described the dragons as agile in flight as dragons of times past. They advised Will to be on the lookout for the beasts and to prepare himself for sudden attack.

As the sun began to hide further behind the mountains, Will decided to spend the night in a small village called Ravenstail on the far western side of the Black Hills. He and his horse had made good time in their travels.

He found a small inn converted from a large barn. Entering slowly, he spotted an old Dwarf carrying in a box from outside.
The Dwarf sized Will up and down as he placed the box on the floor. "Looking for a room for the night?" he asked Will.

"Yes, please," Will answered as he removed his helmet and gloves. The cool night air was fresh on his skin. "Any room will do."

"I suppose you want to eat as well?"

"Ah, no, that won't be necessary," Will answered. Bored of feasting on berries, roots, and mushrooms he could find in the forest, he had instead decided to hunt for meat. He patted his saddle bag where a freshly killed rabbit was stuffed inside.

"Suit yourself," the Dwarf said as he motioned for Will to follow him to where some rooms had been built in the old converted barn. A large structure for such a small town, it had at two stories worth of rooms and a tavern for spirits on the first floor. Several men and Dwarves were smoking pipes and drinking ale together. They hardly noticed the tall handsome knight walking by in his armor. Will supposed they had been drinking for quite a while.

The Dwarf led Will to his room on the second floor. Will looked around at the small bed, table, and candle. The bed had two blankets and a feather mattress that looked very comforting. He had slept on a hay mattress in training, and the thought of goose feathers made him smile.

"Very nice," he said to the Dwarf. "I will go get my bags, eat, and then head off to sleep."

The Dwarf shrugged as Will paid him two coins for the room. Then Will made his way back to his horse outside and unloaded the bags, saddle, and blanket from its back. After preparing some hay and water for his horse, Will unloaded the skinned rabbit from his bag and headed out to a clearing in the field where he quickly made a fire for roasting. Thunder continued to reverberate through the sky as the rabbit roasted on the spit Will had made from long branches. When the meat was roasted through to the bone, he ripped off a leg and feasted. The juicy meat tasted good as he sat underneath the stars that peaked through the passing clouds. He felt a storm approaching in the evening breeze as the smell of rain moved through the hay fields. One by one, candle lights in the houses came on. The townspeople settled in for the night. Tall green grasses surrounded Will. They swayed in the breeze. He found it hard to keep his eyes open as he thought more about that feather bed waiting for him.

When he finished eating the rabbit, Will put out the fire with dirt then made his way back to the barn where he found his horse no longer eating, but resting. Will entered and bought himself a mug of ale. He sat at the small table and drank it slowly, enjoying it completely. The foamy ale was most efficacious for his sore and weary body.

R. A. DOUTHITT

The Dwarf came by to stoke the fire in the large fireplace, and the two chatted for a moment. The Dwarf snorted as he spoke and seemed to be a gruff fellow. He told Will of the history of the small town and how peaceful it was since the war with Lord Caragon had ended.

"A most unnecessary war," the Dwarf said.

"What do you mean?" asked Will as he laid down another coin for more warm ale.

The Dwarf moved to the bar and poured Will another mug of warm ale. "King Alexander acted too rashly. All Caragon wanted was Hildron and the Dragon scales. It seems to me that Alexander went through an awful lot of heartache just to preserve that forest," He grunted as he walked over with the mug. "And the Dragon perished anyway."

"But Caragon was capable of great evil," Will said as he watched the Dwarf clean some tables. "I saw this with my own eyes."

"What evil?"

"Powerful magic. I saw him bring the dead to life to fight us on the battlefield. I saw him create horrific creatures and turn into a black dragon from the air," Will said. "He had to be defeated."

"Bah," the Dwarf said as he wiped spilt ale from tables. "Balderdash."

"And the Dragon?" Will asked.

"What about it?"

"It saved Théadril by giving up its life," Will said.

The Dwarf shrugged his shoulders.

"It is not a tale," Will said as he stood up. "I saw this with my own eyes."

But it was of no use. The Dwarf simply shook his head in disbelief and continued to clean up his small tavern.

Exhausted from the ride, Will excused himself and headed up the stairs to his room. He rubbed his forehead as though disturbed greatly that someone would not believe all that had happened during the battle. Here he was, a veteran of the war with Caragon, and yet this Dwarf did not, would not, believe his stories about what occurred there in the desert plains. Instead, the Dwarf thought it nonsense.

"How many of the townspeople also believe as this Dwarf does?" He mumbled to himself.

Upon entering his room, Will lit the candle on the small table. Then he pulled back the covers from the bed and sat on it. The softness felt good to him as he slumped forward and sighed heavily. He eyed the mud caked on his armor-covered boots. Bending over to unbuckle the armor, he felt a twinge of pain from his sore back. He removed the rest of his armor and stacked it in the corner of his room, but, ever vigilant, he kept his sword with him on the bed. Blowing out the candle, he quietly slipped between the warm soft covers of the bed, and fell asleep as soon as his head hit the downy pillow.

11 ABDUCTION

"My Lord," whispered the servant to Byrén. But Lord Byrén was in a deep sleep. "My Lord!" the servant whispered with such fervency that Lord Byrén opened his eyes and sat up. The fire had died down, but he could see Peter asleep across from the fire pit with its glowing embers. A few sprinkles of rain hit Byrén's face, and he suddenly noticed the cold outside of his downy blanket.

"What is it?" he asked the nervous servant.

"Visitors, my Lord," the servant replied. He pointed to the men approaching on horseback from the west.

Byrén quickly leapt to his feet upon hearing the alarming news.

He ordered his men to quickly wake the Prince. Lord Byrén noticed all the servants had been awake for more than a few minutes as they were all dressed and standing at the ready when the strangers advanced slowly from the west.

§

Peter awoke and stood as soon as he heard the news from the servant. Before he could even respond, the servant was already packing up the bedrolls and putting things into a cart. Other servants hitched the horses. Then, they waited for Lord Byrén's orders to move. Peter could see their hands shake. He knew they were nervous.

As the strangers approached, Peter quickly understood exactly why the servants were nervous. In the moonlight, unobstructed by the clouds, Peter could see the caparison on the horse in front. It was dark with a gold emblem stitched to resemble a dragon. As each horse and rider entered into the camp, it was that the strangers were from the prison, Rünbrior, near Ranvieg. For only Rünbrior has the dragon emblem created by its warden, Valbrand. Each horseman wore a dark steel helmet with a closed visor, a black tunic with Valbrand's crest on the chest, and leather gloves. Their boots were polished to a shine and reflected the moon. Most of the horses were thin and lanky, but the lead horse was a large breed with thick legs sustaining the muscular body. Long hair covered the enormous hooves and it stomped at the damp ground. Its mane was braided down its curved neck. The beast strained against the reins. Peter had never seen such a large breed of horse before. In the cold, Peter saw its breath come from its nostrils as though it were fire breathing. The beast neighed loudly and filled all the men with fear and trepidation. More sporadic rain drops continued to splatter the dirt.

The lead horseman entered into the camp, halted his horse, and then signaled his men to dismount. The men obeyed their leader and Byrén's servants stood their ground cautiously, all except for one. He yelped out and then ran off into the hills revealing to his master and everyone in the camp his fear of being captured. The men watched him run off into the darkness.

Byrén stepped toward the lead rider of Valbrand's men. "What is it you want here this early in the morning?"

The leader, high on his mount, silently turned toward Byrén. Then he methodically turned his head toward the Prince. His eyes inspected Peter's clothing, comparing him to the other men. Lord Byrén swiftly walked over to Peter and stepped in front of him to make Peter seem more like a servant. The dismounted riders combed through the camp and all the belongings inside the carts. A few raindrops pelted their helmets. They were taller men, with thick strong arms. One held onto a long pole that held the Rünbrior banner made of a torn piece of grey fabric with a coarsely painted version of the crest on it. All the men had long steel swords attached to their belts. This fact did not go unnoticed by Lord Byrén. They were armed and ready for any resistance. Their horses whinnied in the cold night air. They made the camp horses nervous including Titan, who neighed loudly, grabbing Peter's attention. As Peter began to walk over to Titan, Lord Byrén stopped him.

"Where do you think you are going?" he shouted to Peter. "Start loading my things into the carts!"

Peter, startled by the orders, stood perplexed at Byrén.

"Now!" Byrén shouted, pushing Peter forward. The other men began to pack up the camp. Peter hesitated to follow along until he realized that Byrén must be treating him as a servant in order to hide his true identity from the strangers.

The leader of Valbrand's men continued to watch Peter move along with the servants.

"I asked you a question," said Byrén. "What is it you want here in our camp so early in the morning?"

"It isn't up to you to ask the questions," said the leader coolly.

One of the riders came toward Byrén. He towered over the elderly Lord.

"So shut your face!" And with that, he slapped Byrén to the ground.

"No!" Peter shouted. He ran toward the stricken Lord lying on the ground. But one of the riders grabbed Peter and lifted him up as his legs kicked beneath him. He twisted and turned in the man's arms, but he couldn't get free. "Let me go!" he shouted.

Byrén's servants grabbed their swords and lunged at the riders, but they were met with Rünbrior swords entering their flesh sending each one to the ground writhing in pain.

"Take him," the leader ordered.

Peter watched each servant struggle on the ground, their blood spewed out all over. Then the rider holding him took him to his mount. Peter saw Lord Byrén, unconscious, lying on the ground.

"Lord Byrén!" Peter shouted. "Master!"

The rider lifted Peter onto his saddle. The rider mounted his horse behind Peter and heeled the horse's ribs. Titan whinnied and neighed as he watched his master being taken from the camp. He reared up and broke loose from the cart.

"Run now!" he yelled. But Titan trotted over to him. "No, boy, run now. Go! Go home!"

Titan obeyed and began to gallop off into the darkness. Peter tried to watch his horse run off toward the hills, but the riders who held him captive all galloped off into the opposite direction leaving seven servants dying on the ground along with a battered Lord Byrén.

Suddenly, the rain began to pour, stinging his face. The rain mixed with the warm tears streaming down his cheeks. The camp disappeared from view.

12 THE CAPTIVE PRINCE OF ILLIATH

Puddles remained on the ground from the night's storms. That next morning, Will awoke from a restful night's sleep. For a minute or two, he forgot where he was. But next to his right hand was his sword. The cold metal against his skin quickly brought him back to the reality of the moment. A new day had come.

After dressing and making his bed, Will made his way to his horse where he covered it with the saddle blanket, saddle, and harness. It nodded up and down while chomping on the bit in its mouth. Will, sensing his horse's impatience, rubbed its long brown nose to settle it.

"Easy now, boy," he whispered.

"Heading off so early?" a voice asked Will. He recognized it as the Dwarf from the previous night.

"Yes," Will nodded. "I have many miles to cover today."

"Ah, the trials," the Dwarf said as he picked up some wood from outside the barn for the fire. "I see you are just starting your journey."

"Yes, how did you know?" Will asked.

"Just a feeling, I suppose." The Dwarf smiled as he carried the wood. "No visible wounds, no marks on your armor, and you're still walking upright. Heh. Don't think you've seen much battle on this journey."

Will smirked. "If you're trying to concern me with the dangers of the trials, you won't succeed. A Royal Knight craves the trials."

The Dwarf chuckled. "And you know all about the trials, do you?"

"What's that supposed to mean?"

The Dwarf struggled with the wood. Will tied up his horse and helped the old Dwarf bring in some wood.

"Each knight must face his own trial," the Dwarf said.

"Understood." Will placed the wood down near the fire pit. "Some will face dragons, some will face the enemy, while others—"

"While others won't know they're facing the enemy until it is too late." The Dwarf took a rag and wiped his dirty hands with it. He handed it to Will.

"I suppose you see Royal Knights ride through here often?" Will wiped his hands.

"More so than not." The Dwarf chuckled. "And they tell me all about their bravery. Yet I never see them after they face the trials. You know what I mean?"

Will handed him the rag.

"Does General Aluein continue to lead the training?" the Dwarf asked as he placed some wood in the fire pit.

"Yes. I'm surprised that you know about Aluein. Do you know him?"

"Aye. He is from these parts. His mother was a Dwarf and his father a man." The Dwarf stoked the fire.

"I didn't know that," Will said.

"Aye. He left here many years ago to fight for the King. He never returned. Don't blame him, of course. Not much excitement around here. But I do see many of the knights he has trained ride through here."

"I am heading toward Ranvieg," Will nodded toward the southeast.

"Yes, I know." The Dwarf lit his pipe then held it between his lips. "I sure hope you're ready for what's out there, lad."

"I am," Will answered as he stood taller. "I spent the last three years in preparation."

"Well, Aluein is a good teacher. I know he taught you well," the Dwarf said while puffing his pipe. "But make sure you are ready for what's to come."

Will exhaled. "I wish you would just come out and say what you mean."

"You are heading into dangerous territory. More than just dragons are out there, you know?" The Dwarf squinted his eyes. "Bedlam," he said as he puffed out some smoke. "He's out there. And he's looking for Royal Knights." He smiled with the pipe in his teeth.

"Bedlam doesn't frighten me," Will said. He relaxed a bit more.

"Well, he should, lad, he should."

Will tried not to show his impatience toward his little friend, but his jaw clenched as though the conversation was getting to him. "I think I had better leave rather than get into an argument with someone ignorant of the ways of war," he huffed. He turned to walk out the door of the large barn. "I thank you for your hospitality."

"Guard your thoughts," the Dwarf shouted. "The enemy doesn't always attack like we think it will."

Will stopped at the doorway, but did not turn around. When his horse spotted him, it whinnied and stomped at the wet ground. At that moment, a loud thunderclap came from above followed by raindrops. Will placed his helmet on with the visor up, mounted his horse, and pulled it to the right. He raised his gloved hand to the Dwarf in a gesture of gratitude then rode off along the pathway leading out of the small township. Smoke came from all the chimneys of the little thatch houses spattered throughout the village. The people were preparing for another day's work. The cool air stung Will's face while he rode. "I can't wait to leave this sleepy town," he said to his horse.

The air was crisp and clean as Will and his horse trotted through the forest. Several hours passed and the sun stood high in the sky ever obscured by rain clouds. More thunder echoed throughout the morning sky. The sound of his horse's hooves on the muddy path and its heavy breathing were the only sounds heard until a black crow broke through with its loud caw. Will glanced upward to see the large bird circling above him and he suspected he was being followed or spied upon. But he decided to continue his way through the green forest, fresh with the scent of ferns and stream water.

Just then, he heard a rumbling in the bushes nearby. He quickly took his sword from its sheath and held it out as he pulled on the reins to stop his horse. He lowered the visor on his helmet and waited for a sound from all directions as his training taught him not to rely on his eyes only, but on all his senses. Sure enough, the rustling sound was now behind him, but he did not turn. He steadied his horse and together they remained calm, ready for any attack. He slowed his breathing down with techniques his trainer had taught him. He gripped his sword tightly with his right hand and used his left hand for balance in case the attack came from behind. Then, he waited.

Will remained unconvinced the sound came from a frightened animal. The black crow cawed above them again, startling his horse. Will squeezed the horse with his thighs and calmed it down. He continued to wait.

"You're good!" said a voice from the bushes.

Will turned to meet the voice with his sword drawn before him. Then, he quickly jumped down from his horse ready to meet his foe. Instead of an attacker, Will spotted a young Dwarf coming from the bushes.

"I waited for you to run off, but you never did," he said as he approached the knight.

"No, and I won't run off now either," Will answered as he pointed the sword at throat of the approaching Dwarf.

"You are a royal knight, yes?" he asked.

"Yes, what is your business out here in the forest?"

"I was hiding."

"From what?"

"Rünbrior guards," the Dwarf answered as he looked back and forth. "That black crow there. One of Valbrand's spies!"

"Rünbrior guards?" Will placed his sword in its sheath. "Which way did they ride?"

"Southwest," the Dwarf pointed.

"Did they see you?"

"No! If they had seen me, they would have taken me with them." He rubbed his arms in an attempt to warm himself. He was clothed only in a short sleeved tunic and pants. He wore no shoes or gloves.

"I wonder what they wanted," Will said.

"Oh, it gets better than that!" the Dwarf laughed heartily. "They had a young boy with them."

"A boy?"

"Yes, captured boy. The Prince!" the Dwarf laughed as he jumped up and down.

"The Prince?" Will asked. "What Prince?"

"Prince Peter of Illiath, you fool!"

Will's eyes widened. Stunned in disbelief by the prospect of the Prince being held captive.

"Are you saying you saw the Rünbrior guards holding the Prince of Illiath captive?"

"Yes!"

"Are you sure?"

"Yes!" the Dwarf shouted as he rubbed his arms. "I saw him. He was being held captive by the guards as they rode through the forest just this morning. They were headed southwest. I am sure they are riding toward Ranvieg."

"And they did not see you?"

"No, but that crow…I am sure it is a spy!" the Dwarf leapt into the bushes once again. "Don't let it see me!"

Will squinted his eyes. Was the Dwarf slightly mad? He hesitated. "How do you know it was the Prince? Have you ever seen the Prince?"

"Yes!" the Dwarf said from the bushes. "I worked at the palace a few years back. I worked in the brewery and I met the King and Queen once. I saw Prince Peter many times. It was him. I know it!"

Will believed him, but he wasn't sure what to do with the information he just heard. "And he was the only captive?"

"Yes. No other prisoners were with them, only the Prince!"

"Where were you when you saw them?"

"Walking along the path heading home, I heard the horses approaching. I turned to see the banner of Rünbrior prison and leapt into the bushes for fear of my life," the Dwarf said as his eyes grew large. He gesticulated with his arms as he described the banner. "No one can forget that banner."

"Why would they take you?"

"They take anyone now," he answered.

"What do you mean?"

"Valbrand orders his men to capture anyone for his prison. He needs men now to do his work."

"What work?"

"You are not from around here, are you?" The Dwarf tilted his head. "Just finished training, eh?"

Will nodded his head yes.

"Ah, then you wouldn't know."

"Know what? What work?"

"Valbrand puts his prisoners to work in the mines near Ranvieg," the Dwarf said. "And in the games."

"Games?" Will asked. "What games?"

"Evil work there at Rünbrior. The forests aren't safe!" the Dwarf's eyes thinned to slits and flickered back and forth.

Will had been warned about Bedlam trying to build up an army.

"I never heard of Bedlam allowing any gaming near this region. I thought Valbrand was in the mining business?" Will asked.

"Bah, it is not about the mining business. It is about the games!" laughed the Dwarf, amused by Will's ignorance of the region.

"What sorts of games are taking place at Rünbrior?" Will asked.

"Valbrand delights in sword fights of his prisoners. He collects large quantities of coin and gemstones for his winners. The games are known all over the southern region. Many come from far off to watch the prisoners fight each other," the Dwarf said as he watched the crow flying above them. "...and the dragons!"

"*Dragons?*" Will stood perplexed. He had heard nothing of these games back in the Crow Valley. He thought of Peter trapped in such an environment. "The prisoners fight dragons?"

"Lots of gold coin to be won in the arena!" the Dwarf rubbed his hands together. "Everybody loves to watch the dragons."

"I've never heard of such a thing," Will looked down the path. "And you're certain it was the Prince? You were in the bushes. Did you see him clearly?"

"Yes!" the Dwarf shouted. "I'm sure it was the Prince of Illiath."

Will nodded to the Dwarf. "I have to do something." He moved toward his horse.

"You must ride back to the castle at Illiath and tell the King!" the Dwarf shouted. "I have to keep moving so the crow doesn't see me." He ran deeper into the forest green pushing ferns and ivy bushes out of his way. "You must ride back!"

Soon the Dwarf was gone.

Will looked around as though he wasn't sure what to do. What would Valbrand do if he discovered Peter was the Prince of Illiath? Would he have Peter killed? Was there enough time?

"I have to go after Peter." Will grabbed the reins and swift mounted his horse. "But the King. He must know what has happened to his son." He looked behind. "Is there time? It will take me days to ride back to Illiath!" Will lowered his visor. "No! I'll go to Rünbrior first and find Peter. Someone will get word to the King. Peter doesn't have much time. I've got to go to him. Move!"

Will dug his heels into his horse and galloped out of the forest heading south toward the prison at Ranvieg.

13 RIDERS OF RÜNBRIOR

The darkened skies were violent with rain and wind as the riders came to a stop near a wooden bridge. Peter's eyes stung from the drops hitting his face. He managed to see a row of other boys close to his own age standing near the bridge. Many were thin and clothed only in tunics and trousers. They shivered in the cold. That's when Peter realized they had been kidnapped as well.

The rider holding onto Peter stopped his horse and dismounted taking Peter with him. When Peter's feet reached the ground, he fell to his knees. His legs were almost numb after several hours of riding on the saddle. The guard grabbed the collar of his tunic and lifted Peter up. Peter forced his legs to move as the guard bound his hands and ankles with leather straps. Then he shoved Peter into the line with the other boys as the hard rain continued to fall.

Peter looked up to find the moon, but it was hidden by the black clouds moving in the wind. The tree tops swayed in the storm as more thunder could be heard in the distance. A bolt of lightning silently lit the sky and illumined the place where they stood. Peter could hear a raging river and spotted the bridge nearby. A darkened path was on the other side of the bridge. He became frightened when he realized his journey had not ended.

Another guard came to the line and connected Peter to the other boys with chains around the leather straps on his wrists and ankles making it hard to stand let alone walk. Peter watched the guards gather together as the leader, mounted on his giant black horse, sat giving orders. Peter saw the men handing over his crossbow to the leader. The man held it up and tried to inspect it in the dark, but decided to attach it to his saddle.

Peter rubbed his arms and shivered. He stood as close to the others as he could, hoping the men did not recognize that he was the Prince of Illiath. To keep his identity hidden would be key to his survival. He looked at the other boys attached to him by the chains. Some were younger than he was and they were dirtier with mud on their faces and bodies. Peter realized that they had been captives for a while. He felt sorry for the boys as he wondered where they came from. Some tried to fight off sleep while they stood and hoped not to collapse for fear of retaliation by the guards. Peter inhaled deeply to keep calm. He tried not to think about where they were headed, but he knew deep in his mind that these guards were from Rünbrior, a most ghastly prison he'd heard about in tales.

Peter thought back to what Theo's history lessons, to what he'd known of Rünbrior. It was a prison carved out of a mountain range of Ranvieg, was created several thousand years earlier. The Elfin King, Kætilfast, used Rünbrior to hold prisoners of war inside his dungeon, but soon the wars increased and the prison grew in size, becoming a useful place to hold prisoners for crimes against the kingdom as well as traitors from faraway lands. Its warden, Kætilrøy, the King's son, was a most gruesome Elf with a lust for wealth. When he discovered many dragons nested within the mountain caves, he sent crews in to mine the caves for the treasure of the dragons. There his men discovered gemstones in the nests of the dragons. They captured the dragons and stole the treasure. That's when Kætilrøy realized he could make a fortune by forcing the prisoners to fight the captured dragons.

Kætilrøy hid himself deep inside the dungeon walls and allowed the prison to rot away from neglect as he used the prisoners for his games. Many weaker prisoners died away quickly, leaving only those fit enough to fight and die in combat.

King Kætilfast began to hear tales of the dungeon from those loyal to him, and so he ordered it closed and his son brought back to the palace at Vulgaard. Many years later, when the peace finally came to the Elfin region, the prison closed until Lord Bedlam was exiled to the Ranvieg region, where he made his fortress. He reopened the prison to house those who dared to go against his fortress. Queen Thordis, current ruler of Vulgaard, sent word to Bedlam that her kingdom would not tolerate the prison nor the games held within. She warned him that her army would destroy Rünbrior once and for all if he did not obey her commands. And for many years Bedlam did comply with the Queen's wishes. But rumors spread about the kidnappings Elves and children. Townsfolk said male children were sent to Rünbrior without trial only to be used for slave labor and the games.

Bedlam's power grew and the darkness spread throughout the lands, enveloping even Vulgaard and sending many of the elves into the forest and mountains for safety. Vulgaard's army dwindled down to a few thousand elves loyal to Queen Thordis, but far too few to fight off Bedlam's growing army of wicked Baroks. So, the prison grew and the mines were captured by Bedlam's men. A warden, Valbrand, was put in place to run Rünbrior and the games began again.

§

Peter tried to stand with the others as long as he could, but his legs grew weary and his eyelids heavy and sore from the stinging rain that continued to fall to the soaked ground, making a thick, heavy mud. The guards stood around a fire pit laughing as they warmed their hands. They seemed to be awaiting orders to move their prisoners across the bridge. Peter wondered why they were taking so long to move. He needed to move his legs in order to stay awake and he feared what would happen to them all if they collapsed to the ground from exhaustion.

The minutes felt like hours. His body ached and his stomach growled from hunger. His bladder, full since the day before, betrayed him and sent his warm urine down his leg, but because it was raining, no one noticed. All the boys could have relieved themselves there in the line and no one would have noticed.

The leader raised his arm and sent his men scampering around like wet rats running from a cat in the night. They quickly mounted their horses and shouted orders to Peter and the others. The line of prisoners moved across the bridge. Peter found it most difficult to move with his ankles chained. He noticed all the boys had the same trouble. The guards didn't seem to mind how slowly the boys moved so long as they moved. As they walked over the bridge, lightning flashed and lit up the sky once more, allowing Peter to see their position and the raging river below. For a moment, he thought about trying to escape by jumping into the rushing water, but he knew it was impossible with the chains binding them all together. Yet he knew he had to try something at some point before his identity was discovered. Slowly, they moved across the wooden bridge to the other side until all they could see were more trees surrounding them like guards. More lightning illuminated the sky.

That is when Peter looked up and saw their destination: The black mountain known as Rünbrior prison.

His body shook uncontrollably from fright. He thought about his father hearing the news of his kidnapping and putting together a rescue attempt.

Soon, he thought, *they will be coming for me soon. I just have to hold on a little longer.*

The group made their way through the trees where they finally parted revealing a set of torches lining a winding pathway up the side of the mountain until the torches disappeared into a cave carved out of the mountainside. Several guards stood at the opening and greeted the riders as they came. The leader, mounted on his horse, trotted by and disappeared into the mouth of the cave, sending men out to retrieve Peter and the others. One by one, the boys were unchained and led into the prison. Suddenly, one boy pushed away from a guard and tried to run into the forest at the base of the mountain. Peter and the others watched as the boy almost made it to the trees when a guard released his crossbow. The arrow pierced the boy's back, sending him to his death. Peter had the answer to his question regarding escape: certain death.

Once inside the cave, Peter saw that the boys were being led deeper inside the prison toward individual cells that had wooden doors closing each one in and burning torches lining the cave walls. Some straw lay on the rock floor. The place smelled sweet from the wet hay and yet rancid from waste and burning oil. Moans and groans from inside the prison cells could be heard. Some voices were young, some were old, and all sent chills up Peter's spine as he realized how many men were rotting inside. He was taught that Rünbrior was for wicked and evil individuals who committed crimes, but now he realized that many could be innocent of any crimes and simply were abducted by the guards as he had been.

His weak body trembled from the cold night air and exhaustion as he walked deeper into the cave until finally a guard shoved him into a tiny prison cell, slammed the wooden door behind him, and locked it. Peter lay on the ground in the dark for a moment before he knelt and inspected his surroundings. There was no window and no light inside his cell, so Peter felt around with his hands. Some straw covered the ground. He crawled and felt the walls. They felt like hard rock on the sides, but the back wall was colder and had some tiny holes in it where some light came through each time lightning struck. He decided that this back wall must face the outside of the prison, or mountain. The side walls were warmer to the touch. Peter's outstretched hands almost touched both walls when he stood in the middle and his arms stretched out as far as he could possibly stretch them. The ceiling was high above him. At least the cell was dry. He crawled over to a side wall, and leaned against it trying to get warm. He curled his body up into a ball. He rested his chin on his knees and gripped his legs with his arms to stay warm as he listened to the other boys march past his cell. He counted at least fifty of them as they passed by. Then, there were no more. No other sound was heard.

In the enveloping dark and eerie silence, Peter shivered. He was afraid. So afraid, that he could not sleep at first. He sat there curled up leaning against the cold stone wall and thought. A flash of lightning lit up the night sky and that's when Peter noticed his cell was not pitch dark as it had been before. Instead, he saw a block of moonlight on the floor a few feet from where he sat. His cell did have a window. He slowly got up and turned to see where the block of light was coming from. There, several feet high above him carved out of the back wall of his cell, was a small square window letting in moonlight. Peter was delighted that the moon had made its way through the rain clouds if only for a moment to light up his dreary residence.

He took advantage of the moonlight and inspected his cell through sleepy eyes. Noticing more straw scattered all over the hard rock floor, he scooped up the straw and made his bed a little softer. He also noticed a wool blanket near the wooden door. He picked it up, shook it off, and then placed it on his straw bed.

"I've got to get out of here somehow," he said to himself.

Walking around the cell, Peter noticed the walls were smooth from years of wear. There would be no way he could climb up to gaze out the window, let alone escape. On the wall, he also noticed some carvings from previous prisoners who once occupied the small cell. Some of the carvings were in languages foreign to him, but one, he noticed, was in his own language. As he read it, he smiled.

"Home again" was all it said, and Peter agreed with its author.

Thoughts of home came to his mind: his soft feather bed, the large palace halls, the kitchens, food, his father's face, and Theo. But then he thought of his current surroundings and how this cell could very well be his new home for many, many years. Tears welled up in his eyes and he buried his head in his arms as he held tightly to his knees. As he cried, he felt his body being released from the weariness and stress of the day until, finally, he gave in. He lay down on the straw bed he had made for himself and covered his tired sore body with the blanket. The wind coming from the window was cold, but at least it blew away the stench of the cell and prison. Soon, Peter found himself in a deep sleep where his dreams took him back the world he loved most…

§

"Peter, how could you!" Annika cried as she gave her adversary quite the stare.

Peter chuckled as he removed her piece from the game board in a flourish of victory. "Easily!" he smiled. "It isn't my fault you aren't very good at this game."

Theo puffed on his pipe as he watched his students play a simple game of battle on a board he had designed himself. The game was used as a teaching tool for helping his students understand war strategy. And so far, it was working.

"I enjoyed the game, Theo," said Simon. "I find it most pleasant to conquer smaller lands with my skill and take possession of them." He grinned an eerie grin toward Annika.

"Pig," she hissed as she placed her pieces back into the game box. "This game is boring."

"What is it you want to do today instead?" asked Peter as he helped clean up.

"Simon, hand me that book," Theo ordered.

A collective moan came from his students who were more than tired of reading and discussing books.

"No, no, I am not going to make you read it," Theo said. *"I wish to show you all something rather interesting."*

As the students all gathered around the large tome, Theo turned the pages gently so as not to harm the ancient text. *"Let's see,"* he said as he turned each page. *"It is here somewhere."*

"What is it you want us to see?" Peter asked.

"I want you to see a model for a telescope that I believe you and Crispin can reconstruct together, Peter. I think you will find it most interesting," Theo said. *"Ah, here it is!"*

The sketch of the telescope was detailed and showed all the working parts. As expected, both Peter and Crispin were very interested in the telescope. *"We could easily build this together, Peter!"* Crispin said. But the others remained uninterested in the project.

"Boooring," sighed Annika. *"What about us?"*

"Well, I believe you still have some mathematics you need to work on as well as some papers to write for me?" Theo smiled with the pipe between his teeth. *"Might as well get to work."*

"How about another game, Simon?" Annika asked. She smiled a repentant smile at Theo who simply puffed on his pipe some more as he watched his students complete their day.

"You know, Theo," Simon asked as he set up a chess board. *"You will miss us when we go."*

"Yes, I do believe I shall," Theo smiled. *"All of you will be leaving here for grand adventures of your own."*

"All accept me," said Peter.

"What do you mean?" asked Simon.

"Well, as King, I will remain here at Illiath to rule my people and the lands," Peter explained. *"After the trials, I must stay here while you will travel all over and have your own adventures."*

"Yes, but the trials!" Crispin said. *"How fantastic will that be?"*

"Yes, Peter," Simon said as he moved his pawn forward. *"I believe you are forgetting that you will be on an adventure of your own."*

"That's true," Peter agreed. *"But once I am back here at Illiath, I will have to stay here to protect the people. My father has never left Illiath since his trials. And you all will be traveling everywhere searching for adventure."*

"I plan on traveling to the east islands with my grandfather," said Annika as she moved her pawn forward. *"We hope to buy horses from breeders as far away as Ibendør!"*

"I love to sail," Crispin said. *"I will sail to other lands with my father. I cannot wait!"*

Peter listened to the others talk of their upcoming travel plans after graduation as he thought about his life ahead of him. Everything had already been planned out for him since before his birth. Being born into royalty gave him no other options but to rule Illiath as his father and grandfather had with honor and self-sacrifice. For the first time, he felt a sense of regret when thinking of his future.

"Adventure can appear to be glorious," Theo said as he puffed his pipe. *"But it can lead one astray as well."*

"What do you mean?" asked Simon as he studied the chess board to make his next move.

"Well, adventure is fine, but over-rated as far as I am concerned," he said as he winked at Peter. *"A set plan for one's life seems more appropriate, don't you think Peter?"*

"Yes, but adventure is freedom! Spontaneity! Excitement!" cried Crispin as he walked around the room waving his arms about. *"What could be more wonderful than that?'*

"But adventure can also be dangerous, frightening, and perilous," sighed Theo. *"One must always be prepared, and nothing prepares someone better than a steady plan."*

"Plans are all fine and good," answered Crispin. *"But they can be dull and boring too."*

"And safe," Theo said as a puff of smoke encircled his head.

Peter knew what Theo was doing. Simon and Annika were too engrossed in their game of chess to participate in the conversation.

"I suppose," said Peter as he stood to leave the room. *"But it would be nice to have a little adventure don't you think?"*

"Ah, to be precarious, courageous, bold..." Theo smiled.

"Exactly," Peter said as he reached the door.

"You mean, for instance, standing face-to-face with a fire-breathing Dragon who then takes you for a ride high above the tree-tops?" Theo said as the others listened. *"Or fighting in a battle to save the kingdom while ghost-like soldiers try to stop you?"*

Peter stopped at the doorway and thought about what Theo said. He smiled at the memory then slowly turned to face the others.

"Yes," he said. "Those are the best adventures ever!"

§

Peter lay motionless inside his cell remembering the conversation with Theo and the others inside the warm and cozy library of Theo's study. He could almost smell the rows of dusty old books and pipe smoke. The voices seemed as real to him inside that cell as they were when he was with them all on that fall afternoon not so long ago.

Adventure, he thought. *What did they know of adventure?* He rested his arms behind his head and stared above at the moonlight coming in through the window of his cell.

Theo was right. It is overrated.

14 THE SPELL

King Alexander was alone in his study once again. He studied maps of the outer regions and read books about the history of Théadril. He wanted to make sure he was prepared for the next meeting of the ten rulers. The quest for the swords remained a most delicate issue as no news from any knight had come for many days. Alexander knew he would continue to find it hard to sleep until his son had arrived safely at the Crow Valley. A messenger was expected to arrive any day to relay the news of Peter's arrival.

King Mildrir entered into the paneled office in the Solar. "Your majesty."

"King Mildrir, my friend, come in." Alexander motioned for him to sit in a large leather chair.

"I will be leaving today to head back to my lands."

"Of course, it has been a long visit."

"Yes, and I need to return to my people," Mildrir said as he sat down. "But there is one thing I feel I need to discuss with you this day."

"And what is that?" Alexander lowered the map and gave his friend his complete attention.

"We must make sure we have a strong plan for the quest before the next meeting," Mildrir said. "I want to leave the other rulers with complete confidence in the plan."

"Of course," Alexander agreed. "I feel the same way."

Just then, a servant interrupted the King. "Your highness, a servant of Lord Byrén has just arrived at the castle."

The King sighed then excused himself from King Mildrir's presence to find Constable Darion.

"I will join you," said Mildrir.

The two men hastily made their way down a long cloister leading out to the courtyard bustling with villagers and workers. All the people were going about their business when the trumpet sounded signaling that the King had entered into the courtyard. All the business stopped as the people stood silent and at attention.

Their sovereign and his guest walked through the courtyard together. Alexander spotted Darion, who spoke with a much disheveled servant being assisted by the King's men. The servant seemed inconsolable.

Alexander stopped walking. "Peter," he whispered.

King Mildrir took his arm. "Alexander, what is it?" he asked.

Alexander felt the blood drain from his face. "I fear...something is terribly wrong," he sighed.

Darion spotted the King and quickly approached him. "Sire," he said as he bowed, "this young man has returned with news of the Prince."

Alexander nodded. "They have arrived at Crow Valley safely then?"

Darion hesitated. "No, my Lord...uh...I am afraid it is not good news at all." He began to wring his hands nervously.

Alexander hastened over to the worn-out squire who had traveled through the night to make it to the palace by morning. Soaking wet and covered with mud, the servant breathed heavily with his eyes opened wide.

"Tell me what happened?" the King asked.

"Sire, let me explain—" said Darion.

The King raised his hand, silencing Darion. "I asked the young man."

"My Lord," the young man huffed. "Peter is gone."

"What do you mean, *gone*?"

"They took Peter. Lord Byrén was struck and my fellow servants killed."

Alexander inhaled. *They took Peter*, he heard the words inside his head. *They...took Peter.*

He stepped back and tried to breathe as though he couldn't fathom what was said to him. He glanced at Darion and King Mildrir, who were equally as shocked. The villagers gasped at the news.

"Say that again?" King Alexander closed his eyes and listened.

"Guards," the servant breathed. "Rünbrior guards came into the camp. They came in with swords. I ran and hid behind a large boulder. I saw them strike down Lord Byrén. There was a fight with his men. Then they grabbed Peter and took him!"

King Alexander opened his eyes.

"I saw them ride off with the Prince!" the young man cried. "His horse ran away. I followed the horse and rode him back here. I alone survived to tell you this."

The townspeople spoke in hushed tones spreading the news of the Prince's fate around the courtyard.

With a fierceness in his eyes, Alexander raised his right hand and struck the young squire across the face, sending him to the ground. The people gasped at the sight of their King striking a young man. Darion winced.

"How dare you!" the King yelled. "How dare you run away without trying to save the Prince!"

The young servant cupped his jaw with his hand as he knelt on the ground in shock. "But sire," he cried.

"Enough!" the King said as he raised his hand again.

The courtyard grew eerily silent.

"Coward," the King whispered, looking down at the squire. Then, he stalked toward the castle entrance with Darion and King Mildrir close behind.

"Your majesty," Darion said, "do not be too harsh on the young boy. He did what he thought was right."

"His sworn duty is to protect his sovereign, the King's son! He was sent as an escort and he failed."

"Yes, your majesty." Darion bowed.

"Where is Titan?" the King asked.

"At the stables."

"I wish to see him," Alexander said.

They hastily walked over to the stables as the frightened townspeople left the courtyard in droves. As the King passed, the stable workers bowed their heads. Titan, covered with mud, stood in his stall. No saddle or blanket was on his back, only his harness.

Alexander inspected the horse. "No one could possibly tell it was the horse of a Royal Prince just by looking at it."

"No, Sire," said Darion.

"Perhaps they did not know he was the Prince." Alexander stroked Titan's nose.

"Did Peter have his shield with him?" asked Mildrir.

"No, only his crossbow," answered Alexander. "Hopefully, they did not see the crossbow."

"It is too hard to tell, my Lord," Mildrir said.

"Yes, his identity may be safe. It will buy him some time if they don't know who he is." Alexander stalked toward the castle entrance. "Ready a search party and have them head out to the plains to find Byrén...or his body. We mustn't leave him out there alone. He needs to be brought back. Send a messenger to the Crow Valley and let them know what has happened," ordered the King as he swiftly walked into the castle followed by Mildrir.

"Yes, Sire," answered Darion, who quickly departed to ready the knights, squires, and soldiers.

Darion stumbled in the entrance way.

"Constable, are you alright?" asked the King's butler.

"Yes, only...no, I am not alright. Prince Peter is in grave danger." Darion stared deeply into the butler's eyes. "We must all be ready to assist the King in any way. Do you understand?"

"Yes, Constable," the butler said.

"Good, now go and tell the others," Darion ordered as he headed to the main gate to talk to the captain of the soldiers. He spotted the captain and the soldiers awaiting orders. "Captain! Ready your men!"

"We heard the news, Constable," the captain said. "I have ordered my men to alert the knights, and I have already sent a group of soldiers out to fetch Lord Byrén."

"Good," answered Darion. He motioned for help to climb the ladder of the outer wall. He winced with pain.

"Are you alright, Constable?" asked the Captain.

"It's my legs. The old battle wounds." When Darion reached the top, he gazed over the western plains and valleys. The land looked so peaceful and serene. Slowly turned his eyes toward the Dragon Forest. It stood as quiet as ever with its towering trees of dark green. Darion wondered just how much longer the peace would last.

§

The wind grew colder on Will's face as he raced on horseback through the forest. Thin tree limbs and branches hit his face from time to time, but he knew he had to make it out of the forest and into the clearing toward Rünbrior as fast as his horse could ride. Ahead he could see where the trees ended and the grassy hills began. They would lead him to the base of the Ranvieg Mountains. He decided he would stay off the main paths to avoid the small towns and villages. He rode over hills swiftly until he heard a noise to his right. It sounded like a woman's scream.

Out of the corner of his eye, Will saw a young Elfin girl standing on a nearby hill. She raised her arms above her head as though trying to catch his attention. Will pulled tightly on the reins to stop his horse. He turned the horse toward the girl and trotted over to her. The sun began its decent behind the tall forest trees, casting long shadows over the green hills. The girl, dressed in a white flowing gown, stood barefoot in the grass. Her long white hair was braided on the sides to reveal her silky skin and blue eyes. She smiled warmly.

Will dismounted, walked his horse over to her, and waited for her to speak. As he looked at her small delicate face, Will was mesmerized by her appearance. She didn't seem to be real at first, until she spoke.

"I am so glad you have finally come to us, Sir William," she said as she held her arms out as though waiting for an embrace.

"I beg your pardon?" Will asked. He could not seem to stop himself. Her stare was mesmerizing. "How do you know my name?"

"It is good that you came," she said.

"Who are you?"

"I am Emelia and I am an Elfin maiden from the north sent here to tell you the great news."

"You have news of the Prince!" Will removed his helmet from his sweaty brow. "Is he alive? If you know where he is, you must tell me!" He stepped toward her small frame.

"The darkness has lifted, Sir William. It has lifted forever. Lord Bedlam has come and he has chosen you to be his messenger!" she said with such joyfulness that Will was once again mesmerized by her soft voice.

Several more Elfin maidens surrounded him. They were small, frail, Elfin girls with long, flowing, hair glistening in the sunlight. Will thought them a vision until they spoke to him in the same manner as Emelia.

"What are you talking about? Who are you?" Will asked again. "Where is Peter? Do you know where he is?"

"This is a great day indeed, Sir William, you have been chosen to usher in the New Age of Théadril! Lord Bedlam has chosen you to spread his message to all the kings of all the regions. He has foreseen this." Emelia lowered her hands down by her side waiting for Will to respond.

"This is a great day!" the other girls chimed in. They slowly approached him.

Feeling threatened, he removed his sword from its sheath sending a few frightened sparrows into the air. "Do you know where Prince Peter is? Have you seen him?" Will asked the girls as they encircled him, but they did not seem to hear him. They seemed to only hear Emelia's voice. Will turned to her again. "What are you doing here? What do you want with me?"

But she remained silent.

"I grow weary of asking this, so I will ask only once more. Where is the Prince of Illiath? Do you know where he is?"

Emelia's face frowned as she looked at Will. Her sudden sadness gave him pause. He thought perhaps she was afraid of his weapon, so he lowered it. But her sadness wasn't because of the weapon.

"The Prince of Illiath is no more," she said.

"What did you say?" he asked in disbelief.

Silence.

"What did you say to me?" he shouted.

"It is true. The Prince of Illiath is no more," Emelia repeated.

The other Elfin girls came and stood by her side as though to comfort her. They grasped hands together forming a wall of bodies.

Will's shoulders slumped from the heaviness of her words. His eyes grew moist and his gaze was distant as though he could not believe what he had heard.

"You are saddened by what I have told you," she said to him, once again raising her arms out as though to embrace him. "He was a brother to you, I know. You loved him."

With those words, the tears fell as he pictured Peter's face the last time he had seen him. "No….it cannot be true."

"He loved you too," she whispered as she stepped toward Will. "Your brave heart is breaking. It is so sad."

Will's body trembled and he stumbled as though weary. He fell to his knees. He could not help but weep as he knelt there in the green grass.

"I failed him," Will wept. "I failed Peter. I failed King Alexander."

"This sadness will soon end," Emelia said. In a soft voice that comforted Will. "I have wonderful news that you must tell the others."

"The King," Will cried. "This news…of his son…will destroy him." He covered his eyes. "I can see him weeping in my mind."

"Lord Bedlam has been watching you for many moons," she whispered. "He has looked deep into your heart. He has chosen you for this great task."

"Stop saying that," Will said as he wiped his eyes.

"He has chosen you to usher in the great New Age of Théadril!" Emelia reached down and touched Will's head.

As soon as he felt her hand on his head, he jumped to his feet and backed away. "Don't touch me!"
But she continued to step toward him with her hand extended. "He has chosen you, Will." She sighed. The other girls smiled.

Will couldn't help but stare into their haunting blue eyes. "Stop saying that." His body grow weak again as he fell to the ground and lay on his back. Emelia knelt down beside his outstretched body and stroked his matted hair and furrowed brow. Will closed his eyes as though he had not slept in years. His mind raced.

"The Dragon is dead," Emelia said sternly. Her voice changed from a soft sigh to a sharper tone filled with anger. "He no longer can save Théadril from our enemies," she hissed. "He has failed. And now because of his failure, Peter is dead too."

Will's face cringed at the words, but his eyes remained closed.

"Hush," cooed Emelia. "Rest now." She stroked his brow and watched his face and body relax again. She gently kissed his parted lips. "Now it is time for the great Lord Bedlam to establish his kingdom in Théadril once and for all," she whispered. "The darkness has finally lifted and the people are now free. Yes, all the people are now free, Will. And of all the people, he has chosen you to take his message of great hope to the rulers of the ten regions. It is you who can bring the people together." She sighed once again.

Will did not stir.

"It is you who will rule Illiath," she said. "You will now become the son of Alexander. You will take your rightful place next to the King and bring peace to the region. Lord Bedlam has foreseen it. He will bring it to pass."

Will lay motionless on the ground as he took in her words. Slowly opening his eyes, he gazed into her gentle face. Then he sat up and looked at the other Elfin maidens. They smiled and waited for his response. But he remained silent.

Among the maidens appeared a tall man dressed in a black cloak. His pale skin tightly stretched across a bony face and he opened his mouth to speak. "Sir William," he said.

Without a word, Will stood up and placed his helmet back on his head.

"Emelia is correct. I have chosen you to do my bidding," he reached out his hand. Many silver rings lined his long thin fingers. Each fingernail was sharpened to a point. "This is a great day indeed, for all the lands to the sea."

Will stood at attention. His body ached no more. "But we all thought you were gone. Exiled to the mountains of Ranvieg forever." Will said.

"Yet here I am. I came here to seek you, Will, because I have great plans for you."

A wooden cane appeared, and the man leaned on it as he made his way around Will. Atop the cane was a dragon's head carved from white marble. Its eyes were formed by two rubies.

"I have watched you from afar. I saw your bravery in the dungeon when you rushed out to save that dying little girl, risking your own life. I saw you on the battlefield fighting for the King. Then I saw your compassion as you helped Prince Peter. Yes, I even followed your progress at Knight Training. I have chosen you, Will, for these reasons and more."

Will stared straight ahead.

"You will ride to Illiath," the man ordered.

Will nodded.

"There you will tell King Alexander of his son's fate. You will then give the Apothecary this." The man handed Will a small crystal vile filled with lavender liquid. "He will give it to the King to drink."

Will took the vile.

"Together, you and I will explain to the great people of Illiath that you are the true Son of the Oath sent to help them during this most difficult time…"

Will looked into the man's black eyes.

"…this most difficult time of mourning." The man leaned on his cane and motioned for the Elfin maidens to depart.

They obeyed.

"Do you understand these orders?"

Will understood. "But will the people believe me?"

The man smiled and revealed rows of yellow sharp teeth. He placed both hands on Will's shoulders. "No. But they will believe *me*."

Will reached up and pulled down the visor of his helmet.

"Now, ride, Sir William." The man pointed his long finger.

A clap of thunder sounded on the plains causing Will's horse to stir as he mounted it. The caw of a black crow cut through the air above him. He watched it circle and then fly off. Turning his horse east, Will stared down at the man.

"Ride and do not stop, understand?" the man said.

"Yes. I understand," Will said. "I understand and obey you, Lord Bedlam."

Will nudged his horse and together they rode quickly toward the path that led to the desert plains and, ultimately, the palace at Illiath.

15 A SEARCH PARTY

The next day, the King's search party arrived at the place where Lord Byrén, Peter, and his men had made their camp. They brought with them the squire who had survived the attack. He pointed out where Peter had been abducted and where Lord Byrén had been struck.

The cart was present as were the motionless bodies of Byrén's men. But Lord Byrén's body was not among them. As the rain began to pelt the dirt, each man dismounted and began calling out for Byrén as the darkness spread. When no answer came, each man decided to ride off in one direction and search for footprints or any sign of the man. The squire asked to stay behind and bury the dead. Watching the King's men ride off into the different directions, the servant went to the cart to see if there were any tools left to use for digging the graves, but only the bedrolls could be found along with Peter's saddle and saddlebags. So, the servant decided to use one of the dead men's swords as a digging tool. He came near to one man and gently turned him over to grab the sword when suddenly he noticed the man was Lord Byrén. He stood back from the shock of seeing his master lying on the ground dressed as a servant.

Then, Byrén moved.

"My Lord!" the servant cried out. "Are you alright?"

He helped Byrén sit up. His face still swollen from where he had been hit, but there were no other signs of violence.

"Yes, oh yes," Byrén said. "Thank goodness you came back."

"What happened? Why are you dressed in a servant's uniform?' he asked Lord Byrén as he helped him to stand.

"After I woke and found my servants killed, I thought perhaps they would be returning to kill me as well. So, I changed into the servant's clothes and decided to hide among the dead in hopes that they would ride away. Where is Peter? Did he escape?" Lord Byrén asked.

His squire's eyes turned away. "They took him," said the servant.

Lord Byrén frowned. "Does the King know already?"

"Yes, my Lord He has sent us to bring you back. A search party has already left to find where they have taken Peter. My guess is they are heading back to Rünbrior."

§

Back at the palace, King Alexander paced the cold tiled floor of the large hall inside the castle. King Mildrir watched his friend agonize over his only child. Darion stood nearby in case his sovereign needed anything to help get him through the long night ahead.

"General Aluein will be expecting Peter," Alexander murmured. "And when he doesn't show by morning, he will send riders out to find them. What a disaster."

Alexander sighed and he stroked his hair with his long fingers. His face looked forlorn and weary. "I should have gone with them."

"You could not have known this would happen," Mildrir said.

"I should have sent knights to ride with them. What was I thinking?" Alexander said. He covered his eyes as though trying to escape from the situation by hiding. "I never should have let them go."

The butler entered.

"Some warm milk for the King. It is going to be a long night," Darion ordered.

"Yes, Constable," answered the butler as he turned toward the kitchen where all the staff waited for more news. They peeked around the corner waiting for the butler's word.

"Anymore news?" the maid asked.

"Nothing," said the butler. "But the Constable wants some warm milk for the King. It is going to be a long night and I do not suppose anyone will be sleeping."

"Perhaps the milk will calm his nerves, the poor man," sighed the cook as she prepared a small metal pot over the fire pit. After pouring some fresh milk into the pot, she stirred it while it warmed.

The staff stood in shock.

"The poor boy." The cook buried her head in her apron and wept. "I have had known Peter since he was born. I had helped his mother care for him." She wiped her eyes. "Oh, what he must be going through this night."

The scullery maids huddled together nodding with tears in their eyes as they thought about him.

"Oh, stop this sniveling!" the butler ordered as he wiped his eyes. "The King needs us to be strong, for Peter. He needs us to be ready to help him. And he doesn't need to see us crying and carrying on." He cleared his throat.

"Yes," the cook sniffed. "You are right. We must remain strong for the King." She poured the milk into the King's cup and placed it on a silver tray for the butler. "I hope this helps calm his nerves."

The butler took the milk out to the hall and waited for further orders as he watched his King continue to pace back and forth. The butler shook his head in sorrow.

§

Several hours had passed and the sun rose. The rains continued to fall as the winds picked up. It was horrible conditions for riding, but the King hoped against all odds that the soldiers had found Lord Byrén and perhaps some clues as the where Peter was taken. The *tick tock* sound coming from the large standing clock in the hall was the only sound as the King paced. He had changed out of his armor and into his tunic and robe. But his mind raced with thoughts of what to do for Peter. Still, he needed to wait for any news from his men who were out searching in the plains.

A servant ended the stillness when he stormed into the castle entrance and ran toward the King.

"My Lord!" he shouted, "A rider approaches!"

16 RIDERS APPROACH

Another morning would soon be upon the prison, and Peter wondered what the day had in store for him. He moaned loudly and rubbed his body which ached from sleeping on the hard rock. The straw only slightly helped. He shivered in the cold air. He rolled over and tried to rest again. Hearing a scratching sound, he looked up in time to see a rat run along the wall searching for food. He cringed and closed his eyes tightly, desperately trying to dream of home once more before morning came. Instead, he felt something inside the pocket of his trousers. On the side of right his leg, was a pocket secured with a button. Peter had forgotten the pocket was there until he rolled over on it. He sat up and unbuttoned the pocket. To his surprise, he pulled out the small golden compass his mother had given him years ago. Suddenly, Peter remembered that Theo reminded him to take it on his journey, and he was glad he had remembered it. He held it in his hand and studied it carefully. He pictured his mother's hand holding it. Then he slowly opened it and saw the small arrow under the glass move. He held it up, hoping something magical would happen like a secret passageway would appear and he could escape. But nothing happened, so he carefully placed it back in his pocket. Somehow, he felt better knowing that a memory of his mother was with him.

At that moment, a loud thump came from outside his cell door and he heard muffled voices out in the corridor where the many other cave-like cells were. He suspected that the guards were out there getting other prisoners up and out. Sure enough, a loud bang came to his door, and it swung open. Peter leapt to his feet out of shock and fear. The guard, dressed in a black tunic with a black metal helmet on his head, black boots on his feet, and the crest of Rubrior on his chest, ordered him out into the corridor.

Peter quickly obeyed and ran out to the corridor where he stood with around twenty other boys all chained together. They were all about his age. The corridor was lit with many torches and the heat from the fires felt good on his cold skin, but the pleasant feeling would not last for long. A few feet down the corridor, the chain of prisoners stopped to gather more boys from their cells. Peter groaned. His shoulders and back continued to ache from his long journey the day before and from his distressful sleep. His stomach growled loudly. Several boys turned to him. He rubbed his empty belly and hoped for food. But he tried not to think about these things as he mentally prepared for what lay ahead in the dark cave that appeared in front of him. He could see flickers of light from torches inside the cave as well as hear voices within. He knew some sort of work was being done in the cave and that they were probably being taken there to work.

The line moved as the guards shouted their orders. Each boy seemed as exhausted as Peter. He wondered where they all came from. As they marched, he saw the thin backs of the boys in front of him. Some wore tunics while others had bare backs and trousers with no shoes on their feet. Some had scars on their backs and others had fresh wounds open and bleeding. Peter shivered and fear began to rise inside him, but he kept telling himself to remain calm. His eyes darted left and right, searching the area for any means of escape.

They entered the cave and Peter caught sight of the workers hauling buckets and pails full of rocks over to a large metal bin where they dumped the rocks. The workers were older men and younger boys around Peter's age. None of the workers spoke or looked around, they all seemed to be in a mindless daze as they moved. Once in a while, they feverishly scratched their arms and hair. Rünbrior guards watched the workers. Some held whips in their hands and others simply held torches as they watched the workers move back and forth deeper into the cave and out with their pails. Peter realized that he must be part of the next shift of workers coming in as replacements.

Soon they moved deeper into the cave. It smelled of dampened dirt. Peter's group kept moving deeper and deeper into the cave until it turned slightly, and they suddenly were ordered to stop. A guard unchained them and told them to pick up a bucket and hammer. Peter grabbed the bucket in front of him on the ground. Inside it was a small hammer. He waited for further orders from the guards as more young boys and older men walked past them. Another loud horn blast sounded, and the guards shouted for them to get to work hammering the rock wall behind them and filling the buckets with rocks.

Peter obeyed, but all the while, he searched the cave for any chance to escape. *I've got to get out of here. There's got to be a way out.*

This work went on for hours. Peter's arms and hands grew weaker and weaker. But he kept hammering more and more into the cave wall with all his might. He decided to work at a cadence he had in his head. The rhythm went to the sound of Titan's hooves on the dirt when he galloped over the plains. He wondered about his horse and if he had made it back to the palace safely. Then Peter wondered about Lord Byrén and if he had survived. Thinking made the time go by faster, so Peter kept thinking. He thought about his friends, Annika, Simon, and Crispin, and wondered where they were sailing to at that moment. Then he wondered about Theo and to whom he was teaching his lessons at that time in the palace. He thought of his father, his room, the forest. Peter studied the guards and noticed when some left the cave. He watched them walk off and turn toward the right. He counted their footsteps.

That must be where they exit. If I could follow them, I'm sure they would lead me to where I could—

"Don't even think about it," said the boy next to him.

The sound of a voice startled Peter out of his thoughts. "What?"

"Don't even think about it," the boy repeated. He hammered the rock wall in front of him.

"What are you talking about?" Peter watched the guards.

"Escape," the boy said. "Don't even think about it."

Peter frowned and dug his hammer into the rock.

"How did you know I was think—"

"Your eyes. Darting to the left then to the right. I've seen it before," the boy said. "You're studying the guards…their footsteps, their path. You're trying to find a way to escape."

Peter exhaled.

"And if I can tell," —the boy looked at the guards— "they can tell."

Obviously, the boy had been there awhile. His hair was long and shaggy on his shoulders and his teeth were darkened by the rock and dirt inside the cave. Peter looked at the boy's hands. They were calloused and dry from the work.

"Why not escape?" he whispered. "There's got to be a way out if there's a way in. I can't stay here. I'm wasting time. Who knows how many days I've wasted in here when I could be at—" Peter stopped himself.

The boy smirked and shook his head. "We all have better places to be. Do you think you're the first to try and escape out of here?" he said.

Peter angrily grabbed his bucket, walked over to the large bin, and dumped the contents in. He continued to watch the guards as they stood together and talked. He waited.

Then came his chance. The guards turned and walked off together.

Peter dropped his bucket, and took off in the opposite direction.

§

King Alexander ran to the entrance of the palace and, in the early morning hours, saw a commotion in the courtyard regarding the approaching rider. He stood into the courtyard with his Constable and Steward. All three men waited in eager anticipation.

"My King!" a soldier cried. "It appears to be the search party along with Lord Byrén."

Alexander sighed with relief hoping that Byrén had some news of Peter.

"Lord Byrén survived," he mumbled under his breath. "How convenient."

"Sire," Darion said. "I'm certain Byrén did all that he could to help Peter."

Alexander shot Darion a stern look.

Darion bowed and took a step back.

All the villagers had abandoned the courtyard earlier and returned to their homes.

Word had already been sent out to the region leaders in hopes of gaining their assistance in bringing Peter home. Alexander awaited the response from each leader.

"I am certain we will hear something from the other leaders soon enough," said Mildrir. Alexander listened.

"Sire, some supper?" asked his Steward who held a tray of food and beverages for the men as they waited with the King.

The King waved him off.

The riders entered in with Lord Byrén. He gave the King a look of extreme sadness.

Alexander turned away in disgust. "Get him inside, question him about Peter, and I'll talk to him later. I'm returning to my room," Alexander stomped off down the hall toward his chamber.

"Yes, your Majesty," Darion said. He turned to Byrén who dismounted his horse and approached.

"Oh Darion," he sighed and placed his hand on the Constable's shoulder. "Some wine, quickly…and food. I've been through so much. The horror! The madness of it all!" He clutched his chest.

Darion swept Byrén's hand off his shoulder and motioned for a knight to come forward. "In time, Lord Byrén," he said rather sternly. "But for now? I must question you regarding Peter's abduction. Take him into the side room there."

Byrén's face became pale as the knight took his arm and led him away.

"What? But I—"

"And the King will want a word with you in the morning," Darion said.

"I doubt he'll remember anything useful," Mildrir said.

Darion nodded then walked off to begin the interrogation of Lord Byrén.

§

Loud crashing came from King Alexander's bed chamber. King Mildrir knocked on the door, then slowly opened it to find Alexander out of breath and leaning on his mahogany desk. Papers, maps, books, and goblets littered the floor. A nearby mirror was shattered. Alexander's eyes looked weary, vacant.

"I failed him," Alexander cried. "I failed my son."

"Nonsense, Alexander," Mildrir said. "Pull yourself together. We'll find him. No matter how long it takes. He will be found."

Alexander only shook his head.

At that moment, he heard a commotion in the palace.

"Sire!" a young soldier cried down the hall. "A rider approaches from the west!"

Alexander threw open the chamber door. "What's this?"

The soldier stood at attention. "A rider, coming from the west."

"Can you see who the rider is?"

"No sire, but he is approaching with great speed," the soldier said between breaths.

Alexander and Mildrir rushed to the palace entrance and waited for the rider to enter into the gates. The rains continued to fall, making large puddles throughout the courtyard. It was desolate and dark in the large open courtyard as the soldiers and guards with their torches lined the curtain walls of the castle. Soon the rider made his way over the drawbridge and under the portcullis.

"Sir William!" yelled a soldier from the wall.

"Will?" said the King, surprised to see the young knight again so soon. Alexander ran into the courtyard to greet him.

Will pulled tightly on the horse's reins and the horse slid to a stop, sending pebbles through the air. He sat there on his horse and gazed around the castle grounds for a moment in the cold early morning air. Will lifted up the visor of his helmet. The rain pelted his face and armor as he watched King Alexander approach him.

"Another rider approaches!" a soldier atop the wall shouted to the King below.

"Will, what are you doing here?" the King asked. He grabbed the reins of Will's horse as he dismounted.

"Sire," Will said as he knelt down before the King.

"Rise, Sir William," Alexander said as he placed his arm on Will's shoulder.

Just then, the other rider entered the gate, trotted over to the King, and waited atop his black horse. The stranger was hooded.

King Alexander stepped toward him and studied his face. When he recognized him, his eyes widened and he stumbled back as though dizzy.

Constable Darion grabbed the King's shoulder to steady him. "Sire, what is it?"

"No. It cannot be," Alexander said. "Guards! Swords!"

The guards ran to the stranger with swords drawn.

The stranger reached up with his long thin hands and removed his hood to reveal his face. "Good King Alexander," the rider spoke. He dismounted his horse and handed the reins to a nearby squire. Then the rider removed a long wooden cane from his saddle. On one end of the cane was a dragon head carved from marble. "People of Illiath. I come in peace. I am honored to be in your presence after all these years."

"Your Majesty, who is this man?" Darion asked.

Alexander turned and found King Mildrir standing with eyes wide open. His mouth open as though ready to speak, but no words came.

"Sire?" Darion asked Alexander. "Who is this man?"

Alexander looked into Darion's eyes, then back at the stranger.

"It is…it is Lord Bedlam," Alexander said.

17 NEWS OF PETER

"What is this?" Mildrir made his way over to Bedlam. "What are you doing here?"

Bedlam raised his hands as the many guards surrounded him with swords drawn. "I heard of Peter's abduction," he told King Mildrir.

"How did you hear about Peter?" Alexander asked.

"It was your riders who took him!" Mildrir shouted.

Bedlam gave him a venomous look. "Nonsense," Bedlam said.

"Come." Darion motioned toward the palace. "Come in out of the rain. Everyone." He touched King Alexander's arm, startling him.

"Yes, let us go into the palace. We have news of Peter," Bedlam said.

Alexander hesitated, but then relented. His guards placed their swords into their sheaths. The men entered the palace. Alexander stood by cautiously watching his guests.

Will stood quietly, looking into his King's eyes. Then he turned to Darion and to King Mildrir. He gazed around the grand entrance hall where he had been knighted not long ago and noticed the portraits of the Queen and King Aléon as well as the Dragon Forest. He remained quiet for a few moments more.

Alexander grew nervous. "What news do you have?"

Will nodded. "I am afraid it is sad news."

Alexander stared intently into Will's eyes. "What have you heard?" he asked as Mildrir walked over to his side.

"The Prince of Illiath…" Will hesitated. "…is dead."

"No!" Darion shouted as he heard the news.

"What…what did you say?" Alexander staggered away from Will as though the words were poisonous daggers entering his flesh. He turned to Bedlam. "This is your doing!" he shouted.

"Sir William, how do you know Peter's fate?" asked Mildrir with furrowed brow.

"Peter is dead," Will said again. "I know because I saw him. I saw his dead body at Rünbrior." He looked at each man standing before him, making sure his eyes met with theirs so that not one word would be misunderstood.

Upon hearing the precise and biting words, Alexander began to collapse until Mildrir caught him.

"It is true," Bedlam said. He removed his cloak and handed it to a nearby servant.

"Are you sure it was him?" Mildrir asked Will.

"Yes," Will answered.

Mildrir grabbed Alexander's arm to help hold up the exhausted King. He ordered Darion, who remained stunned by the news, to bring over a chair.

But Alexander waved him off and began to walk away toward the hall. "No," he whispered and staggered away as though drunk with much wine. "My son."

§

Constable Darion tried to move, but he couldn't. He watched Will, who stood as though made of stone. Something was wrong. Will acted strangely. He walked toward him.

"Where?" Darion asked.

"What?" answered Will.

"Where did you see Peter's body?"

"At Rünbior," Will answered.

"When?" Darion asked.

"Yesterday."

"And you rode all that way in one day to tell us?" Darion said.

"Yes," Will said sternly.

"That is impossible," Darion answered. "No one could ride from Rünbior to Illiath in one day."

"Shouldn't you be looking after the King?" Lord Bedlam dismissed Darion. "Give him some wine to drink. It will help him rest."

Darion looked to Mildrir for assistance.

"He needs rest," Bedlam insisted. "Now, go do as I say. I can see he hasn't slept in a while. He needs rest or he will collapse and the kingdom will be in chaos."

Darion understood and hurried after the King.

"Sir William," Mildrir said, "when were you at Rünbrior?"

"I rode through the forest and saw the guards taking Peter toward the prison. So I followed them. That is when I saw Peter try to escape, and they shot him through the heart with an arrow," Will said without emotion. "Now, get the King to his chambers. Call the Apothecary."

Something was not right. Will had been close to Peter.

"He was your friend, yet you have no sorrow about telling the King this news?" Mildrir suggested. "I see no sign of sorrow on your face as you relayed the news, just rigidity."

"I have had time to grieve, sir," said Will. "It is my anger that you see now. My anger toward Valbrand and his thugs for killing my friend and sovereign is real, I can assure you."

But Mildrir squinted, eyeing Will more closely, unconvinced by his words.

"You should go to the King. He needs you now more than ever." Will removed his gloves.

§

"No, no," Alexander whispered over and over as he was led to the Solar by Darion and the servants. "My son, my son." He placed his hands on his forehead as though trying to keep it from bursting.

Darion helped the King into his room. Mildrir followed close by.

"Something is not right with Will's story. No one can make that ride in one day," Darion said as he placed his hand on

Alexander's brow to ease his aching head. "He is burning with fever."

He and Mildrir helped Alexander lie down on the bed.

"Will is exhausted. Perhaps he has his days confused. Peter was a very close friend. He could be so distraught that he is confused about the details," Mildrir said.

But Darion remained doubtful.

"We'll wait until the morning to announce to the staff all that has happened," Darion said. "I would feel it if Peter were gone. I love him like a son of my own. Yet, I feel nothing."

The butler entered and placed a tray on the table next to the bed. Darion poured some wine into the goblet. The Apothecary quickly came into the room and stood over King Alexander for a moment.

"He needs rest," Darion said to him. "What can you do?"

The Apothecary took out the small crystal vile and emptied the lavender liquid into the goblet filled with wine.

"This should help him sleep," he said to Darion.

"Good," Mildrir said. He sat down on the bed next to Alexander. "He has been without sleep for too long."

Then, Darion lifted the glass to Alexander's lips. "Sire, drink this," he whispered.

Alexander drank.

"And what of Lord Bedlam? Why is he here? Can we trust him?" Darion asked.

Mildrir took Alexander's hand into his own.

"I don't know," he sighed. "I suppose we will have to see."

"My son," Alexander moaned. "He is dead."

"Rest now, Alexander," Mildrir said.

The two men watched their friend slip into a sound sleep. They covered him with blankets and departed from the room. In the hallway, Darion walked with Mildrir to where Bedlam and Will stood waiting.

"Well?" Lord Bedlam asked. He leaned on his wooden cane.

"He is resting peacefully," Mildrir said. "Now, what business is this of yours Bedlam? Why did you come here?"

Bedlam grinned. "You will know why soon enough. But for now, all our attention should be focused on helping Alexander get through this most difficult time."

"I am here to serve the King in any way." Will stepped forward.

"As am I." Bedlam placed his hand over his heart.

Mildrir turned to Darion, who looked as confused as before. "Since when was Alexander's welfare any concern of yours, Bedlam?" Midrir asked.

"Now, Mildrir." He walked over to the King and placed his arm around his shoulders. "During dire circumstances such as this, it is time to let bygones be bygones. Wouldn't you agree?"

Mildrir moved away from him. "I suppose," he murmured.

"What do we tell the people?" Darion said.

"We tell them the truth," Bedlam quickly answered. "They need to know about Peter's fate. They need to help their Sovereign grieve. Alexander needs his people now more than ever before."

Bedlam made his way around the entrance hall, leaning on his cane. He stopped at the portrait of the Queen and study it for a moment. "You watch. The people will be there for him as they were when Queen Laurien died."

Darion nodded.

"Tell them the truth." Bedlam pointed his long finger at Darion. "They will be crushed, but in the end, they will rise up and endure. Mark my words."

Darion looked at Will who remained stoic and motionless. "I suppose I will write the pronouncement," Darion said defeatedly. "Then order the gates to be raised and the bridge lowered. All flags will fly at half-mast. I will meet the people at the gates and make my proclamation that Peter...the Prince of Illiath...is dead." His voice cracked. He hung his head low. "I will do this on behalf of the King."

"Very well," Bedlam said. "How can I be of service to you at this time Constable?"

Darion gave him a stern look. "Pardon my bluntness, Lord Bedlam, but I do not trust you."

Turning, Darion made his way down the hall and stopped to see if he was followed. Assured he was alone, he removed a small golden watch from his pocket and opened it. Upon doing so, the portrait in front of him moved from the wall revealing the hidden passageway behind it. Darion sneaked in and made his way down the dark stairway toward Theo's library.

§

Mildrir turned to Bedlam. "I will go check on the King," he muttered then left the room.

Lord Bedlam and Will watched King Mildrir disappear down the hallway. Then, Bedlam meandered around the grand hall inspecting every item in it. He picked up the corner of a tapestry and felt it with his bony fingers, checked a statue for dust, and then he walked over to the portrait of The Dragon Forest.

"How nice," he said as he studied the details of the painting. He took out another crystal vile from his pocket. He tossed it to Will who carefully caught it. "This should do the trick," Bedlam said.

"How long will it take?" Will asked.

"Be patient," Lord Bedlam walked over and placed his hand on Will's shoulder. "It won't be much longer."

Will understood.

The butler came around the corner into the grand hall, but stopped when he spotted Bedlam and Will talking. He turned to leave, then decided to eavesdrop instead.

"The Constable will make his announcement, the people will be shocked." Bedlam gestured in the air with his cane to illustrate his point. "That's when you will step in and comfort the people. You will be their savior. Your words will assuage their broken hearts. They will look to you to meet their needs, and you will be there for them."

He turned Will to face him. "In time, they will look to you as the next ruler of Illiath," Bedlam said.

"Yes, my Lord," Will said.

The butler leaned in to hear more.

"They will look to *you* as the son of the Oath." Bedlam smiled.

"And when King Alexander is dead, I will be the next King of Illiath," Will said.

"Exactly, my boy," Bedlam said.

The butler gasped when he heard Will's words. He turned and quickly ran off in search of the Constable.

Will walked over to one of the large picture windows.

"Still," he said. "I feel Darion and Mildrir suspect something. They know it is impossible to trek from Ranvieg to here in one day." He turned to Bedlam. "I should've said something else."

"Yes, well, they cannot discover our method of transportation." Bedlam grinned. "At least not yet."

"But what if the fact that Peter is alive leaks out to the people? What if Darion finds out?" Will asked.

"Oh, they will find out. That's part of the plan." Bedlam grinned, revealing his small yellow teeth.

"Although I cannot kill Peter myself." Bedlam studied the top of his cane, stroking the dragon's head like a pet. "I can keep him in that prison until he is killed." He pointed the cane to Will. "In the meantime, you will take his place and gain the trust of the people. They will come to love you. And if Peter ever does reappear, the people won't care. They will want you instead."

"I understand." Will nodded and walked over to the painting of The Dragon Forest. "I will be the son of the Oath," he said.

18 THE WALLS OF RÜNBRIOR

"Halt!" the guard shouted after Peter. "Stop that boy!"

Peter ignored him and continued to run down the corridor as fast as he could. He had no idea where he was headed, only that he knew there had to be a way out. The corridor darkened as he became farther away from the torches. He ran his hand along the rock wall as a guide. When it began to turn left, he could see light ahead, but he also heard the voices of guards. He slowed down. He turned and heard voice of a guard coming up behind him. He searched for and found a crevice in the wall and hid himself there.

As the guards approached, Peter stuck his foot out and tripped the man. He fell flat on his face while his sword and torch flew from his hands. Peter grabbed both and continued to run on ahead. The voices ahead grew louder. He felt the heat from fires as the cave glowed orange. But he kept running as fast as he could.

He ran through a room where blacksmiths hammered swords.

"Hey!" shouted one man who spotted Peter. "Stop him!"

Two men reached for Peter, but they missed. He ran on down another darkened corridor. All he heard was his breathing and his footsteps. He looked behind and saw no one coming after him.

I made it, he thought.

Just then, two men appeared and grabbed Peter's arms.

"No!" he shouted at them. They struggled to the ground. The sword and torch were taken and Peter was hauled off toward his cell.

When he found himself back inside his cell in the dark, he could smell the rain outside.

"Nice try," said the guard. "No supper for you. And the next time you run off, I use this!" He showed Peter the whip then exited the cell and slammed the door shut.

"What?" Peter ran to the door and banged on it. "Please! I need some food and water!"

"Not after that stunt," the guard shouted from the other side.

Peter couldn't remember the last time he had eaten something. He bent over from the hunger pains.

I'll have to try again tomorrow, he thought. *There has to be a way out of here.*

Suddenly, the wooden door opened and an old man placed a small tray of bread and water on the floor of Peter's cell. He motioned for Peter to be quiet.

Peter nodded.

He noticed a small bowl of steaming porridge there on the tray as well. He ran to the tray as the old man closed the wooden door and locked it.

"Thank you," Peter whispered to the man. But there was no reply.

The bread was stale, but Peter did not care. He chewed it slowly, treasuring every bite. Then he spooned up some of the porridge made of wheat and oats. It had barely any taste, but it was warm and felt good inside Peter's belly. He drank all the water and suddenly felt satisfied. He felt his way around his cell to where his straw bed was and then laid on top of the blanket. With his stomach full, Peter felt that he could rest. He closed his eyes and began to dream again of home.

Although the cell was dark, sound sleep escaped Peter on the hard ground. Flashes of lightning and loud claps of thunder woke him every few minutes. Tossing and turning on his bed of straw, his dreams haunted him at night. The Dragon's eyes kept coming to the front of his mind and he wished he could speak to his friend now.

"Is this my trial?" Peter said to no one. "Is this what you meant?"

Peter remembered the images he saw in the lake. He rolled over and desperately tried to sleep. "This cannot be it. I was supposed to go to Knight Training!"

His eyes welled up with tears. He dreamed of the Dragon's fiery breath spewing from its mouth. Peter covered his face then sat up. He could hear the Dragon's voice.

"This is your time, Peter," the Dragon had said.

Peter rested his head on his knees.

"No!" he shouted to no one. "I can't stay here. I must escape."

He stood and paced with clenched fists. "There has to be a way out."

§

"I knew there was a way out!" the man shouted.

"Shut up, you!" the guard dragging him shouted. He motioned for two other guards to help him. They ran up and grabbed the legs of the prisoner.

The rain pelted their bodies as they dragged the man into the mouth of the cave.

"Almost made it, this time, huh?" the man shouted. The guards threw him to the ground at the feet of the Warden, Valbrand, himself.

"I should have you fed to the dragons months ago, Nøel!" Valbrand kicked dirt into the man's face. "Traitor knight!"

Nøel laughed and wiped the dirt off his face.

"Get him inside! No rations for a week!" Valbrand turned to leave the cave.

"Put me in the arena!" Nøel shouted. "I told you I could win more gold for you than any other prisoner."

Valbrand stopped. He turned his head to listen.

"Or I'll escape from here, I swear it." Nøel slowly made it to his feet. "And tell others what really happens here behind these rock walls."

Valbrand turned around and motioned for his assistant, a pudgy little goblin. It handed him a ledger of sorts. Valbrand took it and read it. A tall thin man with little hair and willowy arms, Valbrand was Bedlam's choice for Warden even though Bedlam never trusted him fully.

"This is the third escape attempt in as many months," Valbrand hissed.

"If you had just put me in the arena, you'd be a richer man today." Nøel chuckled. "I was the best knight in Alexander's kingdom and you know it."

"Before you betrayed him and left the quest!" Valbrand spat out the words.

Nøel wiped the spittle from his face. "I told you. The quest has failed. Lord Bedlam has seen to it. I would rather die in this prison than serve him!"

"You may get your wish," Valbrand said. He came closer to Nøel. "Alright. I will give you your chance in the arena. You'd better not disappoint me. Or I swear I will watch them feed you limb by limb to Scathar the great dragon. Understand?"

Nøel laughed. "Understood."

"Get him to the cellblock in shackles! Ten lashes for this attempt." Valbrand quickly departed from the cave.

"Ten lashes? Is that all?" Nøel shouted.

Valbrand could hear Nøel's laughter all the way down the corridor.

19 THE DUKE OF ILLIATH

"I present, the Duke of Illiath!" the captain of the soldiers shouted to the crowd. They erupted in cheers.

Several days after the news of Peter's fate, Will had been named Duke of Illiath by the other rulers. Lord Bedlam asked for a title that the people would respect and obey until Alexander was well enough to rule again.

Will stepped out and raised his hands to quiet the crowd. "Please," he said. "I am your servant."

The people cheered even louder.

"I am here to serve you," Will said. "Together, we will get through this most difficult time in Illiath's history."

Will motioned for his soldiers to begin distributing the bread and fruit to the crowds. They rushed to the cart when they saw the supplies of food.

"Do not shove," Will ordered. "There is plenty for everyone!"

Little children ran to Will who stretched out his hands for them to kiss. Nearby stood Lord Bedlam and Constable Darion watching the proceedings.

"A most excellent reception, don't you think, Constable?" Bedlam asked.

Darion ignored him and turned to head back to the castle. Bedlam chuckled as he watched Darion leave. Then he decided to follow after him.

"I don't understand all this." Darion shook his head. "Why would the rulers make Will a Duke?"

"The people need a leader," Bedlam insisted. "Alexander remains ill and Will is one the people can trust."

Darion continued to ignore him. "The King's condition worsens."

"Yes. Yes, I know," Bedlam said. He tried to look solemn. "I hear the Apothecary is troubled. Seems the King's despair over Peter is killing him."

Darion stopped and gave Bedlam a harsh look. "As if you truly care." Darion pointed his finger at him. "You may be fooling Will and the townspeople here, but you are not fooling me, Lord Bedlam."

"Constable Darion!" a shout from a servant interrupted the men. Darion rushed over to him. "What is it?"

"The Apothecary," the servant huffed. "He says the King's condition is even worse than before."

Darion looked up to King Alexander's window. "Oh no," he ran to the palace entrance.

Bedlam watched, then pivoted to see Will approaching.

"What is it?" Will asked.

Bedlam placed his hand on Will's shoulder. "It is time to put our plan into action, Will. Your time has come."

§

The guard made the loud noise outside the door to Peter's cell yet again and threw it open with his fury rousing Peter to his feet. Once out in the corridor, he chained Peter to the other boys waiting in line as he had the many days before and led them to the cave lit with torches to begin another day of digging rocks out of the cave.

The monotony of it all got to Peter. He noticed all the boys and older men did the same thing over and over. Peter filled many buckets that day as he had the day before and the day before that, but his hands and arms did not ache and the blisters on his hands became calloused. He continued to watch for any sign of possible escape. The guards paced back and forth and kept an eye on Peter every day.

"You see?" said the boy next to him. "I told you. There is no escape from this place."

Peter smirked. "What is your name?" Peter asked.

"Jason," he whispered. "What is yours?"

Peter thought for a second. "Ethan," he lied.

The two shook hands quickly before the guard spotted them. He carried a long black whip draped over his shoulder and had his visor on his black metal helmet down so no one could see his eyes through the slits. No one could tell where he looked.

"How long have you been here?" Peter asked.

"I don't know," the boy said as he scraped the rock wall with his hammer. "I have not seen the sun rise nor set in many months."

Peter frowned.

"I'm sorry," he said. "Where did you come from?"

"Edenland. It is near Vulgaard," the boy sighed. "Where are you from?"

"Ill….." Peter hesitated. "Riverdale." Then he asked, "Why are there only young boys here in the caves?" he whispered.

"That is because Valbrand uses us for his games," Jason answered.

"Games? What games?" Peter asked.

"You have not heard?"

"No."

"Well, once the young boys grow strong, Valbrand takes the strongest for his games in the arena. They fight each other to the death simply for Valbrand's pleasure. Many come from miles around to watch the games."

"What happens if they win?"

"They live to see another day in this beautiful place." Jason chuckled.

Peter nodded.

"I heard it said that the winners can win their freedom, but I am not sure that's true." Jason eyed the guards. "It could be a lie that the guards tell to make the boys work harder."

Peter agreed, yet he couldn't help but think that perhaps one day he would be chosen to fight for his freedom, if he remained in the prison that long.

"They fight with swords?" he asked.

"Yes, but…" Jason's voice trailed off.

"But what?" Peter asked quietly.

"Those who do best against other fighters in the arena eventually go on to fight the dragons," Jason said.

"*Dragons?*" Peter was astonished. "Valbrand has dragons here in the prison?"

"He brings them in for the games. They are deep within the mountain," Jason said as he looked down. "Sometimes you can hear the roar of his favorite dragon from below."

"His favorite?"

"Yes, Scathar. It is his favorite. The fiercest dragon," Jason said as he filled his bucket. "It scares me."

Peter furrowed his brow as he gazed down at his feet, trying to imagine what the dragon looked like.

"It scares us all!" cried another boy who had been listening. "It is the largest fire-breathing dragon around."

"You have seen it?" Peter asked.

"No, of course not," the boy said. "Do I look old enough to fight in the games?"

"Well, no, but—"

"Then why would you ask such an ignorant question?" he said sternly.

Peter frowned. "But then how do you know it is the largest most fearsome of all the dragons?" Peter asked as he lifted up his two buckets full of rocks.

"I just know, that's all," the boy huffed. He walked off with his buckets.

"That's Damon. He isn't very kind. You will have to watch your back around here," Jason said. "We have heard from the guards about Scathar and the other dragons. Sometimes we hear the roar. Sometimes we are allowed to go see its hatchlings."

"Hatchlings?" Peter asked. His eyes lit up.

"Yes. They sometimes send us down to the pit where we feed the dragon hatchlings. You will see soon."

Peter shook his head. "No, not me."

"What do you mean?"

"I'm not staying here long enough to fight in any games." Peter hammered the rock wall.

Jason raised his eyebrows. "You mean, you're going to try and escape again?"

"Of course," Peter said. "I know there is a way out of here."

"Yes! Through the games!" Jason said.

A guard approached so the two boys went back to work.

"If this fool thinks he can escape, let him try," Damon said.

"No, you'll be whipped or killed for sure," Jason said.

"Not me," Peter insisted. "See that guard over there?"

Jason turned.

"He leaves in a few minutes. And when he does, there are no guards here in our section for one minute."

"So?" Damon said.

"So, that's all the time I need."

"But you tried to run away before and it didn't work," Jason said.

Peter looked up. "This time, I climb out." He smiled.

"You're insane," Damon said. "It's well over forty feet to the next level."

"Maybe," Peter said. "But I've got to try."

Peter could not believe how not one of the other boys on the chain had tried to escape by climbing up. The work they did daily built strong muscles over time. But he knew this work would not hone skills for fighting with swords or lances in a joust. He knew he had to get to Knight Training no matter what.

He hammered while the guards spoke in hushed tones. Sure enough, the other guards walked down the corridor while the one guard left the area. This gave Peter his chance.

"So long." Peter threw down his pale and began to scale the rock wall, disappearing into the darkness. All this time, he had been hammering holes in the wall. Now he simply used them as steps to climb up.

Peter easily made it high enough that he could hide in the darkness unnoticed by the guards. But when he realized he could no longer see where to place his hands and feet, panic rose inside him.

Stay calm, he told himself.

He reached over and found a place for his hand. Then, he slowly found a spot for his foot. Below, he could see the new guard replace the other and Jason hammering away at the wall. He inched his way higher and over until he saw the next level. He climbed high enough to pull himself up. There was no one around on the level. He carefully made his way down the corridor, but found no torches lit. He stopped every few feet to listen for guards.

Convinced he had made it, Peter took off down the corridor without looking back.

20 THE DEATH OF THE KING

Darion entered the King's chambers to find Mildrir, the Apothecary, and the butler standing near the bed. Mildrir eyes shone with tears.

"He is gone," he whispered to Darion.

"No!" Darion ran over to the bed and took one of Alexander's hands into his own. It was ice cold. He felt the King's chest for a heartbeat, but found no beat, no breathing, only stillness. Darion wept over his King's body.

"The land is without a King," Mildrir said. "Or an heir."

"Whatever shall we do?" the butler murmured under his breath.

"There is only one thing to do," Lord Bedlam entered the room.

Darion wiped his eyes and gave Bedlam a vicious look. "You get out of here at once!"

"What are you talking about, Bedlam?" Mildrir challenged.

Bedlam looked down at Alexander's the lifeless body. "Illiath is without a ruler or an heir." He motioned toward Will. "But, the people have clearly accepted Will as the Duke of Illiath. They adore him and trust him. He has provided for them since Alexander's illness."

Darion eyed Will, standing at attention in the entrance.

"So, I suggest we make Sir William the ruler of Illiath," Bedlam said. "Uh, for the time being, of course."

Mildrir glared at Will. "Do you know what it means to rule a land?"

"Yes, sire," Will said.

"No, of course you don't. How could you? The son of a peasant farmer."

"Which makes him endearing to the peasants," Bedlam interjected.

"A knight who has never experienced the trials," Mildrir continued.

"The *best* knight at training who has combat experience from battle at a time of war with Lord Caragon, might I add." Bedlam placed his hand on Will's shoulder. "This makes him an able leader of the King's Royal Knights and soldiers. They respect him."

Mildrir shook his head and looked at Darion.

"The war with Lord Caragon was your doing!" seething with anger, Darion rushed over to Bedlam, only to be stopped by Mildrir.

Bedlam raised an eyebrow. "I was never a part of Caragon's ridiculous plan to attack Illiath."

"Liar!" Darion shook his fist.

"There, there," Mildrir said. "Calm down, Darion."

"As you can clearly see," Bedlam said. "Sir William, the Duke of Illiath, can be the ruler of Illiath until all the rulers make a decision."

"I suppose it is the only way, Darion," Mildrir said, rubbing his forehead as though it burned.

"No!" Darion stood. "I don't trust him!"

Mildrir grabbed Darion before he lunged at Bedlam again. "He has proven to be most helpful in the last few weeks since Peter's disappearance. He has provided food for the people, kept commerce going here in the palace, and the people are peaceful."

Darion spun around and walked to the window.

"It is only for the time being, Constable," Bedlam said. He held his wooden cane in his hands. "I understand your hesitance."

"Do you?" Darion turned to Bedlam.

"As you know, since I have been in exile, peace has come to all the lands. Carragon is no more. The dragons are all but extinct. And I have spent much time at Rünbrior making it a successful mining business for the Elves in the region."

"This is true," a voice came from the hallway. King Eulrik entered the chamber.

"Eulrik, what are *you* doing here?" Mildrir asked.

"Word of the King's illness came to me the night before." He stared at Alexander's lifeless body. His mouth fell open as though shocked. "I came to be of any assistance. Then I was told of Bedlam's presence and I knew all was taken care of."

"Nonsense," Darion said. "You came to gloat."

Eulrik's eyes narrowed. "How dare you!"

"All of you, out!" The Apothecary interrupted. "I must prepare the body. Alexander once said he wished to be buried next to the Queen in the palace cemetery. Darion, begin preparations for the funeral procession."

Darion nodded.

The butler assisted in removing everyone from the room. Once everyone was out, he shut the door and stood in the hallway. He motioned for Darion to come to him. "I need to tell you something, Constable," he whispered.

"What is it?" Darion barely listened.

"Not here," whispered the butler. "Come, follow me."

Confused, Darion followed the butler into another hall far away from the Solar. The cloistered hall led to the Queen's sun room far away from the busiest part of the castle. The hall was her favorite as it was lined with stained glass windows depicting scenes from Illiath's history. The men knew they would not be bothered in this area and so they spoke frankly.

"I have seen something. I mean, I heard something and I think you should know what I heard," the butler whispered.

"What is it?" Darion asked with curiosity piqued.

"Days ago, when the King was told of Peter's death," he began, "I returned to the grand hall and overheard Lord Bedlam speaking to Sir William."

"Yes, go on," Darion said as he leaned in close to listen.

"I overheard Bedlam telling Sir William, that *he*, Sir William, would be the heir of Alexander," he said.

Darion stood silent for a moment. "Go on," he finally said.

"He said that Will would rule Illiath as the son of the Oath, replacing Peter," the butler finished.

Darion's eyes widened as he looked away, taking in all that he heard. "Do you think they saw you?" he asked the butler.

"No."

"Do you think they were serious?"

The butler nodded yes.

"So do I," Darion said. "I knew something was amiss."

"Now what do we do?" the butler asked.

"First," Darion said as he looked around to ensure their privacy. He stepped close to the butler. "Have you told anyone else this news besides me?"

He shook his head no.

"Are you certain?"

"Yes," he said.

"I'll have to trust you since we've not much time," Darion said. "Now, much has to be done about this. First, we need to sneak out a message to the Captain of the soldiers without Will knowing. Can you do that?" he asked the butler.

"Yes, I think," he said.

"I will try and meet secretly with the knights when they come for the funeral and see if any of them will agree to remove Will. I am sure some are as suspicious of Bedlam and Will as I am," Darion said as he paced back and forth. "I will inform Theo. I'm certain he has the same feelings that I have about Bedlam."

The butler understood. "I should return now to the kitchen before anyone suspects anything."

"Yes," Darion said. "But first, I need you to swear to me that you will not tell anyone any of these plans. Do you understand?"

He agreed.

"No," Darion said as he grabbed the man's arm. "I need you to swear to me. I need you to swear on the King's crown that you will not tell a soul what you have told me."

He stood silently for a moment contemplating the seriousness of the vow. "I swear," he said with no expression on his face.

Darion nodded and let the man leave. The butler was dismissed, leaving Darion alone in the empty hall. "I suppose I'll have to settle for his word," he mumbled to himself.

He looked uneasy about the plan and wondered what powers Bedlam appointed onto Will. He quickly made his way over to a hidden passageway inside the wall that the Queen had placed there for her private retreat. He grabbed a lit torch off the wall and pushed the wall slightly until it popped open to reveal one of many hidden stairways of the castle.

Darion hastily made his way down the stairs and to a hall that led to Theo's private quarters. The hallway was dark with only glow of the torch bouncing off the walls. He stepped lightly so as not to make much noise.

"Theo," he whispered to the darkness. "Are you there?"

Suddenly, a doorway opened sending light from the room into the hallway guiding Darion to his friend's room.

"Yes," he heard the reply.

Darion quickly entered into the room where he found Theo sitting at his large wooden table covered with maps.

"I have sad news, my old friend," Darion said. "About the King."

§

"Bring him this way," Bedlam ordered.

His soldiers lifted Alexander's body off the bed and down a passageway in the wall. Bedlam told Will to stay behind and pay the Apothecary his reward for lying to the Constable.

"I was told seventy gold coins and a parcel of land," the Apothecary said. "I did what I was told. I gave the King that elixir just as you commanded. Now pay me!"

Will pretended to take out some coins from his belt, but removed a dagger instead. Before the man could react, Will slit his throat with one swipe of the dagger. The blood spewed all over the floor.

"Pick him up," Will ordered Bedlam's men. "Take him to the dungeon. You there, clean up this mess."

The men obeyed.

They quickly followed Will into the secret passageway that led down into the bowels of the palace. Will took a torch from the sconce on the wall and headed down the spiral stairs with the soldiers carrying Apothecary's lifeless body. The air was thick with moisture and the walls went from set stone to rock as he went deeper and deeper into the passageway.

Finally, he saw light coming from underneath a crevice. He pressed on the wall and it opened. Will set the torch back into a sconce. Lord Bedlam stood over Alexander's motionless body. The soldiers came down the stairs and set down the Apothecary's body. They came to Bedlam's side.

"Chain him," Bedlam ordered. His soldiers obeyed.

Alexander's hands and feet were chained to the wall in the dungeon. Bedlam grinned.

"Well done," Bedlam said. He looked at Will and the soldiers. "Leave us."

"But—" Will argued.

"Now!" Bedlam shouted. His eyes flickered red.

They left through the passageway and shut the stone wall door leaving Lord Bedlam alone with King Alexander.

Bedlam stood silent for a moment. Then he harshly kicked Alexander's leg. "Wake up!" he shouted. He took the torch and swung it near Alexander's face.

The King winced from the intense heat and covered his face with his hand. He slowly opened his weak eyes. "Where am I?" he asked.

"Where you belong," Bedlam hissed. "In the dungeon of your own castle."

Bedlam tossed the torch into a nearby barrel of water. The steam rose from the water. Alexander's eyes tried to focus on his surroundings. He spotted bales of hay, barrels, crates, and a dead body nearby. Then, he noticed the chains around his wrists and ankles. He jerked his arms, but saw that it was no use. He was chained to the rock wall.

"What is this? Where am I? What have you done!" He shouted. "Let me go, now!"

Bedlam let out a hearty laugh as he watched his nemesis struggle. "You are in no position for demands." He took out his cane and pointed it at the King. "But I will take a moment to answer your questions."

Alexander pulled on the chains.

"Your people think you are dead."

Alexander's eyes grew large. "What?"

"It's true. Upon my command, your most loyal Apothecary over there gave you an elixir that put you into a deep sleep." He stood over the dead body. "So deep, in fact, that you appeared to be dead."

"No." Alexander closed his eyes.

"Oh yes," Bedlam said. "Very convincing." He walked back to the King. "So, now to all the people of Illiath…you are dead."

Alexander appeared stunned to silence.

"It was only a matter of time before I could put this plan into action. I needed time for the people to trust in peace again." Bedlam tapped his chin with his index finger. "With the Dragon gone and all wars ended, peace had come to the region and the people prospered." He chuckled. "The people forgot all about me. My, my, Alexander." He tapped the King's leg with his cane. "Even *you* trusted me enough to enter your palace. And now look where your trust has gotten you."

Alexander shouted and pulled on the chains. The veins in his neck bulged from his rage.

"Alexander, you know full well that it was determined years ago that I cannot kill you or your heir, correct?" Bedlam paced. "You know full well that my powers are limited."

Alexander searched the room. There were no swords or weapons of any kind in the dungeon. The King frowned.

"And you know full well that until all the swords are together again, my powers will remain limited."

"I demand to be set free!" Alexander shouted. "Let me out of these chains now!"

Bedlam pointed his cane at Alexander again to silence him. "Let me finish."

Alexander shot him a hateful look.

"So, knowing all this, even still you were foolish enough to believe that Peter is dead," Bedlam said.

Alexander sat up.

"Yes, that's right," Bedlam said. "Peter is, in fact, *not* dead. He remains alive and in my prison at Ranvieg."

Alexander closed his eyes and exhaled.

"And since the Dragon lives and told Peter of his destiny, there isn't much I can do to change any of it now." Bedlam admired his cane with its dragon head carved from white marble sitting atop the wood. He carefully fingered the rubies that were used for its eyes.

Alexander squinted his eyes upon hearing of the Dragon. Bedlam mistakenly assumed he already knew. He quickly nodded as though he had known about the Dragon.

"No." Bedlam turned toward Alexander. "I cannot kill you or Peter while the Dragon lives and all the swords remain lost."

He quickly removed a hidden sword from within the cane and thrust it at Alexander's throat.

Alexander stared at the blade, just centimeters away.

"But I can keep that boy in my prison until he rots away just like I can keep you hidden in this dungeon while Will takes over your kingdom, orders the Dragon Forest destroyed, and I take all the swords for my own."

Alexander looked into Bedlam's dead eyes.

"And then," he hissed through pierced lips. "Then I shall have you killed, Alexander. And I will thoroughly enjoy that day." He leaned back. "My power grows. The rulers trust me now more than ever. All the swords will be mine very soon, Alexander," he continued. "And when they are, all the rulers will be under my command and the Dragon destroyed forever. It is what I have been waiting for all these many years."

"So you do *not* have all the swords then," Alexander said.

The devious grin left Bedlam's face. He stood and looked down at Alexander like a mouse stuck in a trap. "No," he mumbled.

"And you are so certain that *I* do not have all the swords yet?" Alexander smirked.

Bedlam took the sword and placed it dangerously close to Alexander's eye. Alexander gulped.

Bedlam turned away in disgust. "Oh, I know you don't have the swords here. She made sure of that."

Alexander jerk the chains. "You leave her out of this!"

"Yes, Queen Laurien made sure that all the swords would remain apart until the opportune time, didn't she?" Bedlam said.

"Because she knew. She knew *you!*"

Bedlam paced. "Perhaps that is true. Although, she served me well in that she helped me with the task. I did appreciate her."

Alexander's eyes were merely slits as he ground his teeth.

"In the end, she had to go. She knew too much. Yes, the Queen thought she was helping her father's legacy by making the swords the final piece of the puzzle. But what she didn't know was that all the swords together can still grant me what I want." He made a fist with his hand. "Power," he said. "Limitless power."

"She never loved you."

Bedlam cringed when he heard those words. He jerked his head toward Alexander. His eyes flickered red. Squatting, he lifted Alexander's chin with the cane. "Know this. I will have that power."

"Not while the Dragon lives," Alexander said.

"If I place all the swords together in the center of the Dragon Forest, not only will I destroy it, but I will destroy the Dragon itself." He showed his small sharp teeth.

Alexander turned his face away.

"And I will destroy all that mattered to her. So, as you can see, Alexander, it's just a matter of who gets to the swords first, isn't it?" He stood and walked to the door of the dungeon. He opened it and allowed three soldiers to enter. "With Peter as a prisoner in Rünbrior forever and you here locked in your dungeon forever…I guess we know who will win this game, don't we?"

"You fool." Alexander pulled on the chains. "Do you really think this plan is full proof? Do you really think you can just enter the Dragon Forest? There is no way you can you get away with this."

The soldiers ran over to where Alexander lay.

"Guard him. Provide one meal a day and some water. I will check on him periodically, understand?" Bedlam ordered. The soldiers nodded.

"In two days, there will be a grand funeral procession for you, King Alexander. The Kings from all regions will come and pay their respects. You will be buried next to your lovely Queen Laurien. The people will mourn. And Sir William will take over as Duke of Illiath, rightful heir to the throne because that was *your final wish*."

Alexander growled. "Somehow, Bedlam, somewhere a mistake will be made," he said. "and you will fail."

Bedlam grinned. "…And all those who disagree with the Duke will be banished from the kingdom," he continued. "or executed for treason."

"No!" Alexander screamed. He knew Bedlam spoke of Theo and Darion. "I will stop this!" Alexander said through clenched teeth. "I will get out of here and stop this!"

"Cheer up, Alexander!" Bedlam said as he stood in the doorway. "Your son is still alive. Isn't that wonderful news? You should be rejoicing!" He laughed heartily. "I know I am!"

Then Bedlam slammed the door behind him. Alexander could hear Bedlam's laughter from the other side.

21 SECRETS OF RÜNBRIOR

Peter continued down the corridor, surprised there were no guards or prisoners in sight. He used his hand as a guide along the wall. When the wall began to curve to the right, Peter noticed the glow from fire ahead. He slowly advanced and heard voices, the crackle of fire, and what sounded like a throaty growl.

Peter stopped and listened intently.

"Hold it back!" the man's voice shouted.

Then came the roar that shook the ground. Peter froze.

"I said hold it!" the man shouted again.

Intrigued, Peter took a few more steps and saw something he had never seen before and never thought he would see in his lifetime.

Several guards held chains that led to a young dragon furiously tugging at the chains. Its scales reflected the fire's glow and its eyes matched the yellow fire. A man with a whip stood near the dragon and shouted orders to the guards.

"Pull it into the cave!" the man shouted and cracked the whip. "Pull!"

The guards obeyed and began to turn the beast neck first. It roared as though in pain from the collar around its neck. It flapped its leathery wings and tipped over a few barrels and swords stacked nearby and it dragged its claws along the rock floor. It roared again revealing its sharp teeth. The man ran over to where a torch rolled near a bale of hay. That's when he spotted Peter watching. "You there!"

Peter jumped.

"What are you doing here?" The man came toward Peter who took a few steps back.

Just then, two guards grabbed Peter by the arms.

"Found you!" the guard shouted. "Come on! Let's go."

Peter struggled, but then the dragon roared. The startled guards stopped moving. Peter's eyes met with the dragon's frightened eyes.

"Don't worry about this one," the man said. "Now get this boy out of here!"

"Back to the mines, boy," the guards carried Peter off.

§

"Get in there!" the guard threw Peter into his cell. Peter fell to the ground.

"I warned you!" the guard removed his whip from his belt. Another guard held Peter up and turned him around. He threw Peter to the wall then whipped his back with one lash. The pain caused Peter to scream and black out for a moment. He fell to his knees.

"That's one," the guard said. "Two lashes and you'll be useless in the mines. Three and you'll be dead, understand?"

Peter moaned on the ground.

The two guards slammed the wooden door behind them.

The air coming in through the window grew colder still. Peter lay on the ground unable to move from the searing pain in his back. After what seemed like a few hours, he rolled over onto all fours and tried to stand. Stumbling, he used the wall to balance. The wooden door opened and the old man slid in another tray of contraband food and water. But Peter couldn't move to accept it. The old man left it on the floor where a rat discovered the bounty.

Peter didn't care. He leaned on the wall watching the rat, envying its freedom to come and go as it pleased through the holes in the wall. Peter tried to take a step, but collapsed onto the ground.

After a while, he opened his eyes and rolled over. He screamed from the pain again and crawled over to his straw bed and blanket. He found it impossible to sleep at night. He heard the scurrying sound of the rat as it ran by. The rodent looked full from the food. It disappeared into a hole in the wall.

Peter tried to find warmth from his blanket, but it was cold from sitting in the dark cell all day. He scratched his head over and over again. The itching from the lice was overwhelming. It was no use trying to sleep. He rubbed his arms to help them get warm and was shocked at how thin they had become. He wasn't sure how long he had been imprisoned, but he knew from his body weight that it had been awhile. Peter tried to think. He tried to devise another plan for his escape, but each time he did he realized its futility. He knew the guard was right. Three lashes of the whip would definitely kill him.

"There's got to be a way," he said to himself.

He wondered why no one from Illiath had come to his rescue. This thought only made him angrier and sadder. So, he gave up trying to explain why his father had not attempted to retrieve him from the prison. Deep down he knew there had to be only one answer: his father assumed he was dead.

Peter knew that if the King had been told that his only son was dead, then he would remain in prison forever. But surely Byrén had escaped and returned to tell the King. Yet not even Lord Byrén knew of his fate. For all he knew, Peter was carried off and killed somewhere. Peter shrugged off all the scenarios in his mind and tried to focus on the present time in his cell. Weakness from hunger and pain overcame him. Hopelessness began to take over his thoughts so he tried to fight it off.

He lay there thinking about what he had seen in the cave. He had never seen a young dragon before. *I guess it's true. They really do fight dragons here.* The dragon's fierce eyes came to his mind. Peter understood the trapped animal's rage against the guards.

He tried to imagine what the games must be like. Perhaps he could train well enough to fight in the arena and earn his freedom. He had already faced a dragon...*The* Dragon...and lived to tell about it, so why couldn't he face another dragon and fight?

He reminded himself he did not have his sword or the scale of the Dragon to protect him from the fiery breath. If he could get his body into shape somehow and practice swordplay in his cell each day, he might be ready to try and fight in the arena. He already knew how to fight with swords and how to ride a horse well enough to joust. He was, after all, a candidate for Knight Training camp because he had proven himself ready. But could he face that young dragon in the arena? Could he win? It's glowing yellow eyes appeared in his mind yet again.

Peter lowered himself to the ground and tried to do some push-ups to build up his chest and arms. He cried out from the pain in his back. It was too overwhelming.

Lying on his side, he wondered about the guards. If he explained to them that he was training to fight in the arena, something the Warden enjoyed, would they be willing to give him at least one extra meal a day? Fearing the punishment of speaking out, Peter decided not to try asking the guards so soon. They were already angry with him for trying to escape. He needed time to prove he was a good and valuable prisoner first.

Suddenly, a most frightening thought entered his mind and sent a shiver through his body. *What if no one ever searches for me? What if I have to stay here forever?*

Peter rubbed his eyes, struggling to keep from weeping. Reaching into his pocket, he pulled out the compass and gently touched it. It gave him hope. Wiping his eyes, he tried to get the negative thoughts out of his mind by concentrating on his next move. He remembered playing chess against Simon in Theo's library. His life now, in the prison, seemed like a game of chess except he was playing against the Warden. He would have to strategize, study his opponent, and know his next move even before he made it. It wasn't check mate yet, but there were only a few moves left until the game would be over, and he would lose more than he could ever imagine.

§

Valbrand entered into his chamber and threw down his cloak. His assistant, a small goblin captured inside the prison years before, scurried to pick it up and hang it on the peg sticking out of the wall. But the goblin, cursed with stubby legs, couldn't reach the peg. He struggled until Valbrand couldn't take it any longer.

"Enough!" he shouted. "Throw it on the chair."

The little goblin obeyed then hopped over to a nearby table.

"Sir," he took out his book of parchment paper and his quill, ready to take notes.

"Not now." Valbrand stepped behind his desk carved out of stone and sat down on his wooden stool. He rubbed his tired face. "Bring me the ledgers!"

"Yes sir!" The goblin grabbed a candle off a table then ran into a dark adjacent room. He screamed a high pitched scream which startled Valbrand.

"What is it now?" Valbrand stood. When looked up, his entire body shook.

Lord Bedlam appeared from the other room followed by the quivering goblin.

"Lord Bedlam here to see you, sir," the goblin wringed its tiny hands.

"Leave us." Bedlam pointed to the creature and it scurried out the door.

"Lord Bedlam." Valbrand bowed his head. "To what do I owe this—"

"Spare me." Bedlam raised his hand. "Spare me the hypocrisy, please."

He slowly moved about the room inspecting its contents with the smoothness of smoke. Finally, he ran his long fingers over the piles of parchment on Valbrand's desk and rudely scattered them onto the dirt floor.

"Your thievery has been well known for quite a while now, Valbrand," Bedlam said in a low voice. His jaw clenched.

Valbrand raised his eyebrows in mock surprise. "What?" He put his hands over his chest. "Why I don't know what you mean, my Lord. I never—"

"Please." Bedlam raised his hand again. "I'm not here to discuss how you've been stealing gold and gem stones from my mines or how you've been gambling on the games and losing my gold in the process."

Valbrand swallowed hard.

Bedlam put his hand to his chin and methodically tapped his index finger on his temple. He turned and looked deeply into Valbrand's beady eyes. "No, we'll save that discussion for another time."

Valbrand bowed. "Thank you my Lord."

"No, I am here for another reason." Bedlam ran his finger along his thin pursed lips.

"Anything, my Lord. How can I be of—"

"Shut up. A prisoner was brought in here not long ago," Bedlam said.

Valbrand narrowed his eyes as though trying to remember something. "That traitor knight?"

Bedlam looked over at him. "What? No. A traitor knight doesn't interest me."

Valbrand tried to think of another.

"A boy was brought in here weeks ago," Bedlam said.

"My Lord." Valbrand cleared his throat. "*Many* young boys are brought into the prison daily."

Bedlam waved his hand and the door swung open. Two riders of Rünbrior entered dressed in their black armor with capes flowing behind them. One held a crossbow. He showed it to Valbrand then threw it on the desk. The crash made an already nervous Valbrand jump.

He studied the weapon for a second or two before he noticed the carvings on the handle.

"P.P" he muttered. Then, he looked up at Lord Bedlam and shrugged.

Bedlam gracefully waved his ringed fingers over the crossbow. "Observe the intricate details in the carvings. Notice the quality of work that went into constructing such a fine weapon." He snapped is fingers.

A rider grabbed Valbrand's bony neck and shoved his face inches away from the crossbow.

"Do you see what I'm talking about?" Bedlam asked.

"Yes," Valbrand squeaked. The rider released him and he stood erect again. "Yes, my Lord." He rubbed his sore neck. "I see the details in the crossbow."

"Good." Bedlam paced the office. His black cloak dragged along the dirt floor. "This prisoner I speak of is none other than Peter, the Prince of Illiath," Bedlam said. He admired the silver rings on his fingers. "He is here within these walls."

"Yes, my Lord." Valbrand shivered at the thought of King Alexander's son in his prison.

"He is here in this prison and I want him to remain in this prison until further orders," he turned toward Valbrand. "Understood?"

Valbrand scratched his balding head. "My Lord," he said. "King Alexander…"

Bedlam motioned for the riders to open the wooden door. "Yes? What about him?" He sighed impatiently.

Valbrand nervously wringed his hands together, took out a handkerchief, and wiped his sweaty brow. "Certainly the King has already ordered a rescue attempt by now."

Bedlam gave no reaction.

"To rescue the Prince. From the prison?"

Bedlam remained silent.

"Uh, the King, he will be very angry I'm sure." Valbrand carefully ambled over to Bedlam. "About his son being captured and mistakenly brought here."

"And?"

"And, so I…well, I…" Valbrand stuttered. "I won't want to be the one to face him when he comes to retrieve his son." Valbrand averted his eyes and patted his face with the handkerchief.

Bedlam firmly placed his hand on Valbrand's thin shoulder and squeezed.

Valbrand winced.

"And you won't have to," Bedlam grinned. "King Alexander is *dead*."

Valbrand looked up. "What?" he gasped. "But how—"

"Yes, it's true. I'm afraid an illness took him much too soon." Bedlam turned to leave. "So, you see? There is nothing for you to worry about."

Valbrand continued to look confused and shocked. "Why hold the Prince here, then?" Valbrand asked. "Why not kill him now and get it over with?"

Bedlam faced him with piercing eyes. "Because I still need the boy, you see."

Valbrand nodded.

"Keep the boy here, Valbrand." Bedlam pointed his cane at the Warden. "Keep him safe until further orders. Understood?"

Valbrand nodded, then bowed his head. He shoved the handkerchief into his pocket as the door slammed shut. "Oh, this is a bother." Valbrand paced the room rubbing his balding head. "Get in here!"

The fat little goblin peeked around the corner from the adjacent room then made his way to his boss' desk. He grabbed his parchment and quill.

"Find me that traitor knight," Valbrand ordered. "He just might be put to some good use after all."

The goblin bowed and ran out the door.

"And find me that boy Prince, too!" Valbrand shouted down the hall.

22 PLANS IN MOTION

Theo sat silently in his chair as Darion finished telling him of Sir William's intentions.

"This news is only part of the story, I'm afraid," Theo said as he slowly stood up and extinguished his pipe.

"What do you mean?" Darion asked.

"I believe Peter is alive, and we must quickly remove Will from the palace before he takes over the kingdom," Theo said.

Darion's eyes grew wide.

"Lord Bedlam is up to more than just taking over Illiath." Theo led Darion to his chamber. "There are darker forces working here."

He took a leather bag out from underneath his bed and began filling it with some books, clothes, and his pipe. Then, he slung it over his shoulder and moved toward the wall.

"And when it comes time for him to remove the obstacles in his way, you and I will be first on his list." Theo pushed open another secret passageway. "I am leaving the palace."

"No, you can't! If Peter is alive as you think he is, then we have to confront Bedlam and Will and go rescue Peter." Darion rushed over to Theo. "We have to act now!"

"We will act," Theo said. "When the time is right…" He placed his hand on Darion's shoulder.

"You stay here and obey Bedlam's commands for now. I am going to find reinforcements. I will return for Alexander's funeral. When I return, I will have a plan. Do you understand?"

Darion nodded. "The knights, I should tell them—"

"No!" Theo raised a finger. "Tell no one. Bedlam's powers are great. He has already selected those who will follow his lead. We cannot take any chances, understand?"

Darion understood. "It sickens me to think of Alexander's funeral." He blinked back tears.

"I know, my friend." Theo said. His voice cracked.

"We've no time now for emotions." He walked into the hidden passageway. "I will be back soon. Stay strong."

With that, he disappeared into the darkened hall. Darion watched as the wall closed shut.

§

The guard threw open the cell door just as he had done many times before. Peter, too stiff to hop to attention, crawled off his straw bed and slowly stood up wincing from the pain.

"Hurry!" yelled the guard.

Peter tried, but could only muster enough strength to walk through the doorway to where the chain waited for him. The other boys, smaller in number since the extreme cold temperatures had taken a few in the night, stood scratching their heads, arms, and legs while waiting to walk. Peter knew they had the lice, too. The tiny parasites tormented him night and day. Walking was good because it helped them stay warm and took their minds off the lice.

As they moved toward the cave, Peter stretched his aching back and yawned, then resumed scratching his hair. *I don't know which is more tormenting*, he thought. *The itching, the physical pain, or the not knowing when I will be freed...if I am ever freed at all.*

As they entered the cave, Peter noticed the guards hovered over a large tin canister. Its contents had been set afire. The fire kept their hands warm as they stood by it and conversed with one another. The boys made their way over to the cave wall where for weeks they had chiseled away at the rock. Peter picked up his hammer and started the day's work.

He had tried running away and climbing his way out, but he was caught. Any new ideas for escape evaded him. With only a few meals here and there, he had grown too weak for any planning.

"How is your back?" Jason asked.

Peter merely shook his head..

"I heard about what happened," Jason said. "I tried to warn you, but—"

Peter raised his hand to stop the boy from talking. "Please."

Jason continued to hammer the rock.

A commotion came from further into the cave and several of the guards ran into it to see what was happening. All the boys stopped working to try and get a glimpse, but Peter was too tired to care about anything except getting warm and eating at the end of the day. He had no idea when it was day or night inside the mountain. All he knew was that when the horn sounded, his day ended and he could eat. The hunger in his stomach burned with each clang of his hammer. Yet he kept moving.

The commotion inside the cave grew louder as more boys stopped to see what happened. Peter, finally intrigued, stopped to see.

As he did, a guard yelled. "Stop that man! Murderer! Stop him!" the guard shouted.

A man with blood on his hands ran out of the cave toward them all. He cruelly shoved a boy out of his way. The boy hit the wall and collapsed. Realizing the man must be the murderer, Peter took his hammer and threw it at the man's feet as he ran past. The hammer hit the man's ankles and he fell forward. As he turned to get up, he tried to strike Peter but he missed because Peter swiftly moved away. Forming a fist, using all the pent-up anger and frustration he had inside, Peter swung and hit the man right on the temple, sending him to the ground.

Stunned silent, the boys froze as the guards made their way to Peter.

"Grab him!" the guard yelled.

Peter squinted his eyes as he waited for the strong arms of the guards to grab him and haul him off to the cell only to be whipped again. But instead they grabbed the man who lay motionless on the ground.

When the guards took the unconscious man away, their leader turned to Peter and stared at him. "What did you do?" he asked dubiously.

"I hit him," Peter said in a voice above a whisper.

"With what?" the guard asked.

"With my fist, sir."

The guard examined Peter's bleeding hand. "Strong fist." He laughed.

Peter just stood quietly by as the other boys watched. The leader of the guards was a tall, husky man with a low, thunderous voice and thick arms. His dark hair was cut short like that of all the guards and he had a few days growth of a beard on his strong jaw.

"Do you know what you did?" the guard asked in that deep voice.

Peter shook his head as he stared down at the guard's muddied boots. He feared making eye contact with him.

"You helped capture the man who took one of my guard's lives," he explained. "He had escaped from the cells below and killed one of my best guards. Then he made his way past several other guards to escape through here...until he met you!" He chuckled. "We'll have to think up some sort of reward for you." The guard studied Peter's thin frame. "How is it a thin boy like you has so much strength?"

"I have been practicing in my cell at night, sir," Peter said.

"Practicing? Practicing for what?"

"For the games, sir. I want to fight in the games one day," Peter explained.

The guard stood silent for a moment. "What do you do in your cell?"

"Push-ups for my arms, lunges for my legs," Peter exaggerated.

"Show me," the guard ordered as he pointed to the ground. Ignoring the pain in his back, Peter obeyed by performing his exercises with great ease. His own body surprised him since only minutes before he felt so incredibly drained and weak.

"Impressive!" The guard laughed. Many of his men had gathered around to watch. Peter stood up and dusted off his hands. "If you keep training like that, I believe one day you will make it to the games. I will make sure the Warden hears of this. Perhaps we can think up some sort of a reward for your bravery," the guard said as he turned to leave.

"I could use..." Peter said quietly.

"Use what?" the guard asked as he turned around.

"More food," Peter said. "It is hard for me to train on one meal a day. I have lost much muscle due to lack of food. Perhaps another meal of bread each day would help me train?" Peter lifted up the sleeve of his dirty tunic to reveal a very thin arm.

"Well, bread will not help you build muscle," the guard said. He rubbed his chin. "I'll see if I can come up with some meat for you."

"And a...." Peter continued.

"Yes?" the guard asked.

"A sword to use when I train?" Peter asked. "You see, I thrust in my cell but without a sword, I cannot practice adequately for the games."

The guard paused, thinking to himself. Peter was not sure if he had angered the guard or not, so he remained silent and waited.

"I have a wooden sword the boy could use for practicing," said one of the guards.

His leader agreed and told him to give it to Peter that night when they returned to their cells. Then all the guards left, carrying the wounded man with them.

At that moment, the leader turned to Peter. "What is your name?" he asked.

Peter froze as the other boys looked at him. "Pe—" he began, but then his voice to trailed off. He decided not to reveal his identity. "Ethan," he said.

"No it isn't!" cried Damon who was down the chain.

"Shhhh!" Jason said to him to keep him quiet.

"Ethan?" the guard said. "Where are you from?"

"Riverdale," Peter lied.

"Well, Ethan of Riverdale, I'll see what I can do," The guard said as he turned to leave. The boys stood by as they watched the guards walk off. Then, they returned to their labor for the day. Peter bent over and picked up his hammer. He noticed his knuckles were bleeding.

"Why did you lie?" Damon cried out.

"You hush!" said Jason. "It is none of your business."

"You hesitated as though your name isn't Ethan," Damon said to Peter. "What's your *real* name?"

"I said Ethan, so my name is Ethan," Peter said.

Damon huffed and then closely inspected Peter's clothes. "I have been to Riverdale. And I have seen the clothes they wear. You are wearing a canvas tunic with gold threading. No one in

Riverdale wears canvas tunics with gold threading. Not even the Mayor!" Damon shouted as he grabbed hold of Peter's tunic. "You are not from Riverdale and you said your name was Peter before."

He stood challenging Peter eye-to-eye as the other boys began to circle around with chains rattling. Peter wanted to hit Damon and twist his arm around behind his back to stop him from touching his tunic, but he also knew he might lose his new privileges if he fought in the cave. Jason stood next to Peter with a confused looked on his face.

"I found the tunic in the forest and put it on one day. Now leave me alone!" Peter shouted as he stepped back and out of Damon's grip.

"I will be watching you," Damon said as he and the other boys returned to their spot along the cave wall.

Jason turned to Peter and waited for an explanation.

"Promise you will tell no one?" Peter whispered to Jason.

"I promise!"

"My name is Peter, but I cannot allow the guards to find out," Peter explained.

"Why not?" Jason asked.

"It is better for you not to know. Just trust me for now." Peter went back to work.

"Do you really plan to fight in the arena?" Jason asked.

"I don't care about the games and all that," Peter whispered. "I want to find out if I can escape through the arena." He looked at Jason. "That's all I care about."

Jason shrugged, lifted his bucket full of rocks, and made his way to the large bin. The day continued on as any other day in the prison.

§

"The plan is going well," Bedlam said to Will. The two men sat at the large table in the dining hall while servants brought them food.

"Good." Will tore into a pheasant and ate the meat.

Bedlam watched.

"And what of Theo and Darion?" Will asked.

"Leave them to me." Bedlam stood and took some wine from the silver tray in the middle of the table. "Wine?"

He offered to pour Will some wine, but Will politely refused, perhaps remembering the elixir that Bedlam had given Alexander.

Bedlam placed the decanter down. "The funeral is ready. Leaders will begin to arrive tomorrow. Theo will be among them." Bedlam walked the room. "Once King Alexander is buried, we will make the announcement to the people that you will be the heir to the throne of Illiath."

"There will be resistance," Will said.

"Of course. And that resistance will be dealt with."

Will stood. "King Alexander's knights?"

"Some will join us." Bedlam took and ate a grape. "Others will not."

"And the other Kings?"

"Each ruler has his own personal interest at stake." Bedlam's eyes narrowed. "They will do as they are told or suffer the consequences."

"And the Dragon Forest?" Will asked.

"Once we have all the players in place, we will begin our attack." Bedlam stood. "And you will lead your people to glory, Will."

Without emotion, Will listened.

"It is only a matter of time." Bedlam walked down the long hallway alone.

23 SIMON'S RETURN

With stempost dividing the waters like a cutlass, the *Gallant* eased into the harbor with its square sails proudly displaying the emblem of King Mildrir. The sailors, some men and some Elves, made their way up the masts onto the rigging to adjust the sails. One by one, they secured the canvas sails to the yard, causing the ship to slow even more. Taller ships led the way into the Eastshore harbor with their large square sails out front and lateen sails in the mizzenmast. They were followed by the class of smaller ships each built from wood and decorated with brass. The *Gallant*, her hold filled with teas and spices, bustled with crew preparing for the dock landing.

The sight was impressive to young Annika as she waited pensively on the pier waiting for Simon to disembark with his guardian. Her eyes, red with fatigue, squinted in the overcast light. Sleep and comfort had abandoned her since hearing about Peter and now his father's death. She would now have to tell Simon the horrible news of their friend.

Her grandfather, King Baldrieg, wanted her to wait until the boy had arrived home, but she couldn't wait. All four friends shared a bond that could never be broken. She had to be the one to greet Simon and tell him herself.

Annika spotted Simon standing on the foredeck with a smile on his face and knew instantly that the trip had been successful. The ship finally settled into the harbor as the plank was lowered, allowing all passengers to disembark. The sailors' rough voices shouted for all to go ashore. One by one, the passengers made their way down the plank to reunite with their loved ones. Annika rose on her toes to spy over the heads and shoulders of the travelers as they moved by her, but she could not see her friend. Finally, she moved through the crowds, apologizing in her most polite way for the crushing of her elbows into ribs and shoulder blades.

Upon reaching the ship, she strained to see if she had missed him, but the crowds had thinned. Only the sailors were left securing the ship to its dock.

"What are you doing here?" said a voice behind her.

Stunned, she turned around to see who it was. "Simon!"

"Annika? What are *you* doing here? I didn't expect to see you here."

Annika faced a much taller Simon standing before her. It had been many weeks since she had seen him. She embraced him tightly, her chin resting on his wide shoulder. "Oh Simon," she said, trying not to shed tears, "it is so good to see you again."

"My dear," Simon's guardian said, "are you here alone?"

"No sir." She wiped tears off her cheeks. "My grandfather is ill and stayed home. He did not want me to come, but I had to. I am here with his Constable as an escort."

"Why did you come?" Simon asked. "Are you alright?"

"Is it your grandfather, the King? Is he alright?" the guardian asked.

"Then you haven't heard…" she said. More tears began to fall. "Peter…Peter is gone."

Simon stood still as he let Annika's words settle. He made sure he heard her correctly.

"Gone?" he asked. "What do you mean gone? As in *missing*?"

They hadn't heard the news, just as Annika suspected. "He was taken, by the guards of Rünbrior, to the prison at Ranvieg," she cried. "And he…he was *killed*."

Simon stepped back a few steps as though struck with a blow to the chest. "What? When did this happen?

"On his way to the Crow Valley after our party at Illiath."

"That many weeks ago? We must go to Illiath immediately." His guardian motioned for the servants to swiftly finish loading their carriages.

"There is more." Annika said as she dried her eyes with the backs of her hands. Simon quickly handed her his handkerchief.

"Upon hearing the news of his son, King Alexander became very ill," she explained. "Sir William has taken over the kingdom."

"Go on," the guardian said.

"And then... and then... King Alexander has died." She buried her face in her hands.

Simon turned away and walked to the edge of the pier. His guardian comforted Annika. "The land without a king...without an heir," the guardian said. "How? How did this all happen?"

"I have come to tell you of the funeral tomorrow. My grandfather is so overcome with grief, he can barely speak."

Simon stared out into the sea for a long moment, taking in everything he had heard. A few gulls flew into the golden sky. His eyes followed them higher and higher. He had just returned from a most memorable voyage and now he stood with a crushed heart. "Peter," he said softly. "My friend."

Striding back Annika, he put an arm around her shoulders and he led her to the carriage. "Does Crispin know?"

"I don't know. I haven't had the chance to visit him," she said.

"So, he is back from his travels?"

"Yes." She wept.

"I'll have to go and see him," Simon said. "We have only been gone on this journey for a few weeks and yet it seems as though the whole world has changed. How could this have happened?" he asked his guardian, who only shrugged.

"Will, who now calls himself the Duke of Illiath, has taken over the palace," Annika said.

"Will?" Simon handed his bags to the driver. "What do you mean?"

Annika entered the carriage. "He was the one who saw Peter's dead body. He told the King and then stayed to take care of him at the palace."

"So no one but Will saw Peter's body? Not even the king? Something seems amiss here," Simon said as he sat next to Annika.

"Only one name comes to my mind regarding all that I have heard this day," the guardian said. "And that name is Bedlam."

"Oh, Lord Bedlam has been assisting the Duke at the palace," Annika said.

"What?" the guardian shouted. "Now I know something is terribly wrong. Let's get back to the castle immediately."

153

The driver shouted at the horses, and they galloped off toward King Mildrir's palace at Thorgest.

§

Alexander sat in the dark dungeon of his very own castle trying to think of a way to escape. He could hear the occasional thumping sounds from people moving around upstairs, water dripping down the walls, and the scratching of rats' claws from between the barrels of oats.

Two of Bedlam's soldiers leaned up against the wall, snoring. Each time Alexander moved, his chains rattled, stirring the men from their sleep.

"Keep still there!" one soldier shouted. "We're trying to get some sleep."

Alexander gave them a look of disgust. His arms and back ached from pulling on the chains. It was no use. They were secured tightly to the wall behind him.

Just then, the door opened revealing Bedlam silhouetted by the light coming from the sconces behind him. Taking a torch, he entered the dungeon.

"Wake up you two." He waved the torch over the two soldiers, and they raised their arms to avoid the flames. "I need you to climb those stairs and open that trap door." Bedlam pointed to the stairs at the back of the dungeon leading up two levels to a small wooden trap door. "Hurry!"

Bedlam walked over to Alexander and smiled. "Your funeral is organized for tomorrow, Alexander. I thought you'd like to know that all the rulers will be represented here at the palace. Some were so grief stricken, they could not make the trip." He waited for a reaction from the King.

"Well, I was moved," Bedlam finally said.

The soldiers opened the trap door and Alexander jumped when he heard a very low but throaty growl. Just then, two large Baroks entered the room pulling two black Zadoks on leashes. Alexander sat up and again tried to pry his wrists from the chains. His eyes opened wide at the sight of the wolf-like beasts coming down the steps. Drool dripped from their snarling mouths. Very sharp yellow teeth glared at him. And their eyes glowed red just as he had remembered from the battlefield.

Yet these creatures were larger and more powerful than the ones he remembered. The Baroks struggled to maintain control when the beasts saw the dead Apothecary's body lying there. Bedlam waved his arm, and the Baroks released the Zadoks to let them feast on the dead body.

Alexander cringed and looked away. The sound of flesh tearing and animals chomping on bones made him sick to his stomach.

"Too much for you?" Bedlam chuckled. "Don't worry. I have them here only to guard you and not to eat you, Alexander."

"You two!" Bedlam shouted to the soldiers. "Come with me. These Baroks will guard the King for now."

The men headed out the large wooden door, leaving Bedlam standing over his prisoner. "I will let you know how the proceedings went. I wouldn't want you to miss a single detail. Especially when Will appears in his new position as ruler of Illiath."

Alexander tried to stand, but the Zadoks growled at him with their blood stained teeth. He sat back down and shot Bedlam a venomous look.

Bedlam tapped Alexander's boot with his cane. "I am enjoying this." He grinned. Then he exited the dungeon and slammed the door shut.

Alexander could hear it being locked from the outside. He turned and saw the Baroks laughing as the beasts tore the dead body to pieces. The pungency of sweat mixed with blood permeated the air. Alexander felt dizzy. He tried to cover his mouth, but the chains kept his hands out of reach.

That's when he noticed the small trap door at the top of the steps was left ajar.

24 THE FUNERAL

One by one, the Royal Knights of King Alexander's kingdom arrived on horseback in the rain and dismounted at the castle entrance to meet their host, the Duke of Illiath. With heads hung low, each knight entered the palace and took his place in the grand hall. Sworn to protect Illiath and their King, now they would walk alongside his casket to the burial grounds. Constable Darion searched the area, but Lord Bedlam was nowhere to be seen.

Darion led the knights to the back of the castle where King Alexander's casket lay in a carriage pulled by eight horses. Each horse had a rider from Alexander's Cavalry. These brave men rode with Alexander to fight off Lord Caragon's evil Baroks in the war. Now, in full dress uniform, they sat pensively awaiting the procession to begin. Alexander's casket lay in the carriage draped in black silk with the golden crest of the lion stitched in.

The King's Knights wore their silver armor polished to a mirror shine, positioned themselves beside the carriage to march in unison as they did in battle with their King. Their scarlet capes draped down their backs caused them to look more regal than battle ready. Their King would have been pleased by the sight.

Behind the carriage, Lady Godden, Lady Silith, Lord Byrén, and the other rulers of the valleys along with each King from the regions stood ready to follow the carriage. Dark clouds hovered overhead and thunder echoed far off. Lady Godden, dressed in a flowing black gown, wept into her handkerchief.

"It's as if all the land mourns the King." She inspected the sky. "This is so tragic. He was so young."

Lady Silith consoled her friend. "I know, but we must remain strong. That's what Alexander would have wanted."

Annika, dressed in a long blue gown, arrived with her grandfather, Baldrieg, King of Glenthryst.

Her long blonde hair pulled back into a bun, she carefully made her way to where the carriage waited. There Simon and Crispin, dressed in their finest tunics, joined her.

"What will happen to Illiath now?" she whispered.

"Never did I think this could happen. Never," Crispin said, still in shock from the news. He gazed over to the carriage. "How could everything that was once so wonderful suddenly become so tragic?"

Simon nodded. "In a way, I am glad Peter is not here to see this."

"It would have crushed him," Annika said.

"Now they are all together again," Crispin said softly.

A young man, dressed in armor and carrying a brass horn, walked out to where the carriage stood. Placing the horn to his lips, he blew three short blasts. All the guests looked up to the tallest of the palace towers. Another young man in armor appeared in the tower. He also held a brass horn to his lips and began to play.

"What is this song he plays, grandfather?" Annika asked.

"He is playing a song written for Alexander's father before the battle of the Cornshire," King Baldrieg said.

The song signaled the start of the procession.

A set of drummers came out of the palace and walked ahead of the carriage, setting the cadence for all to follow. Each drummer wore a tunic representing the crests of Alexander's lineage. The drummers walked and the carriage followed as the horn played.

Slowly the procession made its way around the castle wall. Along the wall, all of Alexander's soldiers saluted the casket as it passed. Some of the young men wept as they watched their sovereign pass in his polished mahogany casket surrounded with roses, peonies, and jasmine from Queen Laurien's gardens.

"The flowers," Annika observed. "They are so lovely."

"They were Alexander's favorite flowers because they reminded him of his beloved wife," Baldrieg said.

Finally, the carriage made its way to the front of the castle near the rushing waters of the Blue River. The people from nearby valleys stood along the roadway leading to the cemetery. The women wept and held their children as the men stood with hands over their hearts. One by one, the peasants tossed flowers onto the casket.

"Long live the King," one man shouted through his tears. "Long live King Alexander!"

The people lowered their eyes as the carriage passed. The horn continued its solemn tune until the carriage made its way through the entrance way of the cemetery. Abruptly, in mid tune, the horn stopped playing.

Annika looked up.

"Why did he stop playing so suddenly?" she asked.

"To symbolize what happened during the war of the Cornshire when an arrow pierced the chest of the young trumpet player as he played during battle," her grandfather explained.

She nodded.

The drummers stopped their drumming. The moment of silence was meant to symbolize the land without a King or an heir.

The only sounds of the women weeping and the carriage creaking its way up a small hill to where the headstones of Queen Laurien and Prince Peter stood. All the guests gathered around the grave as the townspeople observed at the gates of the cemetery.

"Today we say goodbye to King Alexander," King Mildrir spoke first. "A most honorable King, father, husband…and friend."

He gathered some dirt into his hand and, as the soldiers lowered the casket into the prepared hole in the ground, King Mildrir tossed the dirt onto the casket. Each ruler did the same as did each leader of the nearby valleys.

At last, all stood around the grave marker in silence. Thunder rumbled in the distance. The wind through the tall trees.

Off to the side stood Theo, alone.

§

Darion made his way over to speak to his friend. "I cannot understand how all this happened. First Peter, then the King. And now the land without a ruler. Where is the hope?"

Theo nodded toward Peter's three friends, Annika, Crispin, and Simon as they left from the grave site. "There is always hope, my friend," Theo said.

Darion managed a weakened smile.

"Come now. We must be strong in all this," Theo watched as all the mourners passed by the grave. "That's what Alexander would want."

Darion sighed. "Yes, well, at least all the rulers are represented here. There is peace among all the lands."

"Don't look at who is among the mourners," Theo said. "Instead, notice who is *not* here."

Darion paused. "Lord Bedlam." He clenched his fists.

"Exactly. Even he knew it was unwise to make an appearance here. You and I know the truth. Bedlam is behind all this." Theo turned to walk off.

Darion followed. "I know you're right," Darion cringed. "But how could he turn Sir William against the King? What kind of sorcery is this?"

Theo stopped. "Bedlam's power grows, and as it does, he will use the weak-minded for his purpose."

Together they watched Will mount his horse.

"But Will is not weak-minded, is he?" Darion said. "And he loved King Alexander like a father and Peter like a brother."

Theo mumbled something under his breath.

"So how could he turn Will against the King and use him this way," Darion asked.

"Bedlam chooses carefully." Theo raised a finger as he walked. "Be mindful of this. He observes from afar. He knows the intentions of the heart. He senses things unlike other men in this way."

"Where are you going now?" Darion asked.

"To pay a visit to King Isleif." Theo grinned slightly. "It is time to put our plan into motion."

Darion hung his head.

"Don't worry, my friend. There remain a few surprises left." He disappeared into the woods.

Darion overhead the disconcerting conversations of the townspeople as they began to walk back to their villages.

"What will become of us?" one elderly woman said to her husband.

"It will be for the other Kings to decide," he said to her.

She nodded. "If only the Dragon were here again."

"What are you saying? Don't you remember? Lord Bedlam told us the Dragon Forest is the cause of all this suffering." Her husband gave her a stern look. "It's a good thing the Dragon isn't here or we'd all rise up and kill it!"

She frowned.

"Look!" a young girl shouted as she spotted a bird fly by. "A white owl."

The large bird landed on the branch of a tree nearby. Its powerful yellow eyes glowed.

"A winter white owl," the elderly woman said to her.

"A good omen?" the young girl asked.

"I hope so," the elderly woman answered. "I hope so."

§

Inside the palace dungeon sat King Alexander with his mouth bound to ensure his silence.

Lord Bedlam stood by listening to the cadence. "It has begun." He looked up at the stone ceiling. "Your funeral, Alexander." He grinned victoriously at his prisoner. "Of course, we had no funeral for Peter." He exhaled dramatically. "With no body found, we decided not to have a formal funeral, but a headstone was made. Now all three of you are buried together. How quaint."

Alexander tried to kick Bedlam with his feet, but he stood too far away. Alexander screamed, but with a rag stuffed into his mouth, it was muffled.

"Temper, temper." Bedlam stepped several paces over to where a Zadok lay licking its paws and stroked the thick grey fur. "You will be locked up here for many years, Alexander. It's time you come to terms with it."

A few pieces of dirt fell from the ceiling as it vibrated. Bedlam looked up again. "Well, it seems the Royal Knights are all riding off now to their estates." He squatted by Alexander. "They'll need to rest for soon the Duke of Illiath will call on them to do his bidding."

Alexander watched Bedlam carefully.

"Soon they will ride with many soldiers into the Dragon Forest to destroy it, Alexander." Bedlam stood and rubbed his long thin arms. "I get shivers just thinking about it."

Alexander moved his legs again, desperately trying to pull the chains away from the wall.

Bedlam turned and made his way out the dungeon door. "Sleep well, my old friend," he said as one of his soldiers closed and locked the large door. As Bedlam ascended the stairs, he stopped one of his guards. "You there. I noticed the small door at the top of the steps near the haystacks is ajar."

The soldier stammered.

"Idiot!" Bedlam removed the sword from his cane and held it dangerously close to the soldier's throat. "Do you realize how important this prisoner is?"

The soldier stared at the sword.

"Look at me!" Bedlam shouted.

The soldier obeyed.

"If this happens again"—spittle formed in the corners of Bedlam's mouth—"I will gut you like a pig and feed you to my Zadoks. Understood?"

The soldier nodded enthusiastically.

Bedlam replaced his sword inside the cane and continued on his way up the stairs. "Fools. I'm surrounded by incompetence. But only for a short while longer."

The soldier entered the dungeon where two of his fellow soldiers sat chuckling.

"The old man told you off, eh?" one said.

"Shut up!" the soldier said. He leaned against the wall and crossed his arms. "And go close that small door up there!"

"You go close it! He ordered you to do it, not us." The soldiers laughed and drank from their canteens.

Alexander noticed the angry soldier was the youngest of them. He observed him as he went to shut the small trap door at the top of the steps. The boy carefully made his way around the two sleeping Zadoks, then climbed to the top of the steps and slammed the trap door shut. When he came back, Alexander began moaning and coughing.

"Hey, shouldn't we remove that rag from his mouth?" the soldier asked. "Looks like he's having trouble breathing."

Alexander continued to exaggerate his breathing and coughing.

The two other soldiers ignored the question and continued talking amongst themselves. So, the soldier hunched down by Alexander and removed the rag.

The King exhaled and took in a few deep breaths. "Thank you," he said.

"Here—have some water." The young man lifted his canteen to Alexander's dry mouth.

"Hey! What are you doing there?" one soldier shouted.

"Just giving him some water. Keep it quiet," the young man answered. "Lord Bedlam said we could give him water."

Alexander drank as much as he could all the while making eye contact with the young soldier.

"Thank you, my boy," the King said.

The soldier nodded.

"You're not much older than my son, the Prince," Alexander said.

The soldier shrugged. He leaned over and slid a plate with some food on it over to Alexander. "Here. You'd better eat something."

Alexander tried to reach the plate, but the chains were too short.

"Now you've gotta feed him too, huh?" one guard shouted. They laughed at the boy.

"No," he said. Then, he reached over and removed the keys from his belt. He unlocked the cuffs around Alexander's wrists. "Go ahead and eat. Then I'll lock you up again."

Alexander winced as though in pain.

"What is it?" the boy asked.

Alexander looked away as though embarrassed.

"Tell me, are you in pain?"

"It's just that..." the King hesitated. He looked over at the other guards who were eating some food. "It's been many hours since I was able to relieve myself."

The boy seemed to understand. "Oh, alright. I'll see what I can do."

25 MEETING VALBRAND

The food had improved greatly, and Peter was grateful for it too as he sat in his cell eating the boiled meat and bread on his tray. He was now able to eat three meals a day thanks to his bravery in the cave. The guard had proven faithful to his promise to help Peter, and as a result, several days later Peter had gained some weight and strength as he practiced his fighting skills inside his cell each day after the long hours of work in the cave. He was able to sneak a few pieces of meat to his friend Jason.

The guard also provided Peter with a wooden sword to use for his practice sessions in the cell, but he also used it to chase the rat back into its hole. Peter could tell his form had improved as well as his muscular strength. The exercise had helped him sleep more soundly, too. The nightmares eased in this new life. He had sores on his bony hips and back from sleeping on the floor, but he had more to look forward to each day when the guard opened the cell door and ordered him to the cave with the others. Sometimes the guard would leave a book of tales and, in the moonlight, Peter would pass the time by reading about adventures in faraway lands. Although it had been weeks since Peter had entered Rünbrior, he now had a sense of purpose. Once he had a real sword placed in his hands, he hoped he could win in the games and eventually escape.

One morning, Peter walked out the cell door and joined the others who continued to scratch at their itchy scalps while on the chain. As he found his usual spot next to Jason, Peter went on to explain how his training had progressed. But first, he handed his hungry friend a piece of meat.

Jason gobbled it down quickly before any guards spotted him. Peter noticed Jason's eyes were deeply set and his face was thinner. He was showing signs of starvation.

"Thank you, my friend," Jason said. "How is the training going?'

"Well," Peter said, picking up his hammer. "I feel stronger and stronger each day."

"Good!" Jason said. "The first fight of the gaming season is next week. Do you think you will be ready?"

Peter nodded.

"You assume you will be fighting a man," Damon interrupted..

"What do you mean?" Peter asked him.

"Well, do not assume you will fight only men," Damon explained. "They may have you fight a dragon, you know."

Peter hadn't thought of that before. He assumed he would fight a man first.

"It doesn't matter to me," Peter said. "As long as they give me a sword, it doesn't matter who or what I fight."

"We'll see," said Damon.

The hammering continued, and Peter tried to use it to his benefit. He would need strong arms, wrists, and shoulders to last in any fight, and he knew it. A sword seems light at first, but after many minutes of fighting, it could feel like thousands of pales loaded with rocks. As the day wore on, Peter and Jason finished their section of rock and moved to another portion of the cave.

A loud shout came from one of the guards.

"Ethan!" he shouted. Peter ignored him and kept hammering away, deep in thought about home and his father.

"Ethan! Is there an Ethan here?" the guard shouted as he came around.

"Peter," whispered Jason. "I think he is calling you."

At that moment, Peter remembered that he had given a false name to the guard. "Here I am," he reluctantly answered. And with that, the guard grabbed him by the arm and unlocked his wrist cuffs from the main chain.

"The warden wants a word with you," the guard growled.

Peter cocked an eyebrow. He turned to Jason with a concerned look. "So long," he said to his friend whose eyes had grown large with fright.

"Take care," Jason answered.

"Get back to work!" the guards shouted as they cracked their whips.

Jason turned to hammer at the cave wall and Peter was pushed down the darkened pathway. He wondered if he would ever return to this portion of the cave again and where they were taking him.

The dark pathway became lit as they turned a corner and saw torches lining the cave walls.

"This way," the guard said. He shoved Peter toward an opening in the cave. It led to some steps with water dripping down the cave walls. It smelled musty and the air was damp. Peter walked down the steps with the guard closely behind him. So many things raced through his mind. He wondered if he would be punished for something or maybe even set free. *Maybe*, he thought, *my father is here to finally retrieve me!*

But that happy feeling disappeared when Peter saw more guards standing in a room at the end of the stairway. Peter stopped walking. All the guards looked at him. The main guard, who had rewarded him with extra meals, stood in the middle.

"Wait here," the main guard said.

Peter obeyed.

The guard left the room through a doorway that led to yet another room carved out of the mountain rock. Water continued to drip down the cave walls. Peter remained frightened and concerned.

Just then, the guard came back and waved to Peter to follow him. Peter quickly obeyed. He noticed that the other guards were not following him. He walked closely behind the main guard. They stopped in the middle of the next room where a long table stood surrounded by some chairs. An older man stood near the table with a tablet in his hand. He seemed to have some parchment paper and a quill in his hand as though prepared to write something down. His eyes were glazed over with boredom as he stood waiting with Peter and the guard.

A loud voice was heard from yet another doorway that led to yet another room in this labyrinth of sorts. Chains rattled and suddenly guards brought in some young men Peter had never seen before. The young men ranged in age from Peter's to that of his father's age. They were each wearing torn clothing covered in the dark red dirt of the caves Peter was so familiar with. And they each looked as exhausted as Peter from work and lack of good food and rest.

"Stand here," the guard shouted.

The men stopped and turned toward the table. The guards unlocked their wrists and threatened that if they tried to escape, they would be hunted and killed. They were told it was a privilege to be considered by the Warden for the games and they should be appreciative of the opportunity.

The games? Peter thought. *I am being considered for the games?* All the prisoners, including Peter, stood silent waiting for the warden to enter.

The main guard walked over to Peter. "You'll be fine," he whispered. Peter felt more at ease that the man remembered him at all.

Just then Valbrand, a thin man with a narrow face, entered the room with the fat little goblin hopping behind him. Peter watched the little creature as it struggled to climb atop the table. It amused him. Valbrand and the goblin whispered for a moment before the Warden began his inspection of the line of prisoners. Valbrand was taller than Peter. His gray eyes were dry with red rims, like someone who lacked sleep. But he had an air of confidence that caused all the prisoners to fear him. They understood the power this man wielded.

Peter, standing as tall as he could, stared straight ahead avoiding the Warden's eyes as much as he could, but he felt the weight of Valbrand's stare. One by one, the Warden studied each man, looking for strength, size, and fierceness in the eyes. "Pair them off," he shouted.

The guards took the men and grouped them into pairs. Peter was paired off with a young man taller than him, but just as thin. Peter knew he could fight him with ease. He waited for the order.

The goblin scribbled onto the tablet it held as the guards asked for the names of each man.

"Ethan of Riverdale," Peter shouted when asked for his name.

The goblin wrote it down hastily.

Then, Valbrand ordered the first pair of men to begin fighting. They were older, but strong, as they wrestled to the ground together. When one would escape, the other would grab him and throw him back to the ground before Valbrand shouted, "Enough!" to stop the match. Afterwards, each selected man was given a mark on the shoulders and sent into another room.

Finally, Peter and his fighting partner stood alone in the room with the guards, the Warden, and the little goblin watching. For this match, they were given swords. Peter held the large sword in his hands and gripped it tightly. It had been a long time since he had held a real sword and it felt good. He turned to face his opponent. He was already in a fighting stance. Peter wanted to fight in the arena as badly as any man in the prison and was about to prove it.

When the order was given, the two lunged at each other with swords clanging in front. Peter, remembering the moves he had been taught by Will and his father's knights, grasped the sword with both hands, and flung it over head, and brought it down hard on his opponent's sword, making a loud clanging sound that reverberated throughout the cave. Peter spun around and brought the sword inches away from his opponent's throat before it was stopped by iron. His opponent was strong, but Peter felt stronger as he spun around in the opposite direction swiping his sword at the young man's thigh, slicing it open ever so slightly as to send him to the ground on one knee.

Peter knew he had his opponent where he wanted him, so he lunged forward and placed the dull blade at the base of his opponent's throat and waited. When the young man, writhing in pain from the slash in his thigh, began to raise his sword, Peter pushed the dull blade deeper into the crevice of the neck causing him to drop his sword and hand Peter his first victory.

Valbrand remained silent for a moment, then nodded to his guard. As quickly as he had entered the room, he left, followed by the goblin, who continued to scribble onto the tablet.

Peter, breathing heavily, lowered his sword and stood back to allow his opponent a chance to stand, but the young man fell to the ground gripping his thigh. Two guards carried him out of the room as Peter watched. It easily could have been him bleeding and hurt. He was grateful to the guard for helping him with extra meals.

"Well done," the guard said to Peter.

"What is your name?" Peter asked. "So I may thank you."

"Eckert," he said as he padded Peter on the shoulder.

"Thank you, Eckert, for your assistance," Peter said, trying to catch his breath. The fight had taken much energy.

"You have done well for yourself, young Ethan," Eckert said. "The warden was impressed. I do believe you will fight in the games soon and win."

"What happens now?"

"You will be transferred to the other side of the prison where you will begin your training until you fight in the games." Eckert waved his men over. "And then, Ethan, we will see what happens next."

Peter walked behind the guards as they led him to the other side of the prison. He couldn't help but smile. He had hope for the first time in many days since entering into Rünbrior.

§

The palace gates raised and the bridge lowered. The Duke of Illiath walked out and raised his hand. The crowds cheered and little children ran to him.

"Help us!" one woman yelled. "The land. It is dying!"

"We try to garden, but the land yields nothing," one older man said. "The seeds all die!"

A cart full of bread and fruit followed behind and the Duke welcomed the townspeople to enjoy their share of food. Will walked over to the cart and removed some wildflowers. He bent down and handed them to a little girl. She shyly smelled the flowers, then ran to her mother. Will helped the knights and servants distribute the food to the crowds gathered.

"People!" Will raised his arms and the crowd hushed. "People of the Cornshire. I have heard your concerns. Since King Alexander died, the land suffers. But I am here to help you!"

The people ran forward and joyfully took loaves of bread and baskets of fruit. Many walked over and thanked the Duke.

"Oh thank you, Sir William," one woman cried. "Whatever would we do without your kindness?"

"You are too good to us," one man said.

"I am your servant," Will said as he lowered his head. "Come, partake of this bounty." He handed the man bread.

"Take some for your children," Will said.

From atop the outer curtain wall, Lord Bedlam observed all that happened that early morning.

Constable Darion stood beside him. "Just what do you wish to accomplish by giving this food to the people?" he asked.

Bedlam turned to him. "They trust Will. They see how the land is afflicted since Alexander's death. Now they see that Will cares for them. He provides for them. That is what we hope to accomplish."

"Why do I have the feeling there's more to it than mere kindness?" Darion turned to leave. "The land appears afflicted, but do you really believe it is because of the King's death?"

"I don't blame you for not trusting me, Darion," Bedlam said. "But I hope, with time, you can see that I have indeed changed."

Darion smirked. "I know better."

"And I hope that I, in time, can depend on you?"

"What do you mean by that?"

Bedlam leaned on his cane. "Well, my friend, soon the time will come when all the leaders must come together. The Duke will need your support."

Darion squinted. "Support for what?"

Bedlam smiled. "The time will come when everyone will know. But for now, I need to know I can count on you."

Darion's face softened as though he understood what Bedlam was asking. Darion bowed modestly. "But of course. My loyalty lies with King Alexander. His memory, his palace, his wishes." Darion nodded toward the Dragon Forest. "Therefore, if Will's plans align with Alexander's plans, then he has my full support. Always."

The smile left Bedlam's face.

"But if those plans differ in anyway"—Darion's tone grew serious—"I cannot make any promises."

Bedlam lifted his cane. "I understand."

Darion smirked and made his way down the wooden ladder leaving Lord Bedlam alone on the outer wall.

26 THE PALACE AT GUNDREHD

As King Mildrir and the servant approached the large wooden door, the King could hear the giggles of a young woman and the chuckling of King Isleif. The servant hesitated to interrupt, but King Mildrir stood imposingly behind him. Not wanting to wait any longer, Mildrir shoved the servant aside, turned the doorknob, and threw open the door.

Isleif, too busy chasing a lovely young maiden around his large room, didn't notice Mildrir watching. The girl had hiked up her skirt in order to run fast enough to escape Isleif's advances. Giggling, she found herself trapped near the bed.

"I have you now!" Isleif laughed as he approached the girl.

"Isleif!" Mildrir shouted.

The King jumped and spun around in time to see King Mildrir standing in the doorway. The girl screamed, ran passed Mildrir, and left the room.

"Now look what you have done." Isleif laughed. "She has escaped."

"Isleif," Mildrir said, "what are you doing?"

"Well, a king must marry after all." Isleif chuckled as he plopped down on a large chair. "To what do I owe the pleasure of this most unexpected visit King Mildrir?"

Mildrir inhaled and pursed his lips as though trying his best to hide his frustration. He stormed into the room. It was a large room with an impressive wooden bed near the back wall. The bed had four posts several feet high and it was covered with velvet throws. On the floor were many fur skins of animals from faraway lands Mildrir had never seen. Books lined enormous shelves that reached the ceiling at least twenty feet high. Large picture windows of paned glass overlooked the courtyard below. Tables littered with papers, a globe, and maps stood near the windows.

Isleif, son of King Byron, ruled the serene kingdom of Gundrehd near the North Shore. His people had provided the glistening limestone used to build the palace at Illiath. His father was a dear friend of King Aleon, Alexander's father.

"Drinks for everyone!" Isleif ordered. A handsome young man of a hundred man years, he was part Elf and considered young in the Elfin world. Isleif had not married and therefore had no heir, much to the dismay of his mother. He ruled Gundrehd with fairness, but was a youth at heart.

"No, nothing for me," Mildrir said. "We are here on business."

"Ah, I see. Well, you don't mind if I partake of a little refreshment, do you?"

"Isleif, it is still morning."

"Oh come now. I already have a mother and although my father is dead, I do not need another. Come, sit with me."

Mildrir refused. "We are here on urgent business, Isleif." With that, he raised his arm and pointed toward the door. Theo entered.

"Professor Sirus!" Isleif exclaimed. "It is good to see you again. Come, join us. This must be urgent business indeed if Mildrir brought you all the way from Illiath just to come speak with me."

"It is most urgent, Isleif. And it concerns Illiath, the Duke, and," Theo said, "your nephew."

The butler entered with several servants behind. Each carried trays of large cups, pitchers of ale, fruit, and bread. They carefully placed the trays on the large table in the center of the room where many papers and scrolls were scattered.

"Crispin?" Isleif asked as he took a cup of ale from one tray. He sipped it. "What has Crispin done now?"

Theo looked at Mildrir. The two shook their heads in amazement.

"Isleif, it has only been a few weeks since Alexander's death. Or have you forgotten?" Mildrir asked.

"Of course not," Isleif answered. "I have not forgotten. Tragic." He lowered his chin.

"Yes, well, I have traveled many miles to bring you this news," Theo said.

Isleif drank more ale.

Mildrir fumed at the King's lack of urgency. "Sit up and pay attention!" Mildrir shouted.

"Temper, temper," Isleif put down the cup and leaned forward to listen. "Go on. I'm listening."

Theo approached him. "King Alexander is alive."

The snarky smile left Isleif's face. He squinted his eyes and tilted his head. "What?" He leaned forward and looked first at Theo and then at Mildrir then back at Theo again.

Then he tossed his head back and laughed heartily.

Mildrir furrowed his brow.

"What?" Isleif laughed again. "Have both of you gone mad?" He continued to roar with laughter. "Were you not there? Did you not see the casket? At the funeral?"

Mildrir raised an eyebrow. He started toward Isleif, clenching his jaw, but Theo stopped him.

"Now, listen carefully," Theo said with a stern voice. "We were all there. But you and I both know that underneath the palace is a labyrinth of hidden rooms and hallways."

Isleif stopped laughing and wiped his mouth. He nodded. He had been a part of the construction of the palace of Illiath along with Theo and his father. "Go on."

"When I heard of Bedlam's presence, I remained hidden," Theo explained. "And when I heard of Alexander's illness, I became curious. So, one night, I snuck into the King's chambers and inspected his health. It was true, he was declining rapidly. I suspected something immediately."

Isleif leaned forward as he listened.

"I waited a few nights then entered his room only to find the Apothecary forcing wine down the King's throat. When he left the room, I took the goblet of wine and tested its contents. Sure enough, I found this." He held up a small vile of a lavender liquid.

Isleif's eyes opened. "A death elixir?"

Theo nodded. "Yes, exactly."

Isleif stood and took the vile into his hands. He raised it to the light from the window. "Lavender. Just like the one Queen Laurien had swallowed."

Theo took the vile. "Yes. Unfortunately, Peregrine had given her a fatal dose."

"So, where is the King? What happened?" Isleif grabbed his robe and put it on.

"I hid and listened when the Apothecary pronounced the King dead. Darion and Mildrir inspected the body," Theo said.

"He was ice cold, motionless as a statue," Mildrir said.

"A powerful magic is the death elixir," Theo said. "Bedlam knows this."

Mildrir nodded.

"The Apothecary must be dealt with, and swiftly!" Isleif shouted.

"Oh, that has already been taken care of," Theo said.

"What?"

"Oh, yes," he said. "The Duke killed him, then helped Bedlam hide Alexander's body in the dungeon. I saw them carry his body away. I saw this with my own two eyes."

"Squire!" Isleif shouted. Immediately, the squire entered and assisted the King with dressing. "We must go and rescue him now! I can ready a party. Alexander must be freed!"

"Patience, Isleif." Theo raised his hands. "We already have a plan. That is why we are here."

"Good." Isleif turned toward the squire. "Bring me my captain."

"Now, wait and listen to Theo first," Mildrir interrupted.

The squire attached King Isleif's armor to his torso.

"Why? My knights can go and storm the palace now!"

"Because there is more news, you impetuous fool!" Mildrir shouted.

Isleif turned to Theo. "More news? Is this true?"

Theo came toward him. "Yes, now listen carefully."

Mildrir stood close to Isleif, who had waved off his squire.

"I secretly followed Bedlam as his soldiers carried the King's body to the dungeon careful as not to be seen. And I hid away as he spoke to Alexander." Theo paced near the window. "And it was there that I heard the most urgent news of the Prince."

Isleif took a few steps forward. "The Prince?" he asked. "Prince Peter?"

"Yes. Prince Peter." Theo came toward him. "He is very much alive and in Rünbrior prison," he said.

Isleif shook his head. "I don't understand all this hesitance." He sat down and rubbed his forehead. "With all that you know, with all that you can do, why did you not act when you had the chance?"

Theo raised his chin and placed his hand on Isleif's shoulder. "We must be patient."

Isleif stood. "Why? You could have used your powers to end this all right then and there. Why wait?"

Theo turned to Mildrir who shrugged.

"Timing, Isleif," Mildrir said.

Theo walked toward the door. "Because if we wait for the opportune moment, Isleif, all of us can end this once and for all."

27 THE DRAGON MASTER

Peter approached the many fires that blazed in large pits designed for sword and armor making. Smiths hammered melted iron and bronze into crude types of swords to be used for fighting in the games. Next to each pit stood stacks of helmets, polished shields, and breastplates to be worn by each warrior. Peter admired the handiwork. Some warriors hurried by him marching in line on their way to somewhere. He assumed it was the great arena where the battles took place. In their eyes he saw the intensity and ferocity that only men who have faced death possess, and Peter wondered if he had made an enormous mistake in wanting to fight in the arena.

The guard who guided Peter along stopped and gestured for him to enter into a musty room lit with torches. It was a much larger room than his previous cell, and it had two windows with iron bars in the wall. The floor of the room wasn't dirt mixed with hay, but rock that was smooth. The walls were smoothed rock as well and some had carvings on them. On one side of the room was a cot with a blanket and on the other side was a small stove with burning coals. The guard motioned for Peter to enter the room and wait for further orders. Peter obeyed and the guard gave him a sword, knife, helmet, and breastplate brought in by one of the smiths. Peter stood by the cot. He stared incredulously at the weapons and armor.

"These are yours," the guard explained. "You will use them to practice and to fight in the arena. They are the only weapons and armor you will receive, so if they are stolen…you are out of luck!"

The guard and the smith headed toward the cell door.

"And if you try to use them to escape"—the guard pointed at Peter—"you will be bound and fed to the dragons…alive. Understood?"

He and the smith departed the room and slammed the door behind them.

Peter thought about those final words for a moment. He heard the locking of the door which reminded him that, although chosen as a fighter in the games, he was ultimately still a prisoner in Valbrand's prison. Picking up the sword, he inspected it. Looking at the weapons provided, he noticed there wasn't a shield.

"These won't be much use without a shield to block the dragon's fire." He tossed the sword onto the cot.

Peter sat on the cot and unfolded his blanket. He thought about his shield at home in his bed chamber. Removing the compass from his pocket, he slowly opened it. As usual, nothing happened, except that the needle bounced around as he turned the compass. Peter didn't know what to expect. But having the trinket kept him close to his mother. Peter closed the lid of the compass and polished it with his sleeve until it shone. Then he placed it back in his pocket.

Sitting quietly in his new space, enjoying the warmth of the small stove, Peter decided to see what his view was outside the windows of the cell. He scooted his cot over to the wall and used it as a step in order to glance outside. Once there, he looked out only to see that the room was hundreds of feet from the level ground. The whole prison had been carved out of a mountain and Peter's room faced a great precipice overlooking the river. Many clouds hovered over the mountain as the rain fell and bounced into the window. He breathed in the fresh air and smelled the rain. Spiny tree limbs framed the window. The trees looked dead from winter. His thoughts went immediately to his father and why no one had come to rescue him yet. And he wondered about the Dragon.

The door sprang open, startling Peter. He almost fell off the cot.

"You there!" the guard shouted. "Bring your sword and follow me!"

Peter hopped off, grabbed his sword, and hastily followed the guard into the hallway. Together, they jogged over to a large room warmed by stoked fires. Several boys stood in line along the wall. Each held a sword and each one looked as frightened as Peter. He didn't recognize any of them. They all stood in silence until ordered to move.

An older man dressed in armor sat by one of the large pits. Peter curiously studied the man's features. Deep wrinkles lined his forehead and eyes. He looked worn down and weakened by years of imprisonment. He had a long graying beard and thick wiry eyebrows. He whittled a piece of wood with a small knife, raised an eyebrow, and smirked at the young men as they entered the cave which looked more like his work space.

But it wasn't a friendly smirk. Peter sensed the man was being sarcastic. He rubbed his belly as his insides began to ache.

The smell of the cave caught the young men off guard and they gasped from the stench. Peter knew from working in Titan's stall that the stink was from an animal of some sort. A strange sound emanated from the pit nearby. They walked over to the rim of the pit and peered down, only to be met with a stream of fire that singed one boy's eyebrow.

"Watch it now," the man chuckled as he whittled away. "They learned to spew fire this week."

They? Peter slowly leaned over the rim to see a most unusual sight. There in the pit made of stacked stones were several tiny baby dragons scurrying around, chasing each other like puppies Peter had once seen behind the Keep back home. He smiled. One dragon had another's tail in its mouth, and the two fought in a clumsy way. All the boys chuckled.

"Oh yes," the man said. "They are all adorable now, but wait a couple of weeks. You won't be laughing then."

He rose up and placed his piece of wood, which resembled a pipe, next to his stool.

The boys suddenly stood at attention.

"Dangler is the name," the man announced. "I am the Dragon Master here in Rünbrior."

"Dragon Master?" one young man whispered.

Peter had no idea there was such a thing. He assumed all the dragons were captured from the wild and brought to the prison for battle.

"These dragons will be placed into the arena soon." Dangler pointed to the pit. "And you will meet them face-to-face very soon."

They all looked at each other with wide eyes.

"And it will be a fight to the death. You against them," he said.

The little dragons screeched and growled at one another, chasing each other around the pit. Once in a while they would spew their fire, causing the entire pit to glow orange in the light. The boys backed up when this happened. Peter could feel the intense heat on his face.

"Yes, you see?" Dangler said. "Their fire is very real."

"What are we doing here?" one boy asked.

"Good question." Dangler adjusted his armor. "You are here to learn. So pay attention!" He ordered the boys to line up and listen to his instructions. "Dragon fighting is not easy," he said pacing in front of them. "It is a skill, an art form, very similar to that of Knight Training."

Peter stood straight with eyes open. He paid close attention.

"In order to fight dragons, you must learn about them. Best to do this while they are young. You will feed them, clean their pit, and study them while you are here each day."

Amazing! Peter grinned. *I had no idea I would be able to work with dragons.*

"Today, you will come with me to see the slightly older dragons in training." Dangler motioned for the young men to follow him down yet another hallway. As they did, they could hear the clashing of metal and some growls. Peter shivered.

They entered into a small arena where two dragons stood chained to a wall facing a few men in armor. To Peter, the dragons did not look like they were adults. They were longer and leaner with smaller bodies, but they looked as fierce as the mature ones. Peter noticed their eyes immediately. Their anger was apparent. He winced and felt ill at ease. He did not like the notion of these magnificent beasts being chained.

One dragon seemed smaller in frame, so Peter assumed it was the younger of the two. Its scales were a dark green. It had wings attached to its front legs, which made maneuvering difficult. It was meant to fly and not fight on land. The other dragon was definitely older. It was the same height, but stout and more muscular. Its jawline was broader. The horns on its head were larger too. The wings protruded from its back leaving its front legs free to move, like a large horse. It was lithe but not full grown. Its scales were black as night, and reflected the fire glow from the men's torches.

"As you can see, there are many types of dragons." Dangler pointed to the two specimens chained to the wall. "These two were raised here in Rünbrior prison for the sole purpose of training."

He motioned again for the boys to follow him while he carefully approached the beasts. The dragons growled.

"Ajatar, that's the smaller one. It has a keen sense of smell and hearing," Dangler explained.

"Do they breathe fire?" one nervous boy asked.

"No!" came a shout from behind them. The boys turned to see a young man their age dressed in full armor with his visor down over his face, but his eyes could be seen through the slit. Peter recognized the eyes.

"Their fire glands were removed when they were hatchlings," the young man said. He walked over to the others who listened. "Do you think we would actually have two dragons chained within these walls if they could spew fire?" He chuckled at the notion.

"Who are you?" one boy asked.

"Damon," Peter answered.

"Ah, I see you remember me, *Peter*," Damon said as he removed his helmet.

"Ethan," Peter said. "My name is Ethan."

"What are you doing here, Damon?" Dangler asked.

"Valbrand asked me to come and watch the training to make sure it is being conducted properly." Damon handed Peter his helmet. "Here, hold this."

Peter, in his anger, threw the helmet down.

Damon laughed. "You'll soon learn your place here."

"Let us continue," Dangler said.

Damon walked over to the dragons being guarded. He rudely shoved one guard out of the way and drew his sword. The sudden movement made the younger dragon nervous. It rose up and flapped its long wings. Damon, obviously content with the reaction, swung his sword at its head causing it to roar in anger. Damon laughed.

"Enough!" Dangler yelled. "You are interrupting my session!"

Damon stood in a staring contest with the dragon. It hissed at him, desperately trying to breathe fire onto its prey as though it didn't know its fire glands had been removed.

This bothered Peter. He cringed. *This is cruel.*

Damon continued to taunt and anger it. The sight sickened Peter. He made his way over to a pile of swords and walked over to the scene, gripping the hilt tightly in his hand, his anger apparent.

Dangler stopped him as if he suspected bad blood between the two young men. "You will have your chance," Dangler said to Peter who stared at Damon. He turned around and saw the sword in Peter's hand.

"Oh yes, you will," Damon said, laughing at Peter's attempt. "We will definitely have our turn in the arena."

He made his way over to Peter, who gripped the sword even tighter, fully prepared to lunge. Peter did not know where this anger or hate had come from, but he knew taunting these chained beasts was cruel.

"This is nothing but mere vanity and cruelty at its worst," he said.

Damon faced Peter and returned the threatening stare. He grinned.

The two stood face to face. Peter, slightly taller, refused to move.

"Perhaps you would like our turn to be now, here in this place?" Damon hissed in a low voice that only Peter and Dangler, who stood nearby, could hear. "Hmmm? What do you think?"

"I know you have wanted to strike at me for a while now," Peter said. "Although I don't know why or what I have done to earn your hatred."

Damon scowled.

"What you are doing here is wrong." Peter's eyes never left Damon's face.

"Oh my," Damon taunted. "Feeling sorry for the beasts, are we?" He laughed. "Go get this *boy's* mother! We only let men train here." He stepped even closer to Peter who just listened, his jaw clenched.

Dangler carefully watched the scene.

"What do you say?" Damon asked. "Shall we fight now?"

His hand remained on the hilt of his sword as well. Peter knew Damon must have already had been appointed by Valbrand to watch over the training. He had not seen him in many days. To fight him now could prove to be fatal. No, Peter knew their time would have to come later in the arena once he had time to train.

"Soon," Peter answered. "Our time will come soon."

"Ha!" Damon said as he walked off. "I knew it. I knew who you were when they brought you in here. My suspicions were correct. I will be watching you, *Peter*. You and I will have our time in the arena. I guarantee that."

Peter lowered his eyes and handed the sword to Dangler.

"My name is Ethan of Riverdale," he said.

"Whatever your name is, get back with the others and stay there," answered Dangler. "Now, let us resume training," he ordered. "No more interruptions!"

He glared at Damon who smirked and sat down on a stool. Leaning against the wall, he continued watching.

28 THE JOURNEY BEGINS

A few days later, the young soldier entered the dungeon with a tray of food and lowered it near King Alexander. He looked over and saw the sleeping Zadok. The other two soldiers slept in chairs leaning against the wall.

"What have you heard?" Alexander asked. He took the bowl of broth from the tray.

The soldier leaned in to whisper. "The people are frightened. The land seems to be afflicted in some way. But the Duke meets their needs. He gives the people food to help them."

Alexander quickly spooned down the broth and picked up the stale bread to eat. Suddenly, he held his breath. The Zadok growled and rolled over onto its side. Alexander exhaled and closed his eyes. For a moment, he thought the beast was growling at him.

"Horrible creatures," the young man said.

"What is your name?" Alexander said.

The soldier hesitated. "Marek."

"And you are one of Bedlam's guards?"

Marek looked down. "My father…insisted that I assist Lord Bedlam."

Alexander cocked his head. "What do you mean? Who is your father?"

"The Apothecary," Marek said.

Alexander raised his eyebrows. "I had known your father for many years. I remember you when you were a small boy. I had no idea you had grown into a man."

Marek nodded.

"It always surprises me, how time goes by so quickly." Alexander furrowed his brow. "So your father has joined forces with Lord Bedlam?"

"Yes, but..." Marek said. "You must understand, sire. Lord Bedlam had promised my father gold and land, to the north. Beautiful land...if he assisted Lord Bedlam with this plan."

Alexander turned his face away in disgust. "So, he helped fool my people into thinking I am dead all for gold and a parcel of land?"

Marek leaned toward the King. "Please, my Lord. Do not be angry with him. I know he felt a sense of danger in refusing Lord Bedlam. I do not think he meant you harm. We are poor and my father believed Bedlam's lies."

Alexander believed the young man. He knew what Bedlam was capable of—and how he lied, manipulated, and intimidated people to get what he wanted. "Well, Marek, I thank you for your help." Alexander finished off the bread and grabbed the cup of water. "Any more news of Bedlam's plans?"

The soldier stood and walked to an empty chair. He shook his head. "Don't know," he said. "It's been quiet."

Alexander nodded and drank. He never knew when his next meal would be, so he always made sure to eat everything on the tray. He leaned back and raised his arms.

Marek came over and locked the cuffs back onto Alexander's wrists.

"I don't know how to thank you for helping me like this," he said to Marek, who returned to his chair. "I know you are risking much."

Just then, the door opened.

"You! Get over here!" the soldier shouted at Marek who leapt to his feet. "The Duke needs you upstairs. Now!"

Marek left the dungeon without a word to Alexander. The soldier slammed the door shut, leaving the King alone with the other guards and the smelly Zadoks drooling in their sleep.

Marek ran upstairs behind the soldier. When they reached the main floor, there stood the Duke, Lord Bedlam, and several guests mingling in the entrance way of the palace.

"What is it? What's the urgency?" Marek inspected the crowd.

"You're needed to stand guard here, understand?" the soldier whispered.

Marek nodded.

"The Duke wants extra security what with all these rulers from other lands mingling here," the guard said.

"Why? He has Lord Bedlam with him doesn't he?" Marek asked.

"Dunno. Too wary, I guess. Now stand here and don't make any noise," the guard said. "Understand?"

Marek watched the Duke walk his guests through the large hallway explaining something to them. He leaned in to hear what was being said.

"And soon, you will have your choice of the land," Will said to his guest, King Eulrik, who was dressed in his formal tunic and long robe with a leather belt around his thick waist. A ring of gold rested on the crown of his head. Eulrik stroked his reddish-grey beard as he listened.

Marek recognized the King. He took a few steps closer to try and listen further.

"I'd better. You're new to all this. I hope we can trust you, Sir William," the King Eulrik said, scowling as though unhappy about something. "Lord Bedlam has promised us many things."

"And I will fulfill all my promises," Bedlam said as he entered the room. A butler followed close by carrying a tray of drinks. Bedlam took one goblet and handed it to his guest. "You know I will, King Eulrik. Once you sign this agreement with us, you will have all that you wish."

Eulrik rudely took the goblet and drank. Marek followed them as they meandered through the hall. Bedlam continued to speak of some sort of plan. Marek pretended to stand guard when the men stopped walking.

"And who is this beautiful creature?" Lord Bedlam asked.

A young woman stood behind King Eulrik. She wore a scarlet gown made of silk and gold threading. Her flowing red locks reached down her back. On her head rested a golden crown with an emerald in the center. The gemstone flattered her hazel eyes and white skin.

Eulrik took her hand and brought her forward.

"This is my daughter, Esmerelda," he said.

She lowered her eyes and bowed graciously. Then she looked up at Will.

He grinned with politeness and nothing else.

Bedlam took the young lady's hand and gently kissed it, but her eyes never left Will's.

"I wanted her to meet the Duke," Eulrik said.

"Intriguing," Bedlam whispered. "Come this way, my dear." He led her to the table where the meeting would take place.

"And the forest?" another guest interrupted. It was Lord Byrén.

Bedlam gave him a stern look, then handed Esmerelda over to the Duke. They continued on their way with a pleased Eulrik following.

"I assure you, once the forest is destroyed the land will be ours," Bedlam said.

Marek realized he must have said something in his shock because Bedlam turned to face him. Marek stood straight but accidently tipped the butler's tray over, spilling all the goblets filled with wine. The goblets crashed to the floor with such noise the entire crowd was startled silent. They all stared at Marek.

"You clumsy idiot!" Bedlam grabbed Marek and dragged him into an adjacent hall. He waved a guard over. "You inept fool! Get him out of here!"

"I'm sorry, my Lord," Marek said. "It was an accident."

"This way, Marek." The guard led him down the hall.

"Marek?" Bedlam said. "I know you and your pathetic excuse of a father. Keep this fool out of my presence. Do you understand? I only want competent guards and soldiers in my presence."

"My father was a good man." Marek furrowed his brow.

"Your father was an imbecile who failed me!" Bedlam leaned in. "That is why he's dead."

Marek grew angry. "You leave my father out of this!"

"And now his son proves to be just as inept as he was," King Eulrik said with a hearty laugh.

"You'll be dead, too, if you aren't careful. Remove this filth from my sight!" Bedlam made his way back to his guests.

"How dare you!" Marek shouted after him. "My father served you well!"

He struggled with the guard. "Let me go!"

"Are you mad?" The guard shoved him further down the hall. "He'll kill you! Now get moving. Head back to the dungeon. Now!"

Marek stood staring viciously at Lord Bedlam speaking with his guests.

"Now!" The guard grabbed Marek's arm shoved him again.

"All right." Marek yanked his arm away, turned, and hurried toward the stairway leading to the dungeon. He ran down the stairs and ordered the guard to open the door. Once inside, he saw the other guards were fast asleep in their chairs. Crouching near a sleeping Alexander, and nudged him awake.

"What is it?" Alexander rubbed his eyes. "What is it, Marek?"

"It's time," he whispered. "It's time to get you out of here."

§

"Clean up this mess!" Bedlam ordered. He gently led his guests to the nearby dining hall. "Come this way."

Will guided the guests to the large table in the center of the room. Bedlam took his place at the head of the table.

"I've waited many years for this opportunity," King Eulrik said. "To see the end of Alexander's line, the end of this ridiculous quest for the swords, and now the land divided. This is a great time to be alive, indeed."

"Here, here," said Lord Byrén.

Bedlam rubbed his chin as he carefully studied King Eulrik. "Yes, but there remains much to be done before anyone takes up residence on the land."

The guests murmured.

"And what is the plan, exactly?" Eulrik took a drink from his goblet.

Bedlam looked at Will who stood to speak.

"The rulers have been notified that the land will be divided after our armies enter the Dragon Forest and destroy it," the Duke of Illiath said.

"What armies?" Eulrik asked. "King Mildrir and Isleif will never agree to this. They remain loyal to the Oath."

"I was never told of the details of this plan." Lord Byrén stood. "I was only told that I would receive more territory outside of the Crow Valley." He surveyed the entire room. "Was I wrong in this?"

The people did not make eye contact with him.

"Sit down, Byrén." Eulrik seemed embarrassed.

"No, I want to make sure I am correct in my understanding." Lord Byrén scratched his balding head. "I was never told of armies or marching into the Dragon Forest. We in the Crow Valley do not have enough men for this task. I am not prepared to return and ask our generals to send out conscriptions to the men. This won't do at all."

"Sit down!" Eulrik's face turned red.

Lord Byrén ignored him. "No, I want answers. I came here with the idea that I would take over certain territories, that is all." He wringed his hands nervously.

"Shut up, Byrén!" Eulrik stood and shouted.

Lord Byrén's eyes widened and he finally acquiesced and sat down.

Bedlam smirked at the exchange. "The Duke informed all the rulers of this plan. And since you are not a ruler…"

"But I act as ruler of the Crow Valley," Lord Byrén interrupted. "We've no King, so I act as the ruler."

Eulrik shot him one last venomous look that forced Byrén sit quietly.

"As I was saying…" Bedlam stood and made his way around the table as his guests drank wine and listened to their host. His cane clicked on the polished marble floor as he walked. "Times have changed. We know now that the Dragon Forest is the cause of all our troubles. Always has been. The people see this as truth. They will be more than willing to help destroy it if they see this task is in their best interest." Bedlam waved his arm toward Will.

Each guest watched Bedlam with fixed eyes as though under a spell.

"The people have come to trust the Duke as their own leader. He is one of them," Bedlam said. "He has provided for them during this time of famine. Now is the time to use this trust for our benefit."

Byrén shook his head. "This won't do," he whispered.

Suddenly, there was a ruckus coming from the entrance hall.

"What is it now?" Bedlam shouted.

All the guests turned the heads to see what was happening.

Theo, King Mildrir, and King Isleif, and stood in the entrance way next to Annika, Simon, and Crispin.

Lord Bedlam's face turned pale. He gazed over at Will who sat stunned.

"Why Theodore Sirus," Bedlam said in a velvety smooth voice. "To what do we owe the pleasure of your visit?"

Theo walked in first followed by the others. His eyes never left Lord Bedlam. "We come with great news," Theo said without emotion. "I am certain all your esteemed guests will be most pleased."

Bedlam turned to Will, who waved his guards over to Theo. They obeyed and surrounded Theo and the others.

"Surely, you will allow us to share our news," Theo said to Will.

Will swallowed hard then looked to Bedlam, who nodded.

"But of course. You have traveled so far. Please share with us this great news," Bedlam said as he leaned on his cane.

Theo motioned for the three youths to stand before him.

"We have learned through my scouts that Prince Peter is alive and at Rünbrior prison." Isleif came forward.

The guests gasped. Some stood and began murmuring.

"Did he say what I think he said?" one man asked.

"Calm down." Lord Bedlam raised his hands. "Please."

"How do you know this is true?" Will asked.

"I trust my scouts," Isleif said. "They saw him inside the prison. He is being held as a slave. Isn't he, Lord Bedlam?"

The guests all turned to their host.

"After all, it is *your* prison, is it not?" Isleif said.

Bedlam squinted his eyes and smiled a weakly. "I was told of the possibility, but wanted to make sure it was truly the Prince," he lied. "And now we are so very grateful to know that Peter is alive."

The guests continued to talk amongst themselves.

"Then you will have him released immediately, yes?" King Mildrir asked.

Eulrik glared at Mildrir as the guests waited for an answer.

Bedlam nervously bowed. "Of course!" he said. "I will see to it immediately."

As his guests talked amongst themselves, Lord Bedlam approached Theo. He stood dangerously close to the professor and whispered through clenched teeth. "What is this nonsense? What are you trying to do here?"

Theo raised an eyebrow and smirked. He could smell the stench of sulfur on Bedlam. He ignored Bedlam's questions and stepped passed him. "These three youths have stepped forward to volunteer and bring Peter home once he has been released."

The guests looked at one another. Several of them applauded enthusiastically while others scowled.

"What is this?" Eulrik shouted. "Lord Bedlam, I thought Sir William saw the Prince executed? I thought we were here to discuss the dividing of the land among us?"

Theo turned to Bedlam, who looked flush with anger.

"How can this happen if the heir to Alexander's line is still alive?" Eulrik pounded his fist on the table.

"Yes, what trickery is this?" Byrén shouted.

"Oh, shut up, Byrén." Eulrik motioned for his daughter to follow him.

"Oh, I do apologize if we have interrupted your important discussion," Theo said, "about dividing King Alexander's land."

Bedlam waved for the guards to begin removing the guests. "Show our esteemed guests the way out, please, while we continue our discussion in the library."

"I'll be back for some answers, Bedlam," Eulrik shouted. "I was promised more land and I want what I was promised!"

A guard rudely shoved him and his daughter down the hall.

Theo led the youths to the adjacent room as the guests quickly gathered in the entrance hall to their waiting carriages outside in the courtyard.

Once in the library, Theo and the others waited.

§

"What are we going to do now?" Will hastily approached Bedlam with eyes wide open in panic. "How could Theo and Mildrir possibly know?"

"Quiet," Bedlam ordered. "Remain calm. I knew something like this could happen. I am already prepared. You will go into the library, listen to what they have to say, and then give this rescue attempt, or whatever it is, your blessing. Understand?"

"What? What do you mean give it my blessing? This is ridiculous! They are obviously on to our plan and trying to—"

Bedlam shot him a stern look with his inky black eyes. "Just do as I say!"

Will stepped back and grabbed his chest as though he felt a surge of pain. Bedlam pushed open the library door with his bony hand only to see a waiting Theo standing behind Peter's three friends.

"As you can imagine, this news is rather shocking to us," Bedlam said. "But, diligent as ever, the Duke of Illiath has a plan."

Will stepped forward. He reached out and energetically shook the hands of all three of Peter's friends. Theo's eyes never left Lord Bedlam who stood near the door.

"I applaud your bravery. Heading off to Rünbrior is no easy task. The fact that you are willing to risk your lives to bring our friend, Peter, home safely, reveals your love for him," Will said through eyes shiny with tears. "I love Peter as a brother and would die for him."

"Yes, we know," Simon said quietly.

"Go now. You have my blessing. Any supplies they need, we will gladly provide," Will turned to Theo and Isleif.

"No need, Sir William," Isleif said. "I have given them all they will need for the journey."

Will sighed as though relieved. "Well, then, ride safely. Know that the people of Illiath are with you in spirit. Bring our beloved Prince back to us so he can reign as the King he was born to be."

Theo looked up to the ceiling and shook his head as though disgusted. "Hmm, yes, how poetic." Smirking, Theo led the three friends past Bedlam and out to the entrance hall.

"They will ride in the morning," Isleif said to the Duke.

"We honor your commitment and bravery," Lord Bedlam said to Theo's back. There was no response.

When they were gone, Will turned to his master. "Now what do we do?"

Bedlam pursed his lips. "After they leave in the morning, send out your men to kill them."

Will furrowed his brow. "Can't we just stop them and bring them back?"

Bedlam turned to his protégé. "Do as I say."

Will agreed.

"We will set our plan in motion sooner than I had originally thought." Bedlam headed down the hallway leading to the dungeon. "Now I must pay a visit to our old friend, Alexander."

29 FIGHTING DRAGONS

"This dragon is a type of Draco dating thousands of our man years ago," Dangler said as he led Peter to the arena. "Strong legs and large wings are its main characteristics. They kill with their breath and are carnivores."

Peter stood scratching his head and arms.

"Stop scratching!" Dangler shouted.

"I can't help it!" Peter answered back.

"Well, try!" Dangler said.

A few days had passed since Peter began his training with the dragons in the arena.

"My arms." Peter groaned. He rubbed them. "They're killing me."

His body ached from the hard work of wielding heavy swords in practice along with cleaning out the dragon pits. He battled hunger and the ever present sores on his body. But now he was ready to join the crew of young men ready to fight the many types of dragons.

The boys stared at the beast before them. The dragon yanked on the chain connected to the collar around its neck as though testing the strength of the chain links. Peter watched it closely knowing that if those chains did break loose, that dragon would kill all of them in a matter of seconds.

"This one is a type of Wyvern. It has larger back legs, but uses its front legs as sort of arms," Dangler continued. "Wyverns are known for flying and swimming. They, too, kill with their breath."

"How sad to see it chained up here in this arena," Peter whispered. "No wonder these beasts hate us so."

"Did you say something?" Dangler shouted.

Peter shook his head no.

"Good, then let's continue." Dangler walked the boys closer to the arena. The dragons growled and tried to leap at them.

"Notice the claws. Sharp as swords, but also able to grip around a man's body and crush him to death." Dangler looked at the young men. "Notice the teeth—like rows of small daggers in the mouth. No man escapes from them."

Peter and the others stared intently.

"The eyes," Dangler continued. "Beware the eyes. They are strangely hypnotic. Once they get you into a stare, you are captive. There's no escape! They can see into your soul..."

The boys nodded.

"So, how then do you fight a dragon in battle? Especially in the great arena, where some will have fire and others won't?" Dangler asked the boys. "Very carefully, I can tell you that. Very carefully!" He laughed.

Damon chuckled as he watched nearby.

"Grab a sword from the pile there and follow me," he ordered.

Once all the boys had swords, they followed Dangler toward the arena. As they entered, the aroma of sulfur mixed with dirt. The training arena, not as grand in size as the main arena, was several stories high culminating into a large opening in the ceiling revealing an overcast sky. It was the first time Peter had seen the sky in many moons. The arena was carved out of rock complete with rows of steps for spectators to sit and watch the "games" or events. But now only a few fighters practiced in the middle of the arena. Their shouts echoed throughout the large empty space.

"Here is where you will train to fight dragons, each other, and anyone else who challenges you." Dangler pointed to the center of the arena. "At first, you will fight for a position, but later you will fight for your life."

"Position?" one boy asked.

"Yes," Damon answered from behind them. He had placed his helmet on and lowered the visor. "Each time you win a round, you move higher in the ranks. Higher ranks earn more privileges like better food, no labor, and chances to fight dragons." He walked over to the arena, where a squire ran over to him with a sword and shield.

"Damon," Dangler said, "is one of the better fighters. He moved high in the ranks faster than any other."

Damon entered the arena where two other men prepared to fight. But it was only for practice and not a real fight.

"Come now," Dangler said. "Over here we will begin our practice."

Peter watched Damon start his practice. He was swift and powerful with the sword, but clumsy with no Knight Training. Peter had the advantage since he had many chances to observe his father's knights in training and jousts. He knew how to fight with celerity and grace while using strength. Damon's strength impressive, but nothing Peter could not handle.

"Now, as you approach a dragon that no longer breathes fire, it will try to best the sword out of your hand first," Dangler said. "It will use its stare, its tail, the claws, anything and everything to stay alive and kill you!"

He approached the dragon as it lowered its head and opened its mouth in a hiss. It dug at the ground with its front claws in a challenge. Dangler held the sword with both hands and took a few steps near the beast's mouth. Suddenly, without warning, the tail swung around causing Dangler to leap into the air to miss the swipe.

"You see?" he said with satisfaction. "In an instant, you can find yourself without a sword lying on your back about to be eaten by a dragon that enjoys fresh meat." He chuckled. "Alright," he said as he approached the boys who stood staring at the dragon, "Who will go first?"

Peter watched the dragon as its tail swiped back and forth along the dirt. He had figured out a way to approach the beast. Peter looked at the other boys who had not answered. "I will go," he said.

§

Peter carefully approached the bulky dragon. He wore no helmet and no armor, but he had confidence in his sword and in his skill. Knowing that the other boys and Damon watched his every move kept him on task. He knew there would be no living with Damon if he failed to battle the dragon.

"Steady," Dangler said. "Think of your approach. Study the beast."

Peter nodded. Then, suddenly, he felt more aware than ever before. Instead of crouching and slowly approaching, he stood up straight and strode right over to the larger dragon that also raised its head high sensing the surge of strength in Peter's movement.

"What are you doing, boy?" Dangler asked.

"You fool." Damon removed his helmet to have a better look.

But Peter paid them no attention. He vividly remembered his time in the Dragon Forest with the Great Dragon. He could see the eyes glowing. The strength ran through his veins. Gripping the sword with both hands, he moved it between himself and the dragon. It growled as Peter walked toward it.

Then, in one lunge forward, Peter thrust the sword, barely missing the open mouth of the beast. In perfect rhythm, he correctly anticipated the tail swipe and jumped up onto the back of the dragon, confusing the creature. It roared and tried to swing around, but the chain kept it from being able to move accurately. Peter noticed the stunned boys before him as they stared astoundingly at the sight. Damon, too, stood quiet then crossed his arms in front of his chest and shook his head.

Peter, feeling very comfortable on the dragon's neck, prepared to thrust his sword into the back of the beast's head, but hesitated. Dangler did not say a word, but Peter knew it was not time to kill the beast. He only wanted to show the dragon and the others that he *could* kill it if he wanted to. So, he jumped off and ran back to the group before the dragon knew he was away.

"Amazing!" one boy said. The others nodded in agreement.

"Well done," Dangler said. "I have yet to see a fighter with that approach before." He laughed under his breath. "Now, who will go next?" he asked the group.

"I will!" Damon strode toward the dragon with his sword firmly in his hand. The dragon roared at him and clawed at the ground. But Damon kept coming toward the beast. Suddenly, he raised the sword and spun around. The dragon reared its head back as though it would spew fire. Damon, sensing this, swiped at the neck of the dragon and fatally sliced it open. The wounded beast fell to the ground still gurgling for air. Its blood oozed out and mixed with the dirt floor.

"No!" Peter shouted. He started to run toward Damon, but Dangler stopped him.

"What are you doing?" Peter shouted. His face turned red as he clenched his teeth.

"Finishing what you started," Damon said as he stood by the dead dragon. "You coward!"

Peter, wriggled free from Dangler's hold and stood face-to-face with Damon who tried to challenge him.

"Not again." Dangler rushed between the two.

Peter stared into Damon's eyes. "You selfish, ignorant, *foolish* boy! Why on earth would you kill that magnificent beast? To prove that you can?"

"Because that's what we do in here!" Damon yelled. "We kill dragons!" He lunged toward Peter, but Dangler shoved him back. "The sooner you learn that, the better," Damon said.

"There is a time to kill the dragons and a time to learn from them," Peter shot back. "This was not a kill. This beast could not harm you. You slaughtered it out of pride and arrogance!"

"This boy needs to go home to his mother. Only real men fight here," Damon stormed off.

Peter followed him. He yanked Damon's shoulder and forced him to turn.

"Not here!" Dangler ran between the two again, trying desperately to stop an altercation.

Damon stood mere inches from Peter's face. "The next time you touch me," he fumed through clenched teeth, "It will be the last thing you ever do."

"I can hardly wait until we meet in the arena," Peter answered. "If only to watch you die."

"Enough!" Dangler interrupted. He motioned for Damon to leave.

Damon grinned and walked away.

Peter swallowed hard to push all the anger down deep. He inhaled, then exhaled slowly to steady himself. "I cannot believe he killed that dragon."

All the boys stood staring at the dead beast.

"A shame, really." Dangler shook his head. "Now I will have to find another one and train it. What a bother. I don't have time for these messes!" He kicked over his stool.

"Back to your cells!" He waved his arms. The boys frowned and began the walk back, angry to have missed training.

Peter turned to leave, but Dangler called to him. "Ethan," he said. "You stay here."

Peter obeyed.

The two stood alone, while nearby the female dragon sniffed at the carcass and nudged it with her head.

Peter's heart broke. "I thought we weren't supposed to kill these younger dragons."

"You are correct." Dangler motioned for Peter to come sit by the fire pit. "I see some skill in you, Ethan."

Peter sat down on a large stone next to the fire.

"Am I safe to assume you have battled before?" Dangler asked.

Peter shook his head. "I have never battled a dragon before. But..."

Dangler waited.

"I have seen a dragon before. And I have seen dragons fight each other before," Peter explained.

"Really?" Dangler asked.

Peter nodded. "But never in an arena."

"Well, it takes great skill to survive in the arena. You will need to be patient and listen to me," Dangler said. "Understand?"

"All I know is that for the first time since I arrived here in this dark place, I know what my purpose is," Peter explained. "To defeat Damon in the games." His gaze intensified. "No matter what, I will defeat him."

Dangler watched him as he spoke. "I believe you. I recognize the fire in your eyes. I have seen it many times before and never has it turned out for the better." He shook his head and threw a piece of raw meat into the pit where the baby dragons gobbled it up.

Peter hurried toward his cell, and grabbed a sword that leaned against the stone wall. He gripped it until his knuckles ached. As Peter stared at the dull metal blade, he knew this crude weapon along with his skill and hatred would be his way out of the dreaded prison.

§

Lord Bedlam approached the door to King Alexander's chambers. There he paused before entering the large room.

Once inside, he leaned on his dragon cane and gazed out the large picture window overlooking the courtyard. The King's empty bed was off to the side neatly made by loyal servants. The long blue velvet curtains hung alongside the window. Cobwebs had formed on them. Was it any wonder with all the tasks Bedlam had given to the servants that they had not cleaned the King's chambers in weeks? He inspected the massive mahogany table in the center of the room where maps and charts once lay, but now they were filed away in the numerous books that lined the many bookshelves. Lord Bedlam browsed through the many titles. The history of Théadril was chronicled in each leather bound tome.

Meanwhile, in the hallway, Will roamed around looking for his master. He suddenly heard a crash coming from inside King Alexander's chambers. Will pushed open the door enough to hear a throaty growl followed by a familiar voice. A mist exited the room and spilled into the hallway. He leaned in to listen without entering the room.

"What do you mean you've tried everywhere?" Lord Bedlam roared at someone.

"Sire, we have exhausted our resources," the low voice replied.

Will peeked in and saw the reflection of Bedlam in the mirror near the bed. Bedlam's cape had fallen to the ground revealing the man's thin frame. Will could not make whom Bedlam spoke with, but he did notice something strange about Bedlam's hands. The nails were blackened and curled. The long thing fingers were more like claws.

Bedlam leaned on Alexander's desk and gripped it tightly in anger. "We've not much time! Do you understand what this means?" he shouted to the mysterious guest. His voice was lower, almost like a growl.

Will winced.

"Yes, sire," the figure said.

"Leave me!" Bedlam waved his arm and the ghost disappeared.

All Will could see in the mirror was his master's back before he turned toward the books again and frantically pulled them down one by one. He opened each one then threw it on the ground in frustration. As he did this, Will could see something in Bedlam's eyes. They glowed fiery red.

Will leaned in further.

"Where is it?" Bedlam hissed as he searched through the pages. Finally, he stopped, raised a book high, and began laughing maniacally. "There you are!" He turned toward the mirror.

Will gasped when he saw his master's appearance. His skin was scaly, and the hands were indeed claws. When Bedlam grinned, Will saw rows of sharp teeth.

Bedlam opened the book and began to read. "Queen Laurien…came to Théadril with her father. Soon she was betrothed to Alexander, heir to the throne of Illiath."

As he read these words, his hands shook. The book fell to the ground.

Will stood straight.

"No!" A wisp of smoke came from his enlarged nostrils. "We must find it. I've come too far for it all to end now…in this way."

And as Will watched, Bedlam's face changed back to that of a man, and his long bony fingers returned. Will backed away from the room as though in shock.

"I must return to Hildron soon," Bedlam muttered, heading toward the door.

Will ran down the hall away from Alexander's chambers and hid behind a column.

Bedlam exited the room, looked left, then right. Then, he stalked toward the dungeon.

§

That evening, Peter paced inside his cell. He couldn't begin to think of resting. He picked up a stone he found on the ground and threw it against the wall. It shattered. But his rage toward Damon grew.

With a loud crash, the door of his cell flew open and the guards shoved a disheveled looking man into the cell with Peter. Before he could say anything at all, the guards exited and slammed the door shut, leaving the man standing there staring at Peter.

The stranger had dark hair, a chiseled face that appeared hardened from malnutrition, and sunken eyes from lack of sunlight. Yet his body was taught with lean muscles as though he was a fighter of some sort.

"Who are you?" Peter asked. "Why have they brought you here?"

The man titled his head. When he searched Peter's face, his eyebrows raised when he recognized who Peter was. Peter averted his eyes.

"Now it all makes sense." The man knelt down.

Peter took a step back. "What are you doing?"

The man bowed his head. "Your Highness," he said humbly.

Peter raised his eyebrows. He hadn't heard that title in a while. "Get up."

The man obeyed. "Prince Peter. What are you doing in this prison? Does the King know you are here?"

Peter stumbled back even further. "Who are you and how do you know—"

The hardness in the man's face disappeared, and he looked away as though embarrassed. "My name is Nøel. I was once a Royal Knight under your father, King Alexander's rule...before I abandoned the quest for the swords and ended up here in this prison."

Peter listened, studying the man.

"I cannot believe that you are here within these walls," Nøel said. "This must be why Valbrand changed his mind and allowed me to stay to fight in the arena. He must know you are here. He must have put us together for a reason."

"To fight in the arena?" Peter said.

"Exactly," Noel answered.

A smile slowly came to Peter's face.

30 JOURNEY TO VULGAARD

Theo and the others hesitated for a moment as they stood on the edge of the forest right outside the palace at Gundrehd. They were near the north shore.

"Is it safe?" Simon asked.

The King looked back and forth, and then cautiously led the way toward his castle.

"Well, now what?" Cripsin said as they stood at the entrance.

"I'm surprised Bedlam didn't have us killed on the way here." King Isleif removed his belt and sword and handed it to a servant. Another held a tray with several goblets filled with drink. Isleif took a goblet to drink.

"Give Bedlam time," Theo said.

"Kill us?" Crispin furrowed his brow. "Are you serious?"

"Don't worry." Theo patted Crispin on the back, then approached a visibly concerned Simon. He placed his hands on Simon's shoulders to calm him before settling in a chair in the grand hall. "Now sit and listen."

All three former students were enthralled once again by their former master teacher. They slid their chairs near the table and watched as Theo began to tell them many important facts of their journey.

"The covenant Oath sworn by the ten rulers is what has to be maintained no matter what," Theo said. "The land and the King are connected. You will be part of the plan to protect this Oath. This will not be an easy task."

"Peter has always known what his destiny was," Crispin said. "I guess we never really thought about it before now."

"All I know is that we must do everything we can to help him," Annika said, "or what sort of rulers will we be one day?"

"Yes. Exactly," Simon said.

Theo inspected the three youths. "I'm impressed beyond measure." He grinned.

"We know we have to find Peter to restore the kingdom quickly to preserve Théadril." Simon stepped forward. "We are here to do our best."

Theo stood and headed for the door. "Then you must be well armed to venture off to Vulgaard."

"What?" Crispin shouted. "Vulgaard?"

"But, I thought we were headed to Rünbrior," Simon said. "To find Peter and bring him home."

Theo opened the door and motioned to the butler, who carried a large linen bag. Theo took the bag, opened it, and revealed the contents to the three youths: three swords. "That is what we wanted the Duke of Illiath to think. But the journey will take you to the base of the Vulgaard Mountains where the White Forest ends."

"The White Forest," Annika said in a dreamlike voice.

"That is where you will meet up with General Aluein and his men." Theo grabbed the swords one by one and handed them to each of his students.

Simon took his reluctantly, then admired the blade. Crispin held his up near his head as though protecting himself from an imaginary foe. Annika awkwardly held hers with one hand out in front her body as though holding a dead rat. She looked at Theo for help.

"Let me show you, my dear. Hold it firmly in your hand, like this." He demonstrated how to hold her sword.

"Now I understand," she said, carefully studying the blade.

"Understand what?" Simon asked.

"About the sword. The power of the sword. I can feel it." She twisted the sword in her hands. "There is something about the metal. Its strength is almost tangible."

Crispin raised an eyebrow at Simon. "Is she serious?"

Simon gave him a serious look. "I feel it too."

Crispin looked at his sword and shrugged. "I don't get it."

"You will need these swords," Theo explained. "I only wish I could join you, but this is your fight. You will face things that have appeared only in your worst nightmares up until now. You will see things that are beyond the wicked and evil of this world or the next. And you will fight against an enemy that will not stop until it sees the end of Théadril. Are you ready for this task?"

"I am," Annika said confidently.

The two boys cocked their heads.

She pivoted to see them staring at her. "Well?"

"Yes." Simon cleared his throat, straightened his tunic, and stepped forward. "I am ready."

Crispin agreed.

"Very well." Theo pulled something else from the linen sack—a small black lacquered chest. As he opened it, a pungent odor wafted out.

Annika turned her head away to keep from sneezing. "What is that?" she asked as she held her nose.

"I give this to you." Theo held up the little chest. "Inside is a special powder that you mix with water to make a paste. This paste will help heal you."

"I see. It's a sort of magic salve?" Simon took the small chest.

"No. It is not magic," Theo explained. "It is more than that. Magic fools the eye into believing something. This salve is medicine made from—never mind. You'll find out soon enough. It will heal cuts and wounds, but when swallowed it will also heal illness and provide strength as well." He gestured for Simon to place it inside his saddle bag. "You will need some armor. Follow me as we head to the Smith's shack in the courtyard."

The three youths followed Theo out the door. His long robe dragged the ground as he hurried across the large hall inside the palace at Gundrehd to the courtyard. The rain continued to fall, and the muddied ground was filled with puddles.

"I grow tired of this cold rain," Annika said.

"Perhaps the legend is true," Simon mused. "When the King suffers, the land suffers. The King is dead. This is why there is no sunshine."

Theo stopped and slowly turned to face them. "Don't be fooled," he said in a serious tone. "Lord Bedlam is behind all this. Never forget that." His eyes searched the skies.

"He can control nature?" Simon asked.

"His tool is *magic*," Theo said fiercely, "and magic fools the eye into believing whatever it sees."

Simon studied Theo's eyes. "How do you know all this?"

Theo looked away.

"Yes, how do you know all this about magic?" Annika interjected.

"Tell us." Crispin demanded.

Isleif and Mildrir eyed Theo.

"There is a time for everything," Theo said assuringly. "There is a time coming when you will know all the answers to all your questions. And that time will be very soon. I will show you all you need to know. But only when Peter is with you."

The three friends nodded as though they understood. King Mildrir smiled.

"But for now, always be completely aware of Lord Bedlam's presence," Theo warned.

The three searched the skies as well. A crow cawed.

"His spies are everywhere," Theo sighed.

They continued on.

As they entered the smith's shack, they found three breastplates waiting for them. Each one had its own design signifying to whom it belonged. Annika inspected the intricate design on hers and asked Theo to help her buckle it on over her flowing gown.

"My dear, you cannot wear a gown into battle. I have some garments waiting for you all. Then you will be ready to make your way to Vulgaard."

Inside, they were led to a room. King Isleif had provided clothing for the youths and the outfits lay on a table. Annika spotted trousers made of suede and tunics made of canvas. She picked hers up and walked to another room to change.

As the boys changed, Theo went on to tell them they had horses waiting for them to ride out west of the Black Hills.

When they finished dressing, Annika emerged from the room in her new outfit. She touched the canvas tunic as though it felt strange to her. She stood in her new outfit, holding her gown in her arms. She gently touched the silk fabric one last time as though saying goodbye to her former self. She handed the gown to the servant.

"Not bad," she said as she modeled her new clothes for her friends. "These trousers are very comfortable. I can see why men wear them!"

The boys chuckled at her as they adjusted their own pants and shirts. Annika frowned.

"Never mind them, you look fine," Theo said. "But there is one more thing." He turned to look at Isleif who held a knife in his hand. He handed it to Theo, who then returned his gaze to Annika.

"What is that for?" She tilted her head.

"I'm afraid it is for your hair, my dear," Theo said with remorse.

Annika grabbed her golden tresses possessively. "My hair?" She gasped.

"Yes, my dear, it is far too dangerous for you to look like a lovely young woman on this journey. In order for you to participate, you must cut your hair."

Annika looked at the floor of the room as she stroked her long hair. "It was hard enough to say goodbye to my royal clothes, but now you are asking me to give up what makes me feel beautiful...my hair!" She sighed.

Theo walked toward her with the knife, but she raised her hand up to stop him. "I will do it," she whispered. Taking the knife, she swallowed hard. Then, with one hand holding her hair and the other holding the knife, she began cutting her hair off at the nape of her neck. In chunks, the golden tresses fell loosely to the ground all around her feet. When finished, she waited for the reaction of the others.

"Well done, my dear." Theo patted her shoulder.

"Yes," Simon agreed. "You are braver than we are."

"I could have told you that," Annika said as she ran her fingers through her shorter hair. "It's not so bad, is it?"

"You as look lovely as ever," Darion said as he walked through the door.

"Constable Darion!" Annika ran to him, and they embraced. "I am so glad you are here."

"I didn't want you to leave without telling you how proud I am." His voice cracked. "How very proud I am of all of you."

Annika hugged him hard.

When the three fastened their breastplates and were ready, Theo signaled them to listen to him. "This is a most urgent task. A task none of us ever wished upon you." Theo scanned the room as though the walls had disappeared and the land lay before him. "The time has finally come for good to face evil once and for all." He faced them.

Their young faces stared back with blinking eyes.

"And I'm afraid you three will be caught in the middle," he said.

Each of the friends looked at one another.

"But you will be rewarded for your bravery," he said as he approached them. "Not with parades and banners flying as crowds shout your names. No. Your reward will be when you see Peter as King in the palace of Illiath. And together we all will rejoice when Théadril is once again at peace."

Annika smiled and reached up to wipe away a tear.

Theo motioned for them to follow him once again. "Come this way, quietly, to your horses. Then, you can ride out tonight."

"We have everything for you on your saddles. It is a long arduous journey, but I know you will succeed." Darion smiled at his charges.

"Bedlam will try and stop us, won't he?" Crispin asked.

"Most assuredly," Darion said.

Crispin's forehead wrinkled.

"But we had the Duke's blessings," Annika said. "Didn't we?"

"Of course," Theo said. "He has to fool the people into thinking this rescue is his idea. He has to keep up the façade."

Together they all walked down the quiet corridor where no servants worked and made their way to the back exit to the stables. There, waiting for them, stood three horses.

Annika's eyebrows rose when she saw them. "Mountain horses!" she shouted.

"How do you know?" Crispin asked.

"Excuse me, I am a horsewoman," she quipped while stroking one of the horses.

"Ah yes, how could I forget?" Crispin smirked.

"They have strong sturdy legs for long rides and rough terrain." Annika ran her hand down the leg of one horse. She mounted her horse easily. It was tan with a black mane. She had only ever ridden sidesaddle and found the trousers most comfortable for riding.

The others mounted and pivoted their horses toward the opened gate. Mildrir, Isleif, Darion, and Theo stood waiting at the gate. They had concerned looks on their faces.

"They are so young," Mildrir said, rubbing his bearded chin.

"They will be alright," Theo answered as the youths approached. "We will get word to your families as soon as it is clear. They will be angry at first, but in the end they will see it our way."

The youths paused at the gate and exchanged glances.

Isleif walked over to Crispin's horse. "You will be alright," Isleif said to his nephew. "Be brave. Stay together and you will make it. Understand?"

"I wonder when we will see this place again." Simon surveyed the area.

"We will see Théadril restored when we return with Peter to reclaim his kingdom," Crispin said.

"That's the spirit." Isleif patted Crispin's shoulder.

Annika smiled. "For Peter!" She heeled her horse and pulled on the reins to turn it. She galloped over the wooden bridge and through the gate.

"For Illiath!" Simon yelled as his horse followed closely behind.

"For Théadril!" Crispin shouted. He rode alongside the others as they made their way over the plains.

Theo stood with the others as they watched the departing youths make their way toward the Black Hills. The rain continued to drizzle down.

"Perhaps we should have told them about the King lives," Darion said.

"No," Theo replied. "It is best for them not to know too much."

"Is it true, Theo?" Isleif asked. "Will you divulge all your secrets to them one day?"

Theo grinned. "Of course. Better still...I will *show* them."

"Well, Theo," Darion spoke up. "I hope this plan works."

"It has to," Theo answered. "It has to."

31 THE ESCAPE

Alexander heard footsteps coming from behind the locked dungeon door. He glanced over at the two guards fast asleep in their wooden chairs. They each wore coats made from the skins of wolves. Alexander envied them as he shivered in the damp air. He knew autumn was coming, and the dungeon grew colder and colder.

Suddenly, he could hear the door being unlocked. The guards woke up and stood, wiping the sleep from their eyes. One ran over to Alexander and kicked his leg. "Sit up!" he shouted. "Lord Bedlam is coming."

"By all means." Alexander sat up as much as he could with his arms and ankles chained.

Sure enough, Lord Bedlam and two more guards came through the door. Alexander noticed the evil Lord's face looked beat and forlorn with dark circles under his dull eyes. He assumed it must be late into the night.

"You look worn from a long day of deceiving the people." Alexander mocked him.

Bedlam sneered at him. "Well, well, Alexander." Bedlam gestured with his cane. "Somehow, our old friend Theodore has discovered our secret." He scanned the dungeon as though searching for something. "Somehow he discovered Peter is alive. And I'm certain the old wizard must also know you are hidden away in here."

"Theo hasn't resorted to magic in years, you know this," Alexander said.

Bedlam smiled. "If you say so." He walked further into the dungeon.

"What is it? Does he have secret hiding places within the walls?" He looked down at his prisoner. "Hmm? Is that it? A labyrinth of sorts behind these walls?"

Alexander said nothing.

"No bother. I'm afraid it is time to move you to another location. Sleep well, my old friend. For tomorrow we leave here forever." He turned to leave. "Say goodbye to your palace at Illiath, Alexander. When we leave here, it will be the last time you ever see this place, because I will destroy it."

He spotted Marek standing nearby. Bedlam nodded to his soldiers, who grabbed the young man and dragged him to the Zadoks, who were wide awake and growling and straining at their chains.

"My Zadoks are hungry," he hissed.

"No!" Alexander shouted. "Leave the boy alone!"

Marek struggled with the soldiers. Bedlam grabbed the young by the neck and pushed his face closer to the snarling wolf-like beast as drool dripped from its jaws.

"If you ever humiliate me in front of my guests again," Bedlam sneered, "this will be the last thing you ever see."

The Zadok growled and showed its sharp teeth.

The guard threw Marek over to the corner opposite from the Zadoks. They snarled and snapped their jaws. Bedlam petted them to calm them down.

"Come, my pets," he cooed. The guards grabbed the chains and led the large beasts to Bedlam. He led them through the dungeon door. "Tomorrow we head out, Alexander. Tomorrow everything begins." He stood at the entrance and slowly turned around.

"And tomorrow everything ends."

The two guards closed the door and waited for it to be locked from the outside.

Marek glanced over at the King and nodded. "Where do you think we'll move him to?" Marek asked the other guards.

"I don't know and I don't care," one said. "Neither should you care. You're as good as dead." The guard laughed heartily. He walked by Marek.

As he did, Marek reached into the sleeve of his tunic and pulled out a small knife. "Look at this," he said to the guard who turned toward him.

Marek quickly and quietly shoved the blade deep into the guard's throat, severing his vocal cords and a major artery. The guard gasped for air. Marek bent him over. "What is it?" Marek pretended to be concerned. "I think he's choking! You there, come quickly!"

The other guard hastily made his way over. And when he did, Marek shoved the knife deep into his throat as well with one swift stroke.

The first guard fell to the ground gasping in a pool of his own blood. Marek held the knife in the second guard's throat for a few seconds more, and then shoved it in deeper, making sure the wound was fatal. The guard's eyes rolled back as the life drained from him.

Marek lowered him to the ground then quickly removed the keys from the guard's belt. He ran over and began to unlock Alexander's cuffs. "We need to move swiftly. There isn't much time."

"Up there." Alexander pointed to the top of the stairs on the back wall of the dungeon. "That trap door is how we'll get out of here."

Once freed from his chains, Alexander started to run.

"Stop!" Marek said. "Here, put on the guard's clothes."

Together they stripped one of the dead guards of his clothes and Alexander quickly dressed. He stood for Marek's approval. "Well?"

"It'll do," Marek said. "We have to get you pass the guards outside."

Once they reached the top of the stairs, Alexander slowly opened the trap door that led out to the courtyard. Carefully, he peeked out to the left. There was no sign of guards anywhere. Turning to the right, he jerked when he saw what was in front of him. He started to close the trap door.

"What is it?" Marek whispered.

Alexander was pale, as though all the blood was drained from him.

Marek moved passed him and opened the door. He gasped when he saw what stood only a few feet in front of them.

A lithe black dragon rested in the courtyard, its scales reflecting the fire from the nearby torches in the night. It stood at least twenty feet tall with a wing span just as wide.

"Now what do we do?" Marek asked as he closed the trap door.

§

Alexander thought for a moment, and then looked out the door again. The beast was breathing quietly, but it moved its head once in a while, signaling that it was not sleeping. Alexander noticed the dragon had a saddle of some sort on its back with reins and a bit in its mouth like a horse.

"Strange," he whispered. "It's as if someone has been riding it like one would ride a horse."

"We must get out of here now!" Marek said.

Alexander inspected the rest of the courtyard. It was dark. "Everyone must be inside, asleep." He motioned for Marek to follow him. Together they carefully crept out of the door and crawled in the opposite direction of the dragon.

"I know of a secret passage," Alexander said. "This way."

Every few seconds, the black dragon stretched out its long wings as though settling in for the night. Alexander made sure to keep one eye on the beast as much as possible. They successfully crawled toward the side wall where the secret passage was. But then, they heard it—a low growl coming from the dragon.

Alexander turned and saw the beast looking right at them. Its red eyes glowed in the darkness. It snarled, revealing sharp stained teeth.

"Keep moving," Alexander whispered.

The dragon took one step toward them.

"Careful," he said to Marek who continued to crawl toward the castle wall. When he reached it, Alexander told him to push on the limestone bricks.

The dragon hissed. Alexander knew what that meant.

The wall slid open and Marek hastily entered into the dark passageway. "Hurry!" he said to Alexander.

Just as Alexander began to enter the passage, a stream of fire spewed from the dragon's mouth, incinerating everything in its path. Alexander closed the brick wall just in time, missing the flames.

He and Marek sat for a few seconds thinking about what could have happened. They could smell sulfur.

"This way." Alexander used the wall as a guide. They made their way down the corridor and up a narrow flight of stairs in the cold darkness.

Finally, they reached a trap door that Alexander pushed. When it opened, Marek saw that they were on the other side of the outer curtain wall. Shrubs hid the door, but they pushed past them. A ruckus sounded from the courtyard and then the dragon's roar followed.

"They must have discovered that you escaped," Marek said. "We've got to get out of here."

They ran to the bridge over the Blue River near the front of the castle. There guards and soldiers gathered around a small fire, trying to stay warm in the night. Alexander and Marek approached.

"Follow my lead," he said to Marek.

They walked up to the guards.

"You there!" Alexander commanded. "We need your horses now!"

One soldier immediately ran and grabbed the reins of his horse.

But the other guard was skeptical. "What for?"

Marek began to reach for his knife.

"Didn't you hear?" Alexander said. "The King has escaped! Lord Bedlam wants us to ride to the Cornshire in case the King heads in that direction."

"What?" the guard said. "We didn't hear anything—"

Just then, the black dragon roared again. The guard froze, then ordered horses to be brought.

Alexander and Marek mounted the horses.

"Be prepared for anything!" Alexander ordered. "There are many secret passages that the King may use to escape."

The guard looked all around and nodded as though he understood.

Alexander dug his heels into his horse, and together he and Marek made their getaway.

As they rode, Marek shouted, "Sire, where are we going? Shouldn't we be riding north toward Gundrehd?"

Alexander kept his eyes on the forest. "We will. But first I have something I need to do."

§

Lord Bedlam held a torch in the darkened dungeon. He observed the unlocked chains, dead guards, and missing King.

Sir William stood behind him. "Now what do we do, my Lord?"

Bedlam his eyes narrowed. "It has begun." He turned toward Will. "I am heading out to Hildron. Set things in motion. The rulers will follow your lead."

Will nodded.

Lord Bedlam strode by and stood in the dungeon doorway. He stopped and spoke without turning around. "Then, I will destroy this palace."

Will furrowed his brow. "But, my Lord, why? We could use this place to—"

"Silence!" Bedlam roared. His voice echoed down the corridor. "I will not leave one stone of this palace standing upon another."

"Yes, my Lord," Will said.

Bedlam headed up the stairs, leaving Will alone in the dark.

32 THE GREAT ARENA

The next morning, Peter and Nøel entered into Dangler's cave. Several other fighters stood alongside them.

Dangler approached. "Follow me," he said.

Each of the fighters obeyed. Dangler led them through a hallway that reeked of animal waste. Peter recognized the smell of horse droppings mixed with dragon droppings. The air turned humid and cooler. Suddenly, they heard the sound of a large crowd of people chattering like a gaggle of geese.

When they turned a corner, they saw the entrance to the Great Arena. Each man hesitated.

Dangler turned around. "Come on! This way!"

Peter frowned.

Nøel looked at him and tried to give him a reassuring look. "Be prepared for anything."

Peter nodded.

"I planned on this being a training session. However—" Dangler pointed up to the balcony where Valbrand stood with other men from outer regions. "—The Warden decided it was time to see you fight."

A loud throaty roar came from inside a cave at the opposite end of the arena and startled Peter.

"A dragon," one man whispered.

Peter look at Nøel with wide eyes.

"Steady now," Nøel said. "Stay calm."

Peter understood, but inside his stomach turned and his heart beat so hard, it felt like it was in his throat. He swallowed.

A ferocious roar came from inside the cave again.

"Sounds like a large dragon," one fighter said to another. "An adult dragon."

The inside of the cave lit up from the stream of fire coming from the dragon's mouth. Several guards ran from the cave. One was on fire, screaming for his life.

"Definitely an adult dragon," Nøel said. Peter's body shook.

From the balcony, Valbrand looked down at the row of nervous fighters. He chuckled. His little goblin assistant stood nearby tapping its fingertips together nervously.

"Sir, Lord Bedlam said not to endanger the boy, remember?" the goblin said.

"Shut up," Valbrand said. "This boy and that traitor knight will bring in the gold I need. I've been waiting for this chance for far too long."

"Yes sir," the goblin ran off.

"Armor on!" Dangler shouted. The fighters ran to the cave wall where armor leaned against the wall. Nøel grabbed a helmet and handed it to Peter. He showed Peter how to put it on. Then, they helped each other with the breast plates and bucklers.

Peter shivered when the cold metal of the helmet touched his chin. Metal clashed against metal as the fighters practiced with their swords. He could hear the angry shouts of grown men struggling with the beast and smell the dampened dirt. But, most of all, he could hear the roar of that unseen dragon.

"Time!" A guard pointed ahead. "Move!"

Peter and the others slowly moved forward to what would be their first time into the Great Arena at Rünbrior prison.

§

The thick humid air made it hard for the fighters to breathe through their metal helmets as the sweat trickled down their faces. The roar of the waiting crowd sent chills down Peter's back as he stepped foot onto the dirt. Peter had never seen such a sight: forty thousand faces from various lands far away gathered to watch the battles between the chosen men and the captured dragons inside the arena carved from the mountain.

He gripped his sword and shield with sweaty palms and took a deep breath. The blood raced through his veins like the Blue River waters he remembered from Illiath. Cold blood contrasted with his hot skin. His eyes wandered up and over the rows and rows of faces as they climbed higher and higher into the air. The people from strange lands shouted and waved their hands, calling out to each other and to their fighters. Men from Riverdale stood next to men from the Crow Valley. Some had journeyed as far away as lands from beyond Hildron that Peter had never heard about, but always dreamed of seeing. These lands were once plagued by the dragons. Wages had been gambled on each fighter with high hopes of gaining great wealth. But for Peter and Nøel, they only dreamed of gaining their freedom to leave the mountain prison or escape and return to save their King.

"Peter!" Nøel shouted. "Peter, are you alright?"

Stunned out of his trance, Peter nodded to his friend. Barely recognizable, Nøel's armor was hammered out of black metal. His breastplate had strange carvings on it and on his head was a spiked helmet.

"I can barely see out of this thing!" he shouted above the crowd, pointing to his helmet.

Peter stood frozen as though too afraid to speak or move. The others wandered around aimlessly awaiting instructions. Finally, the guard grabbed all the men and forced them to line up along the sidelines while the roars of the dragon could be heard from behind a large black metal gate that covered the entrance to the dark cave—the cave opposite side of the arena many feet away from Peter's shaking hands.

Nøel noticed the Prince seemed tentative. "Peter, I guess this is the real thing. Stay by my side. Together we can fight!"

But Peter continued to stare at the cave's entrance as more roars could be heard. Shouts of men and the cracking of whips rose above the crowd. The guards ran back and forth in front of the men in preparation for something. They seemed nervous.

"You there!" the guards gestured to the two men in line. "You two are first!"

The men, much older than Peter, nodded and walked out onto the red dirt to the center of the arena to thunderous roars from the crowd, while Peter and the others stood by on the sidelines until the guards ordered them to fight. Peter swallowed hard. Part of him wanted to go first, but another part of him deep down inside wanted to run away as fast as he could.

Loud trumpets blasted through the air causing the crowds to cheer even louder. They jumped where they stood and raised their hands into the air. Peter was mesmerized by the sight as he searched the crowds, studying their faces.

"Peter!" Nøel shouted yet again. "Stay with me!"

Peter turned to his friend and nodded.

"Study the battle," Nøel said. "Watch how they fight. Understand?"

"I understand," Peter answered. Then he remembered the reason why he was there: An image of his father's face ran through his mind. A shot of courage ran through his body, and he straightened as the trumpets blared even louder. The gate at the entrance of the cave rose slowly. The two men in the center of the arena took their battle stances. The crowd grew quieter as they all turned toward the cave's entrance.

Peter longed for freedom. But first, he would have to defeat whatever came out of that cave.

§

Mist came from the mouth of the cave along with a low pitched growl that sent a shiver up Peter's spine. Memories of the Dragon Forest and the lake came to his mind. That first encounter with the Dragon with its low pitched growl would stay with him forever.

The two fighters turned to see the guards urge them to shout or raise their arms in challenge. The fighters followed orders and shouted in arrogance as they pounded their breastplates with their gloved hands and bucklers attached to their wrists. The crowd, approving of the scene, cheered loudly. Their blood thirst was apparent. The fighters fed off of the crowd's enthusiasm, mistaking it for support of their efforts when really the shouts were most likely for the dragon. Finally, the dragon's roar grew louder, silencing the crowd. All eyes were on the cave entrance now, and the two fighters remained motionless. Without doubt or hesitation, the dragon sprung forth from the cave. Peter gasped when he saw it.

Longer and leaner than the Dragon of the Forest, this beast appeared to be much younger. A male Wyvern covered in grey scales that sparkled in the light of the many torches. Its eyes glowed red, revealing its rage. With wings attached to its front legs, Peter could see this young dragon was a Wyvern, a flying breed.

Nøel turned to Peter. "It might take flight!" he said loudly over the crowd.

Peter nodded.

"Be prepared for anything!" Nøel shouted.

The dragon inspected the crowd and reared up on its hind legs, proudly spreading its wings wide. The beast opened its mouth revealing rows of sharp teeth the size of a man's hand. Then it lowered its gaze to the men before it. Inhaling air with a slow hiss that Peter recognized, the dragon did what all dragons do best: it spit out fire. A fire so hot that it could easily reduce flesh to ashes in seconds. Glowing yellow and red spewed forth like vomit and engulfed the poor fighter who tried in vain to hide behind his shield. Exposed legs were withered down as his screams rose higher and higher, sending the crowd into frenzy. The poor fighter fell in agony onto his back, but he did not suffer long as the hissing sound came from the dragon's mouth again. Peter turned his eyes away when the dragon sent its fire to burn its victim to death. He could smell the stench of burnt flesh. More roars of approval came from the crowd.

Peter did not know how much more he could take. Yet he knew this was what a dragon fighter did. He had dreamed of becoming a knight to the King in order to fight his father's battles. He knew dragons would be on that list of enemies to fight. But to stand by and watch death come upon a man a few feet away was hard to take.

The surviving fighter remain hidden behind his shield.

"Peter, come with me!" Nøel motioned for Peter to follow him.

He ran along the sidelines to the annoyance of the guards, but Peter followed him anyway. All eyes were on the lone fighter in the arena, and Nøel and Peter were soon to join.

The dragon reared up again and roared its challenge. The fighter held his shield tightly. Then, the hissing sound came again as the dragon raised his head up and back.

"When the fire comes out, follow me!" Nøel shouted.

Peter had an idea what the plan was. He gripped his sword.

Sure enough, the long stream of fire hit the fighter's shield with such force that the man could barely hold it steady. He leaned into the stream with all his might as the metal shield began to glow red from the heat. Peter watched in amazement. *I wish I had my Dragon's scale as a shield now more than ever.*

Nøel shouted and ran onto the arena with Peter closely behind. Nøel raised his sword and threw it at the dragon's shoulder where it sank deeply, catching the beast off guard. It roared from the pain and sent a stream of fire up and over the crowd as spectators scrambled for their lives to escape the flames. Some fell a hundred feet down to their deaths while others ran over each other in desperation.

Peter followed but did not throw his sword. He knew they might need it. He ran over to the fighter who hid behind his shield and helped him up as the dragon turned to face Nøel, who had wisely raised his shield. But the dragon, unable to move as quickly or raise its wings to fly, snapped at Nøel with its powerful jaws. Peter then grabbed the stunned fighter's sword and threw it into the other exposed shoulder of the beast, hoping it would penetrate the scales. It almost fell to the ground as the blade sunk deeply through its scales and into the taut flesh.

Unable to fly with both shoulders wounded, the beast inhaled and let forth short bursts of flames. Peter and the fighter knelt and hid behind their shields trying to elude the fire. Peter was shocked at the force of the bursts of flames, but he held fast. The remaining crowd shouted their enthusiastic approval.

The thunderous applause caused Valbrand to come out of his makeshift office near the arena. He walked over to the perch of his balcony carved out of one of the walls of the great arena where fruit and wine were served. Ignoring the refreshments, he leaned over to inspect the battle below. Shocked to see three fighters battling his dragon all at once, he turned to the guards.

"What is this?" He pointed to the battle below.

"My lord, the other two men joined in the battle," the guard answered with eyes lowered.

The roar of the crowd grew louder, causing Valbrand to stop and watch. He grabbed an apple and sunk his yellow teeth into it, sending juice and pieces of apple down his chin.

"Peter!" Nøel shouted. "Get ready!"

Peter nodded. even though he was not sure what Nøel had in mind. But the dragon hesitated since it could no longer fly. It turned and continued to snap at Nøel who eluded it with great celerity that only a trained knight could possess. He rolled to the right and left as Peter took his own sword and approached the dragon awaiting Nøel's instructions. The muscular body of the beast stood only a few feet away from Peter. He could smell the sickening pungent smell of the blood trickling from its wounds.

"Now!" shouted Nøel, who was having trouble staying away from the large mouth of the dragon. Peter studied the body of the monster and found the perfect place to send his sword. He raised it high above his head and prepared to throw it in when the dragon quickly turned its head toward Peter and butted him to the ground. He rolled a few feet, trying to catch his breath, but he sprung, knowing that if he remained on the ground he would be eaten in one gulp.

"Shield!" shouted Nøel.

But Peter could not locate his metal shield as he held his sword in front of his body. He could smell the smoke and fire. Red eyes glowed from the deep sockets. Then the hissing sound began. He knew he only had but a few seconds before the flames.

Peter looked to his left and right but saw no shield. He quickly flung off his metal helmet, sending it to the ground. The humid air cooled his damp face. He took in a deep breath. The other fighter had run off in fear leaving his shield a few feet away. Peter saw it, but so did the dragon as it studied Peter's face.

Taking a chance, Peter ran to the shield, but the dragon placed its foot in the way. Sword in hand, Peter sliced the foot, sending blood flying and the dragon roaring. Then Peter swerved around the foot and grabbed the shield in time to meet the burst of flames. Excitement race through his veins. To his right was Nøel, who had removed his helmet also. Nøel motioned for Peter to throw him his sword, so Peter grabbed the blade of the sword and sent it flying in the air toward his friend.

The dragon was losing blood and becoming weaker, but it appeared to want its revenge. It roared and limped toward Nøel, who poised, shield and sword in hand, ready to kill his foe. The crowd cheered.

Peter, panting from exhaustion, lacked a weapon. Nøel sliced at the dragon's mouth as it snapped closer and closer, forcing him back. Soon he would be pushed back against the wall of the arena.

Then Peter remembered: Deep inside his boot was a dagger with a blade the length of his palm. He removed it and watched as the dragon moved Nøel closer to the wall where he could send his flames forward, burning his friend to death. Peter had to think fast where he could send the small blade and cause death.

He searched the body of the beast as the crowd cheered louder and louder. He tried to ignore their rants and concentrate. The dragon had tight muscles underneath the shiny scales, but was too young to have impenetrable scales. Peter knew he could slice through them even with a smaller blade. But where?

Nøel yelled at the beast and sliced its mouth from time to time, sending blood spewing onto his breastplate, but this only made the dragon even angrier as it snapped closer and closer to his flesh. Peter knew he had only a few more seconds before Nøel was in too much danger. Then he heard the hissing sounds as the lungs filled with air. The crowd heard it too and roared their approval.

No, Peter thought. *This cannot happen.* Suddenly, he noticed on the inner part of the dragon's neck. *A vessel. Close to the surface.*

Running with all his might, Peter leapt and grabbed hold of the dragon's neck, climbing on board. It was wet with perspiration, but Peter was able to grip and stay on. The beast tried to stop Peter by snapping at his legs, but Peter was too quick. The crowd went insane from the excitement as the dragon tried to grab Peter. It flapped its wings, but the wounded shoulders hindered it from flying. It was too late.

Peter raised his dagger high over his head and lowered it into the beating vessel. When he sliced it wide open, thick red blood spewed out in a steady stream. It screamed from the pain and lurched forward, falling to the ground with Peter on its neck. Nøel ran over to Peter. With on swoop of his sword, Nøel put the dragon out of its misery by removing its head.

Peter struggled to get from underneath the dragon's body. He finally stood with his friend in the middle of the arena. The dragon's headless body lay motionless on the dirt that turned red with the dragon's blood.

The crowd was stunned silent. Only the slow beating of the dragon's dying heart could be heard until it finally stopped. Peter and Nøel stood nearby, panting. Its lifeless head lay on the ground with its red eyes open. They no longer glowed. Its tongue grotesquely protruded from its mouth.

"A mighty foe." Nøel panted.

Peter, trying to catch his breath, nodded at his friend. "A mighty foe indeed," he whispered. He surveyed the stunned crowd.

Then, like thunder echoing over the mountains, the roar of the crowd rose high above them as the people from faraway lands stood on their feet shouting and waving their hands.

Valbrand watched from his balcony above the arena, studying the crowd. Then he turned his eyes to the two fighters as they slowly walked off the arena floor led by guards.

"You see?" he addressed his goblin assistant. "This just might work."

33 THE DRAGON OF THE FOREST

After hours of hiding in the Cornshire and the Cardion Valley, King Alexander and Marek decided it was safe to ride to the entrance of the Dragon Forest just as the sun began to rise.

"Wait here," he said to Marek.

"Yes, sire." Marek dismounted then grabbed the reins of the King's horse.

"I won't be long." Alexander started to head into the forest.

"Sire!" Marek stepped toward him.

Alexander turned. "Yes? What is it?"

Marek lowered his eyes. "I want to apologize…for my father's actions. He brought shame to our family by helping Lord Bedlam. He forced me to become one of Bedlam's soldiers."

"Marek," Alexander said, coming to him, "your father was under a spell. Bedlam's power is strong. It can make men do things they do not want to do. Your father's sacrifice was great. His life was taken from him, and you risked your life to free me."

Marek wiped his eyes then looked at the King.

"Your debt has been paid, my friend." Alexander smiled. "Now, wait here. Do not enter in no matter what you may hear…or see. Understand?"

Marek nodded. Watching as Alexander walked toward the mysterious woods, he noted the warning sign, *Beware the Dragon Forest.* As King Alexander disappeared into the darkness, Marek swallowed hard.

§

The winds blew the tree branches above Alexander as he strode down the dark pathway. They crackled. A few dead leaves scattered around him. Alexander jerked his head to the right as though he suspected he was being watched by both the Dragon and Bedlam's spies from within the trees. A black crow circled high above him.

As he finally made his way into the center of the forest, the mist covered the lake just as he had remembered. The anger inside him brimmed. The veins in his neck pulsated. He drew his sword. "Show yourself!" he demanded. "Show yourself to me! I know you are here!"

But there was only the whistling wind and the crackling of the branches.

"I know you live!" He turned in a circle, searching the tree tops until he staggered from dizziness. "I demand answers!" Alexander shouted with such force, his voice cracked. "Why? Why did you allow this to happen to my son?"

Alexander searched the trees for any sign of the glowing yellow eyes, but saw only the mist rising. "How could you allow this? *He's just a boy*!" With those words he turned his sword downward. "I demand answers!"

He yelled a primal scream that came from his soul and shoved the blade of the sword deep into the damp ground as though stabbing the unseen Dragon.

Immediately, the ground shook, birds scattered from the trees, and a fierce wind whipped twigs and dirt into such a frenzy, Alexander had to cover his face. A flash of lightning lit up the early morning sky and its thunder echoed all around him.

King Alexander fell to the ground trembling.

"Stand up and prepare yourself like a man," came the ominous voice from between the trees. "For I will question *you*."

Alexander slowly stood and stared at the trees. Suddenly, the glowing yellow eyes appeared from between the branches. They rose higher and higher until Alexander could see the form of the massive Dragon approaching.

With each step, the ground shook. Alexander stumbled backwards. His eyes grew wide. "It's true," he mumbled. "You *are* still alive."

"Stand straight," the Dragon ordered.

Alexander obeyed.

"Where were you in the beginning?" the Dragon asked. Its eyes glowed with fierceness. "Were you there when your father's father swore the Oath? Were you there when the regions were formed?"

Alexander couldn't move. The giant beast's sinewy muscles twitched and its magnificent scales sparkled.

"Surely you were." The Dragon lowered its head. Alexander could smell the sulfur. "I have faced the shadows of death and stood at its gates only to fight and destroy them. Were you there with me?"

Alexander shook his head.

"Have you measured the breadth of the entire world, Alexander defender of men? Can you comprehend it all? The creatures of the sea, the dragons of the mountains at Vulgaard, the eagle as she flies...surely you know?" it asked.

Alexander lowered his head. A stream of fire shot near his feet. He leapt back from the heat.

"Answer me!" the Dragon said.

"Please," Alexander begged. He covered his face with his trembling arm. "Spare me! Do not kill me! I only wanted to know about my son."

The Dragon's eyes mellowed. The fierceness left its countenance as it searched the King's heart. Silence came over the forest. "Follow me," it finally said.

Alexander lowered his arm from his face and obeyed. Together they approached the edge of the lake. Ripples glided across the surface.

"Long ago I showed you images in this lake. These images were of your son's future," the Dragon said.

Images appeared again. Alexander leaned in to see his young son led away in chains, fire, thousands of people cheering, and a fierce young dragon.

"These images are of your son's trials."

"But he is not even a knight yet. How could he have trials?"

"It is not his destiny to be a knight," said the Dragon as the images in the water disappeared. "It is his destiny to be *King*."

Alexander somberly walked away, regretting his actions. Reaching his sword still protruding from the ground, he yanked it out. "Forgive me. I had forgotten all that you showed me so many years ago. I need to know. Will I live... to see him return to Illiath?" he humbly asked without looking up.

The Dragon slowly smiled. "Alexander, you will see your son again."

Alexander wept quietly. "Thank you," he whispered, placing his sword back into its sheath. "Now I have to prepare for battle once again."

The Dragon's head rose high toward the east. "You will meet the rulers that remain faithful to the Oath at the palace of Gundrehd. There you will begin to form an army of the land, air, and sea."

"Air? I do not understand—" Then he remembered the dragon at the castle and how it had a saddle and bridle. "You mean...*dragons?*"

"Ride to Gundrehd and begin planning the battle," it said. "You will find your friends, Theo and Darion waiting for you."

"And will you help us yet again?" Alexander approached the Dragon. "Old friend?"

It lowered its large head down to face the King. He saw a warmth in its eyes that he had long forgotten. "It is my destiny to face the forces of evil once again. That is why I returned," it said. "To destroy them once and for all."

Alexander sighed with relief. He headed out of the forest.

"Now ride," the Dragon ordered. And as it spoke, it transformed into the white owl and flew alongside the King.

He ran out of the forest and surprised the young Marek holding the reins of their horses. "Let's go!" Alexander said.

"Are you alright?" Marek shouted. "I heard thunder and saw fire!"

The owl flew right by him nearly missing his head. He ducked out of the way just in time.

"Yes! Everything is alright. Let's go to Gundrehd. We've not much time!" Alexander heeled his horse and rode off toward the east with Marek. The white owl flew high above them.

§

Peter's three friends slowed down their horses so they wouldn't tire as easily as they entered the rugged mountain country.

"We're leaving Théadril now." Crispin glanced behind. "The sun will be coming up soon."

"Do you think it will rain again?" Annika searched the skies above them. She held onto her horse's mane with both hands as it galloped into the desert. The dust matted her hair to her tear-stained cheeks. She turned to her right in time to see Simon on horseback galloping next to her. Crispin quickly appeared on her left. All three of them rode on as loud thunderclaps echoed in the distance.

Simon yelled. "We had better find shelter!"

As they made their way over the dales where the grassy fields gave way to muddy desert plains, the three slowed their horses down in order to look for a place to rest for the night.

"I am afraid," Annika said. "I don't think we should sleep out in the open air. Not if Zadoks or the Duke's men are out there somewhere."

Crispin nodded in agreement and scanned the area. "I remember how Peter described the Zadoks lying on the ground dead in frozen grimaces." He shuddered. "With those large teeth."

"We'll head into the rocky caverns where I am sure we will find a cave. Come. Let's ride over there!" Simon pointed toward the southwest. The three galloped to where the roads ended and the rocky gorges began. They approached a cliff's edge and dismounted.

"We'll have to walk our horses down this cliff if we are to find a cave for the night," Crispin said as he led his horse down the steep cliff.

"Be careful," Annika advised. "His legs are much more vulnerable than yours!"

"Yes, I know miss horsewoman." Crispin rolled his eyes. "Come, follow me."

To her surprise, Crispin's horse maneuvered the cliff with great ease, so she led her horse down afterwards. When all three were finally at the bottom of the gorge, the rain started to pelt the ground.

"I suppose I cannot begin to tell you all how much I hate the rain." Annika scowled.

"Likewise." Simon walked his horse out in front, leading the group down the path. "We have to be careful. This gorge could quickly flood and become a raging river."

"Maybe we should return to higher ground," Crispin suggested.

Just then, the group heard the howl of a creature that seemed desperate in the approaching night.

"On second thought," Crispin said as he searched the top of the cliff. "I think sleeping in a cave tonight might be worth the risk. Don't you?"

Annika nodded.

"Look!" Simon pointed toward the rocks ahead of them. "Did you see something move ahead?"

They each stopped walking. Their horses whinnied and yanked on the reins.

"The horses smell something," Annika said.

"Look!" Simon shouted again. "Did you see that?"

"Yes!" Crispin squinted. "I did see something move behind the rocks."

The three stood frozen midstep.

"Stay here." Simon let go of his horse's reins and walked forward.

Crispin quickly grabbed the horse.

"Simon, no," whispered Annika. "Stop please."

Swiveling toward her, Simon placed his finger on his mouth to shush his friend. She obeyed and held her horse's neck, tightly stroking its mane to keep it calm. Simon carefully walked toward the rock, placing one foot in front of the other.

Crispin's horse nodded nervously as though it smelled something ahead.

"See anything?" Crispin asked Simon.

At that moment, Simon turned ran. Crispin flung the reins back to Simon as all three mounted their horses. But it was too late. They were surrounded.

34 THE DRAGON CHRONICLES

The next day, Peter and Nøel nursed their wounds inside their cell. They enjoyed some extra servings of food sent to them by Valbrand. It was his way of thanking them for the gold coins he won as a result of the victory inside the arena.

Nøel groaned. "Sore back," he mumbled.

Peter chuckled.

Just then, the cell door opened. The guard motioned for Peter to follow him. "The Dragon Master wants a word with you," he ordered.

Peter waited for Dangler in his cave where swords and newly made shields lined the walls. He could hear the growls of the baby dragons coming from the pits nearby.

"I see something in your eyes, boy," Dangler said as he approached. He picked up a stool and sat down. He motioned for Peter to do the same.

Peter sat on the edge of the pit and watched the little dragons fight over pieces of meat.

"You are not from around here," Dangler said. "Who are you, really?"

"What do you mean?" Peter asked. "I am Ethan of Riverdale."

Dangler eyed him carefully. "Yet you fight as though you have had training. In fact, you fight with such confidence that I find it rather difficult to believe you were just a farm boy in Riverdale snatched by Valbrand's men," he said with a quizzical brow.

"What I told you is truth," Peter lied. "I had no choice in the matter. I was taken and brought here."

"Who trained you in the ways of the sword and battle?"

"No one."

"Yet you defeat a young fire-breathing dragon the first time in battle?"

Peter nodded.

"Hmm...I see in your eyes a fierceness I have not seen since Damon."

Peter frowned. He did not like being compared to Damon.

"You have fought well these last few weeks. I feel you are ready for more battles in the great arena, but it isn't up to me."

"I understand," Peter said.

"However, I would be pleased if you also assist me in the instruction of the other boys."

Peter thought about the request. Assisting dangler would mean training with the dragons, and he enjoyed this. Yet assisting in training would mean he'd have to remain in the prison a while longer.

Dangler studied his pupil. "I am not sure I can completely trust you, but I have no choice. You are the best of the group and Valbrand wants only the best in the arena. So be it." He waved off Peter. "But I will be watching you." He took out his knife, picked up a piece of wood nearby, and began whittling.

Peter rose and started to head back to his cell, when something stopped him. "You know much about dragons. But do you know of *the* Dragon as well?"

Dangler stopped whittling and looked at Peter. "The Great Dragon?" he asked.

Peter nodded.

"I knew it! I knew there was something else to you than what you were telling me." Dangler threw down the piece of wood. "Of course I know of the Great Dragon! And so do you. Tell me how."

"Well, when I was a young boy, I ran away from home and entered into the Dragon Forest to slay the Dragon for its scales," Peter explained. "But I felt safe inside the forest. I saw a lake."

"Go on," Dangler said.

"Yes, a crystal blue lake. Then I saw the eyes."

"Behind the trees?" Danglers leaned forward like a small child listening to a tale.

"Yes, glowing yellow, watching my every move," Peter continued.

Dangler reached into his vest and brought out his pipe. He struck a match and lit the pipe sending small clouds of smoke into the air. "And?"

"Then, the beast came out from between the trees and approached me." Peter could almost visualize the Dragon and feel the icy mist on his skin again.

Dangler dropped his pipe and immediately reached down to retrieve it. "You actually saw... *the Dragon?*" he asked skeptically.

Peter nodded. "It spoke to me," he said.

Dangler's eyes were wide now as he continued to smoke. "Amazing," he murmured. "And then?"

"I found it to be most kind and protective. The beast ordered me to climb onto its neck, so I obeyed. Then, it flew me high over the forest and back to the— I mean my home in the valley."

"Never in a million man years did I ever stop to think I would meet someone who had not only entered the Dragon Forest, but met the Dragon." Dangler scratched his forehead. "And lived to tell about it!" His throaty laugh that echoed through the cave.

Peter smiled.

"So, it would seem that you were brought here for a reason," Dangler said. "Wait here, I have something to give to you."

Intrigued, Peter watched the old man shamble off into a dark room. Inside the room, Peter could see fire glow as Dangler lit a torch. Then Peter could hear the sounds of someone searching for something. Peter was amazed with the conversation. Usually, Dangler spoke with great economy of words. But he seemed eager to share his stories with Peter.

Finally, Dangler returned. In his hands was a book, bound in leather dyed red, and had a gemstone on the cover.

Dangler handed it to Peter. "Here. Take this and read it."

Peter held onto the large tome and placed it in his lap. He looked at Dangler as though asking permission to open it. Dangler nodded.

Peter read the cover: *The Dragon Chronicles*. On the cover was some scrollwork in gold and in the middle was a gem stone that seemed to be violet in color. Peter rubbed his fingers over the beautiful stone.

"Amethyst," Dangler said. "A rare and beautiful gem stone of the Dragon."

"Of the dragon?" Peter asked.

Dangler nodded. "Aye. Dragons love their gold and gemstones."

Peter opened the book to the middle. There he read a strange script. He could not read what it said, but it appeared to be someone's story of the dragon. There were many drawings of dragons, maps, and what appeared to be recipes for potions and descriptions of the various types of dragons scribbled all over the margins.

"Study this book from cover to cover," Dangler ordered. "It will help you in the arena."

Peter continued to thumb through the pages. He saw drawings and paintings of dragon eggs with their unique shell designs and colors and he recognized some from the pit he had cleaned. "Amazing" he whispered as he studied each egg design. "Each design is so different."

"As is every dragon," Dangler said. "Everything you need to know about dragons is in that book."

"Where did you get this book?" Peter asked.

"I wrote it," Dangler answered.

Peter looked up from the pages. "You did?" Suddenly, the book seemed even more special.

"I, along with the other trainers, put my knowledge down on those pages to pass on to others." Dangler continued whittling. "So, now I am passing it on to you. Go on, take it and learn the beasts. That way you can assist in training and learn how to defeat them in the great arena."

"Don't I already know how to defeat them?" Peter carefully placed the book down on the ledge of the pit.

"Ha! Maybe in the great arena." Dangler chuckled. He used his pipe as a pointer. "But not out there where they actually live!" Dangler then handed Peter a leather pouch. "Here take this as well."

Peter took the pouch and opened it. Inside he saw a fine white powder. "What is this?" Peter asked.

Dangler chewed on his pipe. "It is a healing salve. You will need it, I promise."

"What do I do with it?"

"Mix it with water to make a paste," Dangler said. "It will heal wounds. You can also drink it and it will heal wounds deep inside. Trust me, you will need it."

Peter closed the pouch. "How do I thank you?"

"By being a good Dragon Master someday. And putting down your knowledge of dragons in that book to pass on to others."

"I enjoy reading books. I find history fascinating," Peter said. The dragons in the pits were all coiled up together sleeping peacefully. Peter stared at them all. "When they are asleep, they do not appear to be so threatening."

"Yes, but don't let them fool you. They will just as soon take your finger off as look at you! Now, about this training," Dangler said. "I see something in your eyes. I see that you have a mission. Could it be to fight against Damon?"

Peter didn't answer.

"Because I thought your mission was to gain your freedom?" Dangler asked.

Peter nodded. "It is."

Dangler scooted to the edge of his stool and leaned forward toward Peter. "Then forget about Damon." He waved the knife for emphasis. "It's useless."

"What do you mean?"

"Damon doesn't even fight in the arena against the dragons," he said as he leaned back again. "He only fights in man-to-man battles and you will fight against the dragons. Great dragons! If you defeat the great dragons, then you earn your freedom."

Peter frowned in disappointment.

"So you can forget all about this fight against Damon and concentrate on how you will survive against the large full grown dragons in the arena, understand?"

"I understand," Peter said.

"You have a gift, Ethan."

"I do?" Peter leaned in.

"And a talent for fighting. I can see it." Dangler pointed his pipe at Peter. "Too bad you couldn't head off to Knight Training up north, eh? You would have done well."

Peter's countenance fell upon hearing those words. He looked away. *Knight training...*

He hadn't thought about it for a while. He sighed. The thought weighed heavily on his heart. He pictured Will in training sitting on his horse in armor that sparkled in the sun. Peter's eyes stung. Tears threatened at the thought of what might have been.

"Yes," he barely whispered. "Too bad." Slowly he reached for the book and stood with the tome in his hands. "Good bye," He headed back to his cell with the special book. The little dragons slept in peace in the pit.

"I can't believe you actually rode on the Dragon. The Dragon of the forest!" Dangler chuckled.

Peter continued to walk away.

"Remember, Ethan, it is all about gaining your freedom!" Dangler called down the hall.

"It is all about returning home to my father's palace at Illiath," Peter said to himself.

§

"I want what I am owed," King Eulrik hissed. He stood in Will's chambers at the palace of Illiath. His daughter waited patiently in the hallway.

"Yes, I know King Eulrik." Will used a calm voice. "Lord Bedlam..."

Eulrik slammed his fist onto the table in the center of the room. But Will was not startled. "Enough!" Eulrik demanded. "I want answers. When will Bedlam return?"

Will picked up a book from the table and placed it onto the bookshelf. "I do not know."

"I don't believe you," Eulrik growled. He walked around the table toward Will. "Nor do I trust you. You're his puppet in all this. He is the real power. From now on I will only speak with him. And I will convince him to have you marry my daughter." Eulrik headed toward the door.

"Really?" Will asked.

Eulrik faced him. "Yes, that was part of the deal. The land and my daughter. You two will be married soon."

Will cocked his head, confused.

Eulrik scanned the room. "Once this palace is destroyed, a new one will be erected for you and my daughter. You two will rule the land as I see fit. Lord Bedlam has agreed to it."

Will stood straight. This was the first time he had heard of this plan.

"That's right." Eulrik crossed his arms. "I know more than you do about Bedlam's plans. As I said, you are only his puppet in all this." He reached for and opened the door. "Don't forget that."

"Emelia," Will said.

With that, the ghost like form of Emelia appeared in the room.

Eulrik jumped when he saw her form. "What's this?"

"Is this information true?" Will asked her.

"Of course not." She smiled with gentleness. She floated over to Eulrik. "This man knows nothing of what he speaks."

"King!" Eulrik shouted. "I am King and I will be addressed as such."

"Well, then." Will turned away. "Remove him from my sight."

Emelia raised her hand then made a shoving motion. Eulrik rose off the ground and flew out the door hitting the wall with such force, he slumped to the ground unconscious before his stunned daughter.

"Father!" She ran toward him and held his face in her hands. Turning toward Emelia, she screamed, "What have you done?"

But Emelia only slammed the door shut in response.

§

"We're dead now." Simon looked behind the group. All around them stood tall angry Ogres staring down at them curiously. No one had dared to enter into their realm without permission.

"Theo said not to stray from the roads," Annika whispered. She began to gnaw on her fingernails nervously. "He told us not to stray."

"Yes, I know," Simon said. "But we had to."

The group did not move a muscle while the Ogres spoke back and forth to each other in their language. Each one held a large wooden club almost the size of each youth.

Crispin stared at the large hands and arms holding the clubs. Peter described the Ogres as brave warriors who had helped King Alexander battle the evil Lord Caragon. "We have come to ask your help," Crispin explained.

"What are you doing?" whispered Simon.

"Reasoning with them," Crispin answered. "Just watch."

The Ogres all turned to listen to the boy.

"We are escaping the Lord Bedlam's soldiers out of Illiath," Crispin continued. "We have run for our lives. Please, help us hide from him and the Duke of Illiath. We are on a mission."

A loud chuckle came from behind them. Many of the Ogres started to laugh as Crispin talked.

"Crispin, what are you doing?" Annika asked.

"You're making them angry," Simon said.

But Crispin again attempted to communicate to the Ogres. "We need your help. We are on a mission to find and save Prince Peter who was taken," he shouted above the laughter.

The Ogres stopped laughing and stared at Crispin. They looked at one another and conversed in their language. The three youths remained cautious.

"Yes, he was taken, abducted in the desert," Crispin said. "And his life is in danger."

The Ogres continued to converse among themselves.

"I wonder what they are saying," Annika whispered.

"They seemed to have recognized Peter's name and title," Crispin whispered back. He stood his ground near the larger of the Ogres, which wore a leather vest and had several tattoos on its large arms. It seemed to be the leader, so Crispin wanted to show how serious he was about their mission.

"I ask you, will you help hide us this night?" Crispin asked again.

The Ogres stopped talking and looked at the three youths. The leader approached Crispin. Each step it took near him shook the ground slightly beneath them. Annika stepped back several inches, holding tightly to the reins of her horse.

The giant beast nodded at Crispin and motioned with its arm to follow it deeper into the gorge.

"It understands me!" he murmured to his friends. "Let's follow them."

"Well," Simon said, "looks like the time you spent with Lord Asgeir was time well spent."

"I am not so sure about this," Annika said to Simon.

But he followed Crispin as the other Ogres walked away.

Annika hesitated. "What if this is a trap? An ambush of some sort?"

"Hush now and follow us," Simon ordered.

Annika reluctantly led her horse along with the others down the darkened path. Night fell. The drizzle of the rain settled the dust on the ground but quickly turned the dirt to mud that stuck to their boots. Annika frowned. She picked up her pace and walked alongside Simon and the others.

"Don't worry," Simon said to her as they walked. "Everything is going to be alright." He smiled at her.

Soon the Ogres led them to a set of caves hidden inside the gorge walls. Many small fires were lit inside the caves and the aroma of cooked meat was tantalizing. Some of the Ogres exited the caves and stared at their visitors walking into the camp, but the lead Ogre grunted toward them as though it were telling them all was fine. Nothing but the drizzle of the rain and the clopping sound of the horse's hooves in the mud could be heard in the night.

Finally, the Ogre led them to a cave and motioned for them to enter in. Crispin stopped the procession and held out his arm. The Ogre grabbed Crispin's forearm in a sort of handshake. He smiled and thanked the large beast as he motioned for Annika and Simon to enter into the cave. Another Ogre handed Crispin a lit torch and some firewood. He let go of his horse's reins to receive the wood and torch as he entered into the cave, lighting it for the others. The Ogre then handed some food in a basket to Annika, who grinned. She placed the basket down, and watched Simon make a fire.

By firelight, Annika unhitched the saddle from her horse and her bedroll. She carried both into the cave. Simon and Crispin followed suit, and soon all three settled in the cave while a small fire burned. Its warmth felt good on their wet skin.

"At last," Annika said. "Rest."

"Yes," Crispin answered as he ate some of the meat. "And food!" He slipped into his bed roll.

"But I will enjoy this sleep tonight. What about you, Simon?" Annika said.

He studied a piece of paper.

"What are you reading?" Annika asked.

Simon lifted the paper to show her. It appeared to be a map that Darion had given him. He worked on plotting out their journey for the morning.

"You really must get some rest, Simon," Annika whispered as she rubbed her eyes. The cave smelled of dust and rain.

"I need to know which way to head out in case," he said.

"In case? In case what?" she asked.

"I want to know where we are just in case we need to leave quickly or in the middle of the night. Now go to sleep," he ordered.

Annika yawned. Peering at Crispin, she saw he was fast asleep. Then, she rolled over and fell asleep as Simon read maps by firelight deep into the night.

35 THE WHITE OWL

Peter sat on his cot admiring his new book.

"So, he just gave it to you?" Nøel sharpened his sword with a stone. "No questions asked?"

"Yes…well, he asked me some questions about the Dragon of the Forest."

Nøel leaned forward. "And what did you tell him?"

"That I had met the Dragon."

Nøel shook his head. "You must be careful. It is best if you remain unknown in this prison. Valbrand may know who you are, but no one else should know."

Peter understood.

He stretched. His body ached from fighting the dragon, and his skin itched from the pesky lice. He knew he needed some sleep, but he couldn't get Dangler's words out of his mind. *What might have been…*

He remembered the camp where the knights trained and his father describing the place as a clearing in a forest with the tiltyard lined with brightly colored pennants flying in the wind. Peter closed his eyes and pictured himself mounted in heavy armor waiting to joust. Then, he opened his eyes only to find himself in the same smelly cell that was his home for many weeks with the same familiar rat across the floor searching in vain for food. It was no use dreaming about what might have been. It was too late.

"You should get some sleep." Nøel lay back on his cot. "You never know when those guards will burst in here and order us to fight in the arena again."

Peter blinked. His eyelids were heavy, but he wanted to continue reading the book about dragons. So, he stoked the fire in the stove and lay on his cot in the firelight,

Turning to page one, he was pleased to find the writing on that page was in an Elfin script, one he recognized thanks to Theo's instruction. He read a few paragraphs. The book listed the differing types of dragons, and the map showed each region where the dragons were located. Peter noticed the Draconis Magnus could be found in the caves of the Ranvieg Mountains and near Vulgaard.

The next pages were in the unfamiliar script, so he studied the many drawings. They chronicled the writer's journey to find dragons. He listed dragon script in the margins. Then there was a chapter on dragon magic. It appeared that certain potions could be made from ground dragon horns, and a special elixir could be made from ground dragon scales. Peter continued to read:

The magic elixir of the dragon scale prolongs youthfulness among men but death in Elves.

Peter kept turning page after page trying to read the script and drawings. Then, as he neared the end, he came upon the pages simply titled, "The Dragon." Peter took notice and sat up

The Great Dragon of the Forest has the most magical and powerful scales of all dragons. Made of the strongest material known to man, the scale can withstand any weapon, venom, and fire. If ground, the powder of the scales can be drunk to promote healing in men as well as strength and vitality. It has been known to bring the dead back to life, but this chronicler has yet to see that with his own eyes.

"Hmmm." Peter sighed. It became clearer to him as to why Peregrine, Lord Caragon, and Bedlam desired those scales more than anything. *An army with those scales would be forever victorious.*

He thumbed through page after page of dragon lore, reading what he could and admiring the many drawings. One chapter was titled, "How to Tame a Dragon" and another was "How to Ride a Dragon." The writer advised taming dragons as soon as they are hatched to ensure they will not return to their wild ways. The removal of the fire glands in the oral cavity was also listed and why. The book described the act of riding a dragon and creating a special saddle to be used in addition to a bridle similar to the one Peter used for his horse, Titan.

"Incredible!" Peter shouted. "Men actually rode dragons through the skies!"

But Nøel was fast asleep on his cot.

Peter noticed the drawings in the margins were not of men, but of Elves. He skimmed back through the pages and noticed the script was similar to the Elfin language he remembered from his father's books on dragons.

There were also drawings of castles high in the mountains. Peter had never seen any other palace besides his father's. He was amazed at the size of the castles carved out of mountains and set high on hills.

After a few hours of reading through the book, Peter's eyes could no longer stay open. The book rested on his chest and his mother's compass underneath his pillow. As he closed his eyes, images of dragons swept through his mind. Some flew, some swam in the ocean. He pictured the dragon hatchlings chasing each other in the pit.

Just then, a noise coming from the window. He stood up and scooted his cot over to the window to try and peak out. Stepping up onto the cot, he peered out at the deadened trees that lined the course, rocky precipice. The moon remained hidden behind the clouds as a cold breeze juggled the dead branches of a tree and wafted across his face. Closing his eyes, he dreamed of home.

Suddenly, he heard the noise again—a familiar screech emerging from the dark and cloudy sky. Just then, the white owl flew in and perched on the branch of the dead tree. Peter stared with his mouth agape at the large bird.

"Is it you?" he asked expecting no reply.

The bird turned its white feathered head almost completely around as it sat regally on its perch. Studying its glowing yellow eyes, Peter felt deep in his heart that it was the Dragon in the form of a white owl.

"I hoped you would come." Peter smiled. "I have so many questions."

The bird shuffled its wings as the cold air blew over its body. Peter knew the bird was there for a reason: *hope*. The owl reminded him of their time together in the forest before he left for Knight Training.

"Please, can you help us escape?" Peter regretted the words as soon as he said them. "No. This is my trial, isn't it?"

Silence.

"At least tell me if my father is well. Why hasn't he come for me? Does he think I am dead?"

The owl stared at Peter.

"Please, say something. I can barely remember my father's voice. I pray he is alright...I hate this place." Peter cringed. "But I know I must endure. I don't want to, but I will."

The owl merely gazed off into the distance.

"What's going to happen to me in this place? Will I ever make it back home?"

The owl shuffled its wings to balance itself.

Peter stared off into the night, not really expecting any answers.

Suddenly, the owl flew away. Peter watched it for a second or two, then quietly scooted his cot back against the wall and sat on it, remembering his time with the Dragon on that fateful day when he swore to uphold the Oath between Dragon and man.

"You are my friend, Peter," the Dragon whispered. *"You and I are brothers."*

Peter nodded through his tears.

"As I have sworn...a son of Alexander...will sit on the throne of Illiath forever," the Dragon declared. *"Your father, King Alexander...was called to be the protector of that covenant Oath. He has fulfilled his duty with honor. And now,"* it hesitated. *"You are the heir of that promise."*

"But, why me?" Peter asked as he looked into the Dragon's eyes.

"This... is your purpose, Peter," it spoke. *"This... is your burden."*

The Dragon turned its head toward Hildron. "Do not seek glory for yourself, Peter. That... is what Peregrine did. And that is what Caragon did." The Dragon turned its gaze toward the castle. More smoke lifted from its nostrils. "The palace...it faces the Dragon Forest," it whispered. "All others built their castles away from it. They cannot see it, Peter. Always remember... to keep the Dragon Forest in your sight."

"Why?" Peter asked.

"That is where your purpose dwells," the Dragon said. The sides of its long snout turned upward as it smiled. "That is where you will get your strength."*

Then, Peter remembered their time in the forest.

"Your love, Peter. Your love for me, your love for your father. Your love for Illiath brought me back." It turned toward the lake and the shadow covered trees. *"I know this is your time. I must be here for your time."*

Peter took in its words.

"As I was there for your father and his father before him," it said. *"I will be here for you."*

Peter exhaled. He could hear the Dragon's voice.

"You must save Illiath, Peter," it said.

"Save Illiath? Me? Surely you must mean my father."

"Your father has fought his battles. He faced his trials on the battlefield and fought valiantly," it said. *"And he was rewarded with a son. Now it is your turn, Peter. You are the Son of the Oath. You are the one to save Illiath."*

"What if I don't want to be *the one?*" Peter asked no one. "I thought I had a choice."

Recalling the compass, Peter located the leather pouch under his pillow, removed the compass, and rubbed it to a shine. His father had explained to him how his mother created spy glasses for star gazing, compasses for his knights, and other trinkets when she had time to work with her hands. *"She was very smart with things like that, Peter,"* Alexander had said. *"You take after her in that area. She was always reading a book and working on some invention."*

Peter smiled as he opened the compass. It glistened in the light of the stove's glow. He placed it back in its pouch and replaced it under the pillow.

"I cannot remember my mother's face," Peter whispered, "or her voice." He scanned the darkened cell. All he could hear was Nøel's deep, rhythmic breathing.

The internal pain was almost too much to bear. He could no longer garner emotion, even though he wanted to. His heart was not yet completely hardened, but callouses were beginning to form.

"What kind of son forgets his mother's voice or his mother's face?" he said, hoping for an answer. But none came. He could feel tears forming, but he refused to let them come. The hardness returned.

He covered his head with his hands. "I cannot escape," he murmured. "Yet I can't stand the thought of staying in this place. I have no choice."

He looked at his armor leaning against the wall lit only by the glow of the fire in the stove and thought of Damon. "Like the dragons chained in the caves, I'm trapped. I have to win in the arena. That's the only way out."

Laying his head on the pillow, and stared off until, finally, he fell asleep.

§

The next morning, the group awoke to the muttering of Ogres outside their caves. When Annika stepped outside, she reported that she could barely see a few feet in front of her. "A fog has covered the camp," she said to the boys as they rose to their feet and rubbed the sleep out of their eyes.

As the fog slowly lightened, the campsite was revealed. All three enjoyed a hearty breakfast of porridge, bread, and warm milk from goats. The Ogres kept a distance as the youths ate and packed up their belongings.

Simon made his way over to the largest of the beasts, whose face was criss-crossed with scars. Tattoos of black ink formed a mysterious pattern on the beast's face and neck. Simon studied the pattern, wondering if it meant something.

"This is a map King Alexander's Constable gave to us." Simon gestured toward the thin paper in his hands. "We are headed to Vulgaard, where we will help rescue the Prince."

The Ogre shook its head.

Simon raised an eyebrow. "What is the matter?" he asked, but the Ogre only pointed toward the north from where his guests had entered the camp.

Simon turned toward Crispin, who only shrugged.

The Ogre looked at the other larger male Ogres and grunted a few times in their language as he pointed to the tops of the cliffs. The others nodded in agreement and one grabbed Simon's hand. Shocked by the gesture, Simon felt overwhelmed by the size of the beast, but decided to follow.

The Ogre led Simon up the side of the cliff. He tried to use his hands to steady himself, but the Ogre dragged him with a sense of urgency.

As soon as Simon reached the top, he leaned over, panting from the work, and dusted the sand off his suede trousers. At last he stood and looked where the Ogre pointed. To the north toward Illiath, Simon could see great clouds of dust rising over the smaller hills of the Theádron desert plains.

"What is it?" he asked the Ogre.

But the beast pointed and grunted its frustration, as if trying to tell him something.

"Riders, from Illiath?" Simon asked.

The Ogre nodded.

"The Duke's men?" Simon tilted his head.

The Ogre nodded.

Simon's worst fears had come true. "We are being followed." He extended his hand as a gesture of thanks to the large beast, and it returned the gesture, in its large hand engulfing Simon's. "Your assistance is greatly appreciated."

Together they hiked back down into the caverns that made up the camp of the Ogres.

"Crispin and Annika," he said, walking toward them, "we've a dilemma."

"What is it?" Crispin asked.

"We are being followed," Simon answered. "Riders are coming this way."

Annika mouthed an "Oh no."

"Our plans to head out have been drastically altered," Simon explained. "We will be safe here among the Ogres."

"But Simon," Crispin said, "what if the Duke's men enter the camp?"

"We'll have to take our chances." Simon hurried toward the cave that would be their home for the next few days. "We've no other choice."

The Ogres gathered in curiosity. The Ogre informed the others of the news, and all turned to spy Simon. He sheepishly waved as the Ogres inspected him, then headed with Annika and Crispin back to the cave, where they fell asleep.

§

Hours later, Annika awoke to a strange sound coming from the cave. She raised her head to find the fire going down, yet providing enough light to see that the others were asleep. Peering toward the entrance of the cave, she saw an Ogre striding rapidly toward them. He grabbed her arm and yanked her up with such force that her bedding came with her.

"What are you doing?" Annika yelled.

Simon and Crispin, awake now, sat up just as the Ogre lifted Annika and headed toward the back of the cave.

"Annika!" Crispin yelled. "What are you doing to her?"

But the Ogre only grunted toward him and bent over to lift something on the ground. He raised a large stone up and grunted again as though trying to tell the boys something. Annika struggled to get loose from the tight grip of the beast, whose arms were almost twice her size.

"Put her down!" Crispin demanded.

"Shh!" Simon whispered. "He's trying to tell us something."

The Ogre nodded and pointed to the hole underneath the stone.

"Oh my," Annika exclaimed, peering into the hole. "It's a passageway."

"Come!" Simon ordered Crispin as he ran to where the Ogre stood.

It lowered Annika into the hole first where her feet met the stone steps leading down a darkened passageway.

Simon followed her down the cold dark cave within the cave with Crispin close behind. Annika noticed the Ogre carried a bucket of water which it used to douse the fire. Once the fire was out, all she could see was the silhouette of the Ogre in the cave entrance. It began to walk toward them again. Once all three were safe inside, the Ogre placed the large stone on top of the passage.

The three stood silent in the dark and cold.

"What now?" Crispin whispered.

"Shh!" Simon replied. "Listen."

First Annika heard horses' hooves faintly outside the cave... then men's voices. "The Duke's men," she whispered. Her whole body trembled.

Simon placed his arms around her. "It will be alright."

They were silent again. Soon the men's voices grew louder, but Annika could not understand the words. The grunts of the Ogres could be heard as well. She supposed they were all gathered outside the cave trying to direct the men away. Next, the sound of goats bleating and scattering could be heard.

A light appeared through the tiny cracks underneath the stone. The Duke's men were inside the cave with torches searching their belongings. More footsteps were heard above them as some dirt tumbled down through the cracks and down the steps. Annika closed her eyes. At any moment the stone could be lifted only to reveal their hiding place.

More Ogres grunted, but they sounded far away. The light disappeared, and once again the youths waited in the darkness. All three trembled.

"This is maddening," Annika whispered.

Simon quickly put his hand over her mouth. Sometimes a soldier would stay behind and hide in order to see if they missed anything in the search. Evidently, Simon thought one man remained in the cave, listening for any sounds of movement. He slowly removed his hand from her mouth. Annika nodded.

A few more minutes passed in the darkness and the cold of the passageway. The stone remained unmoved. They might have to stay hidden all night because the men's voices above could be heard. They could not move to sit down or head further down the steps. They could not risk it.

Annika stared at the stone above, hoping that it would be lifted by an Ogre, signaling everything was safe again. She shuddered from the cold. She covered her face with her hands but did not weep for fear of making a sound. The pain of holding in the tears was almost like suffocating.

The grunts of the Ogres grew louder. They sounded alarmed. The youths could see some shadows. They realized a torch must be inside the cave again. But they could not hear any men's voices. They each stared at the light coming through the cracks underneath the stone. Still, the stone did not move.

Simon looked at Crispin. He shrugged in confusion. Annika began to bite her fingernails. It was a nasty habit that helped calm her nerves. The Ogres grunted above them, arguing about something. Then the light disappeared again, engulfing them in darkness. Annika sighed heavily and gazed down in defeat.

Suddenly, the stone lifted up. Annika gasped. Her eyes were not met with the hateful gaze of the Duke's men, but instead the Ogre stared back. He motioned for them to come out of the passage. They quickly followed.

Their belongings were no longer in the cave. The Ogre gestured for them to follow it outside.

In the moonlight, all three youths were met with a large group of Ogres. One was holding the reigns of their horses which were saddled and loaded with their gear.

"Is it safe?" Simon asked.

The Ogres nodded. One pointed to the south toward Vulgaard.

"Yes," Crispin said. "That is the way we need to go."

Simon walked over to his horse and lifted up one of the saddle bags. He reached in and pulled out the map Darion had given him and offered it to the Ogres.

The Ogre nodded and gently took the map from Simon's hands, as if it knew the paper was old and fragile. It looked closely at the map and pointed out a route to Simon who nodded in agreement.

"Yes, I can see that route is the best way to travel. Will we face Zadoks along the way?" he asked.

The beast nodded.

"Thank you for allowing us to stay here with you," Annika said.

"Yes, thank you for the food and shelter," Crispin said.

"We are off now to search for Peter." Simon held out his arm. "Wish us luck!" He smiled as the Ogre shook his arm.

It grumbled in the broken language of man. "Save Prince." Its large eyes moistened.

The faces of the Ogres looked worn and tired from months of struggling to find food.

"We will do our best," he said as he mounted his saddled horse.

The Ogres gave each youth a coat made of animal fur and helped them put the coats on. Then, one-by-one, Simon, Annika, and Crispin mounted their horses. They were not sure what had transpired in the night, but they knew these gentle beasts saved their lives.

As the three sat high on their saddles with their thick fur coats on and their bed rolls attached, they were ready to ride out. Sunlight fought its way through the thick dark clouds as they galloped out of the gorge.

36 DRAGON FIGHTERS

"Did you know that ground dragon eggshells can be made into a healing paste?" Peter asked as he and Nøel arrived at Dangler's cave.

"No." Nøel reached into the pit and picked up a baby dragon.

"Yes, and their blood is known for healing wounds and giving men strength and vitality," Peter said.

Nøel patted the little dragon on its head and handed it to Peter. "I had no idea," said Nøel. "I was always taught that they were pests that needed to be killed."

"Yes! My father was always trying to keep the dragons from stealing our sheep," said a boy nearby. "He would shoot at them with arrows!"

"I had never seen a dragon before I came here," another boy said.

Peter placed the little dragon with the others and gave each one some meat to eat even though they had no teeth yet. The other boys talked dragons all day. Even when they were learning swordplay and wrestling moves, they spoke of dragons and Peter amazed them with more facts. As they ate their midday meal, Peter explained to them about how a dragon could be trained to fly.

"You mean a man could actually ride on a dragon and fly around?" one boy asked.

"Certainly," Peter said. "It is a common fact that the Elves have trained dragons in order to ride them."

The boys' eyes grew wide as they listened and imagined.

"And they even make leather saddles to use," Peter said. "For comfort....those hard scales, you know."

The boys nodded as Dangler stood by, listening.

"Where did you learn so much about dragons?" another boy asked.

Peter looked at Dangler who shook his head. "From my tutor back home," Peter lied. He knew he couldn't tell them about the mysterious book he read each day, although he truly wanted to.

Dangler rose and began to put all the swords into a pile in the corner of the cave. "You all worked hard today. But now it is time to work on how to *approach* a dragon. Come now, off we go to the arena."

They all swallowed their last bites of lunch and followed Dangler. Peter was last. He felt good about teaching the other boys about dragons. Now maybe they would learn to respect them and fight them fairly.

"I suppose you'll want to take a dragon back to your cell and cuddle with it some more, eh?" a voice from behind said.

Peter turned around and saw Damon standing nearby in a darkened corner of the cave. Damon approached the hatchling pit, peered in, then reached in and grabbed one of the baby dragons.

Peter rushed over. "What are you doing?"

"So you think their cute, do you?" Damon held one of the dragons by the neck. It struggled to get free. "I don't see it."

"Let it go," Peter ordered.

"Or what?" Damon then held the dragon as though he would throw it. The little dragon faintly cried out.

"Let it be." Peter tried to remain calm in spite of Damon's antagonizing, but it was not easy. Anger rushed through his body.

Damon laughed. "Or what?" He threw the little dragon high into the air and caught him as though it were a ball or toy of some sort.

Peter lunged forward to try and snatch the dragon out of Damon's hands, but he missed. Relieved to see that the dragon was caught, Peter did not give in to Damon's taunting.

"These pests aren't cute or funny or anything like that. They are killers!" Damon shouted. "And they must be killed."

"That isn't so," Peter insisted. "They are creatures that have intelligence. Not as we do, of course, but in their own right. Yes, some kill and they should be killed. But not all are evil."

"Is that so?" Damon taunted. "What about this one? Is it an evil dragon or a good dragon?" He held it up to his face and studied its eyes.

The little dragon continued to cry out. Peter knew it was frightened and confused.

"It will be what man teaches it to be," Peter said. "And right now you are teaching it to fear you and hate you."

Damon smirked then continued to look at the dragon. "I hate all dragons. They all should be killed!"

Just then, the little dragon spewed out fire and burned Damon's face. He screamed from the pain and dropped the dragon. It scurried away in fear.

Peter could not help but laugh at the sight of Damon in pain.

"Come on!" Nøel startled Peter. "Get to the arena."

Peter nodded and scratched his scalp.

"You're going to make it bleed again," Nøel warned.

"I don't care," Peter said. "these bugs drive me crazy."

Nøel groaned as though his entire body ached.

"Sore, old man?" Peter teased.

Damon shoved his way passed Peter. "Time to fight," he hissed.

Peter started after him.

"Ethan!" Dangler shouted. He approached Peter who stood with his sword in his hands. He inspected the boy's face. "Are you ready?"

"Let's get on with training." Peter moved over to the line.

Dangler waved the boys over to the wall of the cave and told them grab a sword and shield. Nøel and Peter stood ready with the others.

"Let's continue," Dangler said. "Study each other's moves!" He walked up and down examining each fighter. "Steady your stance! Meet each thrust with a powerful response. See the dragon in your mind. It's there before you. Hold your sword tightly as you approach."

Nøel and Peter practiced with the others when Peter heard the sound. It came from above. He looked up and noticed something moving toward him. It seemed to be a shadow. But then he realized it was a creature. Several more charged down.

"Look!" shouted one boy. The others ran and scattered all over the arena. The creatures screamed a loud and long shrill.

Peter froze. He recognized the sound. He gripped his sword. Only one creature screams with such a long shrill—the Gizor.

"Run for your lives!" one boy shouted. He sprinted across the arena waving his arms as the Gizor swooped down at him time and time again. With large wings attached to their arms and small yet strong legs, the monsters resembled part man and part bat. Peter swung his sword hitting the legs of a Gizor, but three more attacked him sending him to the ground.

Nøel ran to him, but was struck in the back by a Gizor. He flew into the wall and blacked out for a moment. When he came to, he saw several Gizor attacking Peter. They bit Peter's arms and slashed at his face with their claws. Nøel grabbed his sword and swung at the flying monsters. The other boys ran away even though no Gizor attacked them. The monsters only struck at Peter. Nøel knew instantly what was happening.

Damon laughed at the sight.

"Bedlam," Nøel whispered. He searched all over the arena for the menace. He crouched low. He approached Peter who struggled to stand.

Peter swung his sword hitting a few of the monsters, but when one was struck down, another took its place. He finally made it to his feet and continued to swipe at the Gizor sending blood, splattering everywhere. Blood mixed with sweat covered his face.

"Peter!" Nøel ran over to him, but two Gizor grabbed his arms and began to fly away with Nøel in their grasp. He struggled free and fell several feet to the ground.

Dangler yelled for the boys to return and fight, but none would listen. "Come on, you cowards!" Grabbing a sword and began to strike at the monsters as they slashed and clawed at Peter. They turned and began their attack on Dangler.

"Let's go!" shouted one boy. He ran with his sword and entered the fight. Two more joined in. Finally, Peter had relief. His torn face and arms were bloodied. He ran away toward Nøel who was struggling to stand.

"Peter!" Nøel shouted. "Are you alright?"

"Yes," Peter answered. He tried to lift his friend, but another Gizor flew down and hit Peter from behind sending him several feet across the arena. He was isolated again, so the Gizor screamed for its companions to attack.

Nøel cocked his head, realizing this attack was meant for Peter alone. "Over here!" Nøel called, rallying the others.

They raced to assist Peter, who was again on the ground being slashed by the beasts.

The boys sliced their way through the monsters, severing arms and wings, sending blood flying until, finally, the two that were left quickly flew high into the air and disappeared into the shadows once again.

The boys stared up with swords drawn waiting for another attack, but it never came.

"They're gone," Dangler huffed.

The others agreed and threw their swords down. Peter moaned from the pain, but he was able to stand.

"You are a mess, my boy," Dangler said, grimacing at Peter's appearance. "Get him to the apothecary!" he ordered.

"No." Nøel swiftly put Peter's arm around his shoulder to assist him. "I don't trust anyone in this dreadful place. I will take care of him."

"Well, then, you'll need some help." Dangler motioned for everyone to follow him back into the cave.

In the cave, Nøel set Peter down on a wooden stool to rest. Peter panted heavily. Small drops of blood fell one after the other on the dirt floor.

Dangler waved all the boys back, then whispered, "Ethan, the pouch. Remember the pouch?"

Peter nodded.

"Use the powder," Dangler told Nøel. "It will heal him. Tell no one."

Nøel grabbed Peter again and helped him walk out of the cave and down the hall. Once inside the cell, Nøel helped Peter lie down on his cot.

"Rest here," Nøel said. "Where's the pouch?"

Peter pointed to his pillow. Nøel reached under and pulled out the small leather pouch. He opened it and winced at the putrid smell.

"Mix with water," Peter moaned.

Nøel grabbed his water pouch, poured some powder into his palm, the added some water to make a paste. About to put it on Peter's wounds, he hesitated. "I sure hope this isn't poison," he said, not sure he could trust Dangler.

But when Peter groaned again from the pain, Nøel decided to take a chance. He rubbed the paste onto the cuts all over Peter's face and arms. Peter grimaced. Then Nøel gave Peter some water. He sipped some through his swollen lips.

"What happened?" he asked.

"Never mind," Nøel said. "Just drink and rest."

Peter sighed.

Nøel rubbed more paste into the cuts in Peter's legs. Suddenly, Peter began to breath faster. Nøel stopped and examined his friend's face. Most of the cuts were already closing, and the swelling in Peter's face was going down.

Nøel sighed in relief. "Thank goodness."

Before they knew it, the paste had relieved Peter of much pain. He was able to sit and see through his once swollen eyes.

"How do you feel?" Nøel asked.

"What happened?" Peter said.

"What do you remember?" Nøel asked.

Peter blinked several times. "We were fighting. There were shadows."

Nøel waited.

Peter's face grew serious and pale. "Now I remember. The scream."

"Yes." Nøel tucked the leather pouch under the pillow, then collapsed onto the cot and groaned from his own wounds. "Those screams." He rubbed the rest of the paste onto the cuts on his arms.

"Gizor!" Peter said. "They attacked us!"

"Over and over again." Nøel exhaled.

The cuts on Peter's arms were only red slash marks, closed, and healing. "How?" He examined them.

"The powder," Nøel said. "It healed you."

"It's ground dragon horn!" Peter reached for *The Dragon Chronicles* and flipped through the pages until he found the part that explained anodynes and potions.

"See?" He pointed to the drawing of the powder.

"I am concerned, Peter," Nøel said.

"About what?"

"That attack. It was meant for you and no one else."

"But I am alright." Peter held out his arms and legs. "See my wounds? They are almost healed!"

Nøel nodded. "Yes, but those Gizor came for you. They were sent to attack you."

"I know." Peter put the book down. "It isn't over."

"That is my fear. You had better get some rest, because we don't know what will come next."

Peter ran his fingers across the book's cover. "You are correct about that. I think it's Damon."

"Damon?" Nøel asked.

"Yes. He's jealous of me." Peter stretched out his sore legs.

Nøel frowned. "Peter, that boy doesn't have the power to send those creatures to attack you."

"I know." Peter looked serious. "And I don't think he is working alone."

Nøel leaned forward. "You mean, you suspect he's working with Lord Bedlam?"

Peter nodded. "I think Damon knows who I am. And I think he's after me."

"Peter, I—"

"And I'll be ready for him," Peter said. "I'll be ready."

§

As Simon, Annika, and Crispin approached the forest leaving the desert plains behind, groups of smaller, thicker bushes appeared on the horizon at every turn. These shrubs gave way to the sparser trees littering dry grassy hills that once were lush and green in the sunlight, but were now yellow and dead. Yet the constant drizzle had stopped. Drier air blew over the hills and dales, moving the tall dry grasses in the breeze. The sound was soothing and assuaged their weary spirits. A few lone sparrows fluttered high above them heading toward the trees to settle in for the night. The approaching forest was not as dense or beautiful as the Dragon Forest north of Illiath, but it was better than the gorge they had left behind in the desert.

"This is where we must be most careful," Simon warned. His horse had slowed down to a walk. "Keep your eyes open and your hands on your swords."

Crispin sat up tall in his saddle. "Remember Theo's warning about Lord Bedlam's spies that roam the forest trails?"

Simon nodded. He slid his hand from underneath his armor and gripped the handle of his sword.

All three entered into the forest path.

"What is this place?" Crispin asked.

"I haven't a clue, but we will need to camp soon," Simon answered.

They kept riding until they found a place for the night. After tying their horses' reins to trees, they searched for sticks and twigs to start a fire. Then, they gathered around the fire to eat. Simon took bread from his saddle bag and handed a piece to Annika then Crispin.

"So dark out tonight." Crispin gazed up. "No stars in the sky. They're hidden in the clouds."

The three ate in silence then settled in for the night. It didn't take long for them to fall asleep. Their bodies ached from the long ride.

A few hours later, Annika was the first to notice the sound of breaking twigs. Her horse neighed and pulled on its reins, startling the others horses. Their ears flattened and their nostrils flared.

"Simon," Annika whispered, "wake up."

Simon stirred. "What is it?"

"Listen," Annika ordered. "Do you hear it? Something's out there. We're being watched."

"Crispin," Simon whispered more fiercely, "wake up."

Crispin rolled over just as Simon drew his sword.

"Oh no." Crispin sighed. "Bedlam's men?"

Annika nodded and placed her finger on her lips.

Crispin tiptoed to his pack and removed his sword. All three stood ready and waiting. Suddenly, more noises came from the thicket.

The horses neighed again.

"Do you see anything?" Simon asked his friends.

But all around them was only darkness.

"I think we should mount," Annika said.

"Hold still," Simon ordered. He placed his hand up.

A monstrous troll barged through the bushes with his hammer help up high overhead.

"Watch it!" Simon shouted as ran moved out of the way.

The troll attacked the small group. Each youth ran away from the hammer as it swung down with such force, that it shook the ground. The muscular beast, well over 9 feet tall, raised the hammer to strike again. Annika wasted no time untying the reins of the horses quickly leading them away from the attack. The boys raised their swords.

"Move away now, or we will strike!" Simon warned.

The drooling beast roared and raised the hammer high above its head again.

"I don't think it's afraid of us!" Crispin shouted.

"Simon, be careful!" Annika watched from the bushes, clinging to the horses.

The troll scowled at the boys.

"I warned you!" Simon yelled.

He signaled for Crispin to follow his lead, and Crispin nodded. Together they lunged forward plunging their swords into the body of the troll. Then, just as quickly, they retrieved them back. The quick stabs startled the troll, and it clutched its stomach in pain. The hammer dropped.

"Run!" Simon shouted to Crispin.

The boys ran toward Annika, who had already mounted her horse already and held the reins of the others. "Our packs!" she called.

"We'll come back. Now ride!" Simon ordered.

The three rode out of the area and into the night. Annika did not have her sword with her. Behind her was the roar of the dying troll. They stopped their horses and waited. Annika could hear only the heavy panting of the horses and could barely see the boys in the darkness.

"In case there are more out there, we must stay here for a minute or two," Simon whispered.

Some sparrows flew from the trees nearby, stirring the already nervous horses. Then, silence.

Annika studied her horse for a sign. Its body trembled. "We'd better get away from here," she murmured to the others. "Something remains out there."

"Simon," Crispin asked. "What do you hear?"

Simon shook his head. The wind picked up, and the smell of snow remained. Leaves shuffled on the ground in the darkness, breaking the silence. Simon slowly turned his horse, and it made its way over to the others. Annika reached out and touched its mane. But the ears remained flat, signaling a predator was somewhere in the darkness.

"Let's head back to get our packs," Simon ordered.

Crispin hesitated but dutifully nudged his horse to follow the others.

Annika looked to her right and left, trying to glimpse any predators about to attack, but could not see anything. The moon was well hidden behind all the clouds, and the sun hadn't made its way over the mountains yet. "Is it a new moon?" she whispered. "I cannot remember."

Simon motioned for her to be quiet. The eeriness of the woods was became too much for her. Her body trembled as badly as her horse's.

The three continued down a narrow path toward their campsite. The fire had dwindled down to mere embers, but they could see their bed sacks, packs, and the dead troll lying where they left it.

"Oh." Annika spotted the dead troll. About to be sick, she placed her hand over her mouth. "Disgusting."

The beast lay on its side, gripping its bloodied abdomen. Simon dismounted and inspected the creature. Then he signaled that all was well to the others so they could gather their belongings and leave that place.

In silence, they rolled up their beds and secured their belongings to their saddles. Annika stumbled and yawned, but managed to mount her horse. The three slowly headed down the narrow path again.

"The darkness is making it hard to know which way is which," Crispin said. "I barely remember where we are."

"All I know is that a river should be coming up shortly," Simon answered. "If the map I studied earlier is correct."

"Then maybe, just maybe, we can get some sleep?" Annika spoke wearily, her body was giving out from the exhaustion.

"We'll see," Simon sighed. "We must keep going."

Just then, Annika's horse reared up on its hind legs and leapt forward as though escaping something from behind. Annika gripped the reins tightly and followed its lead.

"Ride!" Simon shouted as he heard a loud rumbling coming from behind them.

Crispin nudged his horse and galloped closely behind Simon, who caught up to Annika.

The loud rumbling was very close behind. Several riders galloped toward them at high speed. Leaning their bodies close to their horses' necks, they kicked their horses even harder.

But it was too late. Once they had reached a clearing, they noticed one rider waiting for them alone. His sword was drawn.

37 SURVIVING THE ATTACKS

"I want to fight Damon in the arena," Peter announced to Dangler, who sat whittling away at a piece of wood.

"Not now," Dangler said without looking up. "You're time will come."

"But you don't understand."

"No, *you* don't understand." Dangler placed the piece of wood down. "I do not decide who fights. Valbrand does." Dangler stared at Peter and Nøel standing before him. "And he has decided you two will fight again today."

"What?" Nøel said. "Again? Why?"

Dangler chuckled. "Because he won a sizable amount of gold coin the last time you two fought the dragon." He stomped over to the armor and selected a breastplate. He brought it over to Nøel. "And this time, he hopes to win even more gold coin by watching you two lose." Dangler handed the armor to Nøel.

"Lose?" Peter eyed Nøel.

"Yes." Dangler returned to his stool. "He bets against his own fighters at times. This time he feels he will win big if you two lose. So, he will raise the stakes even higher."

"Oh great," Nøel sighed.

"This way!" the guard shouted.

All the fighters lined up and followed the guard into the arena.

Peter and Nøel followed along in full armor. The guard raised his arm, signaling all the fighters to stop and wait.

"How do you feel?" Nøel asked.

"Good," Peter answered. His wounds had healed, but his body remained sore. He struggled to stand up straight in the heavy armor.

The guard ordered the men into the Great Arena. One by one they jogged in line and took their place along the outer ring. It smelled of dampened dirt. The crowds roared their approval at the sight of the fighters. Peter stood amazed yet again at the size of the crowd. There were more people in the stands than the last time. He realized word must have gotten out about the last battle. Their popularity was growing. He looked straight ahead and noticed several fighters on the opposite side of the arena.

One was Damon.

When Peter saw him, he swallowed hard and felt the air thicken. Beads of sweat ran down his forehead.

"Peter," Nøel called over the shouts of the crowd, "looks like we are fighting man-to-man. Be ready for anything!"

Peter nodded toward Nøel. He gripped his shield and sword.

"Move!" came the shout from the guard.

Peter trotted into the center of the arena. Nøel began to follow him.

"Not you!" The guard pushed Nøel back against the wall.

Peter entered the arena on his own. No other fighters followed, yet on the opposite side, three men and Damon approached.

Peter stood in the center, noticing the men coming forward. He peered up at the balcony where Valbrand usually watched the fights. Sure enough, he was there with his arms folded in approval, gazing down on Peter.

When the trumpets sounded and Peter realized this fight would be against Damon and the three fighters before him, he felt a rush of fear.

"Look at the boy!" Damon taunted. "He is shaking!"

The others laughed and banged their swords and shields together. The crowd responded.

Peter's mind went blank. He tried to think of a strategy, and tried to remember training, but the noise of the crowd distracted him.

Finally, the signal came and Damon sent the three fighters toward Peter. Immediately, Peter realized he was smaller and more agile, so he decided to use his size to his advantage. Once the first fighter reached him and swung at him, Peter easily went down on his knees and missed the swords as he ran by. Then, the other fighters ran toward him. Peter stood up in time to kick one man in the backside, sending him down to the ground. Peter thrust his sword into the back of the other fighter and killed him. Next, he took a stance as Damon pivoted and ran back. Peter quickly removed his helmet and threw it at Damon, hitting him in the face. The third fighter swung at Peter and sliced his shoulder. Peter moved away in time and ran in another direction. His shoulder bled, but the pain only awakened him. The crowd roared.

"Keep moving!" Nøel shouted as he paced.

Two remaining fighters removed their helmets and stalked toward Peter.

"He bleeds!" Damon shouted. He laughed. "Kill him!"

Peter tried to predict which way their bodies would move. Sure enough, one fighter ran to the left and the other ran to the right, so Peter ran up the center and jumped into the air avoiding their swords. He landed on his shoulder and rolled, wincing from the pain which only angered him more.

He quickly stood, hobbling. One fighter ran with sword raised and lowered it in time to meet Peter's sword. He was shocked at the brute strength of the man, but then he remembered this man was fighting for freedom. Peter leaned into the man with all his strength. Both pushed, but Peter wasn't as strong. He fell backward and landed on the dirt floor, sending the crowd into a frenzy. He had lost his shield. The fighter swung his sword around and made his way toward Peter.

The crowd chanted. "Kill! Kill! Kill" over and over again.

Peter could barely movie his arms. But he gripped his sword and slowly began to stand when Damon approached.

"Enough! He's mine!" Damon snarled.

Peter looked over at Nøel, who struggled to get past the guards and help.

"No!" Nøel shouted.

Peter stood firm and held onto his sword with both hands, awaiting Damon. That's when he heard it. *The scream.*

The crowd heard it too. Damon stopped and looked above them. Peter knew the sound and ran away while he had a chance.

"No!" Nøel shouted at Dangler. "Not this again!"

Dangler shrugged and pointed to the balcony.

The crowd grew quiet. Peter noticed shadows moving once again. Suddenly, the flock of Gizor swooped past Damon and Peter, sending them to the ground.

Peter prepared to swipe at the Gizor with his sword. "Go ahead!" he taunted. "Come at me!"

A Gizor screamed as it flew right at him with teeth glaring. Peter grimaced and swiped at it in time to sever one of its wings. But just as he finished that move, three more attacked him. He fell backwards from the blows and hit them with his arms. Three more Gizor flew down and attacked the fighters.

Because the guards watched in shock, Nøel was able to maneuver past them, enter the fight, and help Peter. He sliced at the Gizor with his sword, sending their wings flying and blood splattering. The crowd showed their approval with thunderous applause. Valbrand frowned.

Nøel helped Peter to his feet, and both stood ready for another attack as the crowd cheered. But then Nøel called out to Peter, "Look!" and pointed toward the tops of the stone columns that surrounded the arena. The stone gargoyles that sat atop each column came alive. Their heads turned toward Peter stood on the arena floor, and they grimaced.

Peter couldn't believe his eyes. "Lord Bedlam's magic. It has to be!"

Nøel agreed. "Get ready!"

Damon laughed heartily at the sight of Peter. "He's afraid!" He raised his sword and raced toward Peter.

Instead of waiting, Peter ran ahead to meet Damon.

"No Peter!" Nøel shouted. "Wait!"

But Peter's rage fueled him as he ran toward Damon.

When they met in the middle, their swords clashed. Peter's strength was greater, and Damon fell backwards, but he regained his footing and met Peter's sword again. Then he swung around and sliced at Peter, barely missing his back. Peter turned and swung his sword. Damon moved in time.

The gargoyles leapt from their perches and attacked.

"Come fight me!" Damon shouted at Peter.

"With pleasure." Peter lunged at Damon again, but this time he was pushed to the ground by a gargoyle. The beast stomped on Peter's back. Peter screamed from the pain.

Damon laughed again, of course. The crowd cheered.

Nøel successfully kept the gargoyles off Peter, but not for long. More came from the shadows and flew toward Peter still on the ground.

Damon grabbed his sword and stabbed at Peter, but he rolled out of the way. The sword stabbed the ground instead.

Peter rose to his feet and managed to punch Damon in the face. He flew backwards to the ground. Peter felt the claws of the Gizor above him. He could hear their wings flapping. He swung his sword and hit the legs of one. It screamed, and its blood splattered Peter's face. He winced and wiped it from his eyes.

"Peter! Look out!" Nøel shouted.

But Peter couldn't see with the blood in his eyes. Nøel ran with his sword as Damon lunged at Peter. Nøel thrust his sword to stop Damon just in time. Peter heard the clash and desperately swiped at his eyes. He saw his friend fighting with Damon.

Peter ran to help, but the gargoyle knocked him down with its powerful legs yet again. Peter hit the dirt face first and blacked out for a few seconds. He rolled over in time to see Nøel battling with Damon.

"Peter!" Nøel shouted. "Run to the cave!"

Peter sat up and reached for his sword, but he couldn't find it. A Gizor swept down and snatch it up with its scrawny hands.

"No!" Peter screamed and jumped after it, but it was too late. The creature flew off with it.

"Peter!" Nøel shouted again. "Get out of here! They're coming after you!"

Peter pivoted right as the creature swiped at him. He winced from the pain of his cheek being sliced open. He could hear Damon laugh.

"Enough of this," Nøel struck Damon across the face with his fist.

Damon fell to the ground.

"Now stay there," Nøel shouted. "If you know what's good for you."

Then he turned and made it to Peter as more creatures approached. Grabbing Peter's tunic, he dragged him to the cave. The crowd booed, and the screams from the Gizor stopped.

Peter was barely conscious. Dangler gave Nøel a piece of cloth for Peter's cheek. The gash oozed blood onto the cloth, turning it red.

"Get him out of here," Dangler said. "And use the powder."

Nøel nodded. He lifted Peter up and draped him over his shoulder. He could hear the jeers from the crowd getting louder.

As Dangler turned around, Damon, with face swollen, ran into the cave after them.

"Where is he?" Damon yelled. "I'll kill him!"

Dangler grabbed Damon's shoulders to stop him from chasing after Peter. "Calm down. The fight is over."

Damon kicked over the wooden stool and threw his buckler across the cave.

"No one won this time," Dangler said. He stared toward the arena, noticing Valbrand was not in his balcony. "But there will be a next time."

Damon huffed off toward his cell in anger.

"There is always a next time in this miserable place!" Dangler shouted.

§

The three youths stopped their horses. The riders approached behind them. They were surrounded. The rider before them was in full black armor atop a large horse. The caparison on the horse was unfamiliar to the youths. In the darkness, they could not see to whom it belonged.

The lone rider before them lifted his hand, causing the other riders to remain mounted, visors lowered, on their panting horses. A low flowing river separated them. The rider nudged his horse to enter into the river.

"Who are you?" Simon asked. "Let us pass."

But the rider remained silent.

Simon looked at Crispin, who sat in stunned silence. "Who are you?" Simon repeated. "We seek only to continue on."

The rider, obviously the leader, came closer. He was larger than he first appeared. With the visor of his helmet down and with the darkness, no eyes could be seen. The magnificent horse whinnied and shook its large head, sending its black mane back and forth.

Since the rider was closer, Simon could see the caparison on the horse was that of Ranvieg. He shivered, knowing that Rünbrior prison must be close. He also suspected these must be the men who captured Peter.

Mere seconds passed, yet it seemed like days as they all sat in silence on their horses near the river. As Simon turned to look at Annika, the lead rider raised his hand, causing the other riders to move forward. Some dismounted and began approaching the youths with swords drawn. The scraping of the metal swords removed from the sheaths made Annika's horse nervous and it lurched forward.

"Now!" Simon shouted as he nudged his horse, causing it to run. The others followed suit. He wasn't sure if this move would bring their lives to an end or not, but he knew they could not be captured here. The sudden movements caused the lead rider's horse to rear up and neigh loudly. But one rider grabbed Crispin by the collar, sending him to the ground.

Annika screamed and called, "Simon!"

He stopped his horse and turned it before entering the river, just in time to see Annika grabbed by a rider and thrown to the ground. Her horse ran off into the woods. Simon galloped back to the scene and dismounted. Running to Annika's aid, he too was grabbed by a rider.

The three were forced to stand before the leader with sword blades at their backs. Their heavy breathing and the waters of the river were the only sounds. Then the lead rider dismounted and strode toward the youths. He stood many inches taller than them and impressed them in his black armor. Taking Annika's coat into his gloved hand, he inspected the fabric. He did the same with Crispin. Silently, he nodded to his men.

Annika and Crispin struggled as they were forced toward the riders' horses.

Simon fought against the rider who grabbed him by the arm. "Where are you taking us?" he insisted.

But no one answered.

"I demand to know!"

"You do not make demands here!" One rider slapped Simon across the face.

Annika gasped. Simon gripped the knife attached to his belt, removed it from its small sheath, and with one movement thrust it into the rider's neck. The rider grabbed his throat as blood sprayed all over Simon's face. Annika turned her face away.

Simon was grabbed by two more riders as their leader mounted his horse.

"No!" Crispin yelled while the rider tried to force him onto the saddle of his horse. "Where are you taking us?"

Simon was now held by three strong men. His arms were forced behind his back as they led him to some trees. Crispin thrashed. trying to break free.

Annika mounted the horse with the rider behind her, making sure she did not try to escape. Watching Simon heading toward the trees, she shook, terrified at what they were going to do. The riders quickly leaned Simon against a tree trunk and tied his hands behind him. Once bound to the tree, another rider approached with his bow and arrow. He stood several feet away from Simon and loaded his bow. As he pulled the string tightly back with the arrow aimed directly at Simon's chest, Annika screamed, "No!" revealing that she was indeed a woman. "Let him go!"

The rider seated behind her placed his hand over her mouth. She struggled to get free. The bow remained pulled back. Simon eyes met Crispin's, then he closed them.

With fingers gripping the arrow and arm pulled back, the rider was just about to release the arrow when a loud screech from an owl pierced the silence. Everyone looked up to see a white owl flying down toward the Leader nearly missing his head. He raised his arms to avoid its sharp talons.

At that moment, three large trolls lunged out of the trees with battle cries, their swords and axes raised high above their heads.. One swung his ax down, sending a rider to his death. His body flew several feet. The archer, with bow lowered, stared at an approaching troll, who thrust his sword into the man's chest. Simon could only watch in amazement. The other trolls, apparently angered by the death of their friend, fought with the other riders.

Annika used the distraction to bite deep into the gloved hand of her captor, who yelped from the pain. Leaping off the saddle and onto the ground, she ran into the woods. Crispin also fought with his captor and managed to jump off the saddle toward Simon, who desperately struggled to escape the ropes that bound him. Crispin arrived to cut through the ropes with his knife.

"Come on!" Crispin motioned to Simon to follow him into the woods. The slaughter continued mere feet away. The trolls, in their anger, were leaving no riders alive, but the leader had successfully escaped by riding off through the river and into the woods on the other side.

Simon and Crispin rushed into the thickest part of the woods with the roars of the angry trolls behind them calling out for blood. Tree branches struck their faces as they ran in the dark, not knowing where they were going. The white owl screeched and the bird flew over them as though leading them. He followed it to a clearing where Annika waited. Her helmet was gone, and her cropped blonde hair was partly covering her sweaty face. She was crying, so Simon embraced her.

"Oh thank the heavens you are okay!" She gripped his shoulders. "I thought they were going to kill you."

"It's alright now," Simon reassured her. "It's alright."

Crispin stopped running and bent over trying to catch his breath. The white owl, its eyes glowing yellow, landed on a nearby tree for a second. Then it flew off into the night. The three stood panting in their exhaustion.

"What do we do now?" Crispin murmured. "The trolls will come looking for us soon."

Simon released Annika and nodded. "We must get out of here."

"But our horses remain back there," Annika said. "We cannot continue on foot."

"Those were Riders of Rünbrior," Simon explained. "The good news is that we are very near to Ranvieg. Our journey is coming to an end."

"But we haven't seen the White Forest yet," Crispin argued. "Surely we can't be close to Vulgaard."

"True," Simon said. "But those riders were definitely from Rünbrior."

"They were either going to kill us or take us to the prison," Annika said.

"I know." Crispin wiped his face with his sleeve. "I never thought I would say this, but thank goodness those trolls came when they did!"

Annika stared off into the distance. She shivered.

"Are you alright?" Simon asked, rubbing her shoulders. "We've got to get back and get our things. Annika needs to get warm."

The three headed back into the woods, navigating the trees with a light step. The fighting had ceased, and all was quiet again. Cautiously, they approached the scene of the slaughter and crouched down low so as not to be spotted. No live riders could be seen. Some horses remained nearby, calmly eating some grass.

Annika smiled. "Resilient beasts."

As they slowly came out from the bushes, Simon saw many dead bodies littering the ground. No trolls were killed, only riders. Simon quickly made his way over to his horses and inspected the saddle. All his belongings remained attached. Annika spotted her horse, but Crispin's was nowhere to be found. Annika mounted and offered her hand to Crispin to mount her horse with her. He acquiesced and grabbed her arm. Once seated behind her on the saddle, the two trotted around trying to locate his horse.

"Ready?" Simon whispered to them.

But the two continued to search nearby for his horse. Finally, the creature was spotted eating grass in the middle of the taller trees. Crispin leapt off Annika's horse and mounted his own.

"Don't worry," Simon told Annika. "We'll find a safe place to rest soon."

"Do not worry about me," Annika replied sternly. "I am fine. Let's go."

She nudged her horse and rode off in the lead. The others followed. Once across the river, the three disappeared into the woods on the other side. The sun inched its way over the distant horizon, sending some streaks of light through the thick clouds.

§

Nøel patted Peter's wound with the paste he made from the powder. Peter moaned, but immediately the bleeding stopped.

"Where am I?" Peter asked.

"Back in the cell." Nøel put more paste on the gash and it started to close.

Peter sighed. "I guess we lost the fight."

Nøel shook his head. "No one won this fight."

When the gash became nothing more than a cut, Nøel put the special powder away and leaned back. "I'm certain there is a reason for all these attacks. And I have a feeling it is more than Valbrand wagering against us."

Peter felt his cheek. The wound was completely closed, but it remained tender. "What do you mean?"

Nøel started to remove his armor. "Peter, I think Lord Bedlam is behind all this. After all, this is his prison in the mountains. I have a feeling he knows you are here and he wants to hurt you."

Peter looked away.

"I think your suspicions are correct, Peter. Damon is a part of this." Nøel set his breastplate against the wall and removed his sword belt. "He must be stopped."

38 WOLF TRAP

"We must stop now!" Annika shouted. "Our horses need rest!"

But the others galloped on ahead. Looking at her horse's neck wet with foamy sweat, she nudged her horse to run faster in order to catch up to Simon. Her horse passed Crispin, then reached Simon.

"Simon!" she yelled. "We must stop and give our horses rest!"

"No!" he replied. "They are fine. We must keep going!"

Frustrated, Annika grabbed the bridle of Simon's horse in a dangerous attempt to stop it. It worked, and the startled horse slowed down.

Panting, both horses chomped at their bits.

"What are you doing?" Simon asked.

"We must stop," Annika insisted.

"I tell you, the horses are fine! They are young and can run a good distance in a day," Simon said.

"Listen to me!" Annika warned. "I know horses. And one thing about a horse you should know is this: It will run until it dies just to please its master!"

Simon sat on his panting horse and shot her a perplexed look.

"I know because I have seen it," she explained.

By then, Crispin had arrived. "What's this?" Why have we stopped?"

"To rest," Simon explained.

Crispin nodded. "Oh good," he said as he dismounted. "I thought we'd never stop. My backside is so sore, I can hardly stand it any longer!" He said as he collapsed on the ground.

Annika laughed at Crispin then dismounted. She led her horse over to a small running stream for a drink. She surveyed the area, inspecting it for predators. "How long do you think we have been riding?"

"At least two days." Simon bent over the stream and lowered his leather pouch into the water to fill it. "And at least several hours since we headed out earlier this morning."

"It has to be nearly high noon," Crispin added gazing up at the sun. He unbuckled the saddle from his horse's back and removed it. He, too, led his horse over to the stream. "We must eat something."

"Well," Simon said as he removed his quiver and bows from his saddle, "I suppose we should go looking for rabbits again."

"Rabbit again?" Crispin moaned. "I can't eat yet another rabbit."

"Come now, Crispin." Annika rubbed her horse's back. "No complaining."

Crispin sighed. He rubbed his lower back, then removed his quiver and bow attached with small leather straps from his saddle. "I know, I know. It seems forever ago that I was with Lord Asgeir learning philosophy from him in his courts."

Annika smiled.

"He had the best food! Pheasants, roasted turkey, lime pie...pumpkin bread, fruit pies, bread pudding..." Crispin's voice faded as he walked away.

"Come now, we won't be gone long," Simon said. "Be watchful, Annika."

She nodded. Then the two disappeared into the trees, leaving her alone with the horses. "I wish I had hay for you, but all we have are these oats," she said to her horse. "Still, it is better than nothing."

The horses did find some green tender grass to feed on while Annika removed the saddle and then found a small grooming brush from her pack. She brushed each of the horses, causing them to feel more at ease with their new surroundings.

§

The white owl perched high on a tree, following the black wolf below as it trotted over piles of dried leaves soaked from recent rains. It sniffed the ground once in a while as though tracking a prey.

The wolf suddenly cried out in pain startling several small sparrows into the sky. The wolf frantically licked its wounded paw. A metal trap held its front lower leg. It tried desperately to pull itself free, but could not.

With the sound of human voices approaching, the wolf panted furiously and tried to free its leg. Unable to do so, the wolf transformed itself into a different form: a male Dwarf. He tried to pry open the jaws of the trap, but found it was no use. The trap was too small to cause serious damage, but big enough to make him unable to spy for Lord Bedlam. He heard the voices of the people getting closer. He stopped squirming and decided it was best to wait for them to come to him.

The owl flew off and found another perch nearby the three riders.

Simon and Crispin walked through the forest trying to be as quiet as they could. They listened for the slightest sound coming from the brush.

"I am so hungry," Crispin whispered.

"Yes, I know," Simon said. "How could I not know since you inform me of your hunger pains nearly every second?"

"Don't exaggerate," Crispin said.

The two continued their hunt with loaded bow in hand and ready for launch. Suddenly, a small rabbit scurried out from underneath a shrub causing Simon to release his arrow. The hunt was complete.

"I'm going on for another rabbit of my own," Crispin said.

"Oh, alright," Simon said as he picked up the dead rabbit by the ears. He removed the arrow and headed back to the stream. "Don't be long."

Crispin nodded and continued searching the brush as he walked. Soon he found himself alone in the woods. No longer feeling safe, he decided to return. But when he started back, he could not remember where he was. All the trees were similar, yet unfamiliar. Not wanting to panic, he took a deep breath then studied the paths. Then, the silence was broken by a snap of a twig nearby.

He dropped his bow and removed his knife from his belt. "Who goes there?" he asked. When no one answered, he began walking along a path he hoped headed toward the stream.

Another snap from behind.

Crispin turned and stood silent. "Who is there?" he asked again.

"Ouch!" came a strange voice from the brush. The shrubs shook.

"Who is that?" Crispin carefully approached the shrub with knife in hand.

"Tis I, a Dwarf," the voice answered. "I'm afraid I am stuck in this trap." He winced with pain.

Crispin made his way around the shrub and found a young Dwarf exactly as he had said: trapped in a small mechanism set out for rabbits.

"Funny," Crispin chuckled. "I was out hunting for rabbits and found you in a rabbit trap instead!"

"Yes," the Dwarf said. "Hilarious. Excuse me if I do not laugh, but as you can see I am in a bit of a tangle."

"Sorry," Crispin pried open the trap. "It is a good thing the trap is so small. A larger one would have taken off your foot for certain."

"Well, that is most certainly true!" The Dwarf hopped up. "Who may I thank for this new gift of freedom?"

Crispin smiled at the young Dwarf, whose head only reached up to his chest. "The name's Crispin."

"Thank you, Sir Crispin." The Dwarf held out his hand to shake. "My name is Toomley, son of Elon. I reside in Riverdale."

"Riverdale?" Crispin asked. "Are we anywhere near Riverdale?" He scanned the forest.

The Dwarf began to hobble away down a path. "Yes, we are near Riverdale!"

Crispin followed him. "Wait, I am lost and need to get back to my camp. It is near the stream. Can you help me get back?"

"Most certainly!" Toomley said. "Follow me."

The two walked down a path together.

"Why are you here in these woods?" Toomley asked.

"Oh well, it is a rather long story, but to make it short, we are heading to Vulgaard. Are we near Vulgaard yet?"

"Ha! No, not yet. You are at the base of the Ranvieg Mountains and need to pass through the White Forest. You do have a ways to go. The mountains are covered with snow already and it isn't even winter. Yes, I am afraid you are in for a long journey, my new friend!" the Dwarf explained.

"Wonderful." Crispin frowned.

It was only a bit farther until Crispin smelled the rabbit cooking over a fire and familiar voices. "Hello!" he called.

Annika and Simon replied.

"We made it," Crispin told Toomley. "Stay and join us for rabbit."

"Indeed!" Toomely answered.

They made their introductions and sat around the fire. Simon had already prepared the rabbit. It was skinned and the small carcass was impaled on a stick. It roasted while they questioned their guest. They each had many questions.

"So, how did you come to find yourself in the woods?" Annika asked.

"I hunt these woods all the time, but today I was just out for a stroll. I don't live far from here. There is a small village downstream where a few families live called Riverdale. I can take you there tomorrow. We are busy preparing for the long cold winter that is coming. Stocking up whatever food and wood we can find." He took out a pipe from his jacket made of hide. "So you are heading toward Vulgaard, are you?" Toomley asked.

Simon cringed, then glared at Crispin. "And how is it he knows our destination, Crispin?"

Crispin shrugged in embarrassment. "I supposed I mentioned it."

"Yes, we are headed toward Vulgaard," Simon said.

"Oh my, you have a long journey ahead of you," Toomely explained.

"Another long journey?" Annika asked. Already she sounded exhausted.

"Oh yes," he answered. "See those mountains ahead?"

They all nodded.

"Well, those are the Ranvieg Mountains. You'll have to climb those and on the other side is a small village. Then, past that village is the Vulgaard. But first you must ride through the White Forest. There you will discover the Elves of Vulgaard, I am sure."

"What do you mean?" Crispin asked.

"Well, I suppose they will discover you." Toomley chuckled. "There is no getting through the White Forest without the Elves noticing you as you pass."

The youths studied the mountains in the distance.

"They seem so very far away." Annika sighed and rubbed her neck.

"Aye." Toomley puffed on his pipe. "They are, but you'll be there before you know it."

"I am so very weary of all this riding." Annika sighed again.

Simon decided to change the subject. "Tell us of Riverdale."

Toomley puffed on his pipe for a moment. "I was born in Riverdale and have lived there all my life with my family, before the darkness came. Those were the blessed days of plenty. We were horse breeders. We sold our horses to the Elves. Made a good living at it too. I suppose all good things must come to an end." He rubbed his wounded leg.

"What happened to your leg?" Annika asked.

"It was caught in a wolf trap," Crispin said. "I freed him."

"Aye, he's a good lad. I'm afraid it is very sore." Toomley winced.

"I have something for that." Annika rose and grabbed her saddle bag. She showed Toomley the black box. "Inside is a special anodyne to help heal your leg."

"A what?" he asked.

"A healing salve," she said.

When she opened the small chest, the smell stunned Toomely, who held his nose. Annika used some of her drinking water to mix the paste in the palm of her hand. "Here, place this on the wound," she ordered.

Toomley warily took the salve. "Hmmm," he murmured. "Are you certain?"

Annika nodded.

"Oh, alright," he said as he rubbed the paste onto his wounded ankle. The sting made him wince and grumble under his breath. "I feel something." All three watched in wonder as the redness and swelling left his ankle. "Well, I'll be a donkey's colt!"

"See?" Annika showed him how the wound had healed.

"What is that salve?" he asked. She handed him the box. Toomley inspected it, and his eyebrows raised.

"Now, let's eat!" Simon said. He tore through the rabbit and handed everyone a piece.

"So, someone gave you this powder?" Toomley asked.

Annika nodded her head. "Yes, our friend, Theo."

"Then, my Lord was right." Toomley's voice changed. It sounded much like a low growl. "It *is* you."

Annika stopped smiling and she backed away from the Dwarf.

"Here, have a leg," Simon handed Toomely the meat.

Suddenly, before their eyes, the Dwarf transformed into the black wolf and howled. The three youths jumped back. Annika screamed. The white owl flew off its perch.

"Run!" Simon shouted.

§

"I think Dangler's right. Bedlam wants me alive. I'm worth more to him alive than dead," Peter said. "One thing is for certain. He doesn't want us to win our freedom."

"You must try and eat something." Nøel handed Peter some boiled meat and a piece of bread.

"It's no use. I don't know how much more I can take." Peter bent over and exhaled.

"You must remain strong!" Nøel encouraged him. "These attacks are all part of your trials, Peter. The weaker you become, the more vulnerable your mind will become to Bedlam. He can read your thoughts, you know. He is trying to break you now that he knows you are the Prince of Illiath."

"I know." Peter grabbed his ribs.

"What's the matter? Sore ribs?" Nøel asked.

Peter nodded and grimaced from the pain.

Nøel looked for the healing powder. "I know Bedlam is watching us. He must be. You have to remain strong. Think of your father. Think of your kingdom! You cannot let him stop you."

Nøel had started to make the paste again when Peter heard a sound coming from outside the cell wall. "Listen!"

Nøel sat quiet. "I heard nothing."

Peter slowly stood and inched his way over to the window. "Help me move the cot over to the window," he said.

Nøel brought the cot over to the window. With his bruised body, Peter struggled to step onto it. He looked right and left, and then right in front of him on the same dead tree, landed the white owl.

Peter smiled. "It's the white owl," he whispered.

"The white owl?" Nøel asked.

"Yes. I knew it would come again."

Nøel moved away toward his cot, where he sat down. "What is it about the owl that is so special?" he asked.

Peter stepped down from the cot and sat upon it to rest. "It isn't just an owl."

"What do you mean?"

"It is the Dragon of the forest," Peter said with a grin.

"What?" Nøel tilted his head. "Peter, the Dragon of the forest is—*no more*."

Peter raised a finger. "That is what I once thought."

"Peter, I know you are weary from battle, but try to hear me. The Dragon of the forest is no longer." Nøel knelt beside Peter. "I know you miss it. I know you are probably thinking of home, but listen to me when I say that the owl you see out there in the night is not the Dragon of the forest. It is only a bird"

"No, that is not true," Peter insisted. "It is the Dragon. It has come back to help us."

Nøel leapt to his feet. "Stop this! Peter look at me!"

Peter obeyed.

"I saw the Dragon fight Caragon's black dragon there in the desert. I watched it die. I saw its blood run red onto the dirt as the Baroks attacked it. I saw it breathe its last breath just as you did!"

Peter listened.

"Peter, I tell you, the Dragon is *no more*," Nøel said.

"I know it died! I watched it die too. I saw the blood too."

"Then, why—" Nøel asked.

"But I tell you it lives again!" Peter said. "I spoke with it in the forest before I left home."

Nøel looked into Peter's eyes. "I can see that you are being sincere, but.."

279

"It is here to help us," Peter continued.

"Help us?"

"Yes!"

"*Help us?*" Nøel pushed away from Peter. "Then why won't it show itself? It has the power to free you and end all this. If the Dragon still lives, then why? Why does it allow you to be attacked so relentlessly?"

"I don't know. I should have died a long time ago in this prison. I should be dead now! But I am alive! The Dragon said this is my trial that I must endure."

Nøel rubbed his forehead as though it burned.

"Trust me," Peter said. "The time will come when the Dragon will show itself again and end all this."

Nøel looked at Peter.

"You must believe," Peter said. He winced from the soreness in his side.

"Peter, I do not understand what you are saying. But I believe that *you* believe the Dragon of the forest lives. And because you are my sovereign, I will honor what you say," Nøel said.

"Every knight of the realm must endure his trial." Peter placed his hand on his chest. "This is *my* trial."

"I have pledged my life to your father, and one day soon I will pledge my life to you as my King," Nøel said. "I do not understand, but I will accept what you say."

Peter stood on the cot again and peered out the window. The owl gazed over at him then flew away.

Nøel helped Peter move his cot back over to the wall.

"You must rest now," Nøel said. "If I know Valbrand, we will fight again in the arena sooner than we think."

§

That night, Peter fell into a deep sleep and dreamt of the Dragon.

Suddenly, a loud crashing sound coming from outside the cell woke him. He turned toward Nøel who was also now wide awake. His face was barely lit by the stove's fire glow.

Then, silence. Peter held his breath and waited.

The door burst open and in came two guards who ran over to Peter.

"What is this?" Nøel grabbed his blanket, threw it over the guards' heads, and slammed them together knocking them both unconscious. "Fools!"

When the guards began to stir and wake up, Nøel removed the blanket and saw one guard was bleeding from his mouth and the other had his nose broken. They tried to stand, but Nøel shoved them back down.

"Stay there!" he ordered them.

Peter stood over the guards. "Why are you attacking us in the night?"

One guard mumbled something, but Peter couldn't understand. "What?"

"We are following orders," the guard said through swollen lips.

"Whose orders?" Nøel asked.

The guards said nothing.

Nøel looked as though he knew the answer.

"Whose orders?" Peter asked. He wanted to ask another question, but hesitated. He feared he already knew the answer. But he decided to ask it anyway. "Who sent you?"

The guard looked up at Peter.

"Lord Bedlam sent them," came a familiar voice from behind.

Peter turned when he heard the voice. He stared at Damon, who wore the armor of Valbrand's guards.

"You?" Peter asked incredulously.

"Yes." Damon entered the room. He snapped his fingers, and the two guards hobbled to attention. Then he meandered over to Peter.

"You're working for Bedlam now?" Peter asked.

"Of course." Damon placed his hand on Peter's shoulder. Peter quickly moved away. "I have been working, *spying*, for Bedlam the entire time you've been here."

It took all the strength Peter had left not to wrap his hands around Damon's throat. But he did not move.

"Well done, Peter. I thought for sure the guards would beat you. But your senses are alert." Daman began his inspection of the room. "What's this?" Grabbing Peter's pillow, he picked it up and revealed *The Dragon Chronicles* book. Damon grinned. Then, his gaze focused on the golden compass. Swiftly, he reached for it.

"No!" Peter lunged, but the guards quickly pulled out their swords. One pointed at Nøel and the other at Peter.

Damon laughed. "I'm impressed." He inspected the compass. "This must be one important trinket if you are so willing to risk your life for it."

Peter fumed.

Nøel stared at the sword near his throat.

"I'll consider it a gift," Damon said as he walked away.

"Our time will come." Peter scowled at Damon.

Damon merely sneered back.

"Your plan has failed. I have withstood the attacks in the arena and will continue to be victorious," Peter exclaimed.

"We shall see. You have passed *this* test. That is true. But you and I will have our time in the arena again. I guarantee it." Damon chuckled. Before leaving the room, he stopped. "Will you be able to pass *that* test I wonder?"

"Of course," Peter answered. "Nervous?"

Damon frowned. Then he and the guards left the room.

"So, Bedlam has his spies." Peter faced the locked cell door. "He has me in the arena for his purpose."

"Yes," Nøel said. "He knows he cannot kill you, but he can hurt you and make you desire to die."

Peter kicked over his cot. "My mother's compass! I must get it back."

Nøel took Peter's shoulders. "You will. You will get it back."

"You don't understand." Peter ran his hands through his hair.

"Remember what you told me about the owl? Everything will work out. The anger and hatred you feel now?"

"Yes?"

"Use it when you are in the arena again," Nøel said. "It will give you the strength you need to win."

Peter exhaled. "You are right." His jaw clenched. "This will all work out in the end. I must remember this."

39 THE WHITE FOREST

The wolf stared at Annika. Its red eyes contrasted with its coarse black fur. It growled and slowly approached.

Annika ran to her horse, mounting it as the wolf grabbed her pant leg with its jaws and almost pulled her off the saddle. Her horse reared up and kicked its front legs. The wolf let go and crouched down low to the ground, keeping a safe distance from the horses' hooves. Behind them, more wolves approached, snarling, their red eyes glowing through the trees.

She looked at Simon whose horse snorted and stomped at the ground in defiance. "Should we run off?" she asked.

"Follow me!" Simon galloped passed the stunned wolf. It tried to jump up and bite Simon's leg as he passed by.

Annika and her horse kept up with Simon. The wolves growled behind them—some howled as though calling other wolves to the fight. But they kept riding.

"We're going the wrong way!" she called. They were leaving the river far behind and heading back to the small village they had left before.

"Just keep riding!" Simon called.

Annika glanced back. "They're not following us anymore!"

Simon slowed his horse down, as did Annika. Together they halted, breathing hard, along with their horses. Annika scanned around for any sign of Crispin but could find no evidence of him.

"We must cross the river and head toward the White Forest," Simon said.

"Should we try it?" Annika tried to catch her breath.

"We've no choice." Simon turned his horse and trotted toward the river, swollen from all the melting snow and rain.

Annika followed, keeping an eye out for the wolves. "Where's Crispin?"

"Here I am!" Crispin came galloped up to them with wolves close behind.

"Cross the water!" Simon nudged his horse into the water. It lunged in and the water grew deeper and deeper. The horse tried to maneuver through the water. The rocks were slippery, but it kept going.

"Steady, boy," Simon said, the icy water flowed up to his boots.

Annika watched as Simon's horse waded all the way to the other side. Nudging her horse through the water, she looked back to see if any wolves had gained on them. Crispin and his horse were beginning to wade through the water as Annika made it to the other side.

"Let's try and make it to the bottom of the Ranvieg Mountains," Simon said.

"Wait!" came a shout from behind. It was Crispin. His horse had lost its footing in the water and was struggling. "Help!"

But it was too late. Crispin and his horse were swept down river.

"No!" Annika screamed. "Simon, we've got to go after him!"

Simon tied his horse to a branch then raced down river. Annika followed after him. They searched the river as they ran, stumbling over rocks and dead tree limbs along the bank.

"Do you see him?" Annika shouted above the raging waters. "The waters are getting rough."

Simon stopped. "The current is stronger. I fear a waterfall is ahead!"

"Then we must hurry!" Annika raced passed Simon. Together they sprinted along the bank, calling Crispin's name and dodging tree limbs.

Finally, Annika hopped up onto a large rock protruding from the river water. Simon leapt up next to her. Ahead was the drop-off...and no Crispin.

"I hoped he'd be hanging onto a log or tree branch or something!" Annika cried. But there was no sign of their friend.

"Come." Simon yanked her arm. "Let's go back to the horses."

At first, Annika refused to go. Then, she relented, realizing it was no use. Crispin was gone. The long walk back to the horses was torture. No words were spoken. Annika wept, but Simon refrained from looking back, as though he knew she needed some time to weep.

Ahead their horses waited. Simon untied his and started to mount.

"Should we ride along the river?" Annika asked.

Simon cocked his head. "Why?"

Annika hung her head. "To look for him."

"You saw the waterfall." Simon mounted his horse and adjusted the reins. "It's no use. We have to keep going."

"Maybe we should wait here, just in case—"

"Annika! He's gone. The sooner we accept this, the better. Now we must get going before those wolves cross the river and come after us again."

"How can you say that?" She hurried to Simon's horse and grabbed the reins. "How can you just give up like that? He's our friend!"

Simon closed his eyes and exhaled. "I know he is our friend! But we are also on the run from those beasts, and if we stay here any longer, we could be killed. What good would that do?"

Annika let go of the reins. She turned away in a huff.

"Besides," Simon said to her back. "Crispin would want us to continue. He'd do the same thing!" Simon heeled his horse trotted off deeper into the woods.

Annika grabbed the horn of her saddle and pulled herself up. As she turned her horse, something in the bushes ahead caught her eye. "Crispin?" Then, horrified, she called, "Run!" as she heeled her horse to make it gallop. Instead, it reared and threw Annika to the ground.

Baroks ran through the bushes toward Annika. Terrified, she watched as Simon removed his sword, leapt off his horse, and swung at the first creature that lunged for Annika. She screamed and rolled over in time to miss Simon's sword slicing at the Barok. Its head rolled off onto the dirt, but several more rushed toward them.

Annika ran to her saddle, removing her sword barely in time to swing at the Barok coming for her. But her sword met with metal and the creature's scowl. It leaned in. Annika closed her eyes from the putrid smell of its breath and the drool. It laughed at her. She shoved it back, then struck again, but its sword stopped her. This time, Annika kicked it in the chest, sending it to the dirt. With one thrust, she pierced the creature with her sword, ending the fight.

Simon fought with two creatures, so Annika ran over to help. "I've got this!" he shouted. "Ride off! Now!"

"You can't hold these monsters off by yourself!" Just then, one Barok swung at her. Annika ducked, pivoted, and sliced the Barok's head off.

Simon's jaw dropped.

"See? I told you I can help." Annika wiped the blood off her face.

A loud roar came from the bushes. The Baroks ran off. Simon and Annika stood back to back, panting and wondering what happened.

A frantic Crispin emerged from the bushes yelling and waving his arms above his head like a wild man "Run! Hurry!"

"Crispin?" Annika called as he ran by her.

"I fooled those creatures for now, but they'll be back! Run!"

Simon waved to Annika to get on her horse. "Do as he says!" He mounted his horse and galloped off. Swiftly catching up to Crispin, he reached out his arm, and helped him onto the saddle. Soon, Annika was riding next to them through the forest, leaving the treacherous river waters far behind.

§

"My Lord," Will bowed as Bedlam entered the hallway.

"What is it?" Bedlam stormed passed Will toward the Duke's private quarters, which used to be Alexander's Solar. He hastily removed his gloves. A servant followed with his dragon head cane. Bedlam took it then seated himself in a large cushioned chair.

Will closed the door once the servant exited the room. "King Eulrik paid me a visit. Something needs to be done about him and soon. His incessant whining and complaining irritates me to no end. He demands answers."

Bedlam exhaled. "This is why you summoned me here? King Eulrik?"

"Yes."

"So deal with it." Bedlam waved his hand dismissively. "Why must I be involved?"

Will cocked his head. "He told me you agreed that I would marry his daughter, Esmerelda. Is this true?"

Bedlam smirked, then stood. "I told him what I had to tell him in order to make him come along with our plan." He picked up his gloves and walked past Will toward the door.

"But am I to actually *marry* this woman?" Will asked.

Bedlam opened the door, and headed out into the hallway with a confused Will following. "I don't expect you to do anything you do not wish to do."

"He will continue to harass me," Will argued. "I cannot deal with him any—"

"Then kill him." Bedlam stopped, handed his cane to the waiting servant, and pivoted toward Will. "Settle it once and for all."

Will did not respond.

"What's the matter? Aren't you a knight?" Bedlam chuckled and put on his gloves. "Haven't you been trained to kill?"

"Well, yes, but—"

"But what?" Bedlam motioned for his cane. "You have my powers, you have my blessing. Do it. Kill him." He turned again to leave.

Will bowed.

"It will send a much needed message to the other rulers," Bedlam said. "If they mess with you it is the same as if they mess with me. Understand?"

"Yes, my Lord," Will said.

"Good. I will return soon from Hildron. Things are going very well there." Bedlam strode into the courtyard.

Will watched him for a few seconds then headed back to the Solar.

40 FACING DAMON

Thousands of spectators filled the arena halls yet again. The cheers and calls for battle grew louder as the fighters entered. Peter turned his gaze toward all the other fighters nearby dressed in their black armor holding their shields and bucklers. Damon was not among them.

The fighters placed their helmets on their heads, getting ready to head out to the arena. Already the crowd shouted for battle.

Peter sighed. His body ached from exhaustion. *Fighting dragons will have to end soon. We must make our escape.*

Valbrand stood at his usual perch high above the arena. "I don't care what Lord Bedlam says. This is my doing. I created all this." He spread his arms wide over the sight. "And I'm not about to share my fortune with any of the fighters," he told his assistant. "…or with *him.*"

The goblin nodded.

Peter stood still listening to the roars of the crowd. The pungent smell of sweat permeated the place. He stared at the sword in his hand knowing that each battle could bring him that much closer to escape and freedom. The sword hilt, cheaply made, was worn. The leather straps that covered the metal handle were brittle and tattered. He gazed at his gloved hand and noticed the leather gloves were worn as well. Calluses had formed on his hands. Beads of sweat ran down his nose and lips. He tasted the salt.

He looked over and saw Nøel waving for him to come forward, closer to the dirt of the arena floor. Peter obeyed.

"What is it?" he asked his friend.

"Can you hear it?" Nøel asked.

Peter concentrated, but with his helmet on, he couldn't breathe let alone hear anything over the shouts of the spectators.

"What do you hear?" Nøel asked again.

Nøel took his helmet off signaling Peter to do the same. With helmet off, Peter inhaled the cooler air deeply feeling it enter his lungs. Then he strained to hear the sound. It rose from the rear of the arena near the cave. But only darkness could be seen. Then, he heard it: the slight growl of their foe coming from the darkness yet again.

"Sounds like a young one this time," Peter said to Nøel.

Nøel agreed.

"We'll have to be ready." Nøel put his helmet back on. Peter did the same. Nøel raised his hand. Peter grasped it. "Together we can do this," Nøel said. "Right?"

"Right!" Peter agreed.

The guards approached them. The battle would begin.

Younger dragons meant swifter battles. Younger dragons flew faster and used their brute strength over their underdeveloped fire-breathing skills. This meant less hiding behind shields and more exercising of skills. Peter raised the metal visor of his helmet as he and Nøel walked with the guards.

"After this fight," Nøel said. "We'll make our escape."

Peter squinted. "What?"

Nøel nodded his head toward the cave where the dragons entered. "There. We'll kill the beast, make our way toward the cave, and then fight our way out."

Peter studied his friend's face. He was serious.

"They have horses right outside the cave," he continued. "We can easily make our escape."

"But how?" Peter asked. He saw the guards coming.

"Trust me," Nøel said. "We will use the dragon that comes out of that cave to escape."

Peter observed the cave.

"Follow my lead," Nøel said.

The guards approached. "Who will fight first?" the guard shouted. The other guards laughed.

We will, of course, Peter thought. He gazed up at the highest point in the arena where the warden usually sat. There Valbrand was, seated with his guests. Loud horns signaled the beginning of the battle.

"Let's give them a show," Nøel suggested.

Peter smirked and gripped his sword tightly as he gazed up at the crowd. They cheered wildly and threw rocks at the arena floor.

"The spectators are crazy today. Let's get this over quickly," Nøel shouted.

Together they entered the arena floor. The roar of the captured dragon started low, but rose higher and higher. Peter knew it could see them entering the arena floor. Soon, the ropes that held it down would be severed, and the monster would join them in their quest for freedom.

The dragon, a young and lithe Draco, did not disappoint. As soon as the ropes were severed, it lunged forward to the thrill of the crowd. Peter and Nøel braced themselves for the clash. The beast studied the two fighters before it. Then, it turned to the crowd of spectators who cheered. Peter stood amazed at how the dragon seemed to know the arena was for show.

Its roar made Peter jump. The young dragon was more ferocious that he had originally thought. Without hesitation, it came running toward them with open jaws.

Nøel raised his sword. "Get ready!"

The beast snapped at Peter with its razor sharp teeth. He slashed at it with his sword, but the dragon swerved out of the way of Peter's blade. It was too quick. Peter and Nøel swiped their swords at the beast over and over until the heaviness of their metal swords made their arms ache.

"Enough of this!" Nøel shouted. "Follow me!"

Peter admired Nøel's courage.

He motioned for Peter to run with him around to the back of the dragon. That's when Peter saw the cave. Indeed there were men mounted on horses near the opening, where he and Nøel could make their way out.

The dragon bawled at the crowd mockingly and flapped its wings sending dirt up into the stands. They threw fruit at it, hitting its snout. As the spectators laughed, the Draco spewed its fire at them. The people screamed and ran.

Peter stood ready with his sword. Nøel inspected the cave. There were only a few guards there, but they stood near the cave opening.

The dragon spun around and struck Nøel with its tail, sending him flying across the dirt. Then, it gazed at Peter, who stood his ground. He raised his shield, again expecting fire, but the dragon continued to snap at Peter with its powerful jaws. Peter had to move quickly to keep from losing a leg or an arm. His body ached from all the leaping back and forth to keep away from the dragon. It never relented.

Nøel got to his feet and tried to attack the dragon from the side. It used its wings to protect itself from the swords and its tail swung around again. This time, Nøel avoided it.

Peter could barely catch his breath. He felt the muscles in his back pull. "This isn't working!"

The crowd booed. They wanted blood.

Nøel ran around to where Peter was fighting the dragon. When the beast saw him, it began to inhale. "Here we go!" Nøel shouted.

They ran into the cave and hid behind their shields, hoping the metal would withstand the intense heat. The dragon spewed forth its fire and approached the two fighters still hiding behind their shields. Because the dragon was young, it couldn't hold the stream of fire as long as the mature beasts. When the flames ceased, Nøel knew it was time to act.

But Damon ran onto the arena floor, causing the crowd to erupt in cheers as though he was the favored to win.

Peter looked at Nøel.

The dragon turned its head to see Damon challenging it to a fight.

"What do we do now?" Peter shouted.

Nøel looked at the cave, then back at the dragon. He seemed confused as to whether they should try and escape or not.

"Hurry! What do we do?" Peter shouted again.

The dragon roared and headed toward Damon. The crowd loved the action. Valbrand scowled at them. Peter knew they were losing the fight and the chance to escape.

"We should escape now," Peter decided, "while Damon has the attention!"

But Nøel said, "No, not this time. Come on! Fight!"

Peter gathered up as much strength as he could. Together, he and Nøel ran toward the dragon as the crowd hailed the sight of three fighters going against the young dragon. Peter swiped at the tail before it could strike. The beast turned around in time for Peter to slice at its face.

Damon, sword in hand, shot Peter an look of outrage. "This is my fight!" He started toward the dragon.

"We must win this before Damon does." Nøel raised his sword and threw it at the dragon's chest.

Nøel's aim was true. The blade sunk deep into the beast's chest and it roared from the pain, trying to remove the blade with its front claws to no avail. Peter moved to the front in time for a final stream of flame. The men hid behind their shields one last time as the beast fell to the ground.

The spectators applauded the victory. But Damon stood fuming.

Nøel and Peter watched the dragon slowly die. Then, relieved that the battle was finally over, they bent over and tried to catch their breath.

"Finally." Peter stretched his sore back. "I don't know how many more of these battles I can take."

They looked at the spectators who stood with their arms raised. Some threw flowers at the men. From the balcony, Valbrand scowled at the sight.

Nøel grinned. "I love it when Valbrand is disappointed!"

Peter laughed.

Then Damon approached.

Nøel turned to Damon. "So sorry to have stolen the show."

Damon, eyes narrowed and face reddened with rage, remained silent.

"Another victory for us," Peter said to him.

Together, Nøel and Peter started to walk off the arena.

Nøel pointed at Valbrand. "Not sure if he knew what we were up to or not."

Peter studied the Warden.

"But we couldn't take a chance," Nøel said.

Valbrand's eyes never left them as they walked. Peter sensed something was wrong. He swiveled in time to see Damon following behind Nøel. As Nøel started to remove his armor, that was the opening Damon needed. When Nøel was exposed, Damon thrust his sword into Nøel's side.

"No!" Peter screamed.

The crowd gasped at the unexpected sight. Damon withdrew the blade and came at Peter. Nøel fell to his knees grabbing his side as his blood flowed from the wound. Peter pivoted toward Damon. Without a sword but with his anger burning. Peter ran toward his nemesis.

Damon thrust his sword, but Peter was able to move out of the way in time. He grabbed Damon's neck and threw him to the ground. Damon blacked out for a second. Peter took the small blade out from his boot to stab his nemesis, raised the blade high, and started to bring it down, but Dangler grabbed his arm. Peter was only able to slice Damon's shoulder. He screamed from the wound.

The guards ran out and grabbed Peter and Damon.

"Get them out of here!" Dangler ordered.

Nøel's remained on the arena floor, crumpled up in agony. Peter tried to run out to him, but the guards held him.

"Let me go!" he shouted. He looked wildly at Dangler, who reluctantly nodded for the guards to release Peter. He ran over to his friend.

Nøel's face was pale and his eyes distant. "Peter," he gasped. Blood trickled from between his lips.

Peter grabbed his hand. "I'm here, my friend."

"Peter, you are alright?"

"Yes." Peter tried not to weep. He felt too angry, but the hot tears came anyway. "Hang on. You're going to be alright. We'll get you some help."

Nøel shook his head. "I should have watched Damon." He tried to chuckle. "Never take your eyes off an opponent."

"You fought well. Damon sneaked up on you."

This time Nøel looked deep into Peter's eyes. "This is your time."

"Yes, I know," Peter blinked back the tears.

"No, Peter, you were meant for greatness, not this ridiculous arena."

Peter nodded.

"You must escape."

"I will."

"I'm sorry I failed you," Nøel said.

"No, don't say that." Tears brimmed in Peter's eyes. "You saved me. You helped me more than you'll ever know."

"You are meant to be King, Peter. You are meant for more than these battles in this arena."

Peter understood.

"Valbrand knows this," Nøel's voice was a whisper. "Bedlam knows this."

The tears stained Peter's face.

"Do *you* know this?" Nøel asked.

"Yes." Peter wiped his face.

"Good." Nøel coughed up blood. "I was wrong before, Peter. Don't let your anger and desire for revenge destroy you. Remember *why* you are here."

"I remember."

"This is your trial," Nøel whispered. "This is your time." He squeezed Peter's hand.

"I understand. Hang on. I'll get you the special powder. You'll be all right. It will heal you. Just hold on…"

But Nøel didn't speak. His mouth remained opened, but no words came. Instead, he closed his eyes and breathed his last breath there in the Great Arena.

Peter bowed his head. "No," he cried. Nøel's hand released and dropped to the ground. Peter sat there beside his friend. He couldn't help but remember when the Dragon died. "Don't leave me."

"Good," a voice from behind said.

Peter looked up and saw a satisfied Damon standing over him. The crowds had left, and the guards were dragging the dead dragon off the floor.

Peter got to his feet.

"Now you know that I will not be defeated in this arena," Damon said. "No matter what."

Peter stepped toward him, but the last words from Nøel stopped him from acting.

Damon laughed. "You're pathetic."

Peter just breathed in and out.

Trust me," Damon said as he left the arena. "We will have the last battle."

Peter saw that Dangler watched the scene. The old man seemed worried. Peter approached him. "What will be done with Nøel's body?"

Dangler looked down. "It will be for the Warden to decide, but—"

"But what?" Peter asked.

Dangler sighed. "Dead fighters are never shown respect in death."

Peter understood. He looked back at his friend. "He was more than a fighter. He was a knight of the Royal Realm of King Alexander."

Dangler placed his hand on Peter's shoulder. "I know," he whispered. "Come now. You need to get your rest."

Peter coolly removed the hand from his shoulder and walked to Nøel's body. He stood over it for a second, then stormed off to his cell.

§

"What happened?" Annika asked Crispin, who rode with Simon.

"I don't know!" he replied. "One moment I was drowning…the next I was lying on the bank of the river."

Annika wrinkled her brow, trying to understand. She looked behind them, then pulled on her reins to stop her horse.

Simon did the same. "It seems we've lost them."

Crispin grasped his chest. "My heart feels like it's going to burst."

"You don't remember what happened?" Annika asked.

Crispin shook his head. "All I know is that the river was pushing me under…I struggled to stay afloat…my horse was gone. I thought I would die. Then, all of a sudden, something grabbed me!"

"What?" Simon asked.

"I know it sounds strange, but something grabbed my tunic and put me on the river bank. And that's when the Baroks saw me. I ran for my life!"

A loud screech came from above. Annika looked up and noticed a white owl perched on a high branch. "Look!" She pointed. "An owl. And look at the trees. They are long and white.

"I believe we've made it to the White Forest," Simon said.

"The White Forest," Annika whispered, observing the surroundings. "The trees are beautiful."

Crispin sighed and shook his head. "You're such a romantic. Even as we ride in fear of our lives, you find the beauty in our dire surroundings. Amazing."

"You need to look around more often. This forest is so beautiful compared to the other places we have been through," she said.

"After what I've been through, I believe I have seen enough, thank you *very* much," Crispin said.

Simon quietly chuckled under his breath, but stayed focus on the path ahead, gripping his sword even tighter.

Soon, night fell around them.

"Perhaps it would be best if we kept riding through this forest instead of resting here for the night," Simon suggested.

§

The three friends rode for almost two days after finding Crispin. The way had been as treacherous as the Dwarf, Toomely, had warned.

Annika observed her horse's ears. They would bend backwards if the animal sensed or smelled a predator nearby. The ears remained straight and alert. "All is well for now."

"All I can think of is food," Crispin exhaled. "Lord Asgeir's court had the best food!"

"Yes, we know," said Simon.

"Lamb stew, new potatoes, fish soup." Crispin listed all the foods he could remember. "And the desserts!"

"Yes, we know," Annika said.

"Bread pudding, fruit pies, and butter cookies that melt in your mouth!"

Annika rolled her eyes.

All three went silent. The leafless trees reached much higher than any forest of Théadril. They branched out, growing thinner and thinner the higher they grew. Simon silently performed his watchman duties as leader of the group with Crispin sitting behind him, keeping vigilant watch as well.

The group rode on. The cold and constant riding of their long arduous journey made them weary. Each had sores from sleeping on the ground and their fair share of scratches and scars from riding through thorn bushes and low hanging tree limbs.

Finally after several hours, Annika broke the silence. "We could use a song," she said in a small voice. "What about an old song as old as Théadril itself?"

Simon chuckled. "Why not?"

"A song?" Crispin asked hesitantly. "Now? Is that all you can think of? Singing?" He shook his head. "I'm sleepy enough as it is." He yawned.

"Give us a song, then," Simon said as he continued his vigilant watch.

With a soft voice, Annika began to sing a song she remembered from her childhood.

Of dales and hills stretching far and wide,
Of paths leading homeward bound,
I cry for home as I ride singing
Filled with eternal love ringing.
In my deepest heart.

Oh for the sun and the hope that it brings,
I ride on to hope's ending,
Of paths leading home I come singing.
In my deepest heart.

Her song rose over the trees and softly echoed into the night. The breeze chilled their faces. Annika sniffled as a tear slowly ran down her cold face. She raised a hand to wipe it.

Night surrounded them.

"I cannot remember the next verse," she sighed as they rode deeper into the woods.

"It was lovely," Simon said.

A mist appeared all around them enveloping the horses' hooves

"Thank you," Annika answered, her head hung low. She touched her face and noticed it was so cold and moist. The air began to change. "The forest path is taking us higher."

"Yes. We are entering mountain country. The land of the Elves." Simon's voice sounded uncertain.

Annika studied the white trees—thicker now and more prominent in the night. "Without the breeze, I don't feel as cold. I smell snow."

"Me, too." Crispin yawned again. "I'm not sure we will make it to the other side of these woods."

"We'll try and get as far as we can." Simon raised his eyes to the sky for a moment, then back to the darkness that lay between the trees.

Annika's flesh tingled. She gripped her sword handle with stiff, frozen fingers, the reins clasped tightly in the other hand. Blood suddenly surged through her exhausted body as she mustered enough strength to squeeze the saddle with her thighs, signaling to her horse to be ready at any moment to gallop away. The horse neighed, sending a few sparrows into flight. The other horses responded as well.

"My horse's ears are bent back," Annika whispered. "Something is approaching."

"Shh. Something is watching us," Simon whispered. "In the trees…"

Crispin glanced behind them and grabbed the hilt of his sword. The horse neighed and nodded its head in agitation. With legs barely able to lift out of the snow, its body grew wearier from the climb and from carrying two young boys.

Searching the darkness, Annika pointed. "There!" She pulled sharply on the reins, causing her horse to stop suddenly.

"What is it?" Simon asked, forcing his horse to stop.

All three riders sat motionless.

"I saw two eyes glowing from between the trees!" Annika gestured to her right. The snow fell heavily around them, transforming the dirt path to an icy white. The breath of their horses could be clearly seen in the night air.

"Ride!" Simon urged.

They galloped along the path, sending fresh snow flying into the air behind them. The road climbed and the rocks became larger and larger, making it harder for their horses to gallop.

"Come on!" Crispin shouted. "Faster!"

Just then, Annika heard it. The gurgling sound started low between the trees then grew as it spread all around them…a low, throaty growl that frightened the horses as they ran to get away from it.

"What is it?" Annika cried.

"I don't know, nor do I want to find out," Simon called. "Just ride!" He drew his sword from its sheath and gripped the reins with his free hand.

Crispin removed his sword. Annika followed suit. She was not used to holding a sword while riding and struggled to maintain control of her horse. The heavy blade awkwardly jerked back and forth. She leaned forward with the momentum of her horse's body. Her wrist ached as she tried to grip the sword, but it was no use. With frozen fingers bare in the night air, she couldn't hold tightly enough to the leather grip while her horse moved forward in large leaps.

"Oh no!" she shouted. She watched the metal blade fall to the ground, bounce in the snow, and hit a rock. She pulled on the reins stopping her horse as it reared up from confusion. It did not want to stop. With nostrils flaring, it could smell the predator nearby. But Annika's command was stronger.

She leapt off but held to its reins. The boys continued to ride. Her horse jerked with its neck. It tried to get its owner to move, but she pulled it toward her as she tried to reach for the sword lying nearby.

"Hold still," she ordered as she yanked the horse. But its scream sent chills down her spine. It was neither a normal whinny nor a neigh, but a loud scream as the horse's eyes grew large. Its ears were bent back and its nostrils flared. Annika knew that her horse was mad with fright. She turned to see what was behind her.

There, in the snow-covered path, was a creature staring at her with red glowing eyes and breath panting in the night air. She could hear her own breathing, in rhythm with her own horse's breath. She heard not the sound of more footsteps around her. She heard not the stomps of heavier animals, but the sound of paws in the freshly fallen snow. More eyes glowed red between the dark trees, and the creature stood but a few feet away from her.

Covered with thick dark fur that gave it the look of a wolf, it was much larger and thicker in size, and its growl revealed sharp teeth wet with drool. The red eyes stared at her, daring her to make a move as its brothers quietly surrounded her, studying her as if they could see the blood running through her veins. Not wanting to precipitate a fight of any sort, Annika did not move. It made sense that they wanted to attack her. She was the weakest in the group.

"Zadoks," she whispered. She had heard about them from Peter's tales of battle and Crispin's encounters. "I've never seen one up close before."

They sniffed the air as though they smelled her fear and that of her horse. Annika averted her eyes to try and spot where the sword had fallen. Then she returned her gaze to the Zadok panting a few feet away from her.

"Easy, boy," she whispered to the horse as she slowly bent down to pick up her sword. The creature growled louder and moved a step toward her outstretched hand. It was no use. The sword was too far away. It would have to remain on the ground. She straightened up and kept her eyes on the beast as her horse continued to tug on the reins in her hands. The other Zadoks had encircled Annika and her horse and growled their approval to their leader.

The beast stared down the prey. Its bony frame revealed hunger and desperation. Hip and shoulder bones protruded as it hunched over the front paws. More snowflakes fluttered down between Annika and the creatures. The quiet beauty of the fallen snow seemed so strange in this setting. To die on a peaceful snowy night just wasn't right.

Annika positioned her feet. She had practiced the maneuver over and over again on her stallion that last summer back home. She took a small step backward which allowed the growling Zadok to step toward her. Then, she slowly pulled the reins to the front of her body. "Steady, boy." Never removing her gaze from the red eyes staring at her, she deliberately raised her right foot and placed it in the saddle stirrup as she grabbed the saddle horn with her right hand. In her head she began to count. Then she transferred her weight to her right foot as it entered the stirrup. *One, two...*she counted.

A loud wind rushed behind her, startling the wolf-beasts as they ran forward. Annika knew she had no time to lose so she swooped her body up and over onto the saddle and kicked her horse with one foot. It gladly began to run toward the Zadok in its path. The creature reared up and scratched at the horse, its large paws cutting the flesh and sending bright red blood to the stark white ground. But before any more damage could be done, Annika nudged her horse and took off down the path away from the beasts. She glanced back at the noise behind her.

Evidently, Crispin and Simon had noticed their friend wasn't behind them, so they had returned in time to attack the Zadoks. The beasts had regrouped and attacked Simon and Crispin, who fought on horseback using their swords to slash the creatures as they jumped at the horses. Annika stopped her horse and turned it around to help her friends.

Spotting her sword, she leaned down to the right of her horse, holding onto the saddle horn with her left hand and gripping the sword with her right hand. This time, her frozen fingers were warmed by her anger enough that she could hold on to the hilt and swipe at the attacking creatures one by one.

It seemed a losing battle as all three fought the large beasts with swords, since the Zadoks knew where to bite the horses and pull them down to the ground. Simon's was the first to fall. He and Crispin rolled onto the snow. They regained their footing in time to grip their swords and slash an approaching Zadok, spreading a blanket of blood over white snow. Then, seeing the beast was dead, Simon ran over to his horse and helped it up before the other Zadoks attacked it. One by one the beasts jumped and attacked the horses. Crispin, Annika, and Simon slashed at them with their swords.

At that moment, something zinged between the trees, but they didn't stop to see what it was. A Zadok leapt for Simon. He swung at it and the beast fell to the ground...with an arrow protruding from its neck. It writhed in pain on the ground as three more arrows punctured its dark fur. More cries of pain and yelping were heard from the other Zadoks as they ran off into the darkness with arrows in their sides.

The three youths stood panting in the cold air.

"Did you see that?" Simon panted.

"Yes." Annika spotted several arrows stuck in the trees near them and some littered the ground. Still on her horse, she searched the woods for any signs of men, but saw nothing. Dismounting her panting horse, she noticed that its ears were straight up. After stroking its sweat-soaked neck, she joined her partners in stunned silence. Only the wind could be heard around them. The peacefulness seemed strange.

"Who is out there?" Simon asked.

The others turned from left to right with swords in hand.

"I cannot see anything," Crispin said.

The stillness enveloped them.

Annika's heart pounded. She expected the Zadoks to return at any minute. Crispin picked up an arrow from the snowy ground. As he inspected the arrow, he noticed it was made with the white wood and decorated with a single white feather attached by a thin strip of leather.

Breaking the quiet of the falling snow, a loud screech came from above them as the stark white owl flew to a branch of a nearby tree. It landed calmly, then folded its large wings under its body. Its head turned from right to left as if inspecting the area.

"Look," Simon said as he pointed to the large bird overhead.

"Beautiful." Annika sighed. Then, she heard footsteps approaching from behind them. "Wait! Listen!" she told her counterparts, who swiveled toward the sound and held their swords up. Gazing into the forest, she noticed the trees seemed to be moving in the darkness.

"What is it?" asked Cripsin.

Annika saw a most spectacular sight in the falling snow. Very tall male Elves, dressed in white carrying their bows and quivers, walked toward them. Annika stared intently at the tall creatures with skin as white as the trees around them. One by one, each Elf emerged from behind a nearby tree which camouflaged them perfectly. The white owl screeched above them.

As the Elves approached, Annika noticed that they wore white tunics underneath white leather armor strapped to their torsos with flowing white capes draped behind them. It made for a very magical sight. The tallest one approached Simon. He stood several inches above Simon and wore white leather boots trimmed with fur. Placing his hands on his hips, he inspected the three youths. "Children of men," he said with a startling, low voice.

Simon nodded, speechless.

"I am Thætil, son of Queen Ragnalla of Vulgaard. These are my soldiers and fellow guardians of this forest." He pointed to the other Elves, who had begun to gather around the three youths. Not quite as tall as their leader, each soldier towered over the youths.

Annika carefully eyed each Elf. They were the most beautiful creatures she'd seen in a long time. With skin almost translucent, pale blue eyes that sparkled, and thick white hair that fell below their shoulders, the male Elves stood with an air of confidence.

"The Zadoks are gone for now, but we must make our way out of the forest before they return in greater numbers," Thætil said.

"Where are we?" Simon asked.

"You are in the White Forest," Thætil answered. His long arms stretched out in an attempt to display his surroundings. "The White Forest of Vulgaard, home to the current Queen, Thordis, my sister."

"Then we are near Ranvieg?" Crispin said.

"Very near." Thætil lifted his long arm and pointed toward the dark mountains in the distance. "Dangerously close."

"I cannot believe we made it." Annika lowered her head in exhaustion. "I cannot believe we rode this far." She wept. "It has been so long…"

"I have a map," Simon said as he walked toward his horse. He reached into his saddle and produced the book Theo had given him. "I have a map that shows where we must go. You see, we are on a mission to find our friend and bring him home."

Thætil smiled and nodded. "Yes, we know. We are here to help."

Just then, more footsteps could be heard in the distance. Crunching snow echoed into the night. Crispin reached for his sword, gripping the hilt.

"No need to be afraid." Thætil pointed behind him toward the trees.

Soldiers in familiar armor appeared out of darkness, walking up not in formation but in a haphazard way as though they had walked all through the night and were exhausted. A raspy voice shouted orders.

"General Aluein!" Simon exclaimed.

Finally, they had reached their destination.

"Aye," Aluein replied. "I see you youngsters finally made it!" He chuckled. "It is about time."

He put his hand on Simon's shoulder. "Looks like we made it just in time. Good thing we all came with an ample supply of arrows!" The men laughed, joining with the Elves. "Nothing like those Zadoks to put a little excitement in your night, eh?"

Annika agreed wholeheartedly.

Aleuin smiled at her. "You made it, my dear," Aluein said. "And no one is as proud as I am." He gently touched her chin then embraced her thin frame.

41 THE ELVES OF VULGAARD

"Peter remains deep within the walls of Rünbrior." Thætil lifted his hand and he ordered his Elves to lead the way out of the forest toward the castle of the Queen. "We've no time to lose."

"Aye, we must be moving. I will fill you in on the plan to find Peter when we reach the palace. There you will find food, shelter, and rest." Aluein added.

"Theo was right," Simon said. "He told us we would make it."

"Yes, he was right." Annika smiled.

"Food..." Crispin rubbed his stomach.

They all mounted their battered horses and trotted in between Aluein's men and the Elves with the crunching of hardened snow beneath them. The snow had stopped falling, leaving an icy path along the rocks as the wind sliced at their faces, keeping them awake for the last few miles of their journey. Yet they knew they had accomplished much for Peter. Each one felt closer to their goal of seeing their friend again.

As they marched on, the elusive white owl left its perch and flew into the night air above them sending out a loud screech that pierced through the stillness. Then the bird flew away as though it were a guardian appointed over them.

§

For several more hours they rode through the vast expanse of the White Forest until finally they reached the clearing. When the trees parted, many white capped mountains luminously stared down upon the weary travelers as they made their way toward the palace. Hidden between rocky crevices, the palace of the Elvin Queen Thordis stood in splendor. Two Elves, wearing armor similar to Thætil's own, guarded the gate with long spears. When they spied the travelers, they ordered a younger Elf to mount his steed and ride to the front gate to announce their arrival to the Queen and her Constable.

"I suppose she is expecting us?" Crispin asked.

Simon shrugged. The rims of Simon's eyes were red and they drooped from lack of sleep.

Annika, although exhausted, stared up at the magnificent structure. Built several thousand years earlier for Queen Ragnalla, the castle was crafted of stone carved from the rugged mountains of Ranvieg by the Elves before the Dark Times. Nearby loomed the Ranvieg Mountains that contained the prison known as Rünbior. Its dark edifice made of harsh rock contrasted so vividly with the glistening walls of the Elf Queen's palace and the white snow.

When the younger Elf returned, he gave them their orders to lead the visitors to her entry gate. Nearby, Annika heard the familiar screech of the owl. She twisted her body in the saddle to see behind her, trying to spot the white owl in a tree. The screech echoed through the air again, causing all in the party to search the skies. Suddenly, through the snowy morning, the white owl circled above them, soaring effortlessly in the sky.

Then they each turned their attention toward the Elves, who waved them through the gates and up the steep pathway to the palace entrance.

Thætil led the way to the palace gates, where he instructed his guests to dismount, and his servant took their bone-weary and hungry steeds to the stables for a much needed rest.

Annika watched as the young Elf took her horse along with the others. "Give him oats and hay," she ordered. "Please."

The young Elf nodded and smiled. He seemed to be more than eager to help in any way. Annika turned her gaze to the entrance and studied the two enormous gates that reached high into the sky and they gleamed in the snow. Elaborate designs twisted and intertwined to form symbols on each gate. Annika thought them to be something of Elfin history or language.

As they walked between the open gates leading to the palace, the crunching of the snow beneath their boots made them desire the warmth of the palace all the more. Thætil approached the entrance, and the large wooden doors of the palace entrance slowly opened. He stopped and turned to his guests and waved them through the elaborately carved doors.

General Aluein groaned as he lifted his leg to meet the first of four steps leading up to the doorway. He grabbed his back and winced with pain.

Thætil smiled. "You're not getting old, are you General?"

"You're one to talk of being old," Aluein answered back. Thætil was at least two hundred years old compared to Aluein. "I am just a little weary for these steps. That climb up the mountain was enough for me."

Everyone agreed. The icy pathway leading up to the palace entrance was difficult to navigate, but now they knew rest was close at hand.

"Come now, what's a few more steps when hot food awaits us?" said Crispin, who leapt up all four steps with the energy that only a young man could have.

The others followed suit and found themselves inside the palace they had only heard about in tales told to them by Theo in his boring history lessons.

The inside of the palace did not disappoint. The glimmering white walls, covered with detailed designs carved into each one by a talented mason, led them to the grand entranceway with ceilings that easily reached over seventy feet tall. Gracefully illuminated by a large chandelier made of crystals, the entire area glistened like a diamond bracelet in candlelight. As the weary soldiers were led into the grand hall, Aluein motioned for them to be led to the kitchens. Thætil agreed and whispered several orders to his foot soldier waiting at his side. Then the men were all led away eagerly anticipating a hot meal and the fire's warmth. That left Aluein, Thætil, and the three youths standing beneath the glimmering light of the chandelier.

"Reminds me of the stars," Simon said as he studied the light above them.

Crispin frowned. "I smell food. Why can't we go to the kitchen for a hot meal with the others?"

"Easy now." Simon patted Crispin's shoulder. "We'll eat soon enough. We must remember everything about this place for when we see Theo again."

But Crispin groaned and rubbed his stomach.

Annika slowly walked around the room taking in its splendor. She studied the floor. Each sparkling tile seemed to be made of ice, yet the room was not cold. Seeing her reflection in the tiles beneath her, she ran her fingers over her short hair and frowned. "I had almost forgotten about my hair." Her face was dirty as were her hands. She inspected them front and back wincing as though detesting what they had become—callused, with dirt under the fingernails.

"Can we not go and wash before meeting Queen Thordis?" she asked Thætil. She showed him her hands. "We represent our lands. She cannot see us looking the way we do."

Thætil smiled down at her. "Soon you will be able to wash and eat. The Queen is very impressed with your successful journey, my dear. She has nothing but warm regards for all of you…no matter what your appearance."

Annika continued her inspection of the grand room.

A load trumpet announced the Queen's entrance. All straightened, then bowed in humility before the sovereign. Queen Thordis appeared from behind a corner, regally descending a staircase near the back of the hall with her ladies-in-waiting only a few paces behind her. She leaned on the arm of her son, Thurdin, who appeared to be a youth like Annika, Crispin, and Simon. But he was really over one hundred of man's years. His long white hair flowed with a few strands braided on both sides of his head, revealing a kind face. He smiled at his mother's guests. His light blue silken tunic stitched with silver thread reached reached past his knees almost covering his leather boots.

Queen Thordis was beautiful—her long white hair twisted elegantly into a bun, rested on the back of her small head. Her sculpted face glistened in the candlelight as her almost translucent skin was pulled tightly back. Diamond earrings dangled from each ear and a larger diamond necklace around her neck rested on her light blue silk gown similar to that of her son's. Theo had explained how the elves mined the remarkable jewels from deep inside the protected mountains of Vulgaard. Those mines were the envy of all the rulers.

Her gown reached the floor as the train trailed behind her, creating the appearance of floating. She smiled and asked her guests to rise.

One by one, her guests obeyed and admired the Queen. She walked gracefully near each youth and called them by name. Annika turned her eyes away in embarrassment and placed her left hand on her hair, wishing she could make it grow long again in that instant.

"My dear," the Queen said as she raised her hand and placed Annika's small face in her palm, "you are lovelier now than I remember."

"We have met before?" Annika asked.

The Queen smiled. "Yes, when you were very little. I was there at your family's palace with your grandfather."

Annika nodded as she tried to remember the occasion.

"I find your shorter hair to be so lovely and mature," Queen Thordis said. "And much more practical for such a quest."

Annika smiled and curtsied before the kind Queen. She had never seen eyes so crystal clear before. They were like pools of water.

"Your majesty," Aluein began, "I suppose you have been briefed as to why we are here in your palace?"

Queen Thordis turned to face the General. "Yes, my brother has told me of the plan." She motioned for her guests to follow her into another room off the main entrance.

Crispin gripped his stomach tighter as he followed the group into the large room. "I smell food," he whispered.

Simon grinned and tried not to laugh.

"Come this way," Queen Thordis said as she entered a large white room lit by candles. In the center of the room was a grand mahogany table that stretched on for what seemed an eternity. But it was what stood to the left of the table that captured the attention of her bleary guests.

"Yes!" Crispin shouted, then quickly covered his mouth, realizing he had spoken out loud.

Along the wall was another long table of dark wood carrying rows and rows of platters filled with different foods for the guests to enjoy. There were fruits of many kind, juices, breads, and meats decorating the table beautifully.

"Please," Queen Thordis said. "Partake of the refreshments our cooks have set out for you." She waved her hand leading them to the feast.

Crispin did not hesitate to obey her order. He grabbed a plate and loaded it with the many delicious blueberries, blackberries, and strawberries picked from the nearby meadows. There were various leavened breads such as pumpkin, apple, raisin, along with breads made from whole grains, pastries with thick sugary icings dripping onto the platter, and cookies flavored with rose petals and sweet nuts. Not waiting to be seated before enjoying his bounty, he placed a cookie into his mouth and savored the sweetness. He moaned with pleasure as his belly began to fill.

"Go slowly, my friend," Simon suggested. "You do not want to gorge yourself!" He patted Crispin on the back to wake his friend out of his stupor.

"Yes," Crispin nodded. "Slowly. I'll go slowly." Crumbs spewed from his mouth.

Annika sat with the others at the long table and enjoyed the aromas. "Where did they get all these fruits with the land so stricken of late? And where do they grow all the grain for these breads so high in the mountains?"

Simon shook his head. "I have no idea. But I am grateful to partake of their bounty!"

"Anything but fish and rabbit!" Crispin said.

Annika chuckled and served herself fruit and bread and enjoyed her breakfast as the men talked of the plan to rescue Peter. The apple juice was sweet on her lips as she drank from a bejeweled goblet. It was hard to believe that only a few days earlier they were riding hard trying to find a way from the river's bend and into the White Forest.

"My Queen," Aluein began, "we are ready to put into place the plan we presented to you."

The Queen nodded in agreement. "Indeed. Please do."

Thætil stepped forward. "What has occurred so far?"

"We are waiting for the signal to enter the prison for the games. Once we are in, we put the plan in motion."

"Do we know for a fact that Peter remains inside the walls?" Thætil asked.

Aluein nodded. "Yes. We are absolutely certain."

§

The horrible day that Noel died, the guards had led Peter to his cell. Once the door was opened, they didn't have to throw him inside as usual. Peter stormed inside and threw down his sword. The cell door slammed shut behind him.

He yelled and removed his armor. One by one, he threw each piece against the wall. Then, he ran to his cot and flipped it over in his rage. *The Dragon Chronicles* flew to the ground, but Peter didn't care. He ran to the wall and began pounding it with his fists as hot tears streamed down his face. Swiveling wildly around, he noticed Nøel's cot with the blanket folded on top. Unable to move toward it, Peter simply sobbed.

I can't believe he's gone. He wiped his face. *This can't be happening.*

Peter covered his face with his hands and wept until no more tears came. With his back against the wall, he slid to the floor. Near his foot lay *The Dragon Chronicles*. He kicked it away.

"I'm alone again." He stared at the book. "I can't do this anymore. No more dragons, no more fighting. I'm finding a way out." Observing his sword on the floor, he took a step toward it, picked it up, and raised it as though inspecting it. "But before I go, I'll have my time with Damon."

He swiped the air with the sword, picturing Damon's throat in front of him. "So help me, I will get my revenge. And if one of us has to die, then so be it." Tossing the sword to the ground, he gently sat on Nøel's cot, almost afraid to disturb it.

The silence enveloped him. He yearned to hear his friend's voice asking him about the dragons in the book, his friends, and home.

"I'm sorry, my friend," Peter said to Nøel . "I should've been watching. I should've seen Damon coming. It's my fault you're dead. It's all my fault."

Peter lay down on the cot and fell asleep.

§

A few days, later, Peter found himself still alone in his cell. His name had not been called to fight in the arena, and he was glad to have time to heal both his body and his mind. His mind raced with flashbacks of his abduction in the desert, his time in the arena, and his home at Illiath. So many images flooded in, he became dizzy. He lay down on the cot and stared up at the rock ceiling.

"So much has happened," he said aloud to himself. "So many things I never imagined. How could I have imagined all this? I don't know how much more I can take. All I wanted was to go to Knight Training like Will did. All I wanted was to be a knight and serve my father. What's so wrong with that?"

He rolled over on his cot. "And now look what I've done," he murmured. "Look at what's happened."

As his body began to relax, he closed his eyes. A faint mist spread through the darkness of his mind. The mist felt cool on his skin. He shivered as it grew and filled up the space all around him. Fear spread through Peter's body until he heard a familiar voice coming from the darkness. It seemed to be calling his name, but he couldn't make out the words to be sure. The darkness kept the voice far away. Peter felt his body move through the mist and darkness toward a small light penetrating from afar. The light felt warm, he urgently moved toward it. But the voice remained far off.

Then, as the light grew brighter, Peter could see a hill of green grass swaying in the breeze. The sun shone so brightly, he had to squint. A lone figure stood on the hill. As he moved closer, the realized it was a woman in a long dress with long dark hair blowing in the breeze. She turned and walked down the other side of the hill before Peter's eyes could focus. Suddenly, he was in a hallway in his father's castle. He recognized the space. The hallway was lit only by a single torch in a sconce on the stone wall. He reached out and felt the course stone wall. The air smelled of lavender.

Peter noticed a form moving toward him in the hallway. As the form came closer, he saw that it was his mother.

"Peter," she said.

"Yes," he answered. His eyes were wide open now.

"My son." She held out her hands. But Peter could not move.

"You have become such a strong young man," she continued. "I have been watching you grow."

Peter smiled. His body grew warm.

"You must remain strong, Peter. You must remain true to the cause."

"What cause, mother?"

"You must remain true to the Oath."

He could barely see her face in the dark hallway, but he recognized her voice. She wore a red velvet gown and a thin gold crown that rested on her brow. Peter remembered the dress, the crown, everything about her from his youth.

"Remember what you vowed," she said.

"But, Mother, I am trying."

"Yes, I know my love. But you must stay on the course set before you."

Peter understood.

"I am afraid you have forgotten," she said.

"Forgotten what?" Peter cocked his head.

"Forgotten who you are and why you are here."

Peter looked down.

Peter, yours is a higher calling than most men. You were born into a royal lineage where you are part of the Oath sworn by your father and his fathers before him. You are not of this world. You were placed here for a very special reason...a very special purpose."

Peter listened intently. He agreed. She was right in that he had forgotten who he was.

"Your purpose in this dark prison is not just to fight and win your freedom. There are greater tasks ahead and not much time to complete them all. This desire for revenge is not part of who you are. You must not stray from the path set before you. Look at the compass I gave you."

Peter shook his head. "I've lost it, Mother."

His mother gently smiled.

"I've lost your gift to me." He wept. "Theo told me to keep it safe and I failed."

"Peter. It is not lost. You will see it again and when you do, open it. It will show you the way."

"I've lost my way." Peter exhaled.

His mother shook her head. "Never. You will never lose your way no matter what. As long as you remember who you are....and where you come from." She lifted her hand and placed it under his chin. "Know that I love you, son, and am always with you…"

"Mother!" She started to move away from him. "Don't leave me!"

"Remember this is *your* time for greatness, Peter. You are more than mere vengeance. You are the son of the Oath. Never forget that," she urged.

"Mother, don't leave me alone in here!" He reached for her.

"Never forget…"

"Mother, please! Take me with you!" He tried to touch her garment as she turned away.

Then, she was gone.

Peter sat up in the cot panting as though he had been running. He grasped his chest. His tunic was wet with sweat.

"Mother." He scanned the cell, realizing he had been dreaming. "The Dragon Forest…how could I have forgotten?"

Coming from the window, was the familiar sound. He moved the cot over to the window and stepped up on it. He gazed out the window to see the white owl perched on its usual branch. Peter smiled. The bird, with its ever glowing yellow eyes, flapped its wings as though balancing itself.

"How could I have forgotten what you told me so many months ago?" Peter asked. "I am so sorry."

The bird screeched loudly into the night air.

"I know why I am here now," Peter said. "And I will be true to the Oath. I promise. I will never forget…ever."

The bird flew away into the darkness.

"I promise!" Peter shouted after it.

Peter scooted his cot back near the small stove and sighed. He couldn't stop himself from grinning. He knew he wasn't alone.

"How could I have forgotten?" He said. "My calling isn't to be a knight."

He picked up the sword and gripped it.

"My calling is to be King of Illiath," he studied the sword.

"I will do this," he said. He picked up *The Dragon Chronicles*, dusted it off, and placed it on his cot. "This is the time to act and I will not fail my father, my people, or my land."

He looked over at his armor.

"I will not. I cannot," he said. "for Nøel."

§

"When the Duke of Illiath is dead, we can put forth the plan of attack against the Dragon Forest," King Eulrik explained to his guests. Neighboring rulers of the smaller villages gathered at his table for an elaborate feast and discussion about the Duke of Illiath.

"I understood it to be *his* plan," said one of the guests, "not yours."

"I have a much better plan than he does." Eulrik poured some wine into his goblet and handed it to the servant who stood beside him. The servant sipped the wine then handed it to the King.

"And I can actually fulfill the promises of the pact, unlike that spineless man child Bedlam calls the Duke of Illiath."

"I see you have your wine and food tasted now," another guest noticed.

"Yes. One cannot be too careful these days," Eulrik quipped.

After all his guests had eaten, King Eulrik asked them to join him in his den lined with the mounted and stuffed heads of all the animals he had hunted over the years. The paneled room was warmed by a roaring fire and the guests remarked on how comfortable the room felt on that cold night. Eulrik continued to talk of his plan to enter into a new pact with all the surviving rulers to invade and destroy the Dragon Forest. He explained how the surrounding lands would be evenly distributed to all the rulers except Lord Byrén.

"That weasel won't get one tiny scrap of land while I am in power," Eulrik stated.

His guests remained uncomfortably quiet as he continued to explain.

"So, what is in it for us?" one man finally asked.

"If you provide men and supplies, I will make sure you are amply rewarded," Eulrik explained.

Each man nodded and agreed to the deal. They finished their drinks, and stood to grasp the forearm of their host as a sign of their pact. Each guest departed the palace very pleased with the results of the evening.

King Eulrik, most content with the meeting, watched them depart and then made his way to his quarters. "I want everything cleaned up. And prepare for an early breakfast," he ordered his servants. "I rise early in the morning to head out to Beamoor."

All the servants bowed and then began to clear the table of the dishware.

§

A man dressed in black slipped down the long hallway and into King's quarters.

Eurlik changed out of his tunic and trousers into his long robe made of wolf fur. He inspected himself in the full length mirror hanging on his wall.

"Too much gray." He rubbed his beard with his fingers. "You're getting old, Eulrik. This plan had better work. There aren't many years left for you."

He chortled. As he left his changing area and approached his warm canopied bed, the man dressed in black grabbed him around the neck from behind with enough force to lift him off the ground. The stranger whispered something in the King's ear, and then thrust his sword into Eulrik's back. The thrust was so powerful that the end of the bloodied blade protruded from his abdomen before dying. The man withdrew the sword, sending Eulrik to the ground with a thud that ended the reign of the King of Glaussier forever.

The man inspected his work for a few seconds, then picked up a goblet of wine left by Eulrik's bedside. He raised the goblet to the dead King lying on the ground. "Compliments of the Duke of Illiath," he said, and drank the wine.

Leaving the room, he cautiously crept down the darkened hall. He waited a minute to see if any servants were present. When everything was clear, he swiftly departed through the main entrance and ran through the courtyard where the others waited for him.

Mounting their horses, they rode over the gate in time to hear the shouts of the guards. "Close the gates!"

But it was too late. The ten riders rode under the opened gate and onto the bridge where a lone guard stood with sword drawn.

Hearing the shouts from his superiors, the guard took a stance against the riders even though he was outnumbered. As the horses advanced, the guard winced and prepared himself to be struck down by the riders. But the collision never came. Instead, he stood silently alone. He opened his eyes and no longer saw the riders anywhere around him.

The sudden caw of a raven startled him. He pivoted in time to see ten ravens flying off behind him into the night sky. With mouth open, the soldier watched the birds fly off. He peeked over the edge of the bridge on one side and then ran to look over the other side. He saw nothing but the calm waters of the moat below.

"Where are they?" the captain shouted. He ran across the bridge toward the lone guard who stared at the birds.

The guard pointed at them. "There," he murmured. "There they go!"

The captain watched the birds then looked at the guard's face. "Are you mad?" he asked. He smacked the guard in the back of the head.

42 SECRETS OF VULGAARD

Annika walked with the Queen's youngest son, Thurdin, through the castle. They passed several statues of Elfin warriors from Vulgaard's past carved from stone. Many tapestries hung on the shimmering walls that consisted of diamonds, silver, and stone. Annika couldn't resist touching the tapestries. The smoothness felt good on her dry, rough hands. Finally, the hallway gave way to a large set of doors with glass windows overlooking a large yard with grass green from recent rains. Simon and Crispin stood waiting.

Thurdin opened the doors and led Annika, Simon, and Crispin down a stone path toward the stables carved out of a mountain behind the palace. "Watch your step," he said.

They looked up over the lawn to see a most magnificent view of the mountainous region surrounding Vulgaard. The snowcapped mountains stood thousands of feet high into the crisp, biting. The sight made Annika slightly dizzy. "We are so high up into the mountains."

Thurdin approached. "Yes, my forefathers carved this palace from rock out of the mountain. They wanted the palace and kingdom to be high for protection from invaders."

"Well, it is an amazing sight," Simon said.

Annika took in the entire view of small villages below in the large crevice carved from a river through the mountains. The little villages peppered the mountainside.

"What is it like where you come from?" Thurdin asked.

"My grandfather's kingdom, Glenthryst, is not set in a mountain," Annika said with a chuckle. "But our palace is set high on a hill for protection. We have a small village surrounding the castle and the East Sea is nearby with its cool breezes in summer."

Her eyes had a faraway look. "It is a lovely place that I miss terribly."

"Come. I want to show you something," Thurdin said, changing the subject.

They followed their host along a stone path. Suddenly, a loud roar stopped them instantly.

"What was that sound?" Crispin asked. His eyes were wide.

Before Thurdin could answer, they heard it again. It sounded like the gurgling roar of some creature. Annika, Simon, and Crispin stood frozen in uncertainty. Annika noticed Thurdin was not alarmed.

"Come, I'll show you," Thurdin said.

§

"No!" Esmeralda overturned a table in her bedroom. "It cannot be!"

King Eurlik's Constable brought her the news of her father's death.

"How did this happen?" she screamed and pulled at her hair. "My father, the King!"

"He was assassinated in his own room," the Constable said.

She turned to him as the words left his mouth.

"How? How could someone sneak into the palace and assassinate him?" She came close to the Constable's face. "Without *you* knowing it?"

"Your Highness—"

Esmerelda struck him across the face. "Silence!" Tears streamed down her face. "I don't want to hear your excuses."

Just then, the servants walked by carrying her father's body. It was covered with one of his cloaks. Esmeralda ran over to her father, grabbed his cold hand, and kissed it. The servants stopped.

"Oh, father!" she cried. She removed his ring with her quivering hand and slid it onto her finger. "How could they do this to you?" She clutched it to her chest.

The men continued down the hall with the King's body.

"What will become of the kingdom?" She placed her hands on her face.

"You will take over as Queen, your Highness," the Constable answered. "You will be crowned soon, but your power begins immediately."

She watched them take her father's body away. "I understand." She pivoted to face the Constable. "Who is behind this act?"

The Constable hesitated. "I suspect the Duke of Illiath, your Highness."

"I see," she hissed as she followed after the servants carrying her father. "Send me my head knight. Now!"

§

"Ethan!" a voice shouted.

Peter recognized his mock name and turned to see who was calling him. It was his friend, Jason, from the mines. He looked thicker and stronger since the last time Peter had seen him in the caves. He appeared as though he had been selected for training in the arena.

"Jason!" he called in return as his friend walked toward him. He, too, was dressed in the black armor of Rünbrior.

The two friends placed their hands on each other's shoulders in a gesture of friendship.

"Fighting in the arena again?" Jason asked.

Peter nodded. "Yes. It seems the more you win, the more you fight."

"I have heard many good things about your victories in the arena," Jason said. "This is my first battle." He nervously looked out toward the cave entrance that led to the great arena. "I'm afraid I'm a bit nervous."

"So was I my first time," Peter said. "You will be fine."

"We've come a long way since the mines, haven't we?" Jason asked.

Peter nodded, remembering those early days in the caves when his mind was filled with thoughts of escape. "It feels like a long time ago," he muttered.

Just then, the guards shouted for the men to get ready. All fighters quickly placed their helmets on or adjusted their armor.

Peter swallowed hard. He instinctively turned to Nøel, but then he remembered.

Peter gazed upon the large cheering crowd. Many spectators would pay a hefty amount to see King Alexander's son die in the arena. *If they only knew.* Peter could see the coins changing hands among the spectators. He clenched his jaw and gazed up at the warden's balcony and spotted Valbrand and his group watching.

Peter shook his fist. "After all those attacks on me," Peter shouted over the noise. "You could not defeat me! I am the Prince of Illiath!"

"Peter! What are you doing?" Jason grabbed Peter's shoulder. "Are you mad? You can't reveal your true identity!"

"Don't be concerned with that! Just fight and fight hard!" Peter urged.

Valbrand talked with his guests. He obviously could not hear Peter's shouts.

"Get ready!" the guards ordered, and all the fighters stood straight. Peter tried to remember how he once felt about being a knight. He had dreamed of entering Knight Training, and now here he was fighting in a prison arena desperately trying to stay alive. He was amazed at how, in a moment, everything had changed.

The shouts grew louder and louder as two fighters were chosen to begin the battle. One was Jason, Peter's friend.

Peter stood behind him out of the view of the guards. "Keep your eyes open for anything," he said to Jason, who listened to the advice. "No matter what comes out of that cave, keep your shield and sword at the ready. Keep moving and you will be fine."

Jason nodded.

Just then, Peter saw a guard approach. He turned in time to see Damon place his helmet on.

Glaring at Peter through the visor, he taunted. "No victory for you, this day. I'm afraid it is over for you."

Peter stood silent.

Damon walked up next to him and pointed to Valbrand. "I have my orders," he said.

Peter observed Valbrand laughing with his guests. "Good," Peter said. "I have my destiny."

Damon shook his head. "Today you die in this arena." He stomped off to where the other fighters stood.

Then Peter heard a familiar voice coming from the crowds: a shout that rose high above all the others. He turned toward the voice as it grew.

Peter strained to see until finally he saw an old familiar face that brought a rush of joy. There, among the spectators, stood General Aluein, waving his arms high above his head, shouting as though he were betting on the battle.

"A good sign?" shouted Jason "Do you know him?"

"Yes!" Peter felt hope inside.

Aluein whooped louder than anyone, as if he were a gambler eager to see the fight begin.

The fighters were led out into the center of the arena. Then a loud horn announced the arrival of the enemy. The crowd quieted down. Peter removed his helmet.

"Peter, what are you doing?" Jason whispered.

Peter looked up at Valbrand who chomped on an apple.

"I am Peter, the Prince of Illiath!" Peter proclaimed and raised his helmet.

Valbrand spit out the apple and wiped his chin.

"What did he say?" he asked his assistant. The goblin shrugged.

"I am Peter, the Prince of Illiath!" Peter raised his arms out and turned toward the crowd and other fighters.

The crowd gasped and murmured among each other.

"What is he doing?" Dangler looked around.

The guards stood with shocked faces.

"And I will have victory this day!" Peter shouted. He threw down his helmet and gripped his sword.

Valbrand waved his arms, signaling to the other fighters to go after Peter. They nodded and lowered their visors. All of them obeyed, except Damon. He removed his helmet and threw it down to the ground.

§

Thurdin led his guests down some stone steps that curved alongside the palace walls and descended the side of the mountain. The roar was now louder and deeper in intensity. Male Elves shouted something and the sound of flapping, like sails of a ship in the wind, was heard. Dust rose up and over a stone wall. Yet they kept walking.

"This way," Thurdin said.

Around the stone wall they...froze.

There, only a few feet away, was a male Draco, with rough, dark green scales, standing about twenty feet high on strong muscular legs. Its wings flapped as though it were trying to fly, yet it didn't seem to be in a hurry to escape. What shocked the three youths even more was the fact that several male Elves clustered around the dragon, yet the beast wasn't trying to harm them. The Elves spoke in a language the trio had never heard before.

The dragon wore a bridle around its long snout and chewed on a bit in its mouth. The reins dragged the ground, and on its back near the neck was a leather saddle very similar to those used for horses. It roared again, and all of three friends shook.

"Come, it's alright." Thurdin gestured for them to follow him. He made his way down the steps closer to the dragon.

Crispin shook his head and stepped backward.

"It won't hurt you," Thurdin said.

But he couldn't move forward. The beast roared again, and then it turned its large head toward the strangers. Its eyes met theirs.

Annika gasped.

Thurdin hurried to her. "It won't hurt you, I assure you it won't. Watch!"

He walked to the dragon and ran his hands along its underbelly. The beast shook its head and growled. Thurdin whispered to the dragon in that same strange language. Taking the reins, he placed his left foot into the stirrup and pulled himself up and over the beast.

Seeing Thurdin mounted on the dragon, Annika felt faint. No one could had imagined anything like this. The dragon flapped its giant wings and swished its tail. The dust scattered near Annika and she shielded her face.

"Sorry!" Thurdin called from atop the dragon. "He is clumsy!"

He dug his heels into the dragon's side and the beast flapped its wings even more. Thurdin shouted orders to the other Elves who moved out of the way. With a tug of the reins, the dragon turned and stomped off, its clawed feet dug into the dirt as it walked. Its sinewy muscles twitched under its scaly skin. Thurdin appeared so comfortable on the dragon that Annika stood with her mouth agape. More astonishing was how comfortable the dragon looked.

Thurdin led the dragon down the mountainside into a clearing, then stopped and pivoted the dragon around so he could wave to Annika, who waved back.

"Remarkable!" Simon's voice echoed through the cavern.

Thurdin nudged the dragon again. This time the beast flapped its wings and flew off.

Annika put her hands over her mouth in shock at the sight of Thurdin riding a dragon in flight. "Outstanding," she called.

"He's riding a dragon," Crispin said in awe.

Thurdin rode the dragon high into the air. The beast flapped its wings, then glided along on a breeze, circling above. Its tail was used like a rudder. The lithe body soared easily through the air with the legs tucked under. Thurdin shouted for joy with the wind against his face.

When the thrill ride was over, the dragon came in for a landing. Thurdin handled the beast with ease, causing his three guests to realize this was the norm for the Elves of Vulgaard, something they had never heard of before from anyone in all of Théadril: the Elves possessed the ability to train dragons.

Thurdin dismounted, and then hurried over to his guests. "Well?"

"That was the most amazing thing I have ever seen in my life," Annika said. "How…?"

"How do we train dragons?" He finished her thought.

"Yes."

"Elves can speak the language of the dragons," he explained. He motioned toward the dragon, which was now being fed by the other Elves. "We speak to them, and they speak to us. We live in harmony on these mountains."

"I had no idea." Simon heard more roaring coming from somewhere near. "Are there more?"

"Yes, many more," Thurdin replied. An Elf ran handed him a rag, and he wiped his face. "We have trained many dragons for thousands of years."

"So the dragons live in the mountains?" Simon looked up at the mountain peaks that surrounded them.

"Yes, some do. Some live in the seas, some live in the forests, and some live in the deserts," he pointed behind Simon. "Our dragons live in the mountains guarding their treasure."

"What treasure is that?" Crispin asked.

"These mountains are mined for silver, gold, diamonds, and gemstones," Thurdin explained. "Dragons love gemstones. We discovered that they use them as nests for the eggs. They also use gold for nesting. Interesting, isn't it?"

Crispin's eyes were as wide as his grin.

"These nesting materials are coveted by men everywhere. Unfortunately, men have made a living hunting and killing dragons for the gold and gem stones," he continued. "Tragic, really. That is what made all the dragons hate men severely."

They listened.

"Well, that and many other things men have done to them. The larger dragons were captured by Bedlam for his prison games. So, we spoke to the dragons and explained that Elves are not like men and not at all like Bedlam. We spoke to them and gained their trust. The dragons allowed our forefathers to mine the mountains for gemstones, silver, and gold to build this palace and take care of our people. We protect our dragons and use them for battle against the evil Lord Bedlam, who betrayed the dragons," Thurdin said. "Our hope is with this last battle with King Alexander, the land will be rid of Bedlam once and for all."

Simon lowered his head. "I guess you haven't heard the news." He made his way over to Thurdin. "King Alexander has died."

Thurdin looked over at Annika and Crispin. He smiled. "Friends, I'm afraid it is you who have not heard the great news!"

Annika furrowed her brow. "Whatever do you mean?"

"King Alexander lives!" Thurdin announced with raised arms. "I thought you knew?"

Simon stepped back and stumbled from the shock. "No, no one told us this news." He clutched his chest. "Excuse my shock, but how can this be? We all attended his funeral."

Thurdin placed his hands on Simon's shoulders. "It was an evil trick by Lord Bedlam," he said with seriousness. "We were told that Bedlam held the King in the dungeon at the palace. But the King escaped and made it to Gundhred where he is safe!"

"This is the best news!" Crispin hugged Annika as she wept quietly. "The best news ever! Both the King and Peter are alive!"

The three friends embraced and laughed together.

Then, Annika turned to Thurdin. "Can it really happen? Can we truly be rid of Lord Bedlam once and for all?"

"If we work together and unite as one army." He joined his hands together. "I believe we can win, but we cannot do it without Peter. We need him and the Dragon of the forest. Without them, all will be lost. That is why we must help him escape."

"But the Dragon of the Forest," Annika said. "It is gone, isn't it?"

Thurdin smiled. "That is what you have been told."

"But Peter, he was there. He saw the Dragon die, and—" Simon explained.

Thurdin turned to all three. His eyes sparkled in the sunlight. "I tell you this day the Great Dragon of the forest lives."

Simon stood straight.

"That's it!" Crispin shouted. "That's what saved me from the river! The Dragon!"

Simon studied Thurdin's face. "Crispin's right, isn't he?"

Thurdin grinned. "This is true. We are certain the Dragon has been watching over you throughout your journey."

"I knew it!" Crispin grabbed Annika by the waist and twirled her around. "I knew it!"

"Oh, you did not." Annika laughed. "But I believe you. What else could have plucked you from the water like that?"

"Yes! Exactly!" Crispin smiled.

"How much of Lord Bedlam do you know?" Simon asked Thurdin.

Thurdin's face became serious. "More than I ever wanted to know." He walked a few steps to the precipice overlooking the valleys below. "Lord Bedlam once lived among us here in Vulgaard. He knows the way of the dragon, but he changed and began to enslave the dragons and use them to attack….and *kill*."

Simon shook his head.

"Now he rides a black dragon." Thurdin nodded his head toward the blue skies. "Our war will be up there."

"You'll have to tell us more about him," Simon said.

"There will be a time for that, soon, I assure you. My brother and my mother will tell you all you need to know about the enemy. But first, we have to get you each a dragon and train you how to ride it."

"Seriously?" Crispin's brows rose in concern.

Annika slapped her friend on the back. "Come on, Crispin! This will be exciting!"

Thurdin led his guests down the stone path toward the caves that housed the dragons.

Crispin swallowed hard. "Can't we eat something first?"

43 THE BEGINNING OF THE END

Will stood by his horse outside the entrance to the palace at Illiath. All the servants ran out into the courtyard with whatever possessions they could carry.

"What is happening?" the scullery maid cried to Will.

But he gave her no answer. He refused to look at her. He had his orders.

Bedlam approached dressed in a long leather duster and riding gloves over his thin hands. He stood next to his protégé.

"Everyone has left the palace, my Lord," Will said.

"Good," Bedlam said. "It is time to destroy it. Alexander has seen to that."

Dark clouds began to gather over the castle, blotting out the sun.

"I have waited many years for this moment. I have longed to destroy Alexander's palace and everything that *she* loved," Bedlam grinned. "And now the day is finally here."

Will tilted his head. "She?"

But Lord Bedlam ignored him. The ground began to tremble.

"This is a great day indeed." Bedlam gazed over at Will. "And soon, I will destroy the Prince."

Will furrowed his brow. "But I thought—"

"I cannot kill Peter," Bedlam hissed. "but I can hurt him. I can cut him and make him bleed." He narrowed his eyes. "I can make it to where he begs to die."

Will averted his eyes.

"So, my friend." Bedlam placed his hand on Will's shoulder, "this is your moment as well. Soon, when all is said and done, together we will build you a grand palace right where we are standing." Bedlam surveyed the towers behind them as they crumbled. "Ride out to assure the people that all is well. Tell them this destruction is all the doing of the Dragon of the Forest. Explain that it has returned to wage war on the people. They will believe you."

"Yes, my Lord," Will said. "And where will you be?"

"At Hildron." Bedlam adjusted his gloves and said over his shoulder as he walked away. "Preparing for the last war."

Will nodded.

"Alexander will come at me with all his might." Bedlam mounted his black dragon. It stretched out its wings and growled. He grabbed the reins and pulled them tight. "And that is exactly what I want."

"Yes, my Lord." Will mounted his white stallion. He watched as Lord Bedlam flew off atop the black dragon, followed by several of his guards on their dragons. They disappeared into the darkened clouds.

The ground rumbled as the castle foundation started to crumble. Will lowered his head, then remembered something. Swiftly, he dismounted and ran inside the castle. As he raced down the hallway leading to the King's library, chunks of wall tumbled all around him. The stained-glass windows of the Queen's corridor burst, sending shards of glass everywhere. Will covered his face as he ran toward the King's library. At last he entered, only to find the hundreds of books scattered all over the floor as the ground shook. Tables turned over and so did the large wooden chairs. Will grabbed some books and read their titles. The one he needed wasn't there, so he kept looking even as the walls crumbled and screams resounded.

There it is! In his hands was the book titled *Théadril.* He took it and sprinted back down the hall, but this time he had to climb over large blocks of limestone. When he realized the entire wall had come down, he climbed out and ran to this horse. Healing it, he galloped out the gates, over the bridge, and passed the Blue River where he stopped his horse. The spires that once reached high into the sky had fallen. Some guards and soldiers made it through the gate right before it, too, crumbled to the ground.

In only a few minutes after Lord Bedlam had departed, the Palace at Illiath was indeed destroyed. All that was left after the dust had settled was a pile of limestone bricks where once a glimmering castle stood. The portraits of the King and Queen that once hung in the grand hall were now rubble.

"Sir William." One guard trotted up to the Duke. "Are you alright?"

Will nodded. "Yes. Did everyone make it out?"

"Yes," the guard said.

Will looked to the north and saw hundreds of people running away to their villages.

"I know what Lord Bedlam will have me say to the people," he said with a faraway look. "The Dragon of the Forest caused this destruction."

"Yes, sire," the guard said as he trotted off toward the Cornshire.

"And I know the people will believe every word I say," Will murmured to himself. "Lord Bedlam's powers are that great."

§

The gate of the darkened cave slowly opened. The growl of the dragon inside revealed what the men would be fighting this night, but the growl was deeper and more ominous than Peter had heard before. Smoke drifted from the mouth of the cave, sending the crowd into a fit of excitement. They knew the dragon was not any ordinary dragon. They sensed it must be the prize of Valbrand himself.

The throaty growl sent shivers down Peter's back. It sounded much larger than he had imagined. The ground shook with each of its steps. Red eyes glowed from deep within the cave. The dragon inhaled and blew out fire in one stream which lit up the entire cave, revealing the humongous scaled body.

"This is it, Jason!" Peter warned. "Steady yourself!"

The dragon thundered out of the cave, causing the ground to tremble like an earthquake, catching the fighters off guard. No one expected a large dragon to move so quickly. There before them was Valbrand's prize dragon: Scathar.

The giant dragon stood proud in all its glory at least thirty feet high into the air. Its neck was long and spiked and it had two long horns behind the eyes. The nostrils flared as smoke rose from them. Its long, spiked tail whipped around, sending dust into the air, and landed near Peter and Jason. Scathar seemed to be challenging all the fighters to battle it at once. It turned toward the crowds, who now hid behind each other in fear. A great and powerful Wyvern, the front limbs attached to the wings, making it hard for it to move forward. This dragon preferred to fly. But in the arena, it would have to remain grounded. This seemed to frustrate it more than anything. The lithe body moved quickly with sudden jerks. Peter had never seen such a magnificent beast since the Dragon of the Forest.

"Peter!" came a shout from behind them.

Peter turned around and saw Dangler motioning for him.

"Peter! Come quickly!" Dangler appeared to be holding something large.

Peter ran over to him. "What are you doing here?"

"Never mind that, boy." Dangler looked around, making sure none of the guards saw him. "Here, take this!" He handed Peter something covered with a cloth.

"What is this?" Peter inspected it.

"Just take it, you fool! You've not much time! But you will need this to remain alive." Dangler uncovered it.

What Peter saw astounded him. "A shield!" he cried out. He took it and put it on his arm. "This is a scale…from the Dragon."

Dangler nodded.

"But how—"

"It was given to me years ago, by the Dragon itself. When I realized who you were, I knew I would give it to you at the appointed time. Now get out there and win." Dangler placed his hands on Peter's shoulders. "I feel as though I will never see you again after tonight, Peter. No matter what happens, you must be victorious! I do believe you will win your freedom tonight. You are the best dragonslayer I have ever seen."

Peter noticed something in Dangler's eyes he had never seen before—a great fear.

"You can do it!" Dangler pushed the young Prince away. "Now go!"

"Thank you, my friend." Peter held up the shield. "Thank you for everything!"

Peter ran back to the arena where Damon waited. The other fighters watched Scathar and its every move.

"Remain steady," Peter advised. He raised his hand up to calm Jason, but never took his eyes off Scathar. The dragon impatiently stomped its feet and clawed at the ground. The crowd roared its approval. Then it leaned its head back and roared. Peter could see it was trained for battle. Scathar was ready to begin.

First, two fighters, without hesitation, lunged toward it with their swords. They threw them up and at its chest in one accord. Both swords entered the scaly flesh and stuck there, causing it to roar even louder. The fighters hid behind their shields, waiting for its fury. The dragon did not disappoint. It inhaled quickly and spewed out flames onto their waiting shields. But their puny metal shields were no match for the fire. They yielded. Both fighters became charred bodies in seconds. The crowd erupted in great pleasure.

Peter shook his head as he watched the men die before him. Intense anger brimmed, but he knew he could not lose control. So much was at stake. He turned toward the dragon and took a few deep breaths. To defeat Scathar would mean freedom.

"Come, follow me," he called to Jason.

The two ran behind the other fighters toward the far side of the arena out of the sight of the dragon as it continued to claw the ground, begging for more challengers. They found a place off to the side where they could make their plan.

Aluein shouted to Peter yet again. Out of his flowing cape, he pulled out a familiar shiny object.

Peter saw the object and climbed up into the stands to retrieve it. Aluein handed him another Dragon's scale. Peter grabbed it and jumped back down to the arena floor. He gazed at the shiny scale like an old familiar friend. A strength he had not felt in a long time rose inside him.

"Here!" He gave it to Jason. "You'll need this!"

Jason quickly inspected it, then placed it on his arm.

"Come now," Peter urged. The guards spotted them and were coming for them. "Let's go!"

Together they ran away from the stands and into the arena where four other fighters, including Damon, faced the dragon. The cheers from the spectators rose. Peter gazed up to see Valbrand standing with his arms crossed in front of his chest, but Peter did not care. He held his shield and sword tightly, waiting for Scathar to make its move. It studied each fighter as they took position. Then, the familiar hissing started. The fighters hid behind their armor, but Peter and Jason ran behind the dragon's body while it sent flames shooting forward.

Peter climbed onto its back and plunged his sword deep into the dragon's spine several times. It flapped the wings, hitting Peter and catapulting him to the ground with a hard thud.

Jason gasped.

Peter did not move at first, but then he turned and reached for his shield. The dragon inhaled quickly in order to burn him alive. Sensing this, Jason raised his sword high and brought it down onto its tail with such force that he sliced off the tip of the dragon's tail. Blood sprayed everywhere. The crowd applauded and stomped their feet.

Scathar hissed. The other fighters left the sidelines and joined in, sensing a chance to attack it. One fighter threw his sword, penetrating the chest. But the dragon ignored him as it pivoted to observe Peter.

§

Annika nodded toward Thurdin. She gripped the reins firmly. The dragon she sat upon stretched out its wings and flapped them a few times, sending pebbles and dust flying. Crispin covered his eyes and quickly got out of the way.

"Stay clear of its path!" Thurdin shouted a warning.

The dragon roared, hunched down, flapped its wings, and then lurched forward. Instantly it took off and was several hundred feet high into the air in a matter of seconds. Annika's screams echoed between the mountains.

Annika gripped onto the reins and squeezed with her thighs to stay on the dragon's back. Then, she began to relax, feeling the rhythm of the dragon's flapping wings. They would flap, then stop as the dragon glided along the breeze. The wind was so cold, Annika could barely breathe, but she didn't care. She gazed down below and saw rivers, forests, and the palace. She could see the entire kingdom of Vulgaard with its villages along the river and some homes scattered throughout the mountains. It was a magnificent sight.

The dragon turned on its own and circled back around. That's when Annika saw the Ranvieg Mountains and the prison where Peter was being held. She frowned as she studied the harsh black rock of the mountains far away. The dragon swooped in lower for a landing, and Annika gripped the reins tightly again. She leaned forward as they descended. She yelped and grabbed her middle as though her stomach flipped inside her.

But then the dragon touched down, folded its wings, and roared sending the boys stepping back in caution. When they saw it was safe, they ran toward Annika.

"Are you alright? How was it?" Simon asked.

Annika couldn't speak for a few moments. She was trying to catch her breath. Her face was ice cold, but frozen in a smile and her hair windswept. Finally, it dawned on her that they had landed. "Fine!" she giggled. "I am fine. That was the most exhilarating experience!" She laughed heartedly and the Elves assisted her as she dismounted.

"Amazing!" Crispin said. "You actually rode a dragon!"

"No words can describe it." She grabbed her stomach. "I am still a bit nauseous."

"Any army with dragons would be invincible!" Crispin approached the dragon carefully, and then touched its neck.

"Precisely why Lord Bedlam uses dragons for battle as well." Thurdin motioned for the youths to follow him through the stables carved from the mountain. "Lord Caragon was too stupid to understand this concept and was easily killed because he knew nothing of dragons, but thought he did."

Simon nodded. "Peter told us all about the battle between Caragon's black dragon and the Great Dragon of the Forest."

"Bedlam won't make that mistake twice," Thurdin said. "Come this way."

He led them through large caverns where stalls held the many different dragons. Some were smaller Wyverns and some were smaller Dracos. Near the rear of the tunnel of stalls was where they housed the larger dragons. At the end, the tunnel opened up to a clearing where more Elves worked with the dragons. As the youths approached this clearing, the dragons roared.

"How is it they do not spew fire?" Simon asked.

"We speak to them and reassure them that we are not the enemy," Thurdin explained.

An older Elf approached him, speaking in their language. Thurdin introduced Simon, Annika, and Crispin as the three youths who traveled from Théadril to help find Peter. The older Elf nodded and bowed.

"These are older dragons," Thurdin explained. "They assist us in training the younger ones. These Elves are obtaining further instructions and going over details about the prison and the games that occur inside where Prince Peter is trapped. It is most unfortunate how many dragons are captured for the games. I wish we could rescue all the entrapped dragons within the mountain prison. But right now, our goal is to free Prince Peter."

"From the air," Annika said. "I saw the Ranvieg Mountains. I saw soldiers marching all around. Something is happening there!"

Thurdin nodded. "Yes, as we speak, General Aluein and his men are there ready for the plan to commence."

"May we learn to ride the dragons?" Simon asked.

Thurdin was amused. "That would be most helpful to us. When we ride into battle, it will be on the backs of the dragons!"

"I have enough trouble with horses," said Crispin.

"Well, we will spend the next few weeks training for the battle. Each and every one of us," Thurdin said with intensity in his eyes. "This battle will be most fierce. Lord Bedlam has much to lose. Our people have been held captive by his darkness for far too long."

He appeared pensive, as though remembering times past. Stepping over to the edge of the stone wall that overlooked the village below, he was silent for a moment before turning to his three guests. "This will be the last battle, the last war, and the last chance for *all* the rulers to finally rid our world of Lord Bedlam."

"Then we must succeed!" Annika said.

"We will succeed," Simon assured Thurdin. "Now, show us what we need to know and let's go get Peter."

44 THE ESCAPE FROM THE ARENA

Their eyes met.

Peter and Valbrand's dragon, Scathar, stood mesmerized. Scathar's pupils were black vertical slits inside the glowing red eyes. It panted revealing many long teeth the size of swords.

Jason climbed onto its back and began to stab it ferociously, but the dragon did not take its gaze off of Peter. It seemed to recognize him. It took a few steps forward and inhaled. Peter bent down and hid behind the shield in time to meet the force of the flames hitting him and sending him falling backward. He leaned forward, gaining his footing again. The intense heat was almost more than he could bear, but the shield held fast.

The dragon tilted its head as though amazed that the shield did not yield. It inhaled again, and more fire spewed forth hitting Peter again. He leaned into it, holding fast. The dragon came forward and sniffed the shield as it smoldered from the heat. Raising its head, Scathar whipped its body around, sending the men on its back flying off to the ground. Jason landed on his back, losing his breath. In anger, Scathar stomped on the motionless bodies of the fighters to the approval of the crowd.

Only three fighters remained: Peter, Jason, and Damon. Jason quickly recovered from his fall and joined Peter's side.

Instead of attacking the dragon, Damon lunged toward Peter. He hit him with his entire body, sending Peter to the ground. His shield flew from his arm. Then Damon raised his sword high above Peter's body. Peter rolled out of the way in time for Damon's sword to pierce the ground. Peter rolled again and retrieved his shield. Scathar roared when it noticed Peter.

The dragon, with swords protruding from its bleeding body, did not lose a step. It appeared to be stronger than all the other dragons they had fought in the arena. It dug at the ground, challenging the fighters to charge. The crowd chanted its name again and again.

Damon grabbed his sword and came at Peter again. "I told you we would have our time in the arena!" he shouted.

Peter blocked Damon's attacks with his shield over and over until he used it to hit Damon across the neck. Damon fell back, unable to breath for a moment. Peter grabbed his sword and came at Damon, but was met with Damon's sword and strength.

"I've waited for this moment since I first saw you in the caves," Damon said, hatred filled his eyes. "I knew who you were and I knew *what* you were! The Prince of Illiath."

The two pushed toward one another. Peter could see the hatred in Damon's eyes. Peter pushed him back and regained his footing. The two stood with swords raised.

"How could you have known?"

"I saw you when they brought you in. I noticed your clothing. I recognized it as the tunic of royalty," Damon said. "I was chosen by Valbrand to find out the truth. Now I serve Lord Bedlam! He's coming to destroy you."

Jason tried to keep the dragon away from Peter by striking at it. It spewed more fire, causing him to hide behind his shield.

Damon and Peter engaged in more sword fighting, striking at each other until their arms grew weak. Finally, Damon lunged at Peter again and struck him in the face with his fist. Peter winced, but struck back. Damon staggered.

"Let him come!" Peter shouted. "I am ready for him!"

Damon lunged at him. "You're not ready! You'll never be ready to be a knight let alone *King!*"

"You don't know what you're talking about. I am prepared to be a knight and king!"

Damon swiped at Peter with his sword. Peter leapt out of the way.

"You're a fool just like your father was!" Damon yelled.

"My father is not a fool!"

"Your father is dead!" Damon wiped the spittle from his mouth.

Peter froze when he heard the words and saw the look on Damon's face. "What?" Peter stumbled. "What did you—"

"He was told that you were killed here in this prison." Damon strode toward Peter. "And in his weakness, he died from sorrow, the pathetic fool!"

"No," Peter whispered. "It isn't true." Images of his father flashed before him. "You're lying."

"He's dead, Peter. Now the land has no king!" Damon raised his sword. "And soon you will be dead so the land will have no heir!"

"No!" Peter met Damon's sword and spun him around.

Damon fell to the ground. "Lord Bedlam has seen to it that Sir William will take over Illiath." He slowly rose to his feet. "So, after I kill you, the line of Illiath will be gone...forever!"

"Enough!" Peter shouted. "I'm sick of your lies!" He swiped at him but missed.

"Not until I see you dead!" Damon replied. "Long live Lord Bedlam!"

He came at Peter, who used his shield again to block Damon's blows until the shield flew out of Peter's hands. The two swung their swords at each other. Peter sliced the exposed flesh on Damon's shoulder. He screamed and grabbed the wound. After staring at his own blood, he lunged toward Peter, who met the sword with his own. Peter struck him down again, only this time, the golden compass fell from Damon's tunic onto the dirt. Damon reached for it, but Peter stomped on his hand. Damon screamed from the pain.

Scathar made its move toward Peter, but he saw it approaching. He pushed Damon back then ran to retrieve his shield. The dragon swiftly approached behind Damon.

"Look behind you!" Peter warned Damon.

But Damon ignored the warning and ran to retrieve the compass.

"Leave it!" Peter yelled.

Scathar seemed relentless. Valbrand's dragon wanted Peter.

Damon grabbed the compass, then came at Peter. He blocked Damon again and pushed him back. He fell to the ground. Just then, Peter could hear Scathar inhale.

"Get behind my shield you idiot!" Peter shouted to Damon.

But his nemesis rose and came at Peter again with fierce hatred in his eyes.

"Stop, Damon! Get behind my shield now or you'll die!"

"Never!" Damon said.

But it was no use. Just as Damon ran at Peter with sword Scathar spewed forth fire in time to engulf Damon. Before Peter hid behind his shield, he saw Damon's eyes, alive with hatred and revenge, for the last time.

Behind the Dragon's scale, Peter could hear Damon's tormented screams as the flames hit his unprotected body. When the flames ceased, Peter peeked over the shield and saw the Damon's charred remains. And there, among the ruins, was the golden compass.

§

"I must get out of here," Dangler murmured. He swiftly threw his belongings in a leather bag. His skin grew clammy. The hairs on his arms stood. He scurried from the cave and down the darkened hall. He could hear the shouts from the arena.

Running down the hall, he made his way down some steps that led farther into the mountain. He heard the sound of wind coming from behind him. He stopped. Seeing nothing, he continued down the steps until he noticed the silhouette of a tall thin man before him. He stopped again.

"You fool!" the voice came.

"No!" Dangler shouted.

"Take him!" the voice ordered. Several guards grabbed Dangler and led him down a hallway where he could smell a most familiar smell. Sulfur.

"I had to do it!" he yelled.

But the guards did not relent. They continued to drag him into another cave where a male dragon stood unchained.

"No!" Dangler struggled to get free.

Lord Bedlam approached. He faced Dangler. Then he stepped toward the dragon. Its drool fell to the ground. Bedlam stroked its snout gently.

"What are you going to do?" Dangler asked.

"Did you think you would get away with it?" Bedlam asked.

"You knew it was the Prince!" Dangler insisted. "What does it matter that I gave him the shield?"

Bedlam laughed. "It matters that you and that idiot Valbrand thought you could take things into your own hands. And that must *never* happen." Bedlam walked past Dangler, who struggled with the guards. "Now the battle has begun. You have chosen which side you are on. You must learn your lesson. Release him. And let's go."

The guards threw Dangler toward the dragon's waiting mouth and ran out of the cave. Bedlam made his way up the stone steps to the screams of poor Dangler.

§

Peter picked up the compass and placed it in his pocket. That's when he heard the ominous growl of the dragon behind him.

He also saw Aluein make his way down to the arena level. Disguised as a spectator, Aluein was able to race past the guards. They were too preoccupied with staying out of the dragon's fire to notice Aluein running toward the cave entrance. But Peter had noticed.

"Look!" Peter called to Jason, pointing toward to mouth of the cave. "Our escape!"

Jason nodded. "But not yet!" He jabbed his thumb toward Scathar.

Scathar had had enough of the hesitation from the fighters. The beast began to inhale as the crowd shouted its name.

Peter grabbed Jason and motioned for him to raise his shield. "Get ready!" he ordered. Both knelt down with their shields in front of them as the fire hit with such a force, they almost fell backwards. Peter held his shield with all his might. Jason screamed from the heat. Then the fire stopped as the dragon inhaled again. The other guards perished in the flames. Peter and Jason stayed behind the shield, waiting to hear the hissing sound, but all they could hear were the shouts from the crowd. Still, Peter dared not to look over his shield.

"What is happening?" Jason asked.

"I don't know," Peter answered. "But we must wait for it to inhale again before we run toward the mouth of the cave."

Both boys heard the panting of the dragon. It moved closer to them. The boys swallowed hard. The skin on Peter's arms stung from the heat coming from dragon's mouth. But it did not inhale to spew fire.

Peter looked at Jason, who shrugged. He also wondered why it hadn't attacked them yet.

The spectators chanted, "Scathar, Scathar!" over and over again.

Finally, Peter peeked over the shield to see what was happening.

To his amazement, Valbrand's great dragon stood completely motionless, staring straight ahead as though in a daze. Its eyes glowed red and smoke diffused from its nostrils, but it was not inhaling to spew fire.

The crowd grew quiet until only slight murmurs came from the spectators.

Peter and Jason slowly stood with the shield in front just in case Scathar was toying with them. But Peter studied the giant beast's eyes. He noticed its gaze was not on him or Jason. It appeared to be staring at something behind them. It growled deep within its throat, yet did not move.

"What is wrong with it?" Jason asked.

Peter shook his head. "I have no idea."

When he turned to inspect what was happening behind them, he saw a most magnificent sight.

General Aluein stood behind the boys with the white owl perched on his arm. The snowy white bird, comfortingly familiar to Peter, stared at Scathar with glowing yellow eyes, causing Valbrand's fearsome dragon to remain hypnotized as though they were in some sort of a challenge.

Peter smiled at Aluein, who winked and motioned for Peter and Jason to make their way over to the cave opening where his soldiers waited.

The crowd began to boo and hiss for more action to take place. The white owl flapped its wings to balance on Aluein's arm. This caused the dragon to growl from frustration. It appeared forbidden to move, and the command was maddening. But it did not relent. It continued to stand while its tail swished back and forth along the dirt.

Once Peter and Jason made it near the cave opening, Aluein began to slowly walk away with the owl perched on his arm. Scathar clawed the ground as though it wanted to charge, but something held it back. It followed Aluein with its eyes.

The crowd threw rocks from the stands, voicing their disapproval. They desired more bloodshed.

Valbrand watched the spectacle from his balcony and realized he had been fooled. He pounded his fists on the balcony wall.

"Go seize them!" he ordered his guards, who hustled down the stone steps toward the arena with swords and spears ready. "Bring them to me alive!"

§

Peter heard stone cracking. He looked up to see the gargoyle's atop the columns coming to life again.

"Oh no!" Run to the cave!" he ordered Jason.

The gargoyles attacked the spectators as they ran screaming for cover. One flew at Pete, who swiped at it with his sword, severing its legs.

Aluein released the owl into the air and ran when the owl flew off his arm. He hastily joined Peter and Jason as all three sprinted toward the cave. "Lord Bedlam! He's here!"Aluein called.

The spectators shouted so loudly that Peter and Jason stopped to see what was happening. A monstrous growl rose from the arena. And there, for the first time since the war with Lord Caragon, Aluein and the others saw it.

The owl had instantly transformed into the Great Dragon of the Forest in the middle of the arena.

"Look!" Jason pointed.

Peter stared with mouth agape at the majestic sight.

The Dragon stood towering over Valbrand's prize dragon with wings spread wide. Scathar cowered in fear. The excited spectators cheered and leapt.

Peter, forgetting where he was, walked toward his old friend as though in a dream.

The Dragon turned to see Peter coming toward it. Scathar roared, but the Dragon swung at it with its tail.

It took a few steps toward Peter, who approached the giant beast. He reached out and was about to touch the glistening scales, when a gargoyle shrieked.

Jason screamed, "Peter!"

Peter swung at the creature with his sword, but it shoved him to the ground.

"Run!" Jason yelled.

But the gargoyle held him down with all its might. Peter struggled with the drooling creature. It raised its sharp claws to slice his face, but the Dragon took it in its mouth and threw it into the spectators who moved away just in time.

"We must go now!" Aluein grabbed Jason. He spotted several of Valbrand's guards coming for them. "Out of the cave, move!"

Jason reluctantly left his friend behind and followed General Aluein out the cave where the men waited with horses. They could hear Valbrand's guards coming after them.

"But what about Peter?" Jason yelled.

"He'll be coming soon, trust me!" Aluein turned in time to thrust his sword into the chest of one of Valbrand's soldiers.

Peter's eyes met with the Dragon's. Smoke rose from its nostrils and it lowered its snout close to Peter.

"I remembered you, Peter," it said in a low whisper, "because you remembered me."

Peter reached up and touched the Dragon.

In that instant, dozens of Valbrand's guards met them there with swords drawn.

"This won't do." Peter faced the guards.

"Go now," the Dragon ordered.

Peter obeyed. He knew what he had to do before he escaped. Running out of the arena, he headed into the hallways leading to the prison cells. He spotted some of the boys he had trained

"Ethan!" one boy called. "What do we do? Dangler is gone!"

Peter corrected him. "My name is Peter. I am the Prince of Illiath."

The boys could only stare, speechless.

"You must come with me!" Peter ordered. "Come on!"

He and the boys ran toward the myriad of caves and tunnels. Valbrand's guards racied toward them.

"Let's go!" one boy shouted.

Together they followed Peter, who had already made his way down the tunnels toward the prison cells. He had ordered some to fight the guards there in the training area.

"Together we will keep the guards away from Peter," one boy yelled.

They understood and turned to meet the guards. They could hear the clanging of the armor as the soldiers approached.

45 TO VULGAARD

Scathar grew tired of waiting. The dragon roared and challenged the Dragon of the Forest. Many of the spectators had already made their way out of the arena, frightened for their lives. But some stayed and cheered when Scathar roared.

Scathar spewed its fire, striking the Dragon of the Forest, but to no avail. Its scales were too powerful a match. The beast flapped its wings, trying to fly, but the Great Dragon ended the fight by spewing forth its hot flame, hitting Scathar and sending it to the ground. It rose and lunged at the Dragon with its claws, but the Dragon struck it with its large tail. Scathar struggled to regain its footing. The Dragon spewed more fire, sending the beast to the ground yet again. The Dragon flapped its wings and flew over to the wounded beast on the arena floor. The Great Dragon swiped at Scathar with its claws. Scathar flapped its wings in desperation, trying to take flight, but it was outsized.

"You have chosen to serve evil." The Great Dragon spoke to it in their language.

Scathar remained stunned silent.

"Will you follow me instead?" the Dragon asked.

Scathar opened its mouth revealing rows of sharp teeth.

"Never!" it hissed.

The Dragon swiped at Scathar again, slicing its neck open. Valbrand's great dragon fell to the ground, dead.

The Dragon turned and studied the blood thirsty crowd. It roared scattering the frightened crowd out of the stands. Then it turned and saw Valbrand's guards approaching. The giant Dragon inhaled.

§

Peter grabbed a torch on the wall and that's when he heard the Dragon's hissing sound followed by the roar of fire.

"Listen!" he said to some of the boys with him. Peter smiled because he knew what the Dragon was doing to its enemies back in the arena.

Then Peter and the boys made their way down the different tunnels. He saw many of the prison cells. He stood in front of one door and crushed the lock with the butt of his sword. Pushing the door open, he entered in with his torch. A small boy cowered in the corner, shielding his eyes from the bright light of the torch.

"Come with me!" Peter shouted. Instinctively, the boy rose. "You are free! Follow me!"

Confused, the boy hesitated at first, but then realized it was true. Together they ran toward the next prison cell.

"Peter!" came a voice from behind.

When Peter saw it was Eckert, the guard who helped him, he hesitated.

Eckert, armed with his sword, walked toward Peter and the other boys. Peter wasn't sure whether to trust him or not.

Eckert took a ring of keys off his belt. "You'll need these, your Highness." He handed the keys to Peter who smiled. Eckert bowed his head.

"What? How do you know who I am?" Peter asked.

Eckert grinned.

"I heard your announcement in the arena." He chuckled. "You were very brave today." He glanced at the keys. "Free as many as you can. This prison is done for."

"So, was it you who gave me the extra food when I first arrived?"

Eckert nodded.

"You saved my life. Thank you, my friend." They gripped forearms. "For everything."

"Come on, we've not much time," Eckert said.

Peter he ran toward the next cell and the next until dozens of freed prisoners followed him down the dark tunnels.

As they made their way out, Peter thought he heard a voice coming from one of the caves. He ordered Eckert and the boys to continue down the tunnels to free more prisoners. Then, he followed the voice down a set of steps. When he came to the bottom, he noticed a familiar smell of sulfur and knew a dragon was near. Cautiously, he removed his sword from its sheath and entered the dimly lit cave listening for the voice.

"Help me," came a weak voice from inside the cave. Peter looked down and noticed blood on the ground. He walked toward the voice. It seemed to be coming from behind an overturned wooden table. Peter was about to approach the table, when he noticed the scent of sulfur was strong. He raised the torch and jumped at what he saw.

The dead body of an male dragon lay on the ground. Its throat was slit. Peter studied the body.

"Over here," said the weak voice. Peter stepped close to the table and saw Dangler, in a huddle on the ground. He appeared to be wounded.

"Dangler!" Peter shoved the table aside and knelt by his friend. "You're wounded!"

"Yes," Dangler groaned. "Help me."

Peter hesitated to touch Dangler. "What happened?"

"Bedlam," Dangler said.

Peter frowned.

"We've got to get out of here. He knows you won in the arena. He made his escape, but he will return." Dangler winced.

"I understand," Peter said. "Where can I touch you to lift you?"

Dangler groaned from the pain. "Here, take this." On the ground near his bag lay *The Dragon Chronicles.*

Peter grabbed it.

"You almost left it behind," Dangler grinned, but some blood showed in his teeth. He winced again from the pain.

Peter grabbed the book. He knew he had to take a chance, so he grabbed the old man and lifted him up and over his shoulder.

Dangler screamed from the pain. "Hurry!"

Peter hastily made his way up the stairs and into the cave tunnel, where he spotted Eckert surrounded by many boys. Some looked younger than Peter was when he was first brought to the prison. Eckert assisted Peter by taking Dangler and carrying him off.

"We've got to get out of here now!" Peter shouted to the boys.

But they stood stunned as though in a trance.

Peter raised the torch at them to awaken them. "Come on! Follow me. You are free now, but you need to fight your way out of this prison and I will help you!"

He led them to Dangler's cave and ordered each of the older boys to grab a sword and helmet. They eagerly obeyed. Once they were armed, Peter commanded them to follow him. With a loud cheer, they obeyed and made their way back to the arena and escaped through the cave entrance.

§

Jason, Aluein, and the soldiers had made good progress in battling Valbrand's guards. Several of the guards lay dead or wounded on the ground.

"Where is Peter?" Aluein panted as he pulled his sword from the chest of a dead guard.

"Behind you," Eckert answered.

Peter stood with hundreds of freed prisoners ready to fight their way out of the arena. "Let's go!" He raised his sword.

Aluein jaw dropped in disbelief at the sight.

Loud roars emanated from the tunnels behind them.

Peter turned his head toward the sound. "Bedlam must have loosed all the dragons."

"Whatever we are going to do, we'd better do it now!" Eckert said.

"We need to move away from here!" Peter ordered.

All the boys, along with Aluein, ran as far from the mountain as they could. There, they encountered more of Valbrand's guards.

Peter swung his sword at the guards, and freed boys followed. One by one, they struck at the guards. Peter swiped at one, then spun around and thrust his sword into another, sending blood flying.

Aluein watched atop his horse with eyes wide open in amazement at Peter's fighting skill. The freed boys did not disappoint. They fought until all the guards were lying dead on the ground or so wounded, they couldn't stand.

"We did it!" One boy raised his sword into the air. The other boys whooped.

Peter wiped blood and sweat from his face, laughing heartily.

Then, a trembling of the earth started and rose in concentration of power and force. They grabbed onto each other for balance.

"What is happening?" one boy asked.

Boulders began falling down the sides of the mountain, and the Dragon roared within. The beast flew out of the arena and circled up high into the air as the mountain collapsed. A host of younger dragons flew out of the opening and desperately flew away, joining the Dragon.

The boys cheered and clapped in jubilation.

Finally, one large boulder fell and sealed the entrance to the arena.

The Great Dragon flew over them all. The clouds parted, and there, between the clouds, a colorful rainbow glistened in the sunlight.

Peter slowly walked forward as though under a spell.

"What is it?" Aluein asked.

But Peter remained silent, walking away down the rocky hill toward the sunshine. Aluein followed him. They stopped at the precipice.

"The sun." Peter closed his eyes and drank in the warmth on his face. "It has been so very long since I've seen the beauty of the sun." Peter's eyes welled with tears. "And the green grass, blue sky." He touched the flowers all around them. "My father, Aluein…is he dead?"

Aluein took Peter by both shoulders. "Peter, your father is *alive*."

Peter covered his face with his hands and wept tears of joy.

"Look around you! The land and your father are one. The land lives no matter what Bedlam tried with his foolish magic." Aluein let out a throaty laugh, then grabbed a hand full of grass. He inhaled the sweet smell. "Restoration."

"Yes." Peter gazed over the green valley.

"Your Royal Highness," Thætil said as he approached Peter.

Peter took a step back from the precipice at the sight of the tall Elf coming toward him. "Who are you?"

"I am Thætil, Prince of Vulgaard. You are in the land of the Elves." Thætil motioned his arm to where all his Elfin soldiers stood ready to fight.

The beauty of the elves stunned Peter silent.

"It is over," Thætil said, gazing deeply into Peter's eyes. "You are *free*."

The Great Dragon flying overhead, and its shadow passed over Peter. He wavered in sheer exhaustion and shock.

"Peter, you have come through the trials," Aluein murmured. "You have made it through."

"The trials," Peter whispered. "They are over?" He closed his eyes and repeated the words in his mind. He breathed in the clean crisp air. As he exhaled, he slowly opened his eyes and gazed into the blue sky.

"Yes, Peter." Thætil put his arm on Peter's shoulder. "Each knight must pass the test of the trials in order to serve a King."

"Funny how I never even made it to the Knight Training," Peter said.

"Prince Peter," Thurdin interjected, bowing, "to finally meet you is a great honor. My mother is Queen Thordis." He placed his hand over his heart. "You have survived through some of the most challenging and arduous training any knight could ever hope to endure."

Peter bowed in return. "Prince Thurdin." He surveyed the hundreds of Elves and soldiers side by side on the green hills before him. "Can this all be true? Is this really happening?" Peter asked no one in particular.

Aluein chuckled. "Yes, your Highness. This is really happening."

"I was so foolish," Peter sighed. "I wanted so badly to become a knight, like Will...and like my father." He turned to Aluein. "I wanted to achieve greatness on my own. Now I can see why I was put in this place. I had to lose everything and become a slave to realize greatness isn't about becoming a great knight or winning battles."

Aluein nodded.

Peter glanced behind him at the crumbling mountain and all the former slaves standing nearby. "Greatness is about serving others. I had forgotten that I wasn't meant to be a knight. I was meant to be *king."* He observed the sword in his hand. It was covered with blood. He threw it down to the ground. "I thought I needed to become prepared, but what I learned inside that mountain was that I am already prepared. That's what the Dragon was trying to tell me."

"Each knight must endure his own trial, Peter," Aluein said. "No two trials are the same. Some knights face dragons, some face battle. You faced *both.* Now you can return and serve your father with strength and honor until you become the King of Illiath."

At last Peter truly understood.

"But for now, there is still much work to be done." Aluein turned to the men and Elves and waved. All began to mount their horses. "Your father would be proud, Peter. This is your time."

Peter remembered the same words of Nøel and the Dragon. He grinned.

"I know this is your time," the Dragon said. *"I must be here for your time. As I was there for your father and his father before him, I will be here for you."*

Aluein walked over to his horse.

"Now where do we go?" Peter asked.

"Vulgaard," Thætil answered. He stepped toward Peter. "My sister, the Queen, would like to meet you, Peter."

Peter looked off to the east in amazement. He had heard of Vulgaard all his life, but now he would see the great castle himself. *Can all this be real?*

"Your father's kingdom is in shambles, Peter," Aluein said as he came alongside him on his horse. "Lord Bedlam has bewitched Will. He is a madman. He is planning on entering the Dragon Forest to destroy it. No one man can stop him."

"He has some of the other rulers under his command. Together they have amassed a great army," Thætil explained.

"But why do they want to enter the Forest?" Peter asked.

"Because they know that is where you get your strength," Aluein said. "To destroy the Dragon Forest is to destroy you and your father."

Peter took in all the information. Just then, the Dragon roared above him. All the Elves, men, and freed boys looked up in time to observe the great beast transform into the white owl. It screeched and flew to Peter, landing on his waiting arm.

"My friend," Peter said, balancing the bird on his arm. "And what of my father?" Peter turned to Aluein. "Where is he?"

"He is on his way to Vulgaard, Peter," Thætil said.

"You will be reunited with him there," Aluein said. "Now we must go before Valbrand's Riders come to attack us. I'm certain many escaped with him."

"We'll need more horses," Peter said. He released the owl into the air and watched it fly off.

"No need for more horses. Look!" Thætil shouted. He pointed toward the hill.

Appearing over the hill in a singular motion, flew several dragons with Elves mounted on their backs. Their lithe bodies rushed over the grassy hill then gracefully landed nearby.

Their riders pulled on the reins. Thurdin ran over and took the reins of his dragon.

Peter marveled at the sight. "I never imagined this!" He bowed toward Thurdin.

"Your Highness," Thurdin bowed in return. "We have a dragon for you!"

An Elf walked a young dragon over to Peter and handed him the reins.

"Thank you." Peter studied the beast panting before him. It was a Wyvern with colored scales and bright blues eyes that sparkled in the sunlight. Peter cautiously reached out his hand to touch the snout of the creature. It growled slightly and acquiesced. Peter gently stroked the creature's head, amazed at how docile and tamed it was. "I don't know what to say to all this. Words can't describe it."

The white owl screeched from above as though it approved of everything that transpired there on the hills near the Ranvieg Mountains.

Aluein mounted on his horse and ordered, "Time to ride out!"

Peter watched as all the freed boys followed the Elves toward the grassy hill. Jason was with them. Eckert motioned for the Elves to assist him with Dangler. One Elf took out a black box and began to make the familiar paste to apply to Dangler's wounds. Peter watched the scene, expecting at any moment he would wake to the screams of the guards ordering him back into the caves for another day's work.

"Come on, Peter!" Thurdin mounted his dragon. "It's easy! You remember!"

Peter watched Thurdin fly off on his dragon. As he watched, he remembered the owl. "Thank you, my friend." He waved to it as it circled above in the bright clear sky. "I'll never forget this."

As he watched it fly off, Peter remembered the golden compass. Reaching into his pocket, he pulled it out and flipped it open. Now, along the edge, mysteriously appeared the words *The Dragon Forest.* Peter recalled what his mother had told him.

Raising the compass, he saw the arrow move toward the words *The Dragon Forest* that appeared along the rim. Peter gasped.

"The arrow will always point you toward the Dragon Forest, Peter. That is where you get your strength. Picture the forest in your mind," she said.

The trees and the lake came instantly to his mind as though he stood in the midst of the mysterious woods again. He could hear the sounds of the sparrows, smell the pines, and feel the coolness of the breeze on his face. Then, he found himself walking in the forest with his mother alongside him.

"Remember this place always, Peter. You must never forget who you are or where you came from."

Closing the lid, Peter placed it back inside his pocket. Then, he mounted his dragon.

"This dragon will be loyal to you all your life, Peter," Thætil said.

Peter took the reins into his hand. The dragon turned its head and looked into Peter's eyes. Immediately, Peter felt a bond between them. He looked off toward the grassy hill. There he saw three figures standing on the top of the hill. One waved enthusiastically. Peter waved back. In that instant, Peter recognized the three. *Could it be?*

He shouted as loud as he could, "Simon, Annika, Crispin!"

The three figures shouted and waved. Peter yanked the reins of his dragon and nudged its ribs. "Ha!" he shouted. The dragon took off toward the others.

§

The white owl inspected the sight of all the riders heading east to Vulgaard. When completely satisfied, the bird flew off to the north. As it traveled, the sun's warmth continued to dissolve the dark clouds revealing green grasses and flowers on the plains. The flowers bloomed in a myriad of colors that gleamed in the bright sunlight.

After the long flight north, the owl entered Théadril and flew over the place where the palace at Illiath had once stood. All that remained was a pile of limestone, glass, and rock. It continued over the Blue River and toward the Cornshire. There, in the hill country, men marched in unison. From the east came more men, dressed for battle. They marched on. To the west, the fires of Hildron burned yet again.

As the owl flew on the wind, ahead in its sight was the elusive green forest, still standing, still waiting, still mighty.

The white owl flew over the villagers of the Cardion Valley, who watched the commotion. Finally, after its long journey, the owl approached its final destination with the swift ease of familiarity and placidity. It circled the treetops once, inspecting them again as a general inspects his troops, looking for any sign of weakness or vulnerability. A flock of white doves burst forth from the tree tops.

Then, and only then, did the owl finally and gracefully enter into its realm…the realm of the Dragon Forest.

The End.

ABOUT THE AUTHOR

In 2004, award-winning author R. A. Douthitt decided to write a fantasy adventure book designed to inspire kids everywhere to go out and make their own adventures happen. *The Dragon Forest II* is the second book in this adventure trilogy about knights, castles, and the dragon realm. R.A. Douthitt lives in Arizona with her husband. She is currently working on a ghost story/mystery trilogy. All her books are available online.

Made in United States
North Haven, CT
30 September 2024

58105691R00196